AGE OF HEROES

AGE OF HEROES

JAMES LOVEGROVE

SOLARIS

First published 2016 by Solaris
an imprint of Rebellion Publishing Ltd,
Riverside House, Osney Mead,
Oxford, OX2 0ES, UK

www.solarisbooks.com

ISBN (UK): 978 1 78108 404 5
ISBN (US): 978 1 78108 405 2

10 9 8 7 6 5 4 3 2 1

A CIP catalogue record for this book is available from the
British Library.

Designed & typeset by Rebellion Publishing.

Printed in Denmark by Nørhaven

PROLOGUE

Taklamakan Desert, Northwest China

A HOARSE SHOUT brought Holger Badenhorst from his tent, where he had been treating himself to some alone time with the internet and a box of tissues. As he stepped out into the saffron glare of a desert sunrise, he checked to make sure his shorts were zipped up. He was thinking – hoping – that the shout had been a yelp of triumph. The labourers had finished clearing the way to the third door at last, and someone was keen to bring him the news.

When he saw the face of the man running downhill to the campsite, however, Badenhorst adjusted his expectations. It was Ehmetjan Kadeer, the only member of the workforce who had any English and who was therefore, by default, foreman – or at least go-between, Badenhorst's conduit to the others – and he was not ecstatic. He looked panicked, horror-struck. There was blood on him, too. A lot of it, streaking his hands and smearing his shirtfront in bloom-shaped patches like grisly tie-dye. So much blood that it couldn't have been his own.

The fact that it wasn't Kadeer himself who had been injured came as some relief to Badenhorst. He relied on the man. He even, in as much as he could a non-white, liked him.

Kadeer skidded to a halt in the sand in front of the tent. He was panting hard.

"Sir, up at dig place. In tunnel. Come see."

"What is it?" said Badenhorst. "Whose blood is that? What's happened?"

Kadeer beckoned. "Come see. You must, sir. You must come see."

BADENHORST FOLLOWED KADEER upslope, the pair of them toiling through shin-deep sand against a steep gradient. Badenhorst, pushing fifty, had at least twenty years on Kadeer, who was wiry and fit. Yet he had no trouble keeping pace with him. Toughness and stamina had been bred into him from birth. He had grown up on a kraal some two hundred kilometres west of Johannesburg, on the fringes of the Kalahari, with three older brothers and a widowed father whom a lifetime of farming had hardened to a sinewy tightness, and who prized the body far above the mind. Young Holger had learned from an early age that indolence was not an option. If his bullying brothers hadn't taught him that lesson, his father – free and easy with his belt, especially if he had been drinking – had. You got up, got going, stayed active all day, did your chores, rounded up the cattle, mended the fences, drove into town for supplies, whatever you were told to, and you didn't slack, didn't give up, didn't complain, not ever, not if you knew what was good for you.

He and Kadeer arrived at the mouth of the cleft splitting the face of the rocky escarpment that loomed above the campsite. Within lay a snaking, broad-bottomed valley, which had once housed an ancient town. The remains of habitation were to be seen all around, in the worn, sun-bleached timbers protruding from drifts of sand in irregular rows like the bones of dinosaurs.

This place, whose name was long forgotten, had once been a stopover on the northern branch of the Silk Road. Sheltered in its valley, it had thrived as a staging post and watering hole for merchants and their caravan trains as they crossed the Taklamakan Desert, the most inhospitable and treacherous leg of the journey.

Then, like so many other pockets of civilisation in this arid wilderness, the town had died. Who knew why? Perhaps the subterranean aquifer that fed its cisterns had dried up. Perhaps an unusually severe sandstorm had engulfed the valley. Perhaps the Silk Road itself, its route altered by the Taklamakan's eternally shifting dunes, had veered away, taking with it the passing trade the town relied on. This desert was not somewhere man was supposed to live. It had proved that time and time again, if the ruins of countless other towns which littered the landscape were anything to go by. *Taklamakan*, in the local dialect, meant "Once you're trapped, there's no escape." The desert was also popularly known by the nickname the Sea of Death.

Badenhorst and Kadeer entered a large chamber hewn out of the valley's side. This would have served as the town's meeting hall, or marketplace, or possibly temple. Badenhorst didn't know its original function and frankly didn't give a shit. What was he, an archaeologist? The chamber was big and centrally positioned – that much he did know – and it had no doubt been important to the townsfolk. Even so, it was little more than a rough-floored manmade cave that could have held fifty people at best, with everyone standing.

Currently it was occupied by Badenhorst's workforce, which consisted of a dozen men. Like Kadeer, they were all of them Uyghurs, a Turkic minority principally found here in China's Xinjiang Autonomous Region, its people having colonised the Tarim Basin during the tenth century. They were gathered around something on the floor, and their voices were raised in a babble of consternation.

At a command from Kadeer, they parted ranks, and what Badenhorst saw lying at their feet set his heart plummeting. He had pretty much suspected that this was what he would find; the blood on Kadeer's shirt had been a clue. That didn't make it any less dismaying.

A body.

The man, sprawled on his back, had a round, ragged hole in his torso. Something solid, with the diameter of a drainpipe, had punched into his chest. Within the gory cavity, Badenhorst glimpsed the shattered end of a rib and the glistening fascia of some internal organ. He had seen worse sights in his life, but still he had to fight down nausea.

"*Fokken* hell," he said under his breath.

Already he was making mental calculations. This was going to cost money. There would be compensation for the dead man's family. There would also be a salary hike for the remaining labourers. From past experience, Badenhorst knew they would not go back to work without some form of incentive. The question was how much? How much would they hold out for? How much palm greasing would be required to get the whole show running smoothly again?

Cash flow wasn't a problem in itself. Badenhorst's employer had astonishingly deep pockets. "Money," Badenhorst had been told more than once, "is no object. Getting the job done, that's all that matters. Whatever it takes. Whatever the price. Blank cheque."

What Badenhorst found galling, though, was being held to ransom, being blackmailed by a bunch of unskilled shovel-jockeys. They were already being paid well. Accidents happened. It was only to be expected. Poking around in ancient, long-lost ruins was a hazardous occupation. They had known that when signing up. They should just grow a pair and carry on.

"How did he get this?" Badenhorst said, pointing to the hole in the dead man's chest. "Did he slip and fall onto a sharp rock or something?"

Kadeer looked nonplussed. "Big hurt. He cry out. Men take him here. I try to help him. Stop blood. Too late. He dead already."

Badenhorst simplified. "Yes, but how did he die? What happened?"

Kadeer understood. "This way. I show. Is good thing."

"You mean bad, surely."

"No, sir. Yes, bad," Kadeer said, with a nod at the corpse. "Bad thing for Abdulkerim. But also good thing. For us."

Kadeer set off, and Badenhorst, intrigued – and now just a bit excited – followed.

* * *

BEYOND THE CHAMBER, through a narrow exit in the rear wall, lay two tunnels. One of them led to the town's cisterns, now just a row of empty hollows gouged out of the sheer rock. The other, branching off from the first, had until recently been blocked by a cave-in. Or so it appeared. Badenhorst had overseen enough of these difficult retrievals that he knew not to take anything at face value. While it looked as though the tunnel ceiling had collapsed due to natural causes, there was every chance it had been brought down deliberately. He was dealing with a devious, tricky mind, after all, the mind of someone who had devoted decades of his life to stashing valuable artefacts in far-flung locations around the world in such a way that nobody would stumble across them by chance, or be able to unearth them without considerable expenditure and sacrifice.

The blockage, at any rate, had been no match for a few pounds of mining explosive. But what lay on the other side was a sequence of obstacles, each more obstructive and challenging than the last.

There had been doors. The first was made of a single slab of granite so thick and hard that a jackhammer barely made a dent in it, and only by drilling dozens of holes and packing each with a shaped charge was Badenhorst able to reduce it to rubble.

The second boasted a complex locking mechanism and had pictograms carved into its surface. The images constituted a cryptic code, the solution to which might enable the decipherer to open the door by rotating the concentric stone rings in the middle to the correct configuration, rather like tumblers on a safe.

Having been confronted with a number of similar devices before over the past two years, however, Badenhorst knew better than to attempt to crack the code. It was a hoax, a swindle. Setting the rings in any permutation would spring a trap of some sort. He resorted to explosives again, accepting that the upshot was going to be some new deterrent. In this instance, no sooner was the door breached than ancient gearing groaned into life and huge quantities of sand began to pour from reservoirs embedded above the tunnel, both on this side of the door and beyond, filling it to the ceiling. The unwary explorer might have been swamped and suffocated, but Badenhorst had taken the precaution of detonating the charges remotely by radio signal.

After that it was down to manpower. The labourers cleared the sand away bucketload by bucketload, over the course of a week, until they revealed a third door lying some ten metres along from the second.

It was while excavating the last of the sand from in front of this door that Abdulkerim had met his grisly fate. And Badenhorst could see why.

There was a hole dead centre in the door, of the same diameter as the hole in Abdulkerim. Lying on the floor nearby was a cylindrical chunk of stone, roughly half a metre long. It would have fit snugly and precisely into the aperture in the door, like a plug. One end of it was spattered with blood.

Badenhorst squatted onto his haunches and, with great care, examined both cylinder and hole. Kadeer waited patiently beside him. The portable halogen lamps illuminating the tunnel buzzed softly.

Within the hole, Badenhorst could make out a kind of spring-loaded propulsion system, an elaborate ratcheted catapult that had launched the cylinder outward at high velocity, making it a lethal short-range projectile. A last-ditch attempt to dissuade intruders from venturing any further. Abdulkerim must have inadvertently tripped some switch or trigger... Yes. Down at floor-level, in the door's base. A protruding knob of stone. Badenhorst tested it tentatively with the toe of his boot, making sure beforehand that neither he nor Kadeer was in the line of fire, just in case there was another missile secreted within the door.

There wasn't. But the knob gave under the least pressure, nudging inward. All Abdulkerim would have had to do was touch it with his shovel – which now lay on the ground, blade end first towards the knob – and *blam!* Instant death by blunt force trauma.

"*Ag sies, man,*" Badenhorst muttered. "Poor bastard." It was the closest he would get to a eulogy for the Uyghur labourer.

"Look, sir." Kadeer indicated the hole. "You see? Inside?"

"I've seen. It's a hell of a *blerrie* contraption, all right."

"Inside. *Inside.* You look."

Badenhorst put his eye to the hole again, as urged. Kadeer didn't mean inside the door; he meant *through* it, to the chamber beyond.

Badenhorst had been so preoccupied with fathoming the workings of the trap, he had neglected to consider anything else. *Is good thing*, Kadeer had said.

Of course.

It was only a glint in the darkness. Metal reflecting the light outside. An outline of something gleaming – and sharp.

But it was enough.

Badenhorst had been doing this job for two years: hunting down specific artefacts in isolated and often all-but-inaccessible regions, a dozen of them all told. Two years of his life spent chasing down treasures and piercing the layered defensive measures protecting each one. Two years of travel, preparation, recruitment, discomfort, toil, supervision, setback, slow progress and hard-won success.

Every time, at the moment of final discovery, when the object of his search stood revealed, it was worth it. Every time, he felt like Howard Carter peering through the chink into Tutankhamun's tomb and glimpsing the "wonderful things" within. The exhilaration, however brief, was a fair reward for the days of stress, demand and frustration preceding it. For a few precious seconds, Badenhorst forgot he was helping to lay the groundwork for a string of murders, and could almost believe that he was doing something good instead.

LATER, IN HIS tent, he fired up the satphone and rang his employer. Early morning, China Standard Time, meant it was late the previous evening for the recipient of the call, but Badenhorst had been told never to worry about the hour. Day, night, whenever, he should get in touch as soon as each artefact was found, without delay.

His employer picked up after eight rings.

"Badenhorst. Speak."

The words were fragmented, rumbly, as though bubbling up from deep underwater. The satellite relay might have been partly responsible for that, scrambling the signal as it bounced through low Earth orbit and adding a scrim of static, but Badenhorst was pretty certain that some kind of voice changer software package was in play as well. The distortion was the same wherever he was in the world. It seemed intended to disguise everything about the voice's owner – their age, gender, accent, class – leaving him with absolutely no pointers towards their identity.

That was perhaps the weirdest aspect of the entire undertaking. Badenhorst had no idea who he was working for. Not the faintest clue. His employer had remained anonymous throughout, from the initial exploratory email sent to him from a secure mailer, enquiring whether Badenhorst would be interested in a job so lucrative it would allow him to retire and spend the rest of his life in luxury, to the regular financial transfers he received from a numbered offshore bank account to cover ongoing expenses and fund the project. Every step of the way, Badenhorst had been walking blind, led along by an unknown benefactor. For a man like him, who trusted no one but himself, it had been quite a leap of faith to accept the job offer, no questions asked. Had the payday not been so mouth-wateringly tantalising – twenty million dollars cash, waiting for him in a bank vault on Grand Cayman – he might have baulked.

"We have it, boss," he said.

A pause, a blip of delay. Then his employer said, "Excellent. You're holding it in your hands right now?"

"Not quite. Not as such. But it's only a matter of time. Today, this afternoon at the latest, we'll have extricated it."

"Then isn't this conversation a little premature?"

Badenhorst swatted away a fly that had come to suckle on a bead of sweat on his forehead. "Getting the artefact is a formality now. We've jumped all of the hurdles. My men are wiring up explosives even as we speak, to crack the final door. Then it'll be done and dusted."

"Don't get overconfident," said his employer. "You can't be sure there isn't a last little surprise waiting for you. Sneaky bastard, the man behind all this. He really didn't want the things to be found, and made sure anyone who tried would be punished."

"We have been punished. Lost another labourer this morning."

"How many does that make it in all?"

"Five. He's the fifth casualty. Not counting the wounded, that is. The fifth death."

From the other end of the line came what sounded like a sigh, although it could just have been noise on the line. "Tragic but unavoidable."

"Omelette, breaking eggs," said Badenhorst with practised nonchalance. "Can't get too worked up over some coolie mongrel, *nè*?"

"Your pragmatism does you credit."

Badenhorst couldn't decide if he was being mocked or not; the distortion on the voice masked nuances of tone. He chose to believe that he had just been complimented. There were good reasons for not getting testy with his employer. Twenty million of them, in fact.

"So we're almost finished, eh, boss?" he said. "Eleven artefacts recovered, one to go."

"I'm well aware of that."

"Just making the point that everything's on track, going nice and *lekker*. Where to next? Russia, am I right? That's where artefact number twelve is."

"Correct, but I'm thinking we can do without."

"What?"

"It's been such a long, drawn-out campaign. I'm not sure I can be bothered to hang on any more. We've got enough. Eleven's enough. We can manage without the twelfth. It may prove more useful, anyway, staying where it is. We shall see. No, it's decided. We are bringing this phase of the operation to a close and embarking on phase two. Are you up for that?"

"You're saying this is it? No more digs? I can be getting on with what I'm used to doing?"

"Exactly. It's time to commence enlistment and training."

Badenhorst's true skill set. "I'm happy with that."

"I had a feeling you would be. You've got three months. Will that be enough?"

"Are you asking me or telling?"

"What do you think?"

THREE MONTHS, BADENHORST mused, wandering through the campsite, puffing on a slim joint. Three months to assemble a unit of killers and accustom them to using a suite of weapons they were hardly likely to be familiar with. It was doable. Just. He might have wished for a little more time, but his employer had clearly run out of patience. He or she wanted to accelerate the schedule. Badenhorst would simply have to facilitate that.

A wind was picking up, sending specks of sand swirling through the air. The sand ticked grittily on the windows of the Mercedes-Benz 6×6 G-Wagens parked at the edge of the campsite, which would shortly be carrying Badenhorst and the labourers back to the city of Ürümqi. It would be a seventy-two hour drive along virtually non-existent roads, but superior upholstery and suspension of would make the journey bearable. So would the satisfaction of having his prize stowed in the back of one of the cars, snug in a foam-lined steel flightcase.

Badenhorst smiled.

Three months, and then the killing would begin.

Now *there* was something to look forward to.

THREE MONTHS LATER

ONE

Ushuaia, Tierra del Fuego

THE VOYAGER HAS come to the end of the world.

No, scratch that. Too corny.

The weary travel writer has come to the end of the world.

Nope. Still too corny.

How about: *At the very tip of the South American continent, in the southernmost city on the planet, you can truly believe you have run out of civilisation, and there is nothing beyond and nowhere left to go.*

Hmm. Maybe.

Or why not just have done with it and start like this? *"I sing of arms and the man, he who, exiled by fate, first came from the coast of Troy to Italy, and to Lavinian shores – hurled about endlessly by land and sea, by the will of the gods, by cruel Juno's remorseless anger…"*

Anthony Peregrine looked up from his laptop with a sour expression, half scornful, half rueful.

If in doubt, turn to the classics for inspiration. Even if your chosen quotation was only tangential to the subject matter, it sure as hell lent your copy a touch of sophistication.

Then, of course, there was the plain unvarnished truth. He could go with that option – although there was barely a person alive who would believe it.

The immortal, now with three millennia under his belt, has come to Patagonia to write a series of colour pieces for gofar.com because that's what he currently does for a living: roams the world and cobbles together articles about the places he visits for the benefit of semi-respectable travel websites. It's really just a pose, though, the travel writer thing. A pretext for the wanderlust that has consumed him throughout his extraordinarily long life, ever since the fall of Troy. Something to justify his inability to settle down in any one spot for any meaningful length of time.

The laptop screen remained resolutely blank, the page word-free. The cursor blinked like someone tapping their foot.

Another beer.

Anthony ordered a fresh pint of Hain, the local draught lager, and sipped it, gazing out across the Beagle Channel towards the island of Navarino. He was in Argentina, and across the strait lay Chilean territory. A few boats plied the bleak grey stretch of water, deep-sea fishing vessels mostly, leaving harbour, along with a couple of catamarans taking sightseers out on whale-watching and seal-spotting excursions. A sharp wind from the Atlantic ruffled up small waves and swirled into the open-sided seafront bar, but its bite was mitigated by the heat from a log fire blazing in a raised stone hearth.

The beer didn't bring immediate inspiration, but it did go some way to quenching the ennui Anthony was feeling. He wondered whether this travel writing gig had run its course. He had been at it for – what was it, a couple of decades now? – supplying copy first for airline in-flight magazines and then online outlets. The novelty, such as it was, had worn off. He was running out of things to say, different ways to describe the destinations he fetched up in. It was hard not to lapse into cliché when the world was becoming increasingly homogenised, when diversity and individuality were being drowned by the rising tide of McDonald's, Starbucks and Coca-Cola...

No, he couldn't blame his dissatisfaction on multinationals and the march of globalisation. That was too easy, too trite.

Anthony's problem was that there was nothing new for him, nothing he hadn't seen countless times before, in one form or other. Three thousand years – that sort of longevity took its toll.

So why not just knock it out? It was only a few paragraphs of mindless clickbait that readers would scroll through in seconds, something to link some stock photos together and generate traffic for advertisers. They were hardly expecting James Joyce, were they? Besides, he had promised at the end of his previous article that he'd be writing about Tierra del Fuego in this one. He had fans, a small core of devoted followers, some of whom travelled to the places he recommended. He couldn't let those people down, could he? He had to give them *something*, even if it wasn't much.

So...

Ushuaia is a city of contrasts. The capital of Tierra del Fuego, it nestles at the foot of the snow-capped Martial Mountains and boasts a thriving port and some excellent restaurants. But it's also unfinished-looking and in parts primitive, littered with low, drab buildings that have a Swiss-chalet feel to them but are otherwise architecturally unremarkable. Industrial zones sprawl towards a rugged, wild coastline. Tepid summers give way to bracing winters, the typical climate of subpolar latitudes. Founded by British missionaries, Ushuaia is now staunchly Argentinian, as evidenced by the Malvinas War Memorial occupying a plaza downtown next to –

"Is that a MacBook Pro?"

Anthony stopped typing, glanced round.

The stranger at the adjacent table waved a hand apologetically. "Sorry, mate. Rude of me. I'm a nosy bastard. Just ignore me."

"No, it's okay," said Anthony. "Glad of the interruption. You a Brit?"

"English, yeah. You a Yank?"

"Kind of. More like a citizen of the world."

"You sound a bit Yank."

"Don't all citizens of the world? Brave of you, though, coming here, if I may say. An Englishman. They're not fond of your country in Ushuaia."

The Englishman shrugged. "I'm a big boy. I can handle myself." He motioned at the laptop. "You a blogger or something?"

"Travel writer."

"Oh. Cool. Must pay all right."

"Why?"

"Well, I couldn't help noticing the hardware, could I? Third gen, right? Fifteen-inch Retina display. Flash storage. Extended battery life. Yours looks like a top-spec model, too. I'd love to be able to afford one of those."

They chatted about MacBooks for a while, and about portable computers more generally, and then the conversation strayed to Anglo-Argentinian relations, the *Top Gear* incident, the Falklands, broadening out from there into a sweeping discussion of geopolitics. The stranger's name was Roy Young, and he was intelligent and engaging company. He had clearly travelled himself, although not to the extent that Anthony had – but then no one had to the extent that Anthony had. He was lithe and well-proportioned, early thirties, in good physical condition, with close-cropped hair that suggested military service at some point in his past. He had come to Ushuaia to ski, he said. It was early June and the season hadn't officially started, but snow had already fallen and he had heard there was already good powder up on Mount Krund. He planned to head up to the Cerro Castor resort in the next couple of days and try out the slopes there. Anthony admitted that he did a bit of skiing himself from time to time and had been toying with the idea of visiting Cerro Castor.

Young bought a round of beers, which endeared him further to Anthony, and as the afternoon shaded into evening the two men grew ever friendlier. They ate dinner together at the bar – sausage casserole, spicy fried potatoes, chicken fajitas, rounds of smoked cheese – and at some point Anthony found himself agreeing to accompany Young on a trip aboard the Tren del Fin del Mundo, the narrow-gauge steam railway that ran from Ushuaia into the Tierra del Fuego National Park. It was a horribly touristy thing to do, but then Anthony was a travel writer. Wasn't he supposed to do horribly touristy things and report back about them? Wasn't that the whole point?

*　　*　　*

ACCORDINGLY, HE AND Young met up the next morning, took a taxi out to the "End of the World" station, and were soon trundling along in a little carriage with large windows, hauled by a puffing locomotive, through a rolling, snow-bleached landscape. The train wended its way along Pico Valley, halted at the Cascada de le Macarena station, then continued onward and upward to its terminus, El Parque station, where the two men alighted.

Young had proposed a hike into the forest, which sounded okay to Anthony as it was more adventurous than turning around and going back, which was what the great majority of the train passengers did. Young had brought a rucksack loaded with provisions, and they were both of them dressed for the conditions – walking boots, puffer jackets, thermal gloves. They strode off towards the treeline, Young setting a forthright pace, Anthony ably keeping up.

For the first kilometre or so, Anthony talked about how the railway line had originally been built to serve the penal colony which had been established in Ushuaia in 1896. The trains had brought timber down from a forestry camp so that the prisoners, used as forced labour, could erect houses and help expand the town.

"Funny how a symbol of one era's suffering becomes another's jolly daytrip jaunt," Young commented.

Anthony chuckled. "I might use that line in my piece."

"As long as you tell everyone who said it."

"Never. I'm a writer. I steal. I don't give credit. Everything is fodder for my prose – even people."

"Bastard."

"At least it suggests the world is getting better."

"What, shamelessly pilfering some other bloke's words of wisdom?"

"No. A prison railway becoming a tourist attraction. The present transcending the past. Suffering giving way to leisure."

"Bollocks," said Young. "The world's just the same as it ever was. Something improves somewhere, something else turns to shit. For every peace treaty that's signed, another war breaks out in a different place. For every dictator who gets overthrown, some other extremist regime pops up and embarks on a genocide." He held up his palms and waved them like the sides of a scales: left up, right down; right up, left down. "It all evens out. Checks and balances, yeah?"

"I like to think there's an upward trend nonetheless," said Anthony. "Continual progress. I take the long view. Life is markedly more pleasant and comfortable now, for the majority, than it was even just a century ago. That's an objective, provable, quantifiable fact. People are living longer, they're healthier, there's more to eat, more free time…"

"Yeah, but at what cost? The cushier it gets for us, the faster we bring on climate change. The more we consume – the more of us there are doing the consuming – the bigger a mess we make of the environment. All the oil, the plastics, the heavy metals, the agrochemicals, the manufacturing… We're dooming ourselves, shitting the bed we lie in, but it's okay, doesn't matter, as long as we've all got pizza delivery and smartphones and the latest app. Speaking of which…"

Young produced an iPhone and took a map reading.

"Don't want to get lost, do we now?"

"For someone who bemoans how consumerism is destroying the planet," Anthony said, "you seem to like your tech."

"I never said I was consistent."

They hiked on in silence for a while, the only sound their feet crunching snow. Roy Young, Anthony thought, was an interesting individual, much more complex than he appeared. On the surface, he was affable, competent, droll, but there were dark undercurrents running beneath. If he had once been military – and Anthony knew what to look for and was sure he had been – then he would have been the type who thought hard about every decision, the type who might even question orders if he felt they didn't serve the best interests of himself and his brothers-in-arms.

Anthony knew of another ex-soldier who had not been good at taking orders – a war hero who had, indeed, argued with his general and refused to fight for several days; one of the things that had earned the war hero enduring fame. He even inspired a saying: 'to sulk in your tent'.

Achilles.

Funny. Anthony hadn't thought about Achilles in years. Their paths seldom crossed. He wasn't even sure where Achilles was these days, what alias he was going by, or what he was busying himself with. Fighting, probably. That was the occupation Achilles loved best. When he wasn't having a big schoolgirl strop about not getting his due spoils of war, of course.

They hadn't ever really been friends, he and Achilles. As young men they had, after all, been on opposite sides of the biggest fight going, although they themselves had clashed only once on the battlefield, and that a skirmish more than anything, brief and inconclusive, with more name-calling than swordplay. Since then they had avoided each other more by chance than design, and on the rare occasions they did bump into each other they engaged in wary, bluff banter, never quite able to forget that at one time there had been lethal enmity between them, but equally well aware that life had moved on. It bonded you, whether you liked it or not: the act of desperately trying to kill another person who was desperately trying to kill you. It was as intimate, in its way, as sex.

Young caught Anthony eyeing him sidelong.

"I'm not gay, you know," the Englishman said.

"Neither am I."

"It's just, the way you're looking at me..."

"You remind me of someone, that's all," Anthony said. "Someone from the dim and distant past."

"Oh. Okay. Thought I should clear it up, though, the gay thing. I didn't suggest we go hiking so that I could seduce you, or vice versa."

"In this cold? Are you mad?"

Young laughed. "Too damn right. My dick's so shrivelled up right now, I doubt I could even find it."

"That the excuse you trot out for the girls, is it?"

"Shut it, you wanker."

Definitely a soldier.

Another kilometre, deeper into the forest. Trees rattled their bare branches, and now and then a bird flapped away, a mammal skittered. Young checked their position on his iPhone twice more. Anthony still thought it amazing that he lived in an age when you carried a device in your pocket that told you exactly where you were to within a few metres – among the many other feats it could perform. He remembered a time when sailors navigated by the sun, the stars, landmarks and luck. How could anyone say life had not improved? How could anyone deny that progress was a steady ascent – with, admittedly, the occasional plateau and stumble? Roy Young, with his mayfly lifespan, was simply unable to see how humankind strove constantly to better itself. He was too mired in the now. Give him a few hundred years, time to view the big picture, and he would get it.

The two men came to a clearing. On one side, a slight rise, a three-metre-high bank. On the other, a trickling stream, ice-rimmed, worming its way through a depression in the landscape.

"Coffee?" Young produced a thermos flask.

"Don't mind if I do," said Anthony.

"Fair warning: I've laced it with whisky."

"A sensible precaution."

They sat on rocks and drank from plastic cups. The coffee steamed. Their breath steamed.

Anthony felt good. Yesterday's lapse into self-pity embarrassed him. All he'd needed to lift his spirits was some company. Not being alone reminded you why you existed.

"And now," said Young, rising, "to answer the call of nature. Coffee does that for me."

"Good luck."

"Good luck?"

"Finding your dick."

"I'll do my best. Anthony?"

"Yeah?"

Young seemed on the brink of saying something. Something heartfelt.

But then that wouldn't be very British, would it?

"Doesn't matter. You're a good sort, that's all."

"Thanks. So are you."

Young padded off to find some privacy.

Anthony sat still and listened to his surroundings. The rattle of the stream. The sough of the breeze. The subtle crackle of fallen snow.

Even an immortal should pause and appreciate moments of tranquillity like this.

Especially an immortal.

The bullet hit him a split second before he heard the *crack* of gunfire.

Suddenly he was flat on his back, shoulder numb, gaze fixed on the overcast sky.

Shot.

Somebody had shot him.

Some dumbass son of a bitch had shot *him*.

Pain roared, like a bellows-stoked fire. At the same time a whole volley of bullets came his way. They ricocheted off the rock he had been perched on, which was now shielding him. They kicked up whiffs of snow by his head and feet.

Anthony rolled up tight, making the most of the shelter he had. His shoulder was a mass of flaring agony. There was an in-out wound, the exit point fringed with synthetic fibres from the puffer jacket's stuffing, like a miniature white crown. Now blood, leaking from both holes.

Survivable. He had had worse. In fact, for Anthony, as for all his kind, there was no injury that was not survivable. They healed at the same rate mortals did, but they always healed. Always.

Still the bullets whipped and whizzed towards him. At least three shooters, he estimated. They were situated on the far side of the stream. They had been lying there, concealed, waiting.

Waiting for him?

Or perhaps for Roy Young. Yes, that was more likely. Anthony Peregrine didn't have any enemies that he knew of. None that weren't so long dead that their bones were topsoil. Whereas Young, a former soldier – maybe there was some unfinished business there, some ghost from the past.

Or maybe Argentinians, locals out for payback for the Falklands War. That stood to reason. They had tailed the Englishman all the way from Ushuaia, having singled him out for retribution. Never mind that Young was barely even born when conflict broke out in 1982. To these rifle-toting firebrands, his nationality was enough to make him a legitimate target.

Too bad that they had mistaken Anthony for him.

Too bad for them, that was.

Because Anthony Peregrine did not care for being shot. He was not going to take an insult like that lying down.

Literally.

He sprang to his feet, forbidding his shoulder from hurting. It would not hamper him. He refused.

And he ran.

Not away from the gunfire; towards it.

He ran faster than any mortal could. He ran with god-given speed and agility, jinking, zigzagging, left, right, left, right. To his assailants he would be a blur – moving too swiftly for them to train their sights on him.

They fired nonetheless, but not one of their shots came close.

Anthony hurdled the stream in a single bound, a four-metre leap. He had already noted the position of the nearest gunman: lurking in a stand of evergreens. He dived straight through the foliage, headlong, colliding with the would-be assassin. Together, the two of them rolled and tumbled. A rifle went flying. The gunman let out a grunt of distress. Anthony ended up on top, straddling him. He raised a fist.

The gunman was dressed in fatigues with snow disruption pattern camouflage. He wore goggles and a flak vest, matching colours, white and dark green. He had a holstered sidearm and grenades clipped to a bandolier.

It was all standard military-issue tactical gear, apart from his helmet. That had been modified, sporting a solid crest across the crown from front to back.

Anthony had never seen a contemporary soldier's helmet in such a design before. Nor had he seen a patch of the kind that was sewn onto the man's sleeves: a circle, inset with what looked like the letter M.

He was momentarily taken aback. Things did not compute. This was no Argentinian civilian, no chancer with a hunting rifle and a grudge. This was something else altogether. Something more serious. More dangerous.

Anthony's puzzlement cost him. He took a bullet square in the chest. The impact sent him flying.

He struggled onto all fours. A lung had been perforated. Blood bubbled at the back of his throat. Every breath was a wet wheeze. He could feel nothing between his collarbone and the base of his sternum, just a sense of absence.

But he was a warrior. A Myrmidon, no less.

The man he had knocked flat was scurrying away on hands and knees. Two more men, dressed identically to him, were stalking towards Anthony. Both carried rifles. Anthony couldn't identify make or model – he was no expert in modern weaponry – but these were quality guns, that much he could tell. Nothing so vulgar as an AK-47. Sophisticated, lightweight, top-of-the-range. The men clearly knew how to use them. They were also exchanging positions, one advancing, the other covering. No amateurs, these.

Another pair were zeroing in on him. They had descended from the bank on the other side of the clearing.

Now a third pair, looming from behind.

Anthony stood. Shakily, but he stood.

"Do you know who I am?" he declared in his native tongue, Luwian. "I am Aeneas. Son of Anchises and Aphrodite. Survivor of the sack of Troy. Founder of the city of Rome. A champion. Second only to Hector in the esteem of the Hellenes. I have withstood the hatred of Hera. I have done the bidding of Zeus himself. You gentlemen, whoever you are, have just fucked with the wrong person." His voice thrummed with self-belief and righteous anger. "I am a demigod, and I am about to make each and every one of you suffer for your impudence."

In response, the six men trained their rifles on him, centre of body mass.

A seventh man appeared.

Roy Young.

He sauntered towards Anthony, managing to look respectful and contrite.

"Anthony," he said, "I told you you're a good sort, and I meant it. Another time, another place, we'd have been friends, I reckon. But this isn't that time or place."

Anthony was lost for words. "You... You..."

"Take him down, guys."

Six rifles blurted simultaneously.

Anthony knew only multiple impacts. Multiple sources of pain.

Young stood over him. Anthony's shattered chest heaved. He felt like a jigsaw inside, a mass of jumbled, unjoined pieces. He stared up.

"You're wasting your time," he gasped. "This won't kill me. Can't."

"Maybe not."

Young held out a hand sideways. Someone passed him a hand weapon. A spear. No, a trident. No, only two prongs: a bident.

It was bronze. Just metal.

Yet it seethed. Anthony could sense the power radiating off it, like heat from magma. Rumbling, subterranean power.

Young raised the bident aloft.

"But this can," he said. And he rammed it into Anthony's heart.

TWO

Greenwich Village, Manhattan

THEO'S AGENT HAD chosen a hot new restaurant in the Village for their lunch meeting: Seoul Food, a Korean barbecue place that had got a rave review on the *Huffington Post* and was now taking bookings up to Christmas. How Cynthia had managed to secure them a table, Theo didn't know, but she had. She could work small miracles like that. She had contacts, knew people.

"You've something exciting to tell me," he said after they had ordered. Around them diners chattered, all self-congratulatory smiles, while in the centre of the room an open grill sizzled and flared.

"What makes you say that?"

"I always get the nice-restaurant treatment when it's good news. When it's bad, we go for street-cart hotdogs."

"Am I that transparent to you?" Cynthia said.

"After fifteen years, I'd say so."

"Fifteen? Has it been that long?"

"Almost. Fourteen and change."

"And you don't look a day older than when I first took you on."

"Oh, nonsense," Theo said, deflecting the comment. He knew

she had intended it as a compliment, nothing more, but it was a little too on-the-nose; if she had begun to notice, he would have to be ending their relationship soon, before she seriously started to wonder why he never aged – and that would be a shame, both professionally and personally. Cynthia Klein was a good literary agent. She was also a good human being.

"But it's true," Cynthia said. "Most authors stay perennially young only in their publicity stills. With you, it happens in real life. How do you do it?"

"Clean living. Regular exercise. Botox."

"Ha-ha. I like what you've done with your hair, by the way. Makes you look... distinguished."

He had gone for a more sophisticated cut than previously, and switched his styling gel for a brand that gave a drier, less glossy look. Small alterations in his appearance like this were intended to give the impression that he was maturing. It was a trick he had developed back in the 1930s, when photography became commonplace and created a permanent record of how you looked, something people could turn to if they wanted to make then-and-now comparisons. Photos, unlike memory, were objective. They were evidence.

"Maybe I'm hoping to be taken more seriously as a writer," he said.

Cynthia flapped a heavily bangled forearm. "Forget that BS. Literary respectability? Hah! If you're making it big time in genre, who needs reviews in the *New Yorker*? Believe me, those guys churning out the Great American Novel every five years, they'd kill for your sales figures."

Food arrived: great rectangular slabs of marinated sirloin and cubic chunks of boneless rib, along with a selection of *banchan*, little vegetable side dishes. As Theo and Cynthia tucked in, his phone rang. He checked the screen and thumbed Reject. It probably wasn't important. Voicemail would do.

"Glad to know I take priority over whoever that was," Cynthia said.

"Always, Cynth. So, don't keep me in suspense. How did it go with Simon & Schuster?"

"Congratulations, Mr Stannard. You are now in possession of a brand spanking new two-book deal."

She raised her glass of mineral water, and Theo clinked it with his diet soda. Cynthia was a recovering alcoholic, ten years sober, and out of deference to her Theo only ever ordered soft drinks in her presence.

"Advance?"

"Mid-six-figures per book is the offer, but I'm going to hold out for an extra hundred K for each. They want to keep you, and they know Random House are sniffing around. That's mainland only. We retain overseas rights, of course."

"Of course. And they don't mind that only one of the books is a Jake Killian novel?"

"Jake's the moneymaker, no question, but S&S like the synopsis for *The Golden Thread* very much, and they're willing to take a gamble. The idea of an Ancient Greek murder mystery tickles them. They think it could turn into a series – a second string to your bow. Something maybe to fall back on, if the Jake Killians ever start losing traction, which they won't. I've got to ask, though. We know you're a god among contemporary crime writers…"

"Well, not quite."

"Ah, modesty. I used to know what that was. Good thing you have me to blow your trumpet for you." She had a dirty laugh. "That came out wrong."

"It's easier someone else blowing your trumpet than blowing it yourself."

Now her laugh was positively filthy. "The issue I'm trying to address here is, you've not done historical fiction before. Between us, are you sure you're up to it?"

"Pretty sure," Theo said. "I can do the research. And like I always say when giving pro tips, if you can't find a suitable fact, just make one up. Nobody –"

His phone rang again. He checked. Same caller. As before, he rejected.

"I'm not normally this popular," he said.

"Did I see that name right?" Cynthia had glimpsed the caller ID. "Chase Chance?"

"Yup."

"As in *the* Chase Chance? The *Monster Hunter* fella? From TV?"

"Yup."

"I didn't know you knew him."

"I do."

"How long?"

Almost my entire life, and that's longer than you think. "A while."

"Good friends?"

"Guess you could say so."

Cynthia leaned a little closer, dropping her voice. "Does he have representation? I mean, he must do. He's had at least three tie-in titles published. What I'm asking is, is he happy with his agency? Maybe he'd like to step things up, take it to the next level."

That was Cynthia. Forever hustling.

"Lucky I'm used to you, Cynth," Theo said. "Otherwise I might take offence, you working me to get another client."

"Girl's gotta make her targets."

His phone beeped. Now a text. From Chase Chance.

"Shit. Look, I'll turn it off."

"Is that him again?"

"Yes."

"Well, see what he has to say. He obviously needs to talk with you."

"Okay."

Theo pulled up the text.

Call me. Urgent.

He frowned.

"What's he after?" Cynthia said.

"Don't know. Mind if I deal with it?"

She waved assent. "Just don't forget to ask him about his agent. You know he can't do better than me."

Theo exited the restaurant, and the humid Manhattan heat hit him like a wall, stifling after Seoul Food's air-conditioned interior. The street outside was busy as only Greenwich Village at midday in the summer could be – nose-to-tail taxis, swerving bike messengers, sidewalks crammed with hipsters, wage slaves and tourists. He punched up Chase's name from his contacts list and pressed Call.

"Yeah, Theo, you get my voicemails?"

"Didn't listen to them. Thought you could give it to me straight, whatever it is. Where are you?"

"San Juan."

"That's... Mexico?"

"Puerto Rico."

"I knew that. Filming?"

"You betcha. Look, cuz, this connection's shitty, so I'll just get down to it. You heard about Anthony Peregrine?"

"Who's that?"

"What do you mean, who's that?"

"I'm guessing he's..." Theo lowered his voice. Nobody was eavesdropping. Passers-by passed by, nobody cared. He was just another Manhattanite, on his phone. Still, discretion was your life. You were a member of a highly exclusive club and you took pains not to advertise the fact. "One of us."

"Hell, yes, he's one of us."

"But I can't put a name to... the name. I don't keep tabs on us all."

"Well, Anthony Peregrine is Aeneas's latest alias. Or rather, *was*."

"Was?"

Theo felt something in the pit of his stomach, not quite fear; unease, fear's handmaiden.

"They're saying he's dead," said Chase.

"*They're* saying? Who's saying?"

"Couple of news feeds. Reports from Argentina. I got a ping from Google Alerts earlier today."

"You Google Alert us?"

"Hey, you may not keep tabs. I do. It's fun to know what the relatives are up to."

"The very distant relatives."

"It's not like we have family reunions. Anyhow, that's not the point."

"No. The point is he can't be dead. Aeneas can't be. That's not possible. Unless he's switching to a new identity."

"Yeah, but that's not how we do it, is it?" said Chase. "We don't fake our deaths. Not any more. Because it's too hard nowadays. You can't just get hold of some stranger's corpse, mess up its face and pass it off as your own. Forensic pathology has put paid to all that. So we just duck out discreetly and go be someone else. That's the way."

"Maybe Aeneas has decided to go old-school."

"He's a damn idiot if he has. And Aeneas is many things, but a damn idiot isn't one of them."

"How is he supposed to have died? Do you know?"

"Something to do with an avalanche, seems to be the gist of it. Killed in, by, under, an avalanche in the Martial Mountains, down in Tierra del Fuego."

"So then it must be a mistake. Must be someone else called Anthony Peregrine. That or it's misidentification of the body. Either way, they've got the wrong guy."

"Yeah, that's what I'm thinking. But I'd like to know for sure, one way or the other."

"Me too," said Theo. "You have a number for him?"

"Nope. You're the only family member I keep in touch with – which is a tragedy for at least one of us."

"If not both."

"So I'm volunteering to go down there and do some nosing around. I'm not expecting you to tag along. The great Theo Stannard doesn't leave Manhattan, does he? Superstar thriller writer, with his swish Gramercy Park apartment and his ten-grand-a-year health club and his cute twenty-something publicists with the tits and teeth."

"Not fair."

"But accurate. But as a matter of fact, I don't mind going alone. I'm nearer, and there's no point both of us having a wasted trip, if that's what it turns out to be."

"Okay. Works for me."

"I can't leave Puerto Rico for another two or three days. I'm at the tail end of... something. You know. Business to finish. We've wrapped, but there's one last thing to take care of."

"A world free of monsters."

"Got it in one, cuz. But when I'm done with that, I'll fly south, see what's what."

"Appreciated," said Theo. "It's almost certainly nothing, but keep me posted anyway."

"Will do. And Theo? Remind me. Who's got a constellation?"

Theo groaned. "For fuck's sake…"

"Yeah, but out of the two of us? Is it me or you? Let me think…"

"That never gets old, Chase."

"Sure doesn't," said Chase Chance brightly, and hung up.

"YOU LOOK GLOOMY. Preoccupied."

So said Cynthia as Theo sidled back into the restaurant and retook his seat.

"Do I? Shouldn't. Not with that book deal in the offing."

"What'd he say? Chase Chance, Monster Hunter?"

"He was just – just touching base. That's all."

"Representation?"

"Didn't find out. Didn't come up."

"Ah well. I'll keep badgering you. You know I will." She added, "You do seem worried, though."

"I'm not."

Not yet, he added mentally.

He resumed eating his meal. The food was excellent; he ought to be enjoying himself, but he wasn't.

Cynthia rattled on, in her way. Contract fine print. Royalty thresholds. Foreign markets. A hint of Hollywood interest. Potential this. Probable that. Avenues to pursue, calls to make, trees to shake. Theo heard, but didn't listen.

Aeneas was dead?

Couldn't be.

If he was, what did that mean for the rest of them?

THREE

El Yunque National Forest, Puerto Rico

CHASE CHANCE STALKED through the rainforest. He knew his prey was nearby. He knew, too, that his prey was aware he was there.

The beast had gone to ground. It seemed to have sensed that the man tracking it was no ordinary being. He was implacable; he was nemesis. Chase could almost smell its terror. But terror did not make it any less dangerous. Quite the opposite.

This was the creature he and his camera crew had been pursuing for two weeks, seemingly without success. They had camped out at the edge of the El Yunque National Forest and ventured in every night, shooting on high-def video with a low-light image-intensifying attachment. Along with innumerable mosquito bites, they had gathered a hundred hours of footage. There'd been no direct contact with their quarry, but enough creepy moments – rustles in the undergrowth, flashes of retinal reflection, eerie animal calls – to fill out forty-three minutes of running time and generate another nail-biting, ratings-grabbing episode. Chase Chance, Monster Hunter never actually found any of the monsters he hunted, but viewers didn't seem to mind, aside from a few online grousers who thought that the show was all foreplay and no fuck. The thrill, for the folks at home, was the search, the atmosphere, the possibility…

Chase, in fact, had spent most of the two weeks deliberately steering himself and the crew *away* from where the creature was. He had figured out the location of its lair pretty early on: somewhere in the strip of forest between the western bank of the Icacos River and the El Toro Wilderness Area. Its trails and spoor all led in that direction.

Consequently, he had made sure to stay east of the Icacos, pretending, with all his pop-science authority, that he was busy narrowing down the creature's whereabouts. At one point, out of sight of the crew, he had adapted a mongoose's pawprint in the mud with his knuckles, then drawn it to their attention and speculated whether it might well belong to the animal they were looking for. Both Joey the cameraman and Ahmed the sound guy had fallen for the ploy, as had production assistant Mary-Anne, usually the sceptic in the group. All three became a little more agitated, a little more panicky. Upping the crew's anxiety levels was part and parcel of the show's appeal. If Chase could get them spooked and apprehensive, their excitement transferred to the viewers. Result: subscription channel gold. An audience of four million, domestic, on average. Double that, worldwide.

Chase Chance was US television's premier cryptozoological adventurer. As the show's credits voiceover put it, "He chases the animals that are rumoured to exist, that aren't supposed to exist, that *should not* exist." Over three seasons so far he had gone after yetis, lake monsters, giant earthworms, outsized felids, pterosaurs, owlmen, mothmen, apemen, prehistoric fish, flightless birds, every conceivable kind of cryptid. Wherever one reared its head, or allegedly did, there he and his crew went. Nepal, Mongolia, the Australian Outback, Congo, Cambodia, Cornwall – Chase and team crisscrossed the planet, racking up thousands of air miles in their ceaseless quest. Every time, they came home empty-handed, with nothing to prove conclusively that any such beasts were to be found. That, it seemed, was the abiding message of *Monster Hunter*: there are no monsters. Chase would say as much in his to-camera piece at the end of each episode. He would deliver a spiel about hoaxes, misunderstandings, wrongly interpreted evidence, over-credulousness, the human love of a good mystery. He would say he continued to *want* to believe, but he hadn't yet found anything to make him believe.

It was pure baloney.

There *were* monsters.

And Chase had dedicated himself to eradicating each and every one of them.

Often his investigations turned up nothing whatsoever; the cryptids were genuinely bogus, just local folklore or tourist board flim-flam. Still, he got an episode out of it, airtime filled, no harm done.

Then there were the occasions when he happened upon a real cryptid. Something outside the standard taxonomy. Something anomalous. A throwback to a bygone age.

And he would destroy it.

THIS WAS ONE of those occasions.

His prey was a chupacabra.

For two weeks, Chase had gone to great lengths to disprove the existence of the legendary "goat-sucker", which had first been spotted in Puerto Rico in the mid-1990s before cropping up elsewhere in the world. A rash of recent sightings by villagers living on the periphery of El Yunque had drawn the *Monster Hunter* team to the region. A couple of goats had turned up dead, their throats torn out, which seemed to put the matter beyond doubt. A chupacabra was once again at large, slaughtering livestock in its trademark fashion. The wounds were large and ragged, so it was impossible to judge whether or not vampirism had taken place, but the goats' bodies were sufficiently bloodless that it seemed likely.

Chase had got Joey to shoot footage of a feral dog wandering between houses in one village. Through deft editing and use of commentary, it could be implied that the dog, or another like it, was responsible for the goat deaths. It helped that the animal was stricken with mange. Traditionally a chupacabra was hairless, with spikes on head and back. When people as far afield as Maine and Russia thought they had seen one, what they had in fact seen was a disease-ridden hound with patches of spiky, clumpy fur.

Then, for Chase, it had simply been a case of misdirection, keeping his crew keyed up and jumpy in the rainforest after dark, while artfully avoiding places where they stood any real chance of running into the chupacabra.

The three of them – Joey, Ahmed, Mary-Anne – were presently on their way back to Burbank, to start piecing the show together in an editing suite. Chase had elected to stay on in Puerto Rico for another day or so, to "soak up the culture," he had said. No sooner were they off to the airport, however, than he was back up in El Yunque.

Hunting.

The rainforest, this morning, was all water. Mist hung, streams burbled, leaves dripped. The tree canopy blocked out the sun, but the heat was still tremendous. The air was burning soup. Chase, soaked with sweat, trod through the green, mountainous terrain, stepping over vast rosewood and teak roots and brushing aside giant ferns. A frog screeched shrilly – a five-centimetre-long *coqui*, as loud as it was tiny. A macaw cawed. Hummingbirds shimmered.

Chase could not allow himself to be distracted. There was only one animal he was interested in right now. The rest were just background noise.

The chupacabra's lair was close; just over the next ridge. Chase slowed his progress. Every footstep counted. Every movement must be steady and careful. Stealth was all.

He climbed the incline, placing his feet with precision in the thick loam, toe to heel, so that he wouldn't slip.

He recalled a time. The first time. His first ever monster. He remembered how he had journeyed to her home, an abandoned Hittite temple beyond the river Okeanos, which was reputed to be the source of all of Earth's fresh water, in the region that would come to be known as Mesopotamia. He remembered how he had approached her and her two sisters backwards, guiding himself by the reflection in his shield. He remembered how he had lopped off her snake-haired head with a sickle and stuffed it in a carrying bag, for later use, never once catching its grey, baleful gaze.

Every hunt thereafter had had its moments, its own risks, its own challenges.

But none would ever be quite as terrifying and exhilarating as that first, his victory over the Gorgon Medusa. It had been the moment when he realised his destiny, when he finally understood why he had been born and what he was meant to do with his life. When he stopped being just the bastard son of a god – Zeus, who had impregnated his mother Danae in the form of a shower of gold – and became Perseus, slayer of monsters.

He MISSED THAT sickle. It had been the ideal weapon. A gift from Hermes, its adamantine blade never needed sharpening. Its heft was just right, perfectly balanced in his hand. It cut almost without effort, finding no resistance in the thickest of hide or the densest of bone. He had surrendered it to Odysseus as part of the divine weapons amnesty, the covenant made among the demigods some five centuries BCE. Not a day went by when he didn't regret that decision, even though it had been for the common good.

The combat knife he used these days was a decent implement, no question. A Kizlyar Voron-3, the preferred hand weapon of Russia's Spetsnaz special forces. Fixed-blade. Damask steel. Textured grip. Blood groove. It killed, and killed well.

But it wasn't his sickle.

At last he crested the ridge. Below, in a shallow valley, grew a massive mahogany. Its trunk was split at the base; within this fissure the chupacabra had made its nest. The hollow conical space was the size of a tepee. Nice, cosy and dry.

The beast was waiting for him in there. For all his precaution, it would have heard him coming, scented him. Had Chase simply gone stomping towards it, making no effort to be furtive, it would have bolted. That was how it avoided the tour parties and foraging villagers that strayed onto its home turf. The moment it caught wind of them crashing through the forest, it ran away, returning once they had gone.

With this hunter, the chupacabra sensed that its only chance was concealing itself. Biding its time. Lurking in the darkness of its lair until an opportunity came.

An opportunity to attack.

Chase understood the creature. He understood its desperation. It knew there was no point in fleeing, not from him. Hope of survival lay in sudden, overwhelming force. Do or die. Kill or be killed.

And so it went.

The chupacabra charged. At breakneck speed, it launched itself from the fissure.

It was as ugly as a nightmare. A metre high from paws to haunches, hunched, leathery, brown-grey like a bat, with a stubby muzzle and wide-spaced, tar-black eyes. It snarled as it ran, exposing primary fangs as thick as fingers and a host of splayed secondary fangs like needles, all glistening with slobber. Its claws kicked up sprays of leaf mould. Its spikes were raised, like bristling hackles. Its expression was a concentrated, ferocious scowl.

Chase planted his feet, knife at the ready, braced to meet it.

When it was within striking distance, the chupacabra sprang.

Chase, lightning-quick, ducked.

The beast sailed over his head, but it landed solidly and spun round with barely a pause. Snarling still, it rushed him again. Chase side-stepped and slashed. The chupacabra evaded the knife thrust, twisting like an eel, so that he nicked its flank rather than ripping open its belly. It yipped in pain but was instantly back on the offensive. It wasn't just operating on fight-or-flight adrenaline now; it was affronted, angry.

Jaws wide, fangs bared, it scuttled in low. Its target was the soft parts, the stomach, the genitals. A crippling bite.

Chase skipped backwards, away, knife to the fore. The chupacabra halted, then feinted. Chase stood his ground. The beast feinted again. He stayed stock still. The chupacabra was trying to learn about him. It wanted to see which way he tended to go when threatened, left or right. Then it could exploit that when it attacked for proper.

Smart little fucker.

A third feint, but Chase sprang a surprise by lunging straight at it. The chupacabra, caught on the hop, felt a powerful hand grab it by the scruff of the neck. Next thing it knew, its head was being pressed into the forest floor. The knife was poised, point downward, above its eye.

It fought back, writhing, legs flailing. A claw raked Chase's knee.

Son of a bitch!

He recoiled instinctively, letting go of the chupacabra, which in a flash righted itself. Chase had had the upper hand, a perfect kill position. A lucky swipe of the paw had cost him that. Once more, he and the creature were on an equal footing.

The cut in his knee wasn't deep, but it hurt and hindered movement. The chupacabra went on the attack with renewed ferocity, a rapacious glint in its eye. It had drawn blood, something it never expected to. Perhaps this predator was not as unbeatable as it had first thought.

What followed was a flurry of close-quarter violence. The chupacabra dived, gnawed, danced, leapt. Chase fended, grappled, swerved, retaliated. Together, face to face, they swung about in rough circles. Everything outside of their fight ceased to matter. Monster and demigod vied with all their might for supremacy. Both knew that the struggle would end only when one of them was dead or incapacitated. Both were determined not to be that one.

It was a battle of attrition. Soon the chupacabra was riddled with stab wounds, some of them long scratches, a few penetrating. Chase had lost a chunk of meat from his left forearm and had a couple of lacerating bites on his legs. Blood glistened in the murky green rainforest light. The leaves of various flowering bromeliads around them were spattered with it.

As if by mutual consent, the combatants parted. Exhausted, panting, they eyed each other across a metre of clear ground. The earth between them had been churned up by their feet, as though a small localised hurricane had struck. Loam-dwelling insects, disturbed, exposed, crawled to find shelter.

"Enough," said Chase. "You know as well as I do what the outcome's going to be. Let's get this over with."

The chupacabra growled in response, saying in its bestial language much the same as he had.

It pawed the ground. Chase tensed, muscles quivering.

Now!

They hurtled at each other simultaneously.

There was a jet of blood, a shriek of pain.

They had passed each other, and Chase crouched, down on one knee, knife held backhand, while the chupacabra stood, head bent, very still. They stayed in this tableau, back to back, for four, five, six seconds...

Then Chase turned his head, and the chupacabra did the same.

They shared a look: plangent, fatalistic, resigned.

The blade of the Voron-3 was coated in blood and little shreds of flesh.

The chupacabra let out what sounded like a sigh, as if it had needed to see the knife to confirm what its body was already telling it.

Then, all at once, its innards tumbled from its unsealed abdomen in a huge, wet, yellow-and-purple clump.

A heartbeat later – a last heartbeat – the creature keeled over, utterly dead.

CHASE SANK TO a squat, elbows on thighs, and for quite a long time just stared at the deceased cryptid. The stink of its eviscerated bowels was pungent, almost nauseating, but he was too tired even to think of moving away. He studied the corpse, every hideous inch of it, from pugnacious muzzle to skinny tail tip.

He felt, as he often did in the aftermath of a slaying, both elated and sombre. He wanted to whoop. He wanted to weep.

In the end, sore in a dozen places, clothing tattered and torn, he stirred himself. He rose stiffly and stood over the chupacabra, bowed his head, and offered up a small prayer.

"Zeus, father, this beast's death I dedicate to you, for your glory, and to you, Hermes and Athena, who guided and aided me in a time of need. My triumph is yours. Hear me on Olympus and know that you are respected and honoured."

Finishing, he waited. The rainforest echoed with liquid sounds. There was nothing else. No reply. No sign. Not a hint of divine acknowledgement. Silence, only, from the gods.

No great change there, then. Ever since the Age of Heroes passed, the gods had been conspicuous by their absence. They had withdrawn from the Earth, no longer involving themselves in the lives of men. No more intervention. No more interference. Nothing but lofty indifference. They had relinquished all responsibilities and duties. Their secession had been absolute, even to the point of ignoring their own half-human offspring.

Chase shook his head, grin lopsided.

Then, with his knife, he commenced hacking out a shallow grave for the chupacabra.

TWENTY-FOUR HOURS LATER, he was aboard a Copa Airlines Boeing 737 travelling from San Juan to Panama City, where he would catch a connecting flight to Buenos Aires and from there a third plane down to Malvinas Argentinas Airport at Ushuaia. He had patched up his wounds with bandages, gauze and antiseptic ointment, given himself a tetanus shot, and bought some super-effective painkillers from a pharmacy. A high dose of codeine and a couple of rum and Cokes from the drinks trolley were making him feel very happy indeed, as far above his aches and pains as the airliner was above the Caribbean.

His thoughts were now fixed firmly on Aeneas, a.k.a. Anthony Peregrine. While hunting the chupacabra, he had not allowed himself to give head-space to anything except finding and killing the creature. Able to relax at last, cushioned in a first-class seat, buzzing on booze and pills, he wondered what he would find when he got to Patagonia.

As Theo had said, Aeneas couldn't be dead. It wasn't possible. But if this was him making the transition from one identity to another, ending a life that had outworn its usefulness and embarking on a brand new one, then why was he doing it so publicly, so traceably? Did he reckon, just because he was faking his death in a remote little city at the ass-end of the world, he was more likely to get away with it? Was he hoping some hillbilly Argentinian coroner was simply going to rubber-stamp the cadaver and not perform a proper inquest? Was that the plan? Did he think no one would consult dental records, cross-check with international databases, and do whatever else due diligence required, and spot discrepancies? You couldn't expect to pull off a trick like that, not in the interconnected, information-rich twenty-first century, where every fact about every person was only a mouse click away.

What the hell was Aeneas playing at?

When Chase caught up with him – and he would – he was going to give his nephew a piece of his mind.

FOUR

Republic of Vanuatu, South Pacific

THE TIGER SHARK was getting interested.

Too interested.

At first it had hung off at a distance from the tour group, little more than a grey shark-shaped silhouette in the water, some fifty metres away. It had been curious about them, but had decided that the eagle rays that swarmed about the reef were more alluring. The rays were what the dive tourists had come to see; they were also what the tiger shark had come to eat. It had seemed as though everyone was going to get their wish and there would be no confrontation, no conflict of desires, no overlap.

Then the shark changed its mind. It stopped turning smooth figures-of-eight at the reef's edge and began finning towards where the divers hung in the water in a cluster. It didn't swim directly at them, but patrolled back and forth in front of them, coming that little bit closer with each pass.

Isaac Merrison clutched his spear-pole, hoping he wouldn't have to use it.

The shark was five metres long, a sizeable specimen, though Isaac had seen larger. He estimated its bite radius at fifty centimetres, give or take. This was a fish that would have no trouble taking off a person's arm or leg, and no qualms about doing so either, if provoked. An apex predator that big had no natural enemies, except maybe orcas, and they would challenge it only in numbers, never one-on-one. It certainly wouldn't be scared of a handful of humans in wetsuits.

The divers would be all right as long as they didn't give the shark a reason to feel threatened, and it was Isaac's job, as tour leader, to make sure that didn't happen. He turned to the group and performed a patting motion with one hand, the signal for "Take it easy, relax". The other divers formed "okay" signs with thumb and forefinger to acknowledge. Their expressions, judging by what he could see of faces mostly hidden by wraparound dive masks and primary regulators, were calm and collected.

Isaac turned back to watch the shark. It was still being inquisitive, but it wasn't behaving erratically or aggressively – yet. The moment it dipped its pectoral fins, arched its back or pointed its head downward; that was when it was time to intervene. Isaac had no wish to hurt the beast. It was just a tiger shark, doing what tiger sharks did: scoping out potential meals, assessing danger in the environment, living its blamelessly primordial existence. He would bring the spear-pole into play only as a last resort.

As far as he was concerned, all the inhabitants of his father's realm were sacred, not least sharks. He felt veneration even for the marine creatures he ate. Squid rings, mahi-mahi steaks, Lobster Thermidor – these dishes were a kind of Eucharist for him, a delight for the soul as well as for the taste buds. Treating himself to the Vanuatu speciality, coconut crab, had become a weekly act of worship, one Isaac had indulged in every Sunday lunchtime since he took up resident on the archipelago's main island, Efate, in the early 'noughties. Poseidon received a small vote of thanks both before and after he tucked in.

The shark would only be attacked if it attacked. And that would not occur if everyone in the tour group kept their heads.

* * *

ISAAC WAS CONFIDENT they would; back on land they had struck him as a bunch of capable and unflappable individuals. Usually his tour groups were a mixed proposition, a few experienced divers and an assortment of eager newbies who had only just gained their PADI open water qualification. In each instance, he would assess the ratio of old hands to first timers, make a judgement, and set the dive difficulty accordingly. It wasn't always easy. No one liked to feel mollycoddled, or that they weren't getting their full money's worth. Equally, a single diver who couldn't cope if things got hairy posed a danger to the entire group.

With this lot, Isaac had been comfortable with pushing the safety envelope. They were, all six of them, in fine physical trim. They were all still in their thirties, meaning the chance of some sudden, unexpected health complication was minimal. Each had produced a certificate attesting to advanced scuba skill. Even their forenames sounded solid and reassuring: Hans, Gavin, Sean, Travis, Roy, and the sole woman, Jeanne.

What had impressed Isaac most about them, however, was the thoroughness with which they had checked the scuba equipment they were renting from him. He serviced the gear himself regularly and knew it was good quality and in full working order. Nevertheless, first at his dive shack and again aboard his boat just before they took the plunge, the six tourists had gone through the inspection routine – buoyancy compensator, weight belt, releases, pressure gauge, cylinder, regulator, dive computer – methodically and efficiently. They had divided up into buddy pairs without being asked to, and each half of each pair had helped the other person suit up and then looked for missing items, tangled air hose, loose-dangling straps, and all the rest. Isaac had not felt so relaxed about a tour group in ages. They knew what they were doing, which meant he didn't need to be quite as vigilant as normal. He could enjoy the dive himself all the more because of that.

If the group had a spokesperson, it was the one called Roy, and Roy had told Isaac that he and his friends were keen to see the eagle rays out on Chapel Reef, which lay some ten kilometres due west from Port Vila. Isaac was aware that Chapel Reef boasted some of the best growths of staghorn coral and sea plume in the region, and was home to anemones, nudibranchs, porcelain crabs, leaf scorpionfish and more, marine life in a bewildering, entrancing range of shapes and colours. Even if the rays didn't show, there would be plenty of beauty to gaze at. But the reef was also situated beside a steep seabed drop-off, and the currents there could be complex and hazardous. It all depended on tidal strength and direction. He did some calculations, factored in the group's level of ability, and reckoned there wouldn't be a problem.

EVEN A FIVE-METRE shark wasn't, Isaac thought, a problem. Everybody in the group seemed to be keeping their wits about them. They clustered close together, presenting the shark with what it would perceive as a larger entity, something to be avoided.

There was still a tiny part of Isaac that wanted to attack the shark, just on principle. He could feel the urge inside him. He was tracking the creature's every movement with his eyes – eyes which had once been blinded, then healed, and were still as sharp as any hawk's – and gauging its weak spots. The shark's own eyes, of course, were a good place to drive a spear tip into, as were its gills and its ventral area. Alternatively, he could toss the weapon aside and take the creature on bare-handed, if he felt that way inclined. Wrestle a tiger shark to death? Not impossible, not for him. Flipping it onto its back would paralyse it. Then he could prise apart its jaws until they split at the hinges and leave it to bleed out, or else take the less gory but more stamina-demanding option of holding it still for fifteen minutes so that, with water no longer flowing through its gills, it suffocated to death.

But that was the old him. That was Orion. He no longer killed needlessly, just to prove his greatness. He was not a hunter any more. Not *the* Hunter. He was just a guy called Isaac Merrison who ran a dive tour business on a holiday-destination island in the South Pacific, and lived in a modest beachside bungalow with views across the sea to several of the other, smaller islands that made up the Vanuatu archipelago. The days of his braggart youth, when he repeatedly proclaimed that there was no wild beast he could not catch and slay, and when he repeatedly got into trouble for his arrogance, were far behind him. He hardly recognised any more the man whom Hesiod and blind Homer had written about in their poems. Was that him? Had he really raped King Oinopion's daughter Merope, just because her father welched on a deal? Had he really let Oinopion get him drunk, giving the king the opportunity to blind him in revenge? And Merope wasn't the only female he had forced himself onto. There'd been the Hyperborean virgin, Opis, whom he had ravished mercilessly, and he dimly recalled attempting to do the same with Opis's mistress, none other than Artemis, the only being in all creation whose hunting prowess matched his own. The goddess, of course, had rebuffed him easily, and had almost killed him in a fit of anger by sending a giant scorpion after him to sting him to death. *That* had been a close shave.

He thought of that part of his past only with shame. What a puffed-up, thrusting prick he had been – in every sense. Age had definitely mellowed him. Nowadays he hardly ever looked at a woman in a lustful way, let alone touched one. He was content, instead, to help strangers explore Poseidon's domain and show them its wonders. This was his life. He sometimes thought of himself as an aristocratic heir, taking paying guests through the ancestral home and pointing out its treasures.

The tiger shark continued to veer closer, and Isaac turned to the group again, intending to signal them to terminate the dive and go back to the boat. He still didn't think there was any danger, but it paid to be cautious.

He noticed straight away that one of the group was missing. Where there had been six, now there were five.

What the hell…?

A swift once-over told him the absent diver was Roy. He, of all of them, was the one Isaac had thought least liable to panic. Roy was English, with that kind of imperturbable good humour, as though nothing could ever get past his veneer of irony and diffidence. For him to have turned tail and fled – it was hard to fathom. Yes, the tiger shark was menacing, but he must have realised that the greatest safety lay in sticking with the group. Haring off on his own was asking for trouble. The shark would be attracted to a lone swimmer, particularly one thrashing through the water, as Roy doubtless was. No human stood a chance of outswimming a shark. Roy was more or less committing suicide.

Where was he?

Isaac scanned past the depleted group, looking for him. The water was crystal clear, visibility at 100 metres at least. He could see no sign of Roy. Isaac had turned his back on the group for half a minute. There was no way Roy could have swum out of sight in that time. Unless, that was, he had descended into the thickets of coral with a view to hiding out from the shark down there. Again, futile. The tiger shark's eyesight was extraordinarily sharp, and it could detect bioelectric fields and muscle contractions. If it went looking for him, it would find him.

Damn idiot.

Isaac gave one last glance over his shoulder to check on the shark's position. He would have to leave the group to their own devices while he went in search of Roy. They should be able to manage by themselves, even with a shark prowling. As long as none of them had a sudden brainfart and decided to follow Roy's example...

A column of air bubbles wobbled up from below, bursting around Isaac's flippers.

Roy was rising from the reef, kicking upwards at speed.

He was lugging some sort of weapon.

Isaac felt hands grab him from behind. The other members of the tour group swarmed around him. They were holding his limbs, forcing them backwards, pinioning him. He fought against them, but suspended in the water, with no leverage, it was hard. He couldn't bring his full strength to bear.

Up Roy came, and the weapon was a double-bladed battle-axe with a metre-long haft. It sheared through Isaac's torso, slitting him open from solar plexus to Adam's apple. As it cut into him, he thought he heard a massed battle cry, a thousand warriors bellowing at once as they charged towards the foe, a howl of fear and exhortation. His own howl of agony hooted into his regulator and resounded through his skull.

Then he was floating, no longer held by hands, helpless. The water reddened around him, and he could feel three thousand years of life seeping away, ebbing like a tide, like waves from shore.

Orion the Hunter was dying, and another hunter, the tiger shark, shimmied in to take advantage, drawn by the blood in the water. Its jaws were open wide, dark gullet fringed with a corona of teeth. It took a first tentative bite, then another… then feasted.

FIVE

Gramercy Park, New York

IT HAD BEEN a week since Chase called, and Theo was finding the waiting difficult. He tried to work, but couldn't seem to concentrate. He had a book to write, the first of the two he had just signed a contract for, and there was research to be done, a plot skeleton to flesh out, characters to dream up backstories for. Novels didn't just happen. They didn't pop fully-formed from your brain, the way Athena had from Zeus's brow. They had to be seeded, nurtured, watered, encouraged. You couldn't do that if the soil you were planting in was disturbed.

He still did not believe that Aeneas was dead. But believing it and knowing it to be true were not the same thing.

Waking early on a weekday morning, unquiet, he decided to go out for a run to clear his head. Running was brain-in-neutral time. Once you got a decent, steady pace going, it became difficult to obsess on any one thing. You became a body in motion, nothing more. Your thoughts free-wheeled and you just ran.

Day had not yet broken, but New York was already astir; of course, famously, it never slept. Traffic rolled by, commuters getting the jump on rush hour. Garbage trucks growled like hungry bellies. From Gramercy Park, Theo cut through Stuyvesant, then headed south, crossing FDR via the overpass to the East River Park, where he followed the promenade. There were a few other early-morning runners out and about. Theo knew a couple of them by face, well enough to nod to.

Past the Williamsburg Bridge, he found himself on his own for a stretch, nothing but him, the river and the rhythmic plod of his Saucony Triumphs on the asphalt. The sun was rising to his left, Eos surrendering her brief daily reign, giving way to her brother Helios – or so people would have said, back in ancient times, before science stuck up its hand and gave all the answers. The poets' "rosy-fingered Dawn" was now just dispersal of light through atmospheric particles. Eos's siblings Helios and Selene were just the sun and the moon, planetary bodies. Astronomy and physics had toppled the divine, replacing deity with cold hard fact.

You couldn't blame the gods for going into self-imposed exile. The world had taken away their mystique, their mystery. What did that leave them?

A shout from the park snagged Theo's attention, halting him in his tracks.

It had sounded very much like a cry of distress.

He listened. There it came again. From the other side of the park's amphitheatre. A woman. In trouble.

Theo didn't hesitate. He sprinted in the direction the cry had come from, skirting round the amphitheatre – although to call this concrete pit, with its shallow-raked semicircle of bleachers, an "amphitheatre" was an insult to the grand arenas of Ancient Greece, with their elaborate *skené* backdrops and remarkable acoustics.

A third cry.

The woman, whoever she was, sounded outraged. Indignant. But fearful too.

And there she was. Dressed, like Theo, in Lycra fitness gear. A candy-pink MP3 player strapped to her arm.

Fighting with a man who was also dressed for running.

Theo accelerated. He couldn't help himself.

The man had just yanked the earbuds from the woman's ears. He was bellowing at her. Theo couldn't make out the words clearly. The phrase "goddamn bitch" kept recurring, though, and the man's face was purpled, contorted with fury.

A mugging. The man was trying to steal the MP3 player. The woman punched him a couple of times, to little effect. He was a determined thief. It was worth maybe twenty or thirty bucks, but he was willing to take a thumping to possess it.

Theo hit the mugger in the midriff, taking him down like a linebacker tackling a quarterback. The man hadn't even seen him coming. Within seconds Theo had him lying face down, a knee in his spine, one of his wrists twisted up between his shoulderblades. He was pinned.

"What the fuck!?" the man bellowed. "What the hell are you doing? Are you fucking insane? Get off of me!"

"Shut up or I will break your arm," Theo said. A lie. He wouldn't break it. Dislocate it, maybe.

"You can't do this," the man protested. "This is aggravated battery. I will fucking sue. I will sue you so motherfucking hard, even your grandchildren will belong to me."

"Yeah, get off of him, you bastard," the woman chimed in. "Who the hell do you think you are? Goddamn Batman?"

Theo blinked up at her, perplexed. She was taking the man's side? The guy had just attempted to rob her and Theo had come to the rescue. Shouldn't she be thanking her saviour, rather than lambasting him?

"Honey," said the man, face still squashed to the grass, voice muffled. "Take out your phone. Get a pic of this guy. Call the cops."

"I don't have my phone, babe."

"Well, mine's in my fanny pack. Get it out."

"Wait. Wait." Theo let go of the man's wrist and stood up. It was becoming apparent to him that he had made a serious error. "You two know each other?"

"Know each other?" the woman snapped. "He's my husband!"

"But... I saw him grabbing your MP3 player off you. You were hitting him."

"We were having a row, dumbass."

"What?"

"A row. As in arguing. As in what married people do. Drew accused me of not listening…"

"Because you weren't," said Drew, picking himself up and brushing himself down. "I was trying to tell you about how I'm going to put in a bid for a partnership in the firm, and you had your goddamn earbuds in, and you were just 'uh-huh' and 'yeah' like always."

"I was listening!"

"You weren't, Pam. And you know how it drives me nuts, especially when it's important stuff I'm telling you, stuff that affects our future."

"While we're out jogging isn't the best time to be telling me important stuff. I listen to music when I exercise. Why can't you respect that?"

"Why can't you respect *me*?" Drew retorted hotly. "Don't *I* matter?"

"Okay, okay, I see," said Theo, in a placatory tone. "There's been a misunderstanding. I'm sorry. The way it looked – I thought you were mugging her."

Drew rounded on him. "Do I look like a mugger to you? Seriously?"

"No. No, you don't."

"No, he's an attorney," said Pam. "A prosecutor. With Canterbury, Barnes and Bohm, on Lexington."

Evidently Theo was supposed to have heard of them.

"So when I said I'm going to sue your ass," said Drew, "I meant it. I'm going to take you for every cent you've got. Look at these abrasions on my leg. My shoulder hurts. I got bruising." He rubbed the back of his neck. "I may have whiplash."

"I can only apologise."

"Thought you'd play vigilante, huh? Go all Bernie Goetz on me? Well, you just stuck your nose in the wrong people's business. I'm no street thug. I'm an honest citizen."

Theo couldn't resist. "Well, a lawyer."

"Oh, yeah. Ha-ha. Laugh it up. You won't find it so funny when you get summonsed and have to – Hey. Hey!"

Theo had felt an overwhelming urge to punch Drew in the face. But that would only have made a bad situation worse, so he had opted for the wiser alternative. While Drew was still pontificating, he had turned and run.

Drew, with an irate yell, gave chase. Pam followed. They were both toned, fit individuals, and might well have caught up with Theo had he been a mere human being. As it was, he was faster than either of them. Faster by far. He poured on speed, leaving them lagging in his wake. Soon they were out of sight, and all Drew could do was roar further threats of legal action at him, while Pam lobbed some fairly creative insults his way. They continued to do so until Theo was beyond earshot, and probably kept it up for several minutes after.

A CHAGRINED THEO traipsed from the elevator to his apartment. He showered, trying not to think what an ass he had just made of himself. *Of course* the man hadn't been mugging the woman. *Of course* they'd been a husband and wife having a marital spat. In hindsight, it was obvious. How many muggers went out in running gear? How many muggers robbed their victims without brandishing some sort of weapon?

Theo had seen, not what was there, but what he had wanted to see. He had wanted to catch someone in the commission of a crime. He had wanted to weigh in, fists flying, and dish out justice.

Old habits died hard.

Especially when you'd considered yourself a crimefighter for the best part of three millennia. When that had been your raison d'être ever since the road trip from Troezen to Athens, during which you dealt with a half-dozen wrongdoers and made the route safe for travellers again. When you'd dedicated yourself to becoming a champion of the downtrodden and oppressed, and followed that calling down through the centuries, in various forms and guises, mostly with success.

As he got dressed, Theo debated whether Drew and Pam might have recognised him. He was fairly famous, after all. His novels sold in respectable quantities and he had appeared on network television once or twice, promoting them. They might track him down and press charges. That would be awkward and embarrassing. Not to mention, even if the case was settled out of court, costly.

Then again, if Drew and Pam had recognised him, they'd have said something, surely. Luckily for Theo, authors, even popular ones, were more or less anonymous. Their faces didn't get plastered across the covers of celebrity magazines. They weren't profiled on the *E!* channel. Drew would never find him. In a city this big and populous, the chances of them bumping into each other again were minute. That said, Theo resolved to steer clear of the East River Park for the foreseeable future, just to be on the safe side.

Perhaps he shouldn't have run away. Perhaps he should have stayed put and faced the music.

No. Life was complicated enough as it was. No need to complicate it any further.

He was in the mood for work again, at any rate. The clash in the park had invigorated him. His concerns about Aeneas were relegated to a back burner. It was time to sit down at his desk and get some serious plot brainstorming done.

Jake Killian 5 – working title – was going to be the wildest, most out-there Jake Killian novel yet, or so Theo had promised his publisher. His philanthropist adventurer character had so far faced drug lords, corrupt local politicians, environmental polluters and far-right extremists, and emerged victorious each time. Killian was a reluctant sort of do-gooder. He never sought out trouble, it just came his way. All he wanted was to be allowed to travel the world disbursing the millions he had accrued as a black-market arms dealer. He was trying to make amends for the untold suffering he had caused by selling munitions to unsavoury militias and dictatorships. His conversion to the side of the angels followed an incident in Syria when he had witnessed a religious-fundamentalist terrorist open fire on a crowd in a city square with an unlicensed automatic rifle of just the sort that he, Killian, traded in. The tally of victims stood at 34, schoolchildren among them, and the masked gunman, riding pillion on a scooter, had got away without ever being caught and held to account. The attack had been Killian's Damascus moment (literally, in this case), and he had thereafter employed his knowledge of weapons and the combat skills he had acquired during a stint in the US Marine Corps to stand up on behalf of people who had fallen foul of hostile forces and could not fight back for themselves. If he stumbled across a wrong, he did whatever was required to right it. As the strapline on the cover of every Jake Killian novel said, "When Killian comes to town, the bad guys better run."

This time round, Theo planned for Killian to take on international people traffickers. The setting would be Eastern Europe, for the most part. Research would entail reading books about the region, delving into websites, and maybe visiting a couple of locations, plus talking to journalists with first-hand knowledge of the subject matter.

The first task, though, was to lock down the basic plot structure. The narrative needed to open with Killian encountering some situation that would put him at odds with the villains and provide an imperative for him to roll up his sleeves and get stuck in. That was how the other books kicked off. So, what if Killian was visiting a foundation he had set up for the rehabilitation of child prostitutes in, say, Romania, Lithuania, somewhere like that? And what if a bunch of armed goons stormed the premises in order to kidnap a young girl who had recently been rescued from the clutches of their boss, a sinister Russian oligarch? Outnumbered and outgunned, Killian would be unable to prevent the goons from taking the girl, but there was your plot catalyst, your inciting incident, right there. The rest of the novel would detail his efforts to retrieve her and bring down the oligarch and his private army.

Bingo.

Theo began composing an outline, transferring his ideas up onto the screen, feeling his way from one scene to the next, identifying where the chapter breaks should go in order to maximise suspense, establishing a couple of subplots that would weave around the linear main plot like the serpents, adding depth and texture ...

He had been at it for over an hour when his phone rang.

Chase Chance.

* * *

HE COULDN'T IGNORE the call, much though he'd have liked to. He was in the throes of creativity. He was reluctant to break the flow. But...

"Chase."

"Theo."

"What's the word?"

"Not good." Chase sounded sombre. From someone normally so upbeat, this did not bode well.

"How not good?"

"It's him," Chase said. "It's Aeneas all right. Pious Aeneas."

"You're sure?"

"I got to see the body. I viewed it in the morgue. Pretended I was a relative – not actually a lie, really. Took some doing. A bit of browbeating, a bit of bribing. But I did it. And..."

"Categorically, unconditionally, you're telling me you have just seen the body of Aeneas?"

"Less than an hour ago. Fuck me, Theo, it was him and he's dead."

"Killed-in-an-avalanche dead?"

"Crushed. Mangled. A hell of a mess. Face only just about recognisable."

"So it might not be him," Theo said. "Might be a lookalike. I mean, this is standard procedure, isn't it? Or rather, was. Find a stand-in, a substitute, a corpse that resembles you. Dress it in your clothing. Put your personal effects on the body. *Voilà*. Before fingerprinting, before DNA testing, that's how we did it."

"It was him, Theo," Chase insisted. "I'd know if it wasn't. We can tell, can't we? We recognise our own kind. It goes beyond the visual. What I was just looking at in the morgue of the Hospital Gobernador Ernesto M. Campos in Ushuaia was, so help me, a dead demigod."

SIX

Airspace above the Coral Sea, South Pacific

ROY YOUNG WAS reading a Jake Killian novel on his Kindle Paperwhite as the Embraer Legacy 650 large-cabin jet banked on its ascent from Vanuatu's Bauerfield International Airport, turning northward.

It wasn't a great book, in his opinion. Decent enough story, but the prose lacked finesse. Plenty of narrative oomph, but the author, Theo Stannard, could have crafted his sentences a little better. They were punchy, terse, too much in thrall to Chandler and Hammett, without their masterful, jazzy sense of rhythm. The style seemed intended to bludgeon readers into submission, rather than caress and cajole them along.

The novel was absorbing, at least, and Killian was a compelling wish-fulfilment protagonist. A man with a dark past, trying to bring light. Roy needed distraction, and *Killian's Rage*, the third in the series, was providing it.

As the jet levelled out, Roy heard a seatbelt being unbuckled. From the front of the cabin, Holger Badenhorst headed aft to the toilet. "Got to drop the kids off at the pool," he announced to everyone and no one. He emerged several minutes later, wafting a hand in front of his nose. "Phew! What a *klankie*! I'd leave it a while if I were you. Damn islander food. Plays havoc with the guts."

Roy guessed, from the way he had said it, a momentary hesitation, that Badenhorst had substituted "islander" for a crude racial epithet. The Afrikaner was not what you would call politically correct, but he was making an effort to be, in deference to the sensibilities of the multicultural team he had assembled.

As he made his way back up the aisle between the dual rows of plush seats, Badenhorst shared a word or two with his employees. "How's it today? You okay? Travis, great work. Sean. We got him, *nè*? Pulled it off nice and smooth. Hey, Serge. You'll get a go soon enough, don't worry. Onward and upward, eh?"

Finally he came to Roy. He laid an arm on Roy's headrest and leaned in.

"What you doing there? Reading, huh?"

"Yeah."

A fellow Englander might have picked up on Roy's tone, and left him alone. Badenhorst was not English, and something of a stranger to subtlety.

"What is it? Novel?"

"Yeah. Sort of a crime story. Action-adventure."

"Who by?"

"Bloke called Theo Stannard. Heard of him?"

Badenhorst gave him a complicated look he couldn't quite fathom. "Ha! Interesting. Why'd you choose that one?"

"I like thrillers, and his stuff kept coming up on my Amazon recommendations. Some algorithm obviously decided he was my thing, so I thought I'd give him a shot."

"And...?"

"I don't feel qualified to comment yet. I haven't got very far in, you see."

Again, the brisk summation carried a subtext: *I'm really not interested in talking to you.*

"Well now," said Badenhorst, oblivious. "Listen. I just wanted to say, you've been doing great so far." The Afrikaner raised his voice so that everyone in the cabin, all fourteen of them, could hear. "You all have. You're earning your paycheques, and no mistake. But you, Roy…" He dropped the volume back down to conversational level. "Hiding the axe in the reef beforehand – stroke of genius, my friend. I wish I'd thought of it myself. That stupid *kont* Merrison would never have seen it coming."

"Don't call him a *kont*," said Roy. "If that means what I think it means."

"*Ach*, why do you care what I call him? He wasn't a person to you. Just a job."

"Still. Have some respect."

"Whatever." Badenhorst flapped a hand. "I'm complimenting you. Take the praise. You played your socks off yesterday, just like you did in Argentina. *Ja*, Argentina. That was a hell of a thing, that was. Perfectly sprung trap. Target One thought you were his *chommie*. Trusted you. Went along all meek and mild. Lamb to the slaughter. Didn't suspect a thing. And the idea of the avalanche…"

"It seemed logical. He was a skier."

"Ideal. Plant charges, blow up a snowbank, leave the body at the bottom of the slope to get buried… Too bad that a search-and-rescue team decided to comb the area and found him, but, hey. That's the breaks. We dug the bullets out of him, no alarm bells."

"Maybe not straight away."

"Not ever. And on the off-chance that there are, and our targets get wind of what we're up to, it won't make any difference. We've got what it takes to bring them down, each and every one of them." Badenhorst jerked his head in the direction of the cargo hold, where eleven steel flightcases were stored, along with boxes of armaments, uniforms and other matériel. None of these items was listed on the flight manifest; nor were the names of anyone on the jet. Bauerfield International was a medium security airport, and no customs or immigration checks were performed on private aircraft landing or taking off from there. This was true of every airport the team had used and would be using. As long as they avoided the major international hubs, they could slip in and out of sovereign nations with the kind of impunity reserved for diplomats and monarchs.

"Let's not get complacent," said Roy.

"I never do." Badenhorst beamed from one side of his broad Boer face to the other. "All I'm saying is, you're a true asset to the Myrmidons, Roy. I'm glad I chose you. Well done, me."

"Yeah, well done, you," said Roy. "Now, if you don't mind…" He nodded at the Kindle.

The Afrikaner finally took the hint. "Sure, sure. You get on with it. Not much of a reader myself. But this jet comes loaded with movies. I think there's some Jean-Claude Van Damme stuff on there. Bam! Pow!" He mimed punches. "Give me that over a book any time."

Shortly, Badenhorst was back in his seat up front, headphones on, watching a film on the 9-inch HD LCD monitor that swung out on an armature beside his seat armrest. Almost everyone else in the cabin was doing much the same. They had a long flight ahead of them, a little over twenty-four hours, not including refuelling stops. Movies helped alleviate the tedium, and the tension. There was also the option of falling asleep. Jeanne, the French Canadian sitting directly across the aisle from Roy, had plumped for that. Immediately after take-off she had reclined her seat, collared herself with a neck pillow, and closed her eyes determinedly.

She opened them briefly, catching sight of Roy as he looked at her. He gave a cockeyed smile. She nodded, not in an unfriendly way. Then she aimed a glance forward at Badenhorst, grimaced in distaste, and closed her eyes again.

Roy got it. Smart move. If only *he* had had the idea.

He liked Jeanne. Out of the entire squad, she was the one he got along best with; her and the other Englishman, Gavin. The rest weren't disagreeable by any means, except maybe the German, Hans Schutkeker, who was just a little too full of himself for comfort, and of course Badenhorst himself, who was as aggravating as they come but at least seemed to know it. Gavin Martin and Jeanne… Chevrier? Was that her surname? Something like that. Gavin and her, they had a temperament similar to Roy's own. They didn't enjoy what they did – they didn't get a kick out of it, as some of the others appeared to – they did it because they were good at it and weren't suited for much else.

Outcomes facilitators was the official, somewhat euphemistic term for them.

Myrmidons was the group name Badenhorst had given them.

Assassins was what they were, if you wanted to get down to the nub of the matter.

Paid killers.

Wetworkers.

Currently flying aboard a luxury private airliner from the scene of their last operation to the scene of their next.

Roy tried to settle back into *Killian's Rage*, but the mood was gone. He could no longer concentrate on the novel. Instead, he stared out of the window at the glittering ocean for a while. Then he hoicked his phone from his pocket, opened the pictures folder and scrolled through.

There were photos going back years stored in the phone's memory. Not many; Roy was neither a sentimentalist, nor nor a compulsive recorder of his life, as so many were these days. The images were personal: cherry-picked and cherished.

Here was him and a handful of his mates from the regiment, on one of their tours of duty, stationed at Camp Bastion. Young men grinning in the blinding sunshine outside their billet. Arms around shoulders. Desert camo fatigues. A couple of chests bare. Fun in one of the lulls between tiptoeing around IEDs and returning enemy sniper fire.

Here was him and Karen on their wedding day. Josie as bridesmaid, three years old. Mummy and Daddy belatedly tying the knot, both happy, but as far as she was concerned it was *her* day. Hence the pretty dress, the beribboned bunch of flowers, the tiara in her hair.

Here was Josie aged thirteen, not long after her first stay in a psychiatric unit. Smudges of grey beneath her eyes. Hair long and lank. Her shirtcuff not quite hiding the bandage around one wrist. Trying to smile. Putting on a brave face for the camera during a family outing at the seaside. Studland Bay in Dorset. Cloudbanks on the horizon. Sand and marram grass.

Here she was again, sixteen now, looking almost skeletally thin, brittle, in a shot taken just last year. Her and Roy, in the grounds of the clinic in the Swiss Alps. A spread of lawn. Pines. The elegant but rather severe main building behind them. A ridge of white mountaintops in the far background, sawtoothing a blue sky. Neither of them smiling, at least not so as you would notice, despite the encouragement of Benedikt, the orderly taking the photo. Bodies close but not touching. A portrait of the things money could buy, with the things it couldn't notable by their absence.

Roy closed the folder. It always hurt to see what he had had and didn't have any more. The ache of loss was acute.

But it was salutary too.

Karen was gone. She was out of his life. She had a new man. Divorcee, like her; decent bloke, by all accounts. Kid of his own. Last Roy had heard, they were planning to get married.

Good on her.

Josie was not gone, but she was hanging on by a thread. The clinic in Switzerland, just outside Chur in the east of the country, was doing its utmost to keep her alive and hold at bay the despair that wanted to consume her. The doctors were implementing every therapy in their arsenal, from antidepressants to CBT to transcranial magnetic stimulation. The UK's National Health Service had failed her, repeatedly. So had a string of private British mental health institutions. The Gesundheitsklinik Rheintal, which had an international reputation and counted Hollywood A-listers and internet billionaires among its clients, was her best and last hope. But its services did not come cheap. Far from it. Josie's sanity, and her life, were being preserved only at eye-watering expense.

Roy did not begrudge a penny of the cost. He would gladly have paid double, treble. Anything for his daughter.

Help kill a few people he didn't know?

Anything for his daughter.

SEVEN

New York, New York

THEO MET CHASE off the plane at JFK, two days after they had last spoken on the phone. They shook hands and embraced, and Theo offered to carry Chase's holdall. Chase shrugged. His cousin was a stickler for courtesy, and Chase was a stickler for not carrying his own luggage if he didn't have to.

As they crossed the Departures hall, they had to stop twice so that Chase could deal with people who recognised him. He dutifully chatted with the strangers and then posed for selfies, plastering on the game-for-anything grin that he'd direct at the camera while trekking through mud and worse.

"That's how it is for me, cuz," he said in the cab, en route to Manhattan. "Goes with the territory. *Monster Hunter* fans. Anywhere in public in America, I get mobbed."

"There were two of them. Two separate people. That's hardly 'mobbed'."

"Jealous much?"

"No." Maybe a little. "It does worry me somewhat, though, that you've become so famous. One of the aims when you're someone like us is to try to remain as low-profile as possible, isn't it?"

"Says Mr Bestseller List."

"Touché. But at least my ugly mug isn't being beamed into millions of homes every Thursday evening."

"Not forgetting the reruns on National Geographic."

Theo glanced at the cab driver. The plastic safety partition between them and him afforded some privacy, and anyway the guy seemed to be focused more on negotiating through the heavy, crawling traffic than on his passengers. Every so often he would curse loudly in a thick Ukrainian accent, and at one point Theo heard him say, "Grand Central Parkway? Grand Central Parking Lot, more like." But his voice was muffled, and if they kept theirs low, he wouldn't overhear them.

"Without wishing to get into specifics," Theo said, "how long do you expect to carry on *Monster Hunt*-ing?"

"The execs reckon we can squeeze a couple more seasons out of the format."

"And then? Won't there be demand for some sort of follow-up?"

"If there is, I'll just say no. I realise I can't stay, for want of a better word, a celebrity indefinitely. When I've had my fifteen minutes, I'll slip into a new identity, in another country, and pretty soon everyone will have forgotten about Chase Chance. I'm going to have my fun while it lasts – and of course, you know, clean up what needs cleaning up" – his dangerous beasts – "but you don't need to fret. I'm not going to get careless."

"I just felt the issue should be raised," said Theo. "As it happens, I'm planning to start fading into obscurity myself, in the not too-distant-future. Pull the reclusive author schtick."

"Pynchon, Salinger."

"Yeah. Maybe get myself a house in the woods up in Vermont or Connecticut and communicate with my agent and publisher by email only."

"How about Maine? It's nice there."

"Maine? Scary place, according to its best-known resident. Somewhere to avoid if you don't want to get killed by demonic clowns or eaten by rabid St Bernards."

"Ah, you couldn't stand the competition, that's all," said Chase. "Couldn't live there knowing you'd always be the *other* guy, the Man Who Wouldn't Be King."

"That was quite witty. For you."

"Thanks. I'm pretty pleased with it myself. Of course, you have a bad track record with kings."

Theo smirked. "What's he called now? Evander Arlington?"

"Yeah," said Chase. "Evander Arlington. Don't suppose you've seen the old bastard lately? He's got a place in Midtown, not that far from yours. Super deluxe penthouse. He ever invite you over?"

"Not much chance of that."

"Still hasn't forgiven you, huh? Guy can sure hold a grudge."

"I eloped with his daughter and then ditched her. Not to mention what I did to his, ahem, stepson. You bet he holds a grudge."

They chatted inconsequentially for the rest of the journey. Only once they were at Theo's apartment could they drop their guard and speak freely.

"So. Anthony Peregrine. Aeneas. Here's the deal." Chase fetched out a few pages of computer printout. "I requested a pathologist's report from the coroner in Ushuaia. He couldn't see a reason for one. To him, it was just an accident. Anthony Peregrine went solo-skiing, there was an avalanche, he got caught by it, end of story."

"He a skier?"

"Anthony? Some of his travel pieces have been about alpine resorts and chalets and black runs and the rest, so yeah, I'd say so. Anyway, I kicked up a fuss. Made noises about getting the US ambassador involved. Played the arrogant-American-abroad card. Got my way in the end."

Theo handed him a cup of freshly brewed coffee. Chase clinked it against Theo's own cup, said "Cheers," and took a grateful sip. The overnight flight from Tierra del Fuego had been long and bumpy, and he hadn't slept much.

"This here is a copy of the report," he went on. "How's your Spanish?"

"Poor to non-existent."

"Well, I lived in Spain for a stretch and became fluent, but that was six hundred years ago and the lingo's changed a lot since then. Still, I can just about make sense of what's written here, except for the really technical bits, and... Well, there's something that doesn't quite add up."

Theo frowned. "Go on."

"Mostly Aeneas's injuries are consistent with getting crushed by several thousand tons of snow sliding downhill at a couple of hundred miles an hour. Contusions. Lacerations. Bone fractures. It was what's known as a slab avalanche, one that contains huge chunks of hardened snow. That's way worse than a powder avalanche, the other kind. It's like getting hit by a wave of boulders. However..."

Chase pointed to a section of text.

"There were a number of wounds on the body that Dr Dominguez, the pathologist, noted as '*anómalo*'."

"Abnormal. Anomalous."

"Correct. Some deep gouges that he assumes were caused by loose tree branches travelling at high velocity and perforating the flesh. Except, he couldn't find any traces of wood in them. No splinters, no tiny fragments, as you might expect there would be. Large ragged holes that were clean inside."

"As if they weren't caused naturally at all. As if they were made using a knife?"

"Dr Dominguez wouldn't commit himself that far. He was keen for it to be an accidental death."

"Why?"

"Why? Because ski tourism is big business in that part of Argentina. An avalanche kills a lone skier, that's bad news, sure, but it won't deter visitors. Avalanches are one of the risks you take, especially if you go way off-piste on your own, like Anthony apparently did. They're acceptable. What wouldn't be acceptable is someone getting murdered on the slopes. That would get holidaymakers rushing to cancel their bookings."

"You think someone in authority leaned on him?"

"Not necessarily. I think Dr Dominguez knows how things work and was hedging his bets. Didn't want to be the boy who cried wolf.

The perforation injuries were suspicious, but not enough to warrant taking it any further. Hence, tentatively, judiciously, *anómalo*."

"The fact remains," said Theo, "that however badly Anthony – Aeneas – got hurt by the avalanche, he wouldn't have died. He'd have been hospitalised for months and had a long road to recovery, and his doctors would be amazed that he healed so well. It would be a minor medical miracle, but eventually he would pull through and be as good as new again."

"The advantages of having a dash of divine ichor running through your veins."

"So, if not the avalanche, something else killed him."

"Looks that way. What, though?"

"That's the honking big question. How easy is it to kill a demigod?"

"Total physical destruction can do it," said Chase. "Dardanus, the guy who founded Troy – he was one of Zeus's – he was living in Herculaneum when Vesuvius blew up, several miles closer than Pompeii. The pyroclastic flow cooked him to a crisp. There's no coming back from that. Autolykos of Phokis was at Nagasaki on August 9th 1945. Wrong place, wrong time."

"Keryx was a viscount in France in the late eighteenth century during the Reign of Terror," said Theo. "I tried to save him."

"Oh yeah, your Scarlet Pimpernel routine. Don't tell me." Chase mimed a guillotine blade chopping through his neck and made a squishy slicing sound in the back of his throat.

"Regrettably, yes. I was locked up in the Bastille myself when they took him away in the tumbril to the Place de la Révolution. I did stage a breakout, but too late."

"Couldn't he have tried to escape himself?"

"I think Keryx had been playing the part of the louche aristocrat for so long, he'd gotten soft. You should have seen him as the Vicomte de wherever-it-was. All lace handkerchiefs and beauty spots and full-bottom wigs. A regular at Louis XVI's banquets at Versailles, mincing around with the other nobles. Probably had forgotten he had the edge on his jailers and the *sans-culottes*. He could have struggled free of them if he'd wanted."

"Guess he didn't want it enough."

"Guess not. Even then, I might have brought him back from the dead if I'd been able to find head and body and reunite them, but the revolutionaries were in the habit of carting off the corpses of the guillotined to a tannery, rendering them down and turning the skins into leather."

"Niiice. At any rate, Anthony Peregrine's corpse was all in one piece."

"There's only one thing we know of that's capable of killing a demigod as though he or she were human," said Theo. "One thing that's guaranteed to give a fatal wound."

"One? You mean twelve."

"But all twelve are safely stowed away. Put beyond use. It must be something else."

"You don't think maybe it's just extreme old age?" Chase said. "I was mulling this over on the plane. What if, after three millennia plus, our bodies are finally wearing out? Nothing lasts forever. Even immortality, surely, has got to come to an end sometime." He rolled up one shirtsleeve to expose bandaging. "Something took a big bite out of me the other day."

"What was it?"

"Chupacabra. Long story. And of course I'll get better. Of course the wound will mend and there won't be a trace of it left, not even a scar. But what if, for once, that doesn't happen? What if there turns out to be a limit to our recuperative powers? Could it be that we're coming to the end of the ride? That the god half of us is exhausted, tapped out, and all that's left is the mortal?"

Theo shook his head.

"Are you shaking your head because you don't believe it?" said Chase. "Or because you don't *want* to believe it?"

"Neither. As of right now, I don't have enough information to decide either way. I'm just... pondering."

"Well, ponder this, cousin Theseus. The time of the gods is long past. Our fathers and mothers and all the rest of them, they retired to Olympus, pulled up the drawbridge, and nobody's seen them or heard a peep from them since. Perhaps now, three thousand years on, the time of their offspring is also past. Perhaps now, finally, it's our turn."

CHASE TOOK A long swig of coffee, studying Theo, seeing his words sink in.

"'Theseus,'" said Theo eventually.

"What?"

"It's just... It's been a while since you called me by that name. Since anyone did."

"Yeah, I know it's not protocol. Always use the alias. But, hey, we're alone, just the two of us, just family. And it kind of seemed appropriate, you know? In keeping with the whole portentous vibe I was going for."

"Theseus. Perseus. When I say the names out loud, I don't really think of them as being us, not anymore," said Theo. "First and foremost I think of them as the myths. The ones people have written books about and made movies about. The ones people use as metaphors – consider to have *been* metaphors. Theseus who killed the Minotaur. Perseus who killed the Gorgon Medusa. Not genuine living beings but archetypes. I almost forget that we *were* real."

"Still are."

"Yes, but that sense of dissonance. It's weird. Like the time I went to see *Ariadne auf Naxos* when it premiered Stateside back in 1928. Hopped a train to Philadelphia to catch the first night, and came back perplexed. I'm not even in it. I mean, Theseus isn't. It's about Ariadne after I allegedly abandoned her, and she's pining for me, and then the whole thing degenerates into a broad comedy before she ends up in the arms of Dionysus, only he's called Bacchus in the opera. Strauss clearly didn't care if he mixed up Roman and Greek naming."

"You told me Ariadne was a grade-A ballbreaker. You only hooked up with her because she knew the way through Minos's labyrinth."

"It's not as if she didn't get anything out of it," Theo protested. "That's the point Strauss seems to have missed, probably because

Hesiod, Diodorus and Pausanias all missed it too. Ariadne hated her father. She hated Knossos. I was her ticket off Crete. What we had, her and me, it was mutual need. It wasn't love, or even lust. Well, a little bit lust. She was a beauty, after all. She was…" He gripped the air with his hands, indicating both feminine shapeliness and the manly approach to handling it. "But when we were done, we were done. I didn't dump her. I just had other business to take care of, and she'd got what she wanted, and so we went our separate ways. She was never the jilted fiancée she's been painted as ever since."

"Didn't help that you shacked up with her sister not long after," Chase pointed out.

"Phaedra? That was regrettable. A beauty too, like Ariadne, but at least she seemed more stable, less scheming."

"How'd that work out?"

Theo lowered his gaze. Phaedra's passion for his son Hippolytus – her stepson – had not been requited, but Theo had not realised it until it was almost too late. Believing Hippolytus to be guilty of semi-incest and of cuckolding his own father, he ordered the boy into exile. In Euripides's play about these events, a terrifying bull emerged from the sea and Hippolytus's chariot horses panicked and threw the boy to the ground, although the truth was rather more mundane: Hippolytus whipped the horses to a frenzy, took a corner too fast, and careered head-on into a cypress tree.

Theo cradled the dying teenager in his arms, and there was a reconciliation of sorts, expressions of forgiveness on both sides, but for ages afterward he blamed himself. He held himself accountable for his son's death and was a broken man, a shadow of the stalwart champion he was before. Phaedra hanged herself, overcome with remorse, and had it been possible for a demigod to commit suicide, Theo might well have done so too.

Chase laid a hand on his arm. "Shit, man. Sorry. Didn't mean to dredge that all up again. I'm an idiot."

"No. No. It's all right. Water under the bridge. Way, *way* under. But it's memories like that that remind me. Bring it right home, wham! We were who we were. The memories prove the reality. The fictions are just peripheral noise."

"Peripheral noise. Isn't that a Pink Floyd track?"

Theo half smiled. "You know my musical tastes don't go much past the swing era."

"Oh, you've got some Taylor Swift on your playlist. I know you have."

"Didn't she sing with the Glenn Miller Band?"

"You're thinking of Katy Perry."

"That's right. She stepped in when one of the Andrews Sisters got laryngitis. How silly of me to get the two muddled up."

"It's your age, cuz. Alzheimer's setting in."

Theo shook his fist, mock indignant. "Why, you impertinent cur. I'll try to forget you said that."

"You won't have to try. You'll –"

Chase's phone pinged. He glanced at the screen.

"More about Anthony Peregrine?"

"No..." Chase thumbed through the content of the email. "No, this one's about Isaac Merrison."

"Who's he?"

"'Who's he?' Only your brother."

"My...? You'll have to narrow it down."

"Orion. I mean Orion."

"Half-brother at best. A whole generation after me. Hardly knew him."

The frown on Chase's face deepened to a scowl. "Oh, no. Shit."

"Tell me. Come on, what is it?" Theo didn't mean to bark the words, but he couldn't help it.

"Dude, cool your jets. Just need to read it through to the end... Okay. Yeah. Well. It's from the *Vanuatu Daily Post*'s site. Not exactly the BBC, but not Fox News either. It's saying a local dive tour operator – one Isaac Merrison – is missing, presumed dead. Hasn't been seen or heard from in three days. Not answering his phone. Not at home at his beachfront bungalow. And a piece of a wetsuit washed up ashore in Mele Bay last night, which may or may not be his. It was the brand he used, and it was bloody and shredded, in a way that suggests the wearer was the victim of a shark attack. Vanuatu police are keen to question the group of foreign divers that Merrison took out on an expedition shortly before his disappearance. 'Detectives wish to stress that these people are in no way under suspicion, but may have information regarding Mr Merrison's state of mind in the run-up to what appears to have been a tragic mishap.' Direct quote."

Theo took the phone from Chase and read the short article for himself.

"'State of mind,'" he said. "The implication being, he might have been drinking heavily or something, and went out diving somewhere he shouldn't have?"

"Somewhere shark-infested that got him shark-ingested. It says he was an 'experienced scuba aquanaut' and had been running dive tours in the area for over a decade. I guess the cops think he'd have had to have some sort of mental breakdown and got reckless?"

"Is Orion ever reckless?"

"You tell me. He's your brother."

"Half-brother."

"Guess I hung around with him more than you did. As far as I recall..." Chase thought about it. "He was always kind of an asshole, if we're being honest. At least, to begin with, way back when. Serial rapist, and so far up himself, he'd need a flashlight if he wanted to brush his teeth. But time mellowed him, like it does all of us. I don't know when he and I last ran into each other. Has to have been over a century ago. Nantucket or something, an Atlantic port. Orion had been crewing on whaling ships for years, but had had a kind of epiphany. Seeing so many whales slaughtered voyage after voyage, he'd got sick of it. He told me – I remember this quite clearly – he was going to dedicate himself to preserving his father's realm, not plundering it any more. Later, in the 'sixties, the 'seventies, he became this eco-activist. Greenpeace, the Sierra Club. Protesting toxic dumping in the oceans, deep-sea oil exploration, overfishing, bottom trawling, longline bycatch. Then I guess he got tired of all that and set up as a dive tour guide."

"Seems a logical progression. If you can't save the marine world by campaigning, do it by showing people how to treat it respectfully."

"Shame the marine world didn't return the courtesy."

"That's if he *was* killed by a shark," Theo said.

"You think not?"

"I don't think a shark could kill Orion. Do you?"

"Well, no. Of course not," said Chase. "Any more than it could kill any of us. But maybe he came up against the same thing Aeneas did. Maybe extreme old age caught up with him. He lost his, for want of a better word, powers. The shark was simply the innocent agent of his death, like the avalanche was for Aeneas. His time as an immortal had expired. It was just a question of how, where and when."

"It's a hell of a coincidence, still. Him and Aeneas dying within a week of each other."

"I grant you that. But we don't even know for sure that Orion *is* dead. All we've got is a scrap of torn, bloodied wetsuit which didn't necessarily belong to him. And if it did, well then, who's to say he hasn't just pulled a switcheroo? His Isaac Merrison identity has been jettisoned and he's off somewhere far away from Vanuatu, easing into a new life."

"Could be," Theo said, nodding. "Could be we're making connections where there aren't any."

"You think not?"

"Cousin Perseus," said Theo, "at this precise moment I have no idea what to think. But it would be a mistake, I believe, not to be that tiniest bit alarmed."

EIGHT

Buckinghamshire, England

DEL KARNO LAY on an inflatable in his swimming pool on one of those rare days of a British summer when it was genuinely hot and the sun was shining and there wasn't a cloud in the sky. Thunderstorms were forecast for the evening, because naturally you couldn't have a properly good day's weather in the British Isles without it coming to an abrupt, soggy end. For now, though, there was stillness and brilliance and unstinting warmth, and you relished it all the more knowing that it wasn't going to last.

Del grunted at one of the half-dozen young women sprawling in skimpy swimwear on the poolside loungers. "Drink. Now." The girl sprang to her feet, lithe and lissome, skin agleam with sun lotion, and went indoors, returning a few minutes later with a freshly mixed margarita. She descended the semicircle of steps at the shallow end and waded out to Del, handing him the cocktail in its salt-rimmed glass without spilling a drop. Her reward for her labours was a pat on the cheek and a benevolent smile, and how she preened! Striding out to retake her place beside the other women, she aimed an imperious, smug look at them all. *He touched me*, that look said. *He favoured me*. And her rivals answered with glares of pure envy and spite. A couple of them adopted provocative poses, legs apart, breasts jutting out, in a blatant bid to catch Del's attention. He could almost smell the musk coming off them, the desire to have him, to be had by him. A click of his fingers, and they'd be paddling out to give him a two-girl blowjob right there in the pool, in full view of the rest.

But it was too hot for that. Too hot even to think about sex. Later, when it was cooler, he would indulge, selecting whichever woman took his fancy – maybe all of them. And he would sing to them first, to get them really in the mood. One of his hits from the 'eighties, or perhaps something older, much older, something that would have sounded better accompanied by a cithara or a pandura than by a twelve-string acoustic but still entrancing, ripe with a melodic magic of its own. Something which would stoke a fire of passion in the listener that only an orgy of rampant fucking could put out.

SELF-RESTRAINT HAD NEVER been Del Karno's strong suit. To read any of the biographies about him was to trawl through a delirious catalogue of debauchery and excess. In his early-1980s pop star heyday it was limos, groupies, groupies in limos, backstage parties, hotel-suite revels that went on all night – an endless, globe-spanning shag frenzy fuelled by cocaine and funded by the proceeds from a spate of internationally chart-topping mega-hit singles and albums.

The fun lasted four years – four wild, exhilarating, dick-sore, nosebleed years – and Del loved every minute of it. Then, inevitably, it all came to a screeching halt. There was the drugs bust. The accusations, never conclusively proven, of underage sex. Worse still, the riots at gigs, audiences pressing themselves against the front of the stage in an almost hysterical desperation to get close to their idol, to be within touching distance of him, even just to be looked at by him. These crushes led to the deaths of at least ten fans and left another three crippled for life.

And that was it for his career. All at once, Del Karno was music biz poison. Packs of paparazzi bayed outside his London flat. Tabloids bought exclusives from his conquests, of whom there were so many that the market for their confessions swiftly became saturated and the sums being offered for them derisory. It was over. No one bought his records any more. Our Price and Tower stopped stocking them. MTV stopped playing his videos. He was just another washed-up New Romantic has-been, albeit one who had crashed and burned more spectacularly than most.

He retreated to his 19th-century Buckinghamshire mansion, shielded from press intrusion by security gates and a hundred acres of landscaped grounds. Here, he continued his hedonism, away from prying eyes. Women came. Women went. It was never difficult to attract them. All he had to do was drive to any nearby town, visit a nightclub or a bar, get chatting, sing a few phrases of a song in their ears, and they would follow him home – follow him anywhere. He let them stay at the house, bought them clothes, fed them, looked after them, and bedded them as and when the whim took him. If they were into narcotics, he had a reliable dealer and gave them as much as they could want. Sometimes he indulged, sometimes not. He didn't need coke to make him feel all-powerful or dope to make him feel at ease, but it was a sociable thing to do, and the girls seemed to prefer it if he joined in. It humanised him in their eyes.

Because the girls invariably sensed that he was not quite normal. Even when the aura of stardom was no longer radiating off him like nuclear energy, they knew deep down in their souls that Del Karno was more than just a man. He was rake-thin, raven-haired, elegant, devilishly handsome, with the piercing gaze of a messiah, and when he sang... no one had a voice like that, no one of this world. It was a preternatural voice; a voice that seemed to reach inside you and caress and arouse parts of you which you never knew existed. It was like a cool spring shower, like motes of dust dancing in a beam of sunlight, like snowfall, like a clear night sky.

As aesthetically – and sexually – gratifying as it was, having hordes of young women swanning around his house was proof, to Del, that he had conquered his fear of women, specifically women in groups. He had pushed past a stumbling block that had been repeatedly tripping him up for more years than he cared to remember. There'd been a time when even the sight of a few women together, whatever the context, would bring him out in a hyperventilating panic and he would have to flee. Hence the many sojourns he had had in all-male environments: monasteries mainly, but also merchant ships, boys-only boarding schools, gentlemen's clubs, and workplaces such as academia and the military back in the days when they were exclusive redoubts of masculinity.

Women, together, could be dangerous. He had learned that in Thrace, at the hands of the Maenads. Women, rebuffed, enraged, could tear and rend and rip. There was madness lurking beneath smooth skin, behind lustrous-lashed eyes, in soft mouths. You provoked it at your peril.

Only after he had adopted the stage name and persona of Del Karno and become a bona fide pop icon did he realise that he had no reason to be afraid of women any more. Even when they were in crowds, he could bend them to his will. Their minds and bodies were his for the asking. He had watched the Beatles do it, the Rolling Stones, David Bowie. All those teenybopper bands, too. The Osmonds, the Bay City Rollers. They drove girls wild. They had them eating out of the palms of their hands. All it took was music, and music was his forte.

No wonder he titled his second album *Breakthrough*. In fairly short order, Del went from committed gynophobe to studly sex god. There were centuries of lost time to make up for, and he did so with priapic glee.

Even now, thirty years on from his brief but phenomenal spell of chart success, he marvelled at the way he could casually beckon and his resident fuck-bunnies would come racing to his boudoir. Balls-deep inside them, approaching climax, he would almost roar with delight. The release was as much psychological as physical, a blinding moment of accomplishment.

That take, Maenads.

Screw you and your wine-intoxicated rites and your ivy-wreathed hair and your ululating chants and your flesh-sundering fingernails and teeth.

Screw you; all you bitches.

Screw. You!

*   *   *

As the summer's day grew shadier and the first distant rumbles of thunder sounded to the west, Del and his retinue went inside. When the rain finally came, hitting the mansion's Gothic windows hard as hail, Del was busy watching two of the girls pleasure each other while being fellated by a third. Some very niche German porn played on a widescreen TV mounted above the fireplace. Candles flickered and joss-sticks smouldered.

Later still, after the household had retired to their rooms, Del was restless. He felt thoroughly drained, purged of desire, but somehow not sleepy. He stalked the corridors like a ghost. Lightning flared and thunder pounded. On nights like this, in weather like this, he could not help but think of his wife and of the dark, stormy place he had pursued her to and failed to rescue her from. There weren't many able to say that they had gone to hell and back for a loved one and be telling the absolute, literal truth. Del Karno could.

With his singing he had charmed Cerberus the three-headed watchdog and Charon the ferryman. With his singing he had briefly brought a pause to the torments of the damned – Tantalus, Ixion, Sisyphus – gifting them a few moments of blissful respite. With his singing he had won over Hades and Persephone, king and queen of the dead.

And then, at the very threshold, he had lost his wife again. Not to a snake bite, but to his own insecurity. He had looked back.

And before his eyes, beyond the reach of his outstretched arms, his beloved wife had been whisked away by unseen forces, her cry of despair echoing through measureless caverns and resounding in his ears for years afterwards.

In the slough of grief that followed, it was hardly surprising that he had rejected the Maenads when they invited him to take part in one of their naked, writhing ceremonies of worship to Dionysius.

His subsequent violent disembowelling and amputation was entirely undeserved, and it was a good decade before he fully recovered from it. At least, physically; mentally he was scarred for much, much longer.

*   *   *

DEL'S MEANDERING TOUR through the mansion took him to the kitchen. Perhaps if he fixed himself something to eat, he might feel better. Food was nearly as good at quelling inner disquiet as music. His Polish housekeeper, Bronislawa, kept the fridge well stocked, and mostly stayed out of his way. He got the impression she did not approve of his decadent lifestyle, but she did approve of the huge salary she received from him to keep the place tidy and make sure the bills were paid and any maintenance work done.

The Smeg fridge hummed alluringly. He selected some cold meats and cheeses, and began slicing up a baguette.

He stopped, breadknife poised, the moment he became aware of a presence in the room.

It was a woman.

But not one of *his* women.

She was dressed like a soldier, a paramilitary, with a helmet whose crested design put him in mind of something a Myrmidon or a Macedonian might have worn, or perhaps an Athenian hoplite.

She had a submachine gun. Aimed at Del.

Two more people entered, clad identically to her. The clothes of all three were dripping wet. One of them also had a submachine gun.

The other carried a spear.

The spear had a wooden shaft and an iron head; its butt was capped with a secondary spike, so that the spear could be planted in the earth and to serve as a back-up head should the spear break.

The name for this type of spear was a dory.

Del knew that, and knew that this particular dory was no ordinary weapon. It had been gifted with power, imbued with divine essence. Del could almost hear the ringing of the anvil as the iron was forged and beaten, as a blacksmith god's fist had raised a mighty hammer and brought it down, adding his own sweat and strength to the metal.

"That's…" Del's mouth was oddly dry. "That's Achilles's spear. Made for his father Peleus by Hephaestus. I know it is."

"Don't move," said the man with the spear. "Not a muscle." His accent was Irish, a soft southern burr.

Del nodded numbly. "All right. Whatever you say."

"Cover him," the man said to his two colleagues. They fanned out to either side, guns levelled.

The man looked back at Del. "There are two ways we can do this," he began.

Del raised a finger to interrupt. "You don't have to go on. I understand. I submit."

The man cocked his head quizzically.

"I could sing to you," Del went on. "I could stop you all in your tracks in seconds. It might be a lullaby. It might be fucking 'Happy Birthday to You'. Wouldn't matter. You'd be my slaves. Eager as dogs to do my bidding."

The man shrugged. "You'll have to forgive me, pal. I can't actually make out a word you're saying. Right now we've all of us got one ear blocked up and the other with a monaural comms set plug so that we can hear one another speak through these here throat mics, but nothing else. I'm just going on your body language and the way your lips are moving. I'm assuming you're bargaining for your life. That's not going to fly. We've been told you can be mightily persuasive, so you can, and we're not taking any chances. Keep talking. It won't help."

Del spread out his arms. The gesture was unmistakably one of surrender.

"Here I am, then," he said. "Come and get me. You won't have realised, but I've been telling you: I'm not going to resist."

The man with the spear took a couple of steps forward.

Del puffed out his chest, making himself an easier target.

There was no point fighting. He was never a warrior. Even when he had served in the military, he had chosen non-combat roles – medic, messenger, reconnaissance.

Besides, he was weary. He had had enough. The time seemed right. Here was his opportunity, the one he didn't know he had been waiting for until now.

He missed his wife. After all this time, the centuries of separation, he missed his Eurydice. The love of his life, taken from him long before she should have been.

Now, at last, they could be reunited.

The man with the spear hesitated. This was too easy.

Del nodded graciously.

The man made up his mind and lunged.

The spear tip sank in, piercing Del's heart.

Eurydice.

Belatedly, gratefully, the demigod who had once been known as Orpheus went to join his long-dead wife in the afterlife.

NINE

Lower East Side, Manhattan

THEO ROUSTED CHASE from the guest room first thing the next morning.

"Jet lag," Chase protested.

"Breakfast," Theo insisted.

His favourite diner was on Essex Street, twenty blocks from his apartment. He managed to persuade Chase that they should walk the entire way, to work up an appetite. Chase ordered the mac and cheese pancake; Theo an omelette with bacon, home fries and wheat toast. The waitress – Imelda – knew Theo, but only as a regular; she had no idea that he was a respectable well-known novelist. Whereas Chase was a face off television, and that made him special. He got the full buxom-middle-aged-lady-flirtation treatment with extra helpings of sass and innuendo. Her husband Diego looked on from behind the griddle with an indulgent smile. Imelda knew how to keep the customers coming back.

A morning news show played on a wall-mounted TV set in the corner. The two demigods ate.

"Still stressing about Anthony Peregrine and Isaac Merrison?"

said Chase. It wasn't a question, not really. Chase could see that his cousin was distracted, preoccupied.

"Trying not to," said Theo, "but it keeps going round and round in my head. There's a part of me that can't help looking for patterns. I can't switch it off."

He thought of the "mugging" he had intervened in just the other day. About the risk of jumping to conclusions.

"There is such a thing as coincidence," Chase said.

"There's also such a thing as gut instinct," Theo replied, "and mine's saying something more is going on here."

Chase glanced around. None of the nearby booths was occupied. Imelda was kibitzing with Diego behind the counter; the TV supplying background noise. They couldn't be overheard.

"I'd be willing to respect that, cuz, but when was the last time you were an actual crimefighter? How long ago has it been since you were out there making the mean streets safe for law-abiding folk to walk down?"

"The 'seventies."

"Exactly. The 'seventies. Forty years. Now you *write* about people righting wrongs, instead of doing it yourself. No offence, but maybe your crime radar is malfunctioning. I see two unrelated, possibly unsuspicious events; you see a conspiracy. It's called catastrophising. It's what people with anxiety disorders do, put the worst conceivable spin on a situation and act as if that's what's bound to happen."

"It's what authors do too, only we call it drama."

"Same difference. I'm just putting it to you that Aeneas is dead, yes, but maybe there's a simple, reasonable explanation for that."

"And Orion?"

"Your half-brother has pulled a disappearing act, not the subtlest or cleverest of ones, but that's all."

"How do you account for the two incidents occurring so close in time to each other?"

"Sheer dumb luck. The bad kind."

"Okay, but weren't you the one who volunteered to go down to Argentina to check things out?"

"I did that mostly as a favour to you."

"And now you're saying there's nothing to worry about?"

"I'm saying there's nothing to be gained by worrying," said Chase. "All the same," he added, "when I look at you now, with that little knot between your eyebrows, hardly touching your meal..."

Theo glanced down at his plate. He had had only three meagre mouthfuls and been toying with the food the rest of the time.

"... I have to admit I think it's pretty cool."

"My lack of appetite impresses you?"

"No, what it signifies. The old Theo. The guy who used to be so driven, used to have such a firm sense of purpose. Theseus once more. You haven't had a crime to solve, an enemy to fight, for four decades – apart from the ones you make up stories about."

"Just because I haven't been active on the vigilante front..."

"That's it. In a nutshell. You haven't been. And I don't think it was good for you, retiring from all that. You were, what, a 'consulting detective' in London in the late Victorian era?"

"I was."

"Locating Lady Ponsonby-Wildebeest's missing pearls and figuring out if it was Colonel Mustard, in the library, with the lead pipe."

"More like catching child abductors and foiling inheritance swindlers."

"Then you came to America in the 'thirties and set up shop in LA as a private investigator."

"Had a licence and everything."

"Everything except the whisky habit. Then you moved east and became a masked urban avenger, putting on a balaclava and busting crooks' heads from Times Square to Coney Island."

"It needed to be done. New York was a cesspool back then."

"So you cleaned it up. Rudy Giuliani with a baseball bat."

"Made it a little less messy."

"And those are just your most recent exploits, the tail end of a long, long list going back through history. You put in the hours, Theo. You did good. There are thousands of mortals, alive and dead, who have you to thank for making their lives that little bit better, saving them from predators and scumbags. But then you gave up and you became just... aimless."

"I had a mission," said Theo, "the same mission I'd been pursuing since the Age of Heroes. And I got tired. I felt I'd done enough. I'd *had* enough. All I could stomach. How it was in America in the nineteen-seventies, the way everything became seedy, more depraved than it ever used to be – innocents getting hooked on drugs, kids having awful things done to them, corruption in the highest places – I just got sick of it. After a while I felt I wasn't making a difference any more. I was a Band-Aid on a haemorrhage. I hated it. It wasn't satisfying. It was just a grind."

"Tell me about it. You became so grim. You hardly ever smiled or cracked a joke. Whenever we met up, your whole conversation was about this gang boss, that pimp, and how the cops were all morons or on the take and always got in your way. You never lightened up, dude. You made Christian Bale's Batman look like Woody fucking Woodpecker. You were – I'm going to be frank here, maybe brutally so – not such a nice person to know back then."

"I wasn't?"

"You were kind of a douche, as a matter of fact."

Theo laughed, unamused.

"I'm your cousin. Your family. Your friend. If I can't say this sort of stuff to you, who can? You weren't mean, you weren't nasty. Not to me, at least. But jeez, your people skills sucked."

"Sugar-coat it, why don't you?"

"No one's blaming you for it, but you weren't you. Things got on top of you, and you were right to take a break from it all. It was almost like you had some kind of a breakdown – a midlife crisis. But now this guy" – Chase pointed his fork across the table – "this guy I'm looking at today, he's refreshed and renewed and ready for the fray again, raring to go."

"So, if I'm following your logic," Theo said, "being concerned about Aeneas and Orion, which you seem to think may be unnecessary, is a good thing?"

"I'm saying it's bringing your mojo back. Whether it turns out to be for no good reason doesn't matter. Could be this is the long-awaited spark that reignites the purifying fire that is Theo Stannard."

"I don't know. I'm pretty happy with the way things are." Even as he said it, it didn't ring true to Theo's ears. "I've got my literary career. I've got a comfortable daily routine. I've got life pretty much how I could want it. If I start back down the road of crimefighting, wouldn't that jeopardise everything I've...?"

He realised Chase wasn't listening.

"Chase? Chase?"

"Shhh." Chase's attention was on the TV. Rapt.

Theo tuned in to the morning show's burble. It was the top of the hour. The anchorman had reached the overseas segment of the round-up. In other news...

"British police still aren't saying if the fire was set deliberately or an accident," the immaculately coiffed man said. "All that's known, as this helicopter footage shows, is that the building was entirely engulfed in flames and has been gutted. So far, the death toll stands at seven. Controversial 'eighties pop star Karno had house guests staying, although the exact number is unclear, but it has been officially confirmed that he himself is among the victims. Meanwhile, over in China..."

The topic switched to the cloud of severe toxic smog in Beijing which had claimed several lives.

"Why did we have to listen to that?" Theo asked.

"Karno," said Chase. "Del Karno. He's dead."

"I have no idea who..." The penny dropped. "Damn. One of us?"

"Orpheus. Del Karno is – was – Orpheus."

"You're shitting me."

"Come on, you must have known that was him. You must have seen him on TV back in the 'eighties. You'd have recognised him as Orpheus even with the guyliner and the Flock-of-Seagulls 'do."

"I was... elsewhere in the 'eighties."

"You'd have to have been hiding under a rock not to have heard of Del Karno."

"I was. Well, Ayers Rock. Near there, in the middle of the Australian Outback. No phone. No TV. Not even a radio."

"Oh, yeah. Your post-vigilantism drying-out hermit period. I forgot. But he was everywhere for about three, four years, was Orpheus. Hit the big time. Had a meteoric rise-and-fall pop career.

Went out there after a lifetime of seclusion and just had a blast. You'd have disapproved, but he seemed to be enjoying himself while it lasted."

"He's not enjoying himself anymore," said Theo, stolidly. He clenched a fist on the tabletop. "Okay, so that makes three now. Three of us in a matter of days, either dead or apparently so. Don't you tell me not to worry any more, Chase. Something is going on. This isn't coincidence."

Chase sighed heavily. "I can't disagree. I wish I could, but I can't, not now. But what? What's going on?"

"We're being picked off, one by one. Targeted and assassinated."

"Yeah, and whoever it is, they're going for the big dogs too, aren't they? Aeneas, Orion, Orpheus. The names. Not any of the small fry like, I don't know, Asopos."

"Who?"

"Exactly. One of Poseidon's other kids, conceived with that nymph he couldn't keep his hands off, what's her name – Pero. Or my half-brother Zagreus, another of Zeus's spawn. *There's* a demigod languishing in the where-are-they-now file. Even I don't know what's become of Zagreus. But it doesn't seem as though he should be looking over his shoulder right now. It's only the likes of you and me who should be nervous. The ones with constellations named after them. Oh wait, that's not you."

"Ha-ha."

Chase set his mouth firmly. "You know who I think we should go and talk with, cuz?"

"No."

"Odysseus."

"You can't be serious."

"He's connected. He's smart – smarter than either of us. He has channels."

"He's also a class-A prick."

"Leaving that aside, if anyone can dig around and rustle up intel, it's Odysseus. He is the 'resourceful one', after all. The 'great tactician'. The 'man of twists and turns'."

"Don't come at me with your Homeric epithets. He's also 'hot-headed', 'the sacker of cities' and 'the man of pain'." Theo drew a deep breath. "But I accept he could be useful to turn to in an emergency. Where does he call home these days?"

"Where do you think?" Chase grinned. "Where all the conceited, conniving creeps hang out. Washington, D.C."

TEN

Aylesbury, England

As he had every single day for the past few years, without fail, Roy Young performed a half-hour exercise routine designed to keep him in shape and to quieten his inner demons. It was a mixture of Pilates and isometrics, using his own bodyweight for resistance and requiring an area of floorspace only one metre by two metres. It could be carried out anywhere: in a tent, on a balcony, in a ship's cabin, even in a prison cell, should that eventuality arise.

He finished off with a few rounds of *nadi shodhana pranayama*, a yoga breathing technique involving pinching off the nostrils alternately. This aligned and synchronised the two hemispheres of the brain and calmed the sympathetic and parasympathetic nervous systems. Roy had perfected it to the stage where even just five minutes spent sitting cross-legged, focusing on his inhalations and exhalations and nothing else, left him with a clearer mind and a strengthened sense of self-confidence. The doubts that plagued him and threatened to undermine him were, for the time being, held at bay.

When he was done, he showered, dressed and headed out.

Currently the Myrmidons were holed up in a pricey but nondescript chain hotel on the outskirts of Aylesbury, some forty-odd miles northwest of London. The three-person team, chosen by Badenhorst, had been scheduled to return from their mission sometime during the small hours, but Roy had had no contact with them since their departure at nightfall. In the meantime he had stayed in his room, keeping himself to himself. He assumed the operation had been a success. He would surely have been apprised if it had not.

The strike team had consisted of Sean Wilson, Hans Schutkeker and the only other female Myrmidon apart from Jeanne, a brusque Scandinavian called Gunnvor Blomgren. Roy was not disappointed not to have been included. He had taken point on the first two executions; let someone else do the dirty work for a change.

The hotel had a central lounge, a kind of hub from which three two-storey room blocks branched out. A bar and a restaurant abutted the lounge, with the reception lobby perched in front. The hotel was busy at present. A midsized firm of medical equipment suppliers was using it for its annual conference. The corridors teemed with suited men and women who seemed to be competing as to which of them could act the most businesslike and efficient. If they weren't bent over their phones and tablets, they were huddled together discussing marketing strategies and sales targets. The Myrmidons, in their smart-casual civvies, didn't quite blend in, but they too conducted themselves with an air of quiet professional competence. They might not have had seminars and presentations to attend, but they nonetheless looked as though they, like the white-collar brigade around them, were staying at the hotel for business. Last night Roy had overheard a middle-management type from the medical equipment company air the opinion that they were either international lawyers or members of an investment consortium, here for a team-building retreat. Miles wide of the mark, but as long as that was the impression the Myrmidons gave, they would pass unnoticed and remain forgettable.

Gavin Martin and Jeanne Chevrier both happened to be in the lounge, taking tea together. Gavin shunted out a spare chair at the table with his foot, and Roy took it. He ordered a pot of Earl Grey and a toasted muffin.

"Any word about the job?" Roy enquired.

"Not seen Badenhorst all day," Gavin replied, "but we'd know if it had gone tits up, wouldn't we? We'd be on the plane and in the air pronto if it had. Safe to say that Sean and co. pulled it off and are in their rooms catching up on sleep."

"I'm surprised old biltong breath didn't pick you this time," said Gavin. "You're his golden boy."

"I think he wants to keep us fresh. Rotating the squads helps with that. And we're all getting paid the same, regardless of how many jobs we go on. As long as the bank transfer comes through at the end, I don't care how much or how little I have to do to earn it."

"Wise words, mate." Gavin was a stocky Midlander with a gregarious nature and an easygoing smile. To look at him you might never have suspected that he had once been a sergeant in the UK's elite commando force, the SAS. He seemed the kind of bloke who'd be at his happiest fly-fishing, or sinking a pint with his mates down the pub, not parachuting behind enemy lines to gather recon data and slit throats.

"Did you hear about the fire, Roy?" Jeanne said.

"What fire?"

"It was on the lunchtime news. The hotel staff are all talking about it. Some place nearby burned down last night. Stately home belonging to this musician guy."

"Del Karno," said Gavin.

"Name rings a bell." Roy searched his memory. "Yeah. I remember seeing him on *Top of the Pops* a couple of times when I was a kid. He wore terrible baggy silk pantaloons and a button-down tunic. Played one of those guitar keyboard things. Lots of dry ice and lasers. 'Visions of You', wasn't that one of his? Catchy little ditty. Is he dead, then?"

"Looks that way," said Jeanne. "Him and at least six others. All women. He had this kind of harem thing going on."

"All right for some," Gavin said.

"Is that your dream? Sharing a house with six women?"

"Isn't it everyone's?"

"Not mine." She chucked a sugar sachet at him.

Gavin deflected it with a laugh. "What about six men, then?"

"One would be more than enough." The French Canadian aimed a swift glance at Roy as she said this. It was scarcely more than a sideways flick of the eyes. He almost missed it. He was glad he didn't. Jeanne was lean and elfin, with a lively face and a bawdy sense of humour. Exactly his type. Maybe when all this was over...

"So it was an accident, this fire?" he said.

"No one's sure yet," said Gavin. "Might have been faulty wiring. That's one theory. It was an old building. A stray spark could have set the whole blaze off. They're going to investigate as soon as it's safe. But Karno was a bit of a naughty boy by all accounts, fond of the narcotics, and he may have caused it himself. Like he knocked over a candle or something by mistake and was so out of it he didn't realise."

"Sounds plausible. How far is his house from here?"

"A few miles. One of the waiters said Karno used to visit the hotel sometimes to pick up girls."

"Do you think...?" Roy began.

"Do I think what?"

Roy grimaced. "I'm wondering if Del Karno was the job."

Gavin frowned. "One of our targets was an 'eighties pop star?"

"Seems unlikely, I know, but he lived up the road, and a house fire is an excellent way of erasing evidence."

"I guess it's a possibility," said Jeanne.

"But that would make the others who died in the fire collateral damage," said Gavin.

"Unless they were targets as well," said Roy. "Which doesn't fit the pattern of the jobs so far."

"You seem pissed off," Jeanne observed.

"Not as such. But I think I'm going to go and have words with Badenhorst."

ROY HAMMERED ON the door to Badenhorst's room. The Afrikaner opened it wearing nothing but one of the hotel bathrobes, securing the draw cord under his barrel-like belly. His cheeks were flushed and he was evidently annoyed to have a visitor, although he tried to mask it. Roy had interrupted something.

"Afternoon, Roy. Not being rude or anything, but there's a Do Not Disturb sign hanging on the door handle. Did you not see it?"

"You got a moment?"

Badenhorst glanced back over his shoulder into the room.

So he had company. Probably the kind of company you paid for. By the hour.

"Can it wait?"

"I suppose. How long?"

"Give me thirty minutes."

Roy returned half an hour later. In the corridor leading to the room he passed a woman coming the other way. She was heavily made-up and wearing stiletto heels and a leather micro-skirt, with a shiny ash-blonde wig that contrasted sharply with her dark skin. Her perfume was pungent, strong enough to disguise much worse smells. Badenhorst's "company", had to be. Roy watched her totter along to the stairs and click-clack down them. From the way she held herself, a slight stiffness in her gait, she looked to be in some discomfort. He imagined Badenhorst had purchased extras.

The Afrikaner, this time, gave a better rendition of someone who was pleased to see Roy.

"Come in, come in. Something from the minibar? It's on me. Well, on our employer. No? I'm going to have a whisky myself. Sure you won't join me? *Ach*, never mind."

The room reeked of the woman's perfume. There was also a mustier undertone, the aroma of sweat and effort. The bed had been made, though not as neatly as if a chambermaid had done it.

"It was Del Karno," Roy said.

"Straight to the point, eh?" Badenhorst uncapped a miniature of Famous Grouse and downed it at a gulp. "I presume Sean told you, or Hans or Gunnvor?"

"No. Haven't seen them yet. I worked it out for myself."

"Well done, you. Yes, it *was* him. Del Karno was the target. So what? You a fan of his?"

"And the team set a fire afterwards to cover their tracks, yes?"

"They put a frying pan full of cooking oil on the gas stove, lit the gas ring, left it. I think they placed some dishcloths and a roll of paper towel nearby, to help speed things along when the pan caught alight. It's a pretty standard method for making arson look like a domestic mishap. You may have used it once or twice yourself. Within forty minutes the whole kitchen was in flames. The rest of the house followed soon after. Again, so what?"

"Did they know about the women who were staying at the house?"

Badenhorst's smile remained in place, but his face hardened around it. "Ah, so this is what's bugging you."

"Were they targets too?"

The Afrikaner weighed his reply carefully. "They weren't what you might call 'on the list'. But, Roy, think about it. What else were the team going to do? Leave the guy's body lying there with a dirty great stab wound in it, for those women to find in the morning? We're about making these deaths as inconspicuous as possible. That's our prime directive. Which, if it means a few others have got to die, it's a pity, but..." He shrugged. "Unavoidable."

"There must have been some other way. Whose idea was it to start the fire?"

"Sean's. He was leader, and he made an field decision. They'd caught Karno in the kitchen. A kitchen fire therefore seemed the logical solution. But don't blame him. Sean ran it past me over the comms and I gave him the go-ahead. The buck stops here." Badenhorst jabbed a stubby thumb at his own chest.

"How very noble of you."

"That's how chain of command works, Roy. And don't you forget it. I must say, I'm a little surprised you're being so squeamish all of a sudden. You've been an outcomes facilitator how long? Three years? In that time you've got to have had some byblow from one of your jobs, surely."

"Never."

"Never?"

"I've never killed anyone I wasn't being paid to kill."

"What, you've never blown up someone's car and there were passengers in it besides the target?"

"Never."

"You've never had to take out bodyguards who're standing between you and the target?"

"Never."

"You've never eliminated witnesses?"

"Never."

Badenhorst whistled softly. "Well, it's no wonder you're so highly thought of in the circles we move in, Roy Young, even after such a short career. You're a *blerrie* human smart missile, you are. You only hit what you're aimed at."

"I don't like mess," Roy said. "I don't like overspill. I especially don't like harming innocents."

"Depends on how you define innocent, doesn't it? Targets don't necessarily have to be bad people, after all. They can just be a business rival, a political opponent, a union agitator, a spouse's bit on the side. They don't have to deserve to die; they only have to stand in the way of someone who has money and probably *is* morally corrupt. Do you ever consider that? That maybe it's the person paying you who's the one you should be killing, not the person you're being paid to kill?"

Roy had indeed considered it. Long and hard. All too often.

"Yeah," said Badenhorst, seeing his expression. "Thought as much. You can get up on your *fokken* high horse, Roy, but it's no higher than anyone else's. You just think it is. You're compromised simply by being in the business you're in. Pretending you still have ethics is fooling no one, least of all yourself."

"There could have been another way." It sounded lame and Roy knew it. "Those women didn't have to die too. At the very least they could have died more cleanly. Being burned to death is a horrible way to go."

"*Ach*, they were most likely knocked unconscious in their sleep by the smoke. They wouldn't have felt a thing."

"You don't know that for certain."

"No, but I'll tell you what: I can believe it, and that's enough.

Means I don't lose a wink of sleep about it. You and this conscience of yours, Roy. Is it making you have second thoughts? Would you like to back out of the project?"

Roy wanted to say *yes*. He really did.

"Because you're welcome to." Badenhorst made an ushering motion. "Feel free. You won't get paid for services rendered, of course. It might put a dent in your professional reputation as well. I mean, if someone were to come to me for a reference further down the line, I could hardly give them a glowing one, could I? 'Roy Young? Bit of a *moegoe*, if you ask me. Can't handle pressure.' That's what I might tell them. *Moegoe* means 'coward', by the way. Pussy."

"I gathered that," Roy said, tight-lipped.

"Not everyone is familiar with Afrikaner slang, that's all. And I know how much you need the money, my friend. Don't think that I don't. I know about your daughter. What's her name? Josie. I know she's the reason you got into this line of work in the first place. Poor little Josie."

Roy felt his fists clench. "Be very careful what you say next, Badenhorst."

Badenhorst grinned. "Oh, I'll say what I like, and you'll have no choice in the matter. Because I hold the purse strings, don't I? And you want what's in the purse. You need it. For Josie. Who's a pretty young *bakvissie* but who's also a bit crazy. A bit wrong in the head. A bit..." Badenhorst twirled a forefinger at his temple and rolled his eyes. "That's why she's at that Swiss booby-hatch and you're paying a fortune to keep her there."

Roy glared at him.

"Oh, *ja*, Roy, I know about that. I know about you. About all of you Myrmidons. I do my *blerrie* homework, don't I? I do my background checks. That's my thing. I'm thorough. Your Josie has severe bipolar disorder. I've read her case notes and psychiatric evaluations. Doctor-patient confidentiality, my arse; it's amazing how easily doctors forget the Hippocratic Oath when you wave a wad of cash under their noses. She's had manic-depressive episodes since puberty, repeated and acute, resulting in self-harm, anorexia, bulimia and attempted suicide. She is, in layman's terms, one *fokked*-up young lady."

Roy's fists clenched tighter. He heard his knuckles crack.

"Such a shame," Badenhorst went on, "because she's a *choty goty*. I've seen a picture of her. I'd tap that like a shot, if she weren't a nutter and likely to cut my balls off with a pair of scissors."

The Afrikaner had gone from taunting to openly goading Roy. His round, meaty face was almost bursting with smug contempt, challenging Roy to react, inviting him to take a swing. And the instant Roy snapped, Badenhorst could fire him. He'd be out on his ear, without a penny in wages. The three months he had spent in training under Badenhorst, and the two operations he had so far carried out, would all be for nothing. Those were the terms of the contract which Roy and the other Myrmidons had signed. You either saw it out to the end, or you were in breach. No non-refundable downpayment. No stepped increments. Take it or leave it.

As deals went in the wetwork trade, it was an unusual one. Normally you were paid something even if the mission failed or had to be aborted. A retainer, expenses. You were never completely out of pocket, whether or not the end-result was a successful kill.

Roy had gone along with it, despite his misgivings, because the final fee was so fantastically huge. An average one-off job netted him fifty to a hundred thousand US dollars; in this instance, each Myrmidon stood to receive a lump sum of ten million. It was too tempting an amount to say no to, in spite of the unorthodox conditions attached.

Ten million, properly invested, would yield enough interest to cover the bills at the Gesundheitsklinik Rheintal amply, for as long as was necessary. Josie's continued treatment would be assured. This in turn meant that Roy would not have to work as an outcomes facilitator ever again. He could quit and do something else – anything else – for a living. Drive a bus. Stack shelves at a supermarket. Sweep streets. *Anything*. He would not have to take one more life in order to save his daughter's. He would no longer have to buy her future with the blood of others.

A single punch to Badenhorst's face would change all that, and they both knew it. Killing the Afrikaner with his bare hands – and Roy was sorely tempted – would be just as counterproductive.

Without Badenhorst there to oversee it, the entire project would collapse. Whoever his employer was would be forced to pull the plug. Badenhorst, as mastermind and liaison, was indispensable. An ugly, gloating lynchpin.

Roy made himself relax, prying his fingers out of his palms and willing his hands to unclench. It took every ounce of self-control he had.

"If you" – his voice was strained and quavering – "if you ever talk about my daughter like that again... If you ever even mention her again... I'll..."

"Yes?" said Badenhorst. "You'll do what?"

Roy did not answer.

"I thought as much," said the Afrikaner.

Roy left the room. He didn't slam the door behind him. It would have been petty. It would have made no difference. He went straight to his own room and ran through his exercise routine a second time, and then a third for good measure, until his clothes were soaked with sweat and every muscle ached. A full quarter of an hour of *nadi shodhana pranayama*, and he was almost calm again.

Almost.

ELEVEN

Washington, D.C.

"I STILL DON'T know whether this is a good idea or not, Chase."

Theo and Chase were sitting in a rental car across the street from a large federal-style mansion in the Georgetown district of Washington. They had driven down from New York that morning, completing the trip in a shade under five hours, not bad time at all considering there had been roadworks on the I-95 southbound outside Baltimore. Theo had been at the wheel the entire journey while his cousin made work-related phone calls and napped. Theo couldn't say which he found more irritating: Chase schmoozing television executives or Chase snoozing in the passenger seat.

Now, stationed in a leafy thoroughfare in the capital's toniest and most expensive neighbourhood, they were weighing up their options.

"I mean to say," Theo continued, "if he hasn't returned your calls, what makes you think he'll let us in when we come knocking at his front door? You left half a dozen messages for him yesterday. I can't believe he never checked his phone in all that time. No one doesn't check their phone for that long. He's stonewalling us."

"Maybe he is," said Chase. "Or maybe the number I dug up for him is an old one. Either way, all the more reason we try and see him in person, man to man."

"What are you proposing? We go up to the gate and press the buzzer?"

The house was set in walled grounds, with an automated gate barring access to the short driveway. There were surveillance cameras, at least three in plain sight, undoubtedly more of them hidden from view.

"Why wouldn't that work?" said Chase.

"For the same reason phoning him hasn't worked. He can just ignore us."

"We can always sneak in round the back."

According to the images on Google Earth, the rear of the property overlooked parkland. Theo reckoned it was possible they could steal up on the house from there unobserved, using trees and undergrowth for cover, but their final approach would be across open lawn, and if there were cameras out front, there would be cameras out back. The homeowner would see them coming and almost certainly had countermeasures he could implement. It would get messy.

"It wouldn't help our case," he said. "It'd make us look shifty and duplicitous."

"This is Odysseus we're talking about here," said Chase. "Shifty and duplicitous are his middle names."

"Meaning we'd be more likely to ingratiate ourselves with him if we behave the same as he does?"

"Endear ourselves, even."

"I don't know." Theo shook his head. "I'm beginning to think this was a mistake. The whole thing. Perhaps we don't really need him."

"Hey, I didn't drive two hundred miles only to turn around and go back empty-handed."

"You *didn't* drive two hundred miles. I did."

"Whatever. Hang on. What's this?"

A three-vehicle motorcade was wending its way towards them up the street: two identical black Cadillac limousines, followed by a black Chrysler SUV. All three cars had impenetrably black-tinted windows, and all three slowed as they neared the house.

Simultaneously, a quartet of black-suited, sunglassed security men emerged from the building – a personal protection detail. The gate rolled open. The motorcade turned in. The protection detail waved the limos to a triple garage, the doors of which closed immediately they were inside. The SUV stayed out front. The gate rolled shut.

"Holy crap," said Chase. "What was that?"

"Visiting dignitary, obviously. Somebody fairly important, given there were two limos: one of them'll be a decoy. The SUV's got a bunch of Secret Service guys inside. This is a senator, a congressman, somebody at that level."

An hour later the motorcade departed, crawling along the street in the direction it had come like some sinister giant caterpillar.

"Right," said Chase. "So he's had his political heavyweight chum over for lunch. Now it's our turn."

"Wait. Wait!"

But Chase was already out of the car and crossing the road. Theo could see no alternative but to follow him.

Chase prodded the button marked *Callers* on the entry console inset into the left-hand gate pillar.

From the speaker, a gravelly voice growled, "Who's this?"

"Yeah, hello, is that Harry Gottlieb?" said Chase.

"No."

"Didn't think so. Well, we're pals of Harry's. Old pals. We just happened to be passing by and we thought we'd come and say hi. He in?"

"State your names."

"Dick Zuckerman and Phil Macavity. We're gay porn stars. You'll definitely be familiar with our work."

"All right, wiseass," said the man at the other end of the voice feed. "You have five seconds to get your butts back to whatever goddamn rock you crawled out from under. Otherwise we'll come out there and deal with you, and you seriously do not want that to happen."

Theo shouldered Chase aside. "Okay, sorry about that," he said into the console. "My associate has a sense of humour – or what he thinks passes for one."

"I resent that!" Chase said.

"We are, genuinely, old friends of Mr Gottlieb," Theo said. "Distant relatives might be more accurate. Anyway: Theo Stannard and Chase Chance. If he doesn't recognise the names, tell him... Tell him we were around in his travelling days."

"Mr Gottlieb does lots of travelling."

"It's a particular Mediterranean voyage I'm referring to. He'll know exactly what I mean. He kind of got lost."

There was silence from the console. It dragged on for a minute. Two minutes.

"Well, that was successful," said Chase.

Then the front door of the mansion opened and out stepped the protection detail again. The four men strode down the driveway with purpose. They were uniformly thick-necked and bulky, and the cut of their suit jackets only partially disguised the sidearms holstered at their armpits.

"This looks like it's going to get interesting," said Theo.

"I hope 'interesting' is another word for 'fun'," said Chase.

"Please let's do this my way. We should at least try to negotiate."

"Aw, you're such a spoilsport, cuz."

So saying, Chase grasped two of the spikes surmounting the gate. It was eight feet tall but he vaulted over it at a single bound.

"Sir!" yelled the nearest of the men. "Sir, stand down immediately! Do not come any nearer. This is private property and I am authorised and legally within my rights to deploy lethal force against you."

Chase charged, ramming the heel of his palm into the security man's throat, poleaxing him instantly. He'd gauged the blow so that it incapacitated rather than killed; the guard might have to breathe through a tube and be fed intravenously for the next few weeks, but he would live.

Handguns were drawn. Chase was already moving to the next target. Theo, heaving a sigh, leapt lightly over the gate himself. His cousin could be so damn hot-headed at times. Like a teenager in a three-thousand-year-old body.

The remaining security men tried to draw a bead on Chase, but he was too quick. He dispatched the second of them at a run with an outstretched arm, like a WWE wrestler clotheslining an opponent. The man went down so hard his scapula and collarbone snapped.

The third guard managed to loose off a round before Chase caught up with him, but the shot hit nothing but shrubbery. Then the gun, a Ruger SR9, was no longer in his hand. Chase snatched it from him by the muzzle, reversed it, and used the butt to club him into insensibility before tossing the weapon aside.

Meanwhile Theo was zeroing in on the fourth and final member of the protection detail. The man saw him coming; he pivoted; his gun swung up.

To Theo's eyes, he did all this in slow motion, like something out of a movie dream-sequence. There was time for Theo to skirt around his field of aim, to dart in from the side, to knock him cold with a single right hook to the jaw, all before the man's finger could even tighten on the trigger. He pulled the punch, using only a small fraction of his deity-derived strength. Even so, the man's head rocked to the side and Theo felt bone splinter under the impact. Any harder and he might have left him with permanent brain damage. You had to be so careful with mortals. They were so frail, even the tough ones.

In total, from Chase jumping the gate to Theo taking care of the fourth security man, the fight lasted just under ten seconds.

In the aftermath, the two demigods looked at each other. Neither was even panting. Chase offered his cousin a loopy, doglike smile. Theo, refusing to be won over, responded with a stern stare.

"Oh, bravo."

The voice came from the top of the steps leading up to the mansion's main entrance, where stood a dapper, distinguished-looking man who appeared to be in his mid-fifties, beautifully turned out in a tailored suit, liquorice-black Oxfords and a Windsor-knotted striped silk tie. He gave a round of sardonic applause.

"Well, you've succeeded in getting my attention," said Harry Gottlieb, the political strategist formerly known as Odysseus. "You may as well come inside."

* * *

GOTTLIEB SETTLED THEM in the living room and went to make a couple of phone calls. Within half an hour the injured security men had been removed from the front lawn and whisked off to a private hospital, and a new protection detail had arrived to take their place. Washington's Metropolitan PD had been placated at the very highest levels, with any police officers who had responded to reports of a gunshot in the Georgetown area now assured that it had been a prank, kids letting off a firework somewhat in advance of the Fourth of July. The whole incident was wiped away as though nothing had happened.

"Couldn't take a hint, could you?" Gottlieb said after he had returned from fixing the situation.

"Couldn't answer a simple voicemail, could you?" Chase shot back.

"I would have gotten round to it eventually."

"So you did receive the messages."

"Oh, I received them. You weren't terribly specific, though, were you? All you said was you had something of great urgency to discuss with me, or words to that effect, and you became increasingly irked and curt each time you rang; which frankly made me *less* inclined to pay attention. Besides, I had important matters to attend to."

"That motorcade we saw go in and leave," said Theo.

"My regular monthly lunchtime meeting; I was devoting all my energies to that. Foreign policy and deficit reduction were both on the agenda, and I had to research and prepare accordingly. I like to be up on my brief going in."

"How high-up *is* your lunch buddy?"

"Very high."

"Senate high?"

"Higher. As high as you can go. Let me put it this way; normally his car has flags on the front."

Theo chuckled in disbelief. "You and the President of the United States meet privately every month?"

"We do," Gottlieb replied equably. "More, during a crisis. It's been that way since the early 'eighties, with successive incumbents of the Oval Office. Before then, it was my father Solomon Gottlieb they saw."

"Also you."

"Also me. The handover occurred right in the middle of the Reagan administration. I had been gradually dyeing my hair white, like now; then I left on sabbatical for a few months, let my normal hair colour grow back in, and returned as Solomon's son and heir. Dear old Ronnie, bless his limited mental capacity, was none the wiser. At first he was wary about dealing with Gottlieb Junior rather than Senior, but soon as he realised he was getting the same sound counsel, he stopped worrying. I doubt I could pull that trick with the present Commander-in-Chief. He is far sharper-witted."

"I'm surprised he needs your advice at all."

"Oh, they come," said Gottlieb airily. "Democrat or Republican, they come, month in, month out. It's a kind of pilgrimage, and just as much a part of Presidential tradition as the Correspondents' Dinner or the Thanksgiving turkey pardoning. I'm a Beltway fixture, the Sage of Georgetown. I have sway. Any POTUS shuns me at his peril. Or *her* peril," he added, "mustn't rule anything out."

"I knew you were a mover and shaker, but..." Chase sounded impressed, in spite of himself.

Theo chose to be more phlegmatic than his cousin. "Is that the only reason you refused to see us? Because you had a date with the President?"

"Well, no. Frankly, I couldn't stir myself to be interested. I don't really belong to your little club, do I? Why should I be bothered if you've got some sort of flap going on? I have worldwide concerns. I have the ear of the most powerful man on the planet. Decisions I make ripple out from here across the globe. I work on the broadest imaginable canvas, and your concerns are – no offence – petty."

Gottlieb said this evenly, with no discernible spite. Chase bristled, and Theo put a hand on his shoulder to restrain him. You handled a man like Harry Gottlieb diplomatically. Rising to his bait simply affirmed his superiority and lowered you in his estimation. You played him at his own game or not at all. It was the only way to win, or at least draw.

"You say you don't belong to our club," he began.

"I am not, by the strictest definition, a demigod," Gottlieb said. "My paternal grandfather is Zeus and my maternal great-grandfather is Hermes. Via them I have been bestowed, like you two, with immortality; but I lack your physical prowess and vigour. I am not able to leap and run and perform feats of strength above and beyond the capacity of any mortal. It is my mind that is extraordinary – cunning and intelligence."

"The cunning and intelligence which came up with the Wooden Horse of Troy, and which saved your ship's crew from countless deadly hazards on your way home to Ithaca."

"Your point being...?"

"Nothing. I was just –"

"Just trying to soft-soap me by listing my best-known accomplishments?"

"There was also the theft of the palladium from Troy."

Gottlieb smirked. "Ah, yes. Crawling through the city's sewers to retrieve the little olive-wood thing. The oracles had said Troy would not fall as long as the palladium remained within its walls; true or not, I figured the Myrmidons would be disheartened by the loss of their sacred trinket. It was psychological warfare long before anyone coined the term."

"Wasn't Diomedes with you?" said Chase.

Gottlieb fixed him with a steely-eyed glare.

"Yeah, and you tried to kill him on the way out. So's you could claim the credit all for yourself?" Chase went on.

"Yes, now is probably not the time to bring that up," said Theo.

"Why not? It's true. He's a big old glory-hound."

"We've come to him for help, not to piss him off."

"Oh, it's quite all right," said Gottlieb, breezily. "For the record, I didn't actually try to kill him. That is a calumny perpetrated by both Homer and Apollodorus of Athens. I may have drawn my sword as we were returning to camp and Diomedes may happen to have looked over his shoulder and seen the glint of moonlight reflecting off the blade, but the truth was I had heard a noise and unsheathed my sword to defend myself. *Not* that I was preparing to stab him in the back and bring the palladium to the Greeks on my own. How treacherous and self-serving would that have been!"

"Very," said Theo. "Which is why we're more than happy to

accept your version of events. Aren't we, Chase? You were there, after all. Homer and Apollodorus weren't. What did they know?"

"Thank you, Theseus," said Gottlieb.

"I'd prefer Theo, if you don't mind."

"Humble apologies. You stick with your aliases all the time, don't you? So that you're less likely to slip up when in mixed company."

"It's simpler that way."

"Another reason I don't associate with you lot. The etiquette you abide by. The painstaking efforts you make to blend in, to be as like mortals as you can."

"There's nothing wrong with that."

"No, no, nothing whatsoever. There's no harm in fitting in. It rather does a disservice to our heritage, though, doesn't it? I like it that mortals come to consult me. I like having the most powerful of them at my beck and call. To be the unseen power behind the throne – that's where the real ruling happens. That has been my calling ever since I was banished from Ithaca for killing my Penelope's suitors."

"Oh yeah," Chase drawled, "you've been a major influence on all the greats."

Gottlieb nodded. "I count history's finest as my clients." He began checking them off on his fingers. "Alexander, Caesar, Charlemagne, Queen Elizabeth, Lincoln…"

"Also Genghis Khan, Napoleon, and some guy called Hitler."

"You have been keeping track, haven't you? Clever fellow." There was a steely edge beneath the compliment, a razor blade hidden in candy.

"Ear to the ground. I ask around. I make demigod business my business."

"So you do. So you do. Well, as to the Hitler connection, I won't deny it: I helped him on his rise to power, his self-described 'struggle'. Adolf had some good ideas. He sincerely wished to rescue Germany from penury and shame. His was a noble goal. But when I realised how far he was going to take it, that was when I made my excuses and left. I spent the war flitting between Britain and America, chivvying Churchill and rallying Roosevelt."

"Which makes everything okay."

"Why, Chase Chance, do you persist in antagonising me," said Gottlieb, "when by your own admission you and your cousin are seeking my aid?"

"Maybe I can't help it. Maybe you rub me up the wrong way. All your high-and-mighty talk."

Theo jumped in. "Chase has strong feelings and isn't always good at controlling them. To his credit, he was the one who suggested we meet up with you. I wasn't completely in favour."

"Be that as it may, you have put me to some trouble, the both of you," said Gottlieb severely. "You have cost me a set of bodyguards, an appurtenance I have to have, not because I fear any attempt on my life but because someone like me must be seen to take his personal safety seriously. You have inconvenienced me and lobbed insulting insinuations at me. Why on earth should I extend you the benefit of my assistance?" He slapped the air with the back of his hand. "Some vague familial affinity? A commonality of origin that I tangentially share with you?"

"Because you are the man of stratagems," said Theo, "and we need stratagems. Okay, cards on the table. Here's how it is. Listen and then decide if we've wasted your time and ours."

"Very well."

"There's a fairly good chance that someone is killing demigods. Someone is singling us out and murdering us. Trouble is, we have no clue who, why or even how. It's a mystery. A conundrum. It demands a mind like yours to unravel it."

"Killing demigods?" said Gottlieb. "Well, why didn't you say so earlier?"

Theo observed a tiny spark in those bright, knowing eyes. Harry Gottlieb was intrigued.

"Chase didn't want to get into it in a voicemail. Too complicated. Plus, you know, discretion. Anyone might be listening in. Also, we're not even a hundred per cent sure that *is* what's happening. It looks that way, though."

"But killing demigods is impossible. Almost impossible. We can recover from virtually any injury you care to name."

"But there is a way. One that doesn't necessarily involve chopping us up into tiny pieces or burning us to cinders."

"Yes. The twelve artefacts. The divine weapons and protections. Gifts variously given to demigods to aid them in their quests or as a token of parental affection."

"Which you stowed somewhere safe."

"I did," said Gottlieb. "And they should still be there, where I left them. They cannot have been recovered. I went to great pains to ensure that."

"But what if they have been? What if someone has gotten hold of them and is using them against us?"

Gottlieb, for the first time during the conversation, sat down. Up until then he had been pacing the room, while Theo and Chase remained perched on a brocade-upholstered sofa, lecturing them like a pair of wayward pupils.

Now, at eye level with them in an armchair that matched the sofa, he said, "Tell me everything."

TWELVE

Southern Somalia

THE BUS RUMBLED along unmarked two-lane tarmac under a pitiless late-afternoon sun. The vehicle was reputed to have air-conditioning, but if the rumour was true, Roy wasn't feeling any of the benefits. His jeans were adhering to the vinyl seat covering and his shirt was piebald with patches of sweat.

He was sitting at the rear of the bus, next to Gavin Martin. All the other Myrmidons were ranged before him, the entire complement, with Badenhorst at the front next to the driver. Every time the wheels hit a pothole in the road – which was more or less once a minute – Roy saw their heads bounce in unison, as though they were agreeing avidly with something someone had said.

Outside the dust-caked windows, the landscape alternated between countryside and farmland. There was the occasional breezeblock smallholding or ramshackle village, but otherwise it was scrubby savannah broken up by banana plantations, sorghum fields and swathes of parched pasture. The southern region of Somalia was the country's agricultural hub, reliant on two major rivers, the Jubba and the Shebelle, for irrigation. It was also the area most affected by civil war and sectarian bloodshed. Every so often the bus passed the blackened shell of a building, either burnt out or bombed. At one point an open-back Land Rover came trundling the other way laden with ragtag paramilitaries, their rifles jutting out at all angles like the quills of a gunmetal porcupine. Islamist slogans were spray-painted on walls, mostly in Arabic script, but now and then an *Allahu Akbar* in the Roman alphabet.

The locals, nonetheless, went about their business as normal. Here were some kids scurrying around after a football; there a goatherd driving his flock along the roadside. Two women waddling homeward with string bags full of groceries. Either they were so accustomed to the background presence of violence they no longer noticed it, or they had taught themselves to behave as if it didn't exist.

Roy nudged Gavin. "Mate? You got a moment?"

Gavin looked up from the game he was playing on his phone. "Sure. What is it?"

The bus's diesel engine gave off a continuous churning growl, loud enough that Roy would have had to shout to be heard by the people sitting in the next row of seats. Still, he kept his voice low.

"What are we doing?" he said.

"Travelling to an anti-insurgency training camp, where we're going to take down target number four."

"Yes, thank you for being so literal."

"You're welcome."

"But what are we *doing*? This whole project. What's it all in aid of?"

"It's in aid of me making enough dosh so that the missus and I can move to Malaga with the kids and live out the rest of our days drinking sangria by the side of our own swimming pool. That's what." Gavin returned his attention to the phone.

"Fair enough," said Roy. "Let me put it another way. What is it with these antique weapons? What's the story there? Why do we have to use them? Why are we having to get up close and personal with the targets, when a sniper round to the head from five hundred metres away ought to do the trick?"

Gavin paused the game. Candy Crush Saga could wait.

"You have a lot of questions, Roy," he said. "Ever hear that saying about gift horses?"

"Well, here's one more question. Who are these people we're eliminating? They don't seem to have anything in common. They're complete randoms: a travel writer, a dive tour guide, a former pop star, now a mercenary. It's like someone's sticking a pin in an international phone directory. They must all be connected in some way, but how?"

"I don't know. I don't want to know; I don't need to know. A job is a job. If you start wondering about it, you're not going to be able to do it. Don't think about the who. Just think about the dough." Gavin motioned at his phone. "Now, can I finish this?"

"Go ahead."

"Cheers."

The advice was sound, but Roy somehow couldn't take it. He couldn't overlook the fundamental strangeness of the project. Not any more.

The weapons were the weirdest part. What did it mean, dispatching the targets with spears and axes and so forth? What was it supposed to signify? There was something almost ritualistic about it, as if the targets were sacrifices. Was that it? Was that the point? Or was it to send some oblique message? Make some statement that could be understood only by a specific audience?

Then there were Anthony Peregrine's last words: *This won't kill me. Can't.* Said after he had taken two 5.56mm bullets in the torso. And after that weird, long speech of his, in some unfamiliar, primordial language.

On the flight from England to Somalia's Kismayo International Airport, Sean Wilson had described Del Karno's final moments to the rest of the team. He had told them, with relish, how Karno submitted to the spear thrust, not resisting, as if welcoming it. "I couldn't hear a thing the eejit was saying, but he just held out his arms, he did, like fecking Jesus Hisself, and I stepped in, and that was that. Easiest kill ever."

Why had Badenhorst insisted on the strike team wearing earplugs for that job? What difference would it have made, them being able to hear Karno speak? And why had Karno greeted death so willingly, with open arms?

Roy was becoming more than curious. He didn't mind Badenhorst keeping secrets from them; that was standard procedure. It didn't do to know everything. As long as you had all the facts that were relevant, the rest was superfluous.

But he was starting to think that he and the other Myrmidons were being kept *too much* in the dark, that Badenhorst was withholding certain vital pieces of intel. The secrets were big ones. And big secrets made for big threats.

THIRTEEN

Washington, D.C.

THE EIGHTEENTH AMENDMENT, the cocktail bar where Gottlieb had suggested they meet, sat on the corner of an intersection a half-dozen blocks east of the White House. At first glance Theo judged it a poor choice of venue: it was crowded, the clientele almost exclusively political advisors, lobbyists and journalists. There was little elbow room and seemed to be even less privacy.

He quickly gathered, however, that the bar-goers were paying attention to nothing except the sound of their own voices. Everyone was too busy braying and whinnying at everyone else, as drunk on self-importance as they were on alcohol. You could hold a conversation here in the absolute certainty that it wouldn't be snooped on. These people were barely listening to one another.

Gottlieb arrived shortly after 10PM, an hour later than he had said he would. He sailed through the throng unremarked and unhindered. Possibly the most powerful person on the premises, yet he was anonymous.

"*Kal'espera, o kyrioi,*" he said to Theo and Chase.

"Perhaps we should stick with English," said Theo.

"I thought ancient Hellenic might be prudent," said Gottlieb. "So that we may talk freely."

"I don't think that's a precaution we need to take here. More to the point, if someone does tune in to our conversation and can't understand a word, they might assume the worst. Three men speaking in a foreign language, with pretty swarthy complexions, a stone's throw from Pennsylvania Avenue. This is America. There will be profiling. There will be police called."

"Very well," said Gottlieb. "At any rate, I trust you've made the most of your time in our fine city. So many sights to see. The Smithsonian, the Washington Monument, the Lincoln Memorial…"

"Do we *look* like tourists?" Chase snapped. He was well into his third whisky sour.

"Chase took the car and left me stranded for the afternoon," said Theo. "I found a coffee shop and caught up on correspondence. Fanmail, business stuff, social media."

"The life of the author of potboilers," said Gottlieb. "So banal."

Theo smiled as though he had the words *FUCK YOU* etched into his incisors.

"And where did you go, Chase?" Gottlieb asked indifferently.

"Out in the hills to the north, just over the state line."

"Maryland? Whatever for?"

Theo said, "He wanted to see if he could pick up any trace of the… What did you call it, Chase? Sounds like a character off of *Sesame Street*?"

"The Snallygaster," said Chase. "It's a cryptid that was named by German immigrants back in the seventeen hundreds – *Schneller Geist*, 'quick spirit'. It's a cross between a bird and a reptile, with steel claws and beak and a demonic face. Plucks you up off the ground and flies off with you to its roost where it sucks your blood at its leisure."

"And did you meet with success?" said Gottlieb.

"I drove around a bit. Headed on foot into the woods around the Patuxent River. Not a thing. It was kind of a long shot, but it never hurts to try. If I'd had time I might have looked for the Dewayo as well, up in Frederick County. It's the Snallygaster's mortal enemy. Something like a werewolf. But I had to get back here."

"You and your monsters. It's quite the obsession. Are there still any left? You seem to have done a pretty thorough job of making them extinct."

"Some remain. And they bite." Chase revealed his bandaged arm for Gottlieb to see. "Proof."

Gottlieb twisted the corners of his mouth down, a half-hearted stab at an expression of empathy. "Poor you. I presume your motives are purely altruistic."

"What do you mean by that?"

"You kill monsters so as to keep the public safe."

"Of course. Why else?"

"And not because you get a thrill out of it."

Chase eyed him over the rim of his tumbler. "The fact is, as civilisation spreads, there are fewer places for monsters to hide in. Their habitats are being encroached on. But you can't keep them in a game reserve, like lions or elephants; they have to stay in the wild. Upshot is you're going to get more clashes between them and humans, and one or other side is going to regret it."

"So it's better that you kill them first, is that it? A kind of pre-emptive strike."

"That's it. Simplifies things, too. This is an age that doesn't have room for anything people can't identify or classify. It's an age of rationalism, and monsters have no place in it."

"Rationalism?" Gottlieb laughed hollowly. "Have you not noticed how many religious zealots there are out there? All those monotheist fundamentalists obeying the edicts of their One True God? Washington has more than its fair share."

"And they don't want monsters in the world either. I'm performing a useful community service, Harry. I'm getting rid of the last few vestiges of the past – *our* past, when heroes and monsters were commonplace. I'm sweeping away the things that no longer belong."

"Well, if you insist."

"I do." Chase finished off his drink.

Gottlieb held up two fingers, attracting the attention of a waitress. "Over here, my dear." To Theo and Chase: "My round. What'll it be?"

Yet another whisky sour for Chase, a second rum and Coke for Theo, and a gimlet for Gottlieb.

After the drinks came, Theo said, "So, what's the news?"

"No more small talk?" said Gottlieb. "You really do have the bit between your teeth, Theo."

"I'm taking what's happening very seriously."

"You're a very serious person. Always have been. Like Chase here, you can't seem to escape who you were."

"Nor, for that matter, can you."

"Fair point. We are set in our ways, aren't we? You'd think, after all this time, we'd have changed. Perhaps we can't."

"Isaac Merrison did," said Chase.

"Who? Oh, yes. Orion. But then he had to. He couldn't go on the way he was, so angry, so consumed by the desire to conquer and dominate. The rest of us, we just tread over the same old ground, wearing new boots."

"You've made enquiries, I take it," said Theo.

"Patience, patience," said Gottlieb. "Yes, I have. I've placed a few calls, set wheels in motion. Principally I've pulled some strings with the Director at Langley. As we speak, CIA drones are winging their way from various US airbases around the world to the places where I buried divine artefacts. The pilots' brief is to reconnoitre only, look for signs of disturbance at the sites. The pilots have been told that these may be the locations of terrorists arms caches. Beyond that, they are in ignorance, as is the Director. I don't anticipate anyone reporting back until tomorrow morning at the earliest. I chose each site for its remoteness and inaccessibility, after all. That was the whole point, putting the things where they wouldn't be stumbled upon by accident."

"And booby-trapping them, for anyone retrieving them on purpose."

"Daedalus himself would have envied the job I did," said Gottlieb. "I spent months devising and perfecting those traps. Tripwires, crossbows triggered by pressure plates. Pools of mercury, sliding portcullis blocks. Deluges of sand. Water-activated counterweights. Fragile plugs of concrete stopping up channels connected to underground reservoirs. I used as little metal as possible in the construction, and any I did use I coated with chromate to prevent it rusting. The traps were intended to remain dormant but effective for centuries."

"Until Lara Croft comes along and somersaults past the lot of them," said Chase.

"Who is Lara Croft?"

"You're kidding me. Seriously? You've never heard of *Tomb Raider*?"

"Is it another lowest-common-denominator television show, like yours?"

Chase, ignoring the barb, shook his head wonderingly. "You probably don't know who Indiana Jones is either."

"Him I'm familiar with. Reagan was a big fan of the films. He would sometimes act out scenes for me while we were in conference. It was… tiresome."

"Trying to keep us focused…" said Theo.

Chase shot him a you're-no-fun look.

"Chase may not realise it, but he has a point," Theo continued. "Let's presume someone was able to beat all the traps, cunning as they are."

"Not beyond the bounds of possibility, I suppose," Gottlieb said.

"Would the artefacts still be potent, after all this time?"

"Still imbued with divine essence, still deadly to us? I don't see why not. We are, aren't we? The divinity in us, such as it is, has preserved us well past man's allotted threescore and ten. We remain in a state of perpetual youthfulness. Some of us more than others." He aimed a wry sidelong glance at Chase. "Why shouldn't it be the same for the twelve artefacts?"

"The gods are no longer around, that's all."

"And the artefacts need constantly topping up with power, like a laptop's battery needs charging? I don't think it works that way. Once each of them was bestowed its godly imprimatur, it had it in perpetuity. That's why they struck me as so hazardous, why they had to be collected and buried, like toxic waste. They would always pose a risk."

"And only you know where they were."

"Only me," Gottlieb said with a nod. "That is the status quo, and it has served us well so far."

Something jangled in Theo's mind, like a tiny, distant alarm. What Gottlieb had just said didn't ring entirely true, but he was damned if he could figure out at that moment what was bothering him. He had so many memories, too many to search easily. It was like finding a specific tree in a vast forest. He shook his head; it would come to him.

"I believe, under the circumstances, that the status quo should be revised," he said.

Gottlieb eyed him with scepticism and a touch of indignation. "You're asking me to divulge the locations of the artefacts to you? To break a sacred trust I have held for three thousand years?"

"Yes."

"Whatever for?"

"Because it's about time. Because we deserve to know."

"You deserve to know!" Gottlieb echoed with sharp disdain. "You don't deserve anything of the sort."

"It's a big damn secret for one individual to keep. Sharing it is long overdue."

"Preposterous. Never."

"Look at it this way. If it does turn out that the artefacts have been unearthed, then the point's moot anyway."

"And if they haven't been, you'll have got me to surrender up knowledge I have assiduously kept to myself my entire life, for nothing."

"I'm insisting that you do this, Harry," Theo said. "Whether or not Aeneas, Orion and Orpheus were killed with the artefacts, the rest of us have a right to be told where you stashed them. We may have accepted, back then, that it was sensible for wise Odysseus to be the artefacts' sole custodian. But the world has moved on. Things are different now."

Gottlieb squinted at him askance. "If I didn't know better, I might infer that you have your suspicions about me, Theo Stannard. That you think I me the culprit behind the deaths."

"No," Theo said firmly – maybe a little too firmly. "That's not my reasoning at all."

"I very much hope it isn't. I would be deeply disappointed if it was. I would also become thoroughly uncooperative, which I am sure you would not wish."

"All the same, I'm still insisting."

"With the implication that – what? If I don't comply you'll hurt me? Here? In full view of all these people? Dozens of witnesses, some of them members of the national and international press?" Gottlieb snorted.

Theo realised then that the choice of venue for this meeting had been neither accident nor miscalculation. Gottlieb had prepared for a clash; worse, he had his own suspicions about Theo and Chase.

It was paranoid. But then Theo was starting to feel a tinge of paranoia himself.

"Look," Theo said. His tone was as mollifying as he could make it. "I'm not asking much." He slid a cocktail napkin across the table to Gottlieb. "Just jot them down on this. The what and the where. Then we're all on an equal footing."

"Why does it matter to you, this knowledge? How is it going to help?"

"At the risk of sounding bleak, what if something happens to you? What if, heaven forfend, you go the way of the other three?"

"I'm too wily for that."

"One can't be too careful. I'm asking you for a gesture of trust."

"Trust? Seems more like mistrust to me. You don't think I'm being straight with you. You don't think I've arranged for those drones at all."

"Perhaps I like to cover all the bases."

"And should I agree to do as you ask, what will you do with it? This could all be a charade, a scheme to wheedle the locations out of me, enabling you to get your own hands on the artefacts."

"You know me," said Theo. "You said just now that we don't change, and you know the sort of person I am. I'm not a murderer."

"You've killed."

"Those who deserved it. Thieves, extortionists, torturers. And, yes, murderers. But not fellow demigods."

"Some demigods have been thieves, extortionists, murderers and worse. Orion was no saint. Neither was Aeneas, for all that called him Pious. He mistreated Dido of Carthage egregiously, his conquest of the Latins was far from peaceful, and he didn't show the warlord Turnus any mercy when they duelled. Orpheus too was hardly a paragon of good behaviour."

Theo almost laughed. "Come on. If I'm the guy who killed them, why would I have come to you for help?"

"As a ruse, to allow you to add me to the tally. I'm sure there are things I've done that the self-righteous Theseus would disapprove of."

"That's crazy. Besides, if I'm already using the divine artefacts to go on a slaughter spree, why would I be asking you to tell me where they are?"

"Another ruse. You don't have them yet. You want them, and you've set this all up to get hold of them."

"Crazier still. What's it like in your head, Harry? All these thoughts going round in circles, chasing their tails, eating themselves? You've been in politics too long. You can't see anything for what it is any more. You can only see motives behind motives, wheels within wheels, plots inside plots. Just write down where the artefacts are. For my sake, for yours. Think of it as an insurance policy. You must see the sense in that."

Gottlieb was silent for a long while. Cogs were turning in his intricate brain. Theo wondered if he had pushed him too hard. It was conceivable Gottlieb might just stand up and walk away, and then what? Could Theo pursue him and beat the information out of him? Of course he couldn't.

He didn't even want to know where the artefacts had been stowed, not that badly. He was just keen for Gottlieb to give some indication that he was on the side of right. With a man as slippery as Odysseus, you needed a show of earnest, a bargaining chip, to keep him honest. Otherwise he would treat you as just another malleable fool to toy with and manipulate. Gottlieb would not be a reliable ally until he had proved beyond all doubt that he could be.

Slowly, reluctantly, the self-styled Sage of Georgetown reached into an inside jacket pocket and produced a beautiful fountain pen, a Montblanc Meisterstück with solid gold nib and black resin barrel. He applied it to the humble cocktail napkin, writing neatly for a couple of minutes. Then, capping the pen, he slid the napkin back to Theo.

"There. Happy?"

Theo scanned the list of artefacts and their locations:

In no particular order:

Trident (Poseidon)	Deception Island, Antarctica
Bident (Hades)	Atacama Desert, Bolivia
Bow (Apollo)	Svalbard, Norway
Bow (Artemis)	Pitcairn Island, South Pacific
Hammer (Hephaestus)	Kerguelen Archipelago, South Indian Ocean
Axe (Ares)	Tristan de Cunha, South Atlantic
Helm of Darkness (Hades)	Novy Tolkatui, Siberia
Spear (Hephaestus)	Motuo, China
Sickle (Hermes)	Taklamakan Desert, China
Aegis (Zeus)	Socotra Island, Yemen
Scythe (Kronos)	Cape York Peninsula, Australia
Club (Dionysus)	Ittoqqortoormiit, Greenland

Chase, peering over his shoulder, let out a whistle. "Holy shit. I've been remote places, but there's some there even I haven't heard of. Novy Tolkatui? Socotra Island? And I'm not even going to try to pronounce that last one."

"Imagine travelling to such far-flung destinations in the days before airliners," said Gottlieb. "Before helicopters. Before even steam. Imagine how damn long and arduous the voyages were. Sail, then mule train, slogging across ice or sand dune or mountainside for mile after mile, lugging building materials and urging on slaves who were reluctant at best, at worst mutinous... Made my ten-year journey home from Troy look like a two-week pleasure cruise."

"Is this all true?" Theo said, indicating the list.

"You mean have I made any of it up? No. Do you think me capable of coming up with a dozen obscure place names right off the top of my head?"

"Look on it as a compliment that I do. I have to point out, too, that you've not been very specific. The Atacama Desert, for instance – that's big. Where in the Atacama Desert?"

"You were hoping for GPS coordinates, perhaps?" Gottlieb's smile was smug. "I'm not going to give away *everything*, Theo. You've plenty there to be getting on with, and it's all you're going to have, for now." He stood to leave. "I would say that it's been a pleasure, but I doubt you'd believe me. I will be in touch as and when I have anything further to impart. Goodnight."

LATER, LYING IN bed in his hotel room, wakeful, Theo mulled over the conversation. Typical Odysseus, laying down his hand while keeping some up his sleeve.

Then, all at once, it hit him. He remembered.

"And only you would know where they were."

"Only me."

But that wasn't quite accurate, was it?

FOURTEEN

Piraeus, Athens – 5th Century BCE

ODYSSEUS WAS LATE.

Six weeks late.

But, Theseus thought, that was hardly unexpected. The man was famous for arriving well behind schedule. Known for it, some would say.

Besides, they had arranged this rendezvous twelve summers ago. What was a few weeks extra, in light of that? Relatively speaking, nothing.

He would turn up. Of that Theseus was confident. Odysseus had his failings, but when he set himself a goal he kept on going until it was met.

So, for six weeks, Theseus had been kicking his heels in Athens. Every morning he would set off from the city along the narrow strip of land that ran between the Long Walls, the fortified defences built recently by General Themistocles as a bulwark against invasion by the Spartans. The Long Walls offered a safe corridor between Athens and its port, and fenced enough territory that in times of crisis the entire Athenian populace might be afforded a refuge, with room to cultivate crops and graze cattle for the duration of any siege.

Reaching Piraeus, Theseus would take a table at a taverna in Kantharos, the harbour's commercial sector. From there he would watch the merchant ships put in, offload their cargos and set sail again. Around him, sailors drank and roistered. They were of many nationalities, predominantly Greeks but with Phoenicians, Persians, Carthaginians, Nubians and even the occasional Iberian mixed in. Their voices were a polyglot babble.

Just visible from this vantage point were the other two sectors of the harbour, Zea and Munichia, between them providing berths for the entire Athenian navy, the three-hundred-strong fleet of triremes which gave the city-state unsurpassed supremacy in the Aegean and Ionian Seas. During peacetime, as now, the ships were drawn up above the shoreline and housed in pillar-sided sheds, to protect them from the elements and keep their timbers from rotting in the water. Slaves were engaged in scraping barnacles off the hulls and slapping on a coating of tar and wax.

Every day Theseus would eat lunch, usually lentil soup, flatbread, fruits and vegetables, washed down with a *skyphos* or two of thinned wine; and he would wait. Odysseus had been precise in his instructions. They were to meet this year at noon on the *noumenia* – the first day – of Hekatombaion. The meeting place was this taverna or, if for some reason it had closed down, whichever one was closest by.

Hekatombaion passed with no sign of Odysseus, and Metageitnion began, and by the middle of that month Theseus was finding it hard to think of a reason to remain. Summer was at its height, and Athens was dusty, stinking and hot. He was lodging at a tolerably well-appointed inn, but missed the comforts of home, which at present was a small farm up near Thessaloniki where cooling breezes blew even in humid weather and cypresses offered scented shelter from the sun.

There was the theatre, so he wasn't starved of entertainment. There was the state-sanctioned Solonian brothel in the Kerameikos district, so that was another need taken care of. He could socialise in the Agora if the mood took him, or attend a symposium. These were all pleasures.

But there was no getting around it: he was becoming bored and impatient. He had taken to roaming the streets after dark, on the prowl for thieves and rogues, cutpurses and rapists. Athens had its police force, the *astynomia*, but they did not patrol at night, and when the sun went down, the lawlessness went up. The clusters of narrow streets nestling at the foot of the Acropolis became dark, winding warrens of danger. Several times Theseus was set upon by cudgel-wielding gangs or lone knife-men, all of them keen to relieve him of his money and, if he refused to surrender that quietly, his life. He taught them the error of their ways.

The irony was not lost on him. Here was the city he himself had for a time been king of, and had fostered and helped grow. Now, centuries on, he came to it as a visitor, an outsider, and while Athens still flourished and was everything he could have hoped it would be, the world's pre-eminent nation-state, it had also developed social cankers, as all great cities did. Parts of it festered and demanded to be purged, just as a person in ill health must be bled in order to restore the balance of the humours. Its one-time monarch now fulfilled the role of secret surgeon.

On the day he seriously began to contemplate leaving Athens and heading homeward, Odysseus at last showed up.

The wanderer trudged into the taverna, looking footsore and exhausted. Theseus remembered Odysseus as lively-eyed and neatly turned out, his beard trimmed, his curly locks oiled, his clothes always freshly laundered and pristine-looking. This man was gaunt, sunburnt and unkempt. His beard straggled, as did his hair. His chiton and cloak were worn, torn and threadbare. Several of the leather thongs on his sandals had broken and been knotted back together rather than replaced.

He sat down at the table, helped himself to wine, and was silent for such a long time that Theseus began to wonder if he had lost the power of speech.

Then he croaked, "It's done."

"All hidden?" said Theseus.

"All. I said it would take twelve years, a year apiece, and so it did. You have no idea the places I've been. To the ends of the Earth and back. The storms I've weathered. The conditions I've endured."

Odysseus's Ithacan accent, which he had contrived to shed since his ignominious expulsion from the island of his birth, was back thicker than ever. For all his articulacy, it made him sound like a bumpkin. It seemed that the further he had travelled on this globe-girdling mission of his, the more he had returned to his roots.

He talked of a desert at such a high altitude, higher even than the peak of Mount Olympus, that the air was almost too thin to breathe. Of flyspeck islands so far from any land, you found them more by chance than by skill. Of icy wastes so vast and desolate, the sunlight glaring off the snow could turn you blind. Of uncharted wildernesses inhabited by bears and wolves that had no fear of humans because they had never encountered any.

In spite of all that, all the hardships and privations, the harshness of the environments he had ventured into, he had accomplished what he had set out to do, pulling off a feat he had thought nigh impossible. By comparison, Heracles's Twelve Labours were nothing. Theseus's Six Labours, likewise, were nothing. The poets would sing of the Labours of Odysseus, they would compose epics on the subject, if only they knew of them. Which of course they would not. Not ever.

"And you aren't going to tell me where the artefacts are," said Theseus.

"No. That's the whole point, isn't it? It's not that I don't think you're trustworthy. Of all of us, I adjudge you probably the most trustworthy there is. But knowledge as important as this needs to be contained. After the fate Pollux meted out on Castor, we can't afford anyone else gaining access to the artefacts, least of all one of our own."

The murder of Castor had been the impetus for Odysseus collecting and sequestering the divine artefacts. The final straw. Castor and his twin had squabbled over the women they wished to marry, Phoebe and Hilaria, who happened to be their cousins and, as it happened, married already. The row had escalated, ending with Pollux bludgeoning his sibling's head to a bloody pulp with a hammer.

The hammer was not just any hammer but one forged by Hephaestus himself, presented it to his son Philottos, to help him slay a Mormo, a vampiric creature that was attacking and killing children in Philottos's kingdom. Destroying the Mormo was a noble feat, unquestionably heroic, but Philottos was a conflicted, complicated figure, prone to vice and rashness. Running out of money during a drunken game of dice with Pollux, he staked the hammer on the result of the next throw – and lost.

After Pollux used the hammer to murder Castor, a rumour had gone round that Castor had been merely mortal, Pollux inheriting the full dose of their father's godhood at his twin's expense. There was also talk that the women's husbands Idas and Lynceus were the actual culprits. Theseus reckoned Odysseus was the one who had spun these webs of disinformation, in order to veil the truth: that there were weapons capable of felling demigods as surely as if they were human. The vast majority of mortals were unaware that demigods still walked among them, but some knew, and some of those who knew might be glad to learn that they were not as indestructible as they were reputed to be, and might try to exploit that vulnerability. In addition, demigods themselves, as Castor and Pollux had amply shown, could be their own worst enemies. Hundreds of divine offspring had been born during the Age of Heroes, and that number was still being added to, although the rate was tailing off steeply as the gods interacted less and less with mankind. Disputes and feuds cropped up among them, sometimes simmering for decades before suddenly turning bloody. The divine artefacts made it that much easier for them to slay one another, and that much likelier.

At any rate, after a long and determined campaign of cajoling and browbeating by Odysseus, a consensus was reached among the principal demigods. The vast majority of the divine artefacts had been reclaimed by their creators; they had been on loan only, each a gift given for a specific purpose and duly returned to the gods once that purpose had been fulfilled.

Twelve, however, still remained on Earth. Either the gods had forgotten about them or didn't require them back. Gods weren't known for their consistency, or their mindfulness. They were as profligate with their gifts as they were with their philandering.

These twelve artefacts, it was agreed, should be handed in to Odysseus for disposal. They could not be destroyed; the divine numen was too strong in them for that. Even the heat of a furnace would not so much as singe them, and throwing them into the ocean was no guarantee that they might not later wash ashore. But through Odysseus's cunning they could be put beyond use.

Achilles was loath to give up his spear, but he did. Heracles did not want to lose the bow which Apollo had bequeathed him, but was persuaded. Orion was the hardest of all to convince to part with his own bow, which had been gifted to him by his one-time lover, far-darting Artemis. Odysseus had had to work on him for days before he could be made to see sense.

"For this amnesty to succeed," Odysseus said to Theseus in the taverna, "it has to be total and unbreakable. I can't have, for instance, Heracles come bleating to me at some future date, asking please can he have his bow back, and getting all stroppy when I refuse to tell him where it is. He might threaten to kill me unless I confess, in which case I can simply point out that if I die, he'll never find out. That should be enough to deter him, or at least leave him so paralysed with indecision he'll give up." Odysseus sniggered. "Poor Heracles. Blessed with great brawn but little brain. It's almost too easy, bamboozling a lummox like him."

"So you're willing to stake your life on the fact that only you know where the artefacts are?"

"Nobody would want to call my bluff; it would be entirely self-defeating. Heracles, or whoever, could dangle me over an active volcano, but wouldn't dare drop me in."

"Let's say someone does, though, or you meet with some horrendous accident from which even a demigod can't recover. What then? How will we ever find the artefacts if we need to?"

"Why would you need to?"

"I don't know. The situation might arise. And it's not like you not to have a contingency plan, Odysseus. Something to fall back on in case of emergency."

The man of twists and turns gazed out over the wine-dark sea. "You know me too well, Theseus," he said eventually. "That, in fact, is the reason for the delay in my returning. I took a small detour along the way, to deposit something."

"Namely...?"

"I have made provision in the unlikely event that I die and the even unlikelier event that I forget where I cached the artefacts. I have drawn maps of the locations and written detailed itineraries, describing how and where to reach them. I have even drawn sketches of the landscape surrounding each spot. These instructions cover several sheets of vellum, which I have sealed up in a set of copper cylinders and left with a certain person of our acquaintance."

"Who?"

"I am," Odysseus said, "a man without a permanent home. So I have entrusted the cylinders to the safekeeping of someone who has several homes, all of them fairly impressive."

"Who?" Theseus asked again. He had some inkling which person Odysseus was referring to, but he wanted to hear the name said.

"You, of all people, are not going to like the answer. But then, why should that matter?"

A third time, more insistent: "Who?"

"King Minos."

FIFTEEN

Washington, D.C.

"Lied to us. The son of a bitch lied to us. Right to our faces."

Theo thumped the steering wheel, inadvertently prompting a hoot from the rental car's horn.

They were stuck in traffic, virtually at a standstill. The driver of the car in front leaned out of his window and shouted, "Hey, buddy, nobody's going anywhere. Gridlock. So just cool it, okay?"

"Yes, sorry," Theo replied. "It was a mistake."

"Sure, sure," said the other driver. "Mistake *this*, asshole," and he flipped Theo the bird.

When Chase had finished laughing at his cousin, he said, "Duh. Of *course* he lied. Odysseus, remember? Guy has the integrity of a roadside crow."

"I mean, I suppose it could just have slipped his mind..."

"Not him. He lied, plain and simple."

"I should have called him on it at the time. I sort of knew. I just couldn't put my finger precisely on what it was he'd said that was bugging me."

"Well, we're going to fix that now, aren't we?"

"Damn straight. If this traffic will ever let us get to his house."

"Washington ties with Chicago for the honour of having the worst road congestion in America. It's because no building in the city is allowed to be taller than the width of the street it's on. That leads to urban sprawl, leads to inadequate road infrastructure, leads to..." Chase nodded at the stationary queue of vehicles ahead.

"Cameras aren't on, Chase. You don't have to travelogue."

"Just helping to pass the time."

"Well, don't."

Half an hour later, they had made it through Foggy Bottom and into Georgetown. Ten minutes after that, they were outside Harry Gottlieb's house.

Theo pressed the entry buzzer button several times, without effect. No one responded, not even a security man.

"Okay," he said. "The hard way it is."

Chase was poised to leap over the gate, but Theo had other ideas. He grasped two of the bars, planted his feet, and heaved sideways. The gate began to roll, squealing, grinding, shuddering, resisting. Theo gritted his teeth and shoved harder. There were crunching and cracking sounds as piston rams buckled and the hydraulic motor broke. He managed to create a gap a full metre wide before the mechanism was so severely damaged that the gate just stuck firm and not even a demigod's strength could budge it any further. He let go and dusted off his palms. His hands had dug into the steel of the bars so hard, leaving dents like the moulded grip on a combat knife.

"Oh, boy, you are not a happy bunny," said Chase. "How much is that going to cost to repair?"

"Harry can bill me," said Theo, stalking off up the driveway.

He was braced for the protection detail to come barrelling out of the house, guns waving, but this did not happen. As he climbed the steps to the front door, he grew more and more certain that there was no one home. Somehow you could tell from close up when a house was empty, and this one was. The air was too still.

Hence he didn't bother with the doorbell, opting instead for a hard, well-placed, jamb-splintering kick.

He and Chase stood in the grand hallway as the echoes of the door slamming open died away.

"Hello?" Chase called out. "Anyone? Jehovah's Witnesses. We're here to discuss the End Times. We can leave a copy of *The Watchtower* and come back later if you're too busy right now."

They performed a rapid search of the downstairs. Theo was in no doubt that his forced entry had triggered some kind of silent alarm. In ten minutes, fifteen at most, the cops would arrive.

Gottlieb was gone; that much was obvious. And he hadn't left long ago. In the kitchen there were the remains of breakfast. He hadn't tidied away the dishes, and the coffee percolator jug was half full and still faintly warm. They had missed him by half an hour at most. Damn traffic.

Upstairs, in the master bedroom, the doors of the walk-in closet stood ajar and a couple of the drawers in the dresser hung open. Gottlieb had packed his bags. He wasn't merely out for the day, then.

"Theo?"

That was Chase, calling up from below.

Theo joined him in Gottlieb's study. A flatscreen monitor sat atop a venerable cherrywood desk – a desk that rivalled the *Resolute* desk in the Oval Office for enormity and ornateness. The monitor was connected to a Dell Precision tower, and stuck on the keyboard in front of it was a yellow Post-it note. On the small square of paper someone – Gottlieb – had drawn an arrow pointing to the return key and written the words "*Press me*". Beneath he had added, "*(This is not a trick)*".

"It's a trick," said Chase. "We hit the key and, I don't know, maybe a bomb goes off and we get blown to kingdom come."

The same thought had crossed Theo's mind. That Gottlieb had fled Washington in such a hurry because he was guilty; that he was the one slaying other demigods, for reasons best known to him. With Theo and Chase sniffing around, he had begun to feel the heat and got out of Dodge.

And what better way to prevent them pursuing him than wire up his house with a bomb? The explosion might conceivably not kill them, but it would at the very least put them out of action for a while – long enough for Gottlieb to hightail it to the middle of nowhere and for his trail to go stone cold.

Then again, Gottlieb could have arranged for a bomb to go off the moment anyone opened the front door. A much simpler and more dependable method than inviting them to push a button and be the authors of their own destruction.

By the same token, Gottlieb might be counting on them thinking just that. Telling them to hit the return key was so obviously a ploy that it must not be a ploy, which meant it must be a ploy.

This, after all, was the man who convinced the Cyclops Polyphemus his name was Outis – 'Nobody' – and then put his eye out, so that when the giant screamed for help from the Cyclopes in neighbouring caves, and they asked him who had hurt him, he replied, 'Nobody,' and they decided he didn't need help.

Theo hesitated, unsure what to do. Time was ticking. He didn't fancy a run-in with the authorities; too awkward. Should he and Chase cut their losses, ignore the Post-it message, and just go? That seemed the most sensible option.

But what if the message was genuine? What would pressing the return key do? Was there something on the computer Gottlieb wished them to see?

"Oh, fuck it."

Theo, bracing himself for the worst, jabbed down with a forefinger. The flatscreen monitor sparked into life.

Two lines of text appeared against a blue background, with an empty box in between.

Input my son's name.

Otherwise the hard drive will erase
itself in 30 seconds.

As they watched, the 30 changed to a 29.

"His son's name," said Chase. "Does he not know the first thing about choosing an unguessable password? That's Computer Studies 101. Never use a relative's name."

"As far as anyone who knows Harry Gottlieb is concerned, he doesn't have a son," said Theo. "This is meant for us, to make sure we are who we hopes we are."

"Okay, but which son? Odysseus had a bunch of kids, like the rest of us. He didn't exactly keep it in his pants. He got Circe pregnant three times and played hide the salami with Calypso on Ogygia. After Penelope, there was Queen Callidice of Thesprotia, Princess Euippe of Dodona…"

"Only one of his sons really mattered to him. The one who went searching for him when he didn't return home, and who helped him get his wife back after he did."

The countdown had reached 3 seconds. Theo leaned in and typed the word TELEMACHUS.

The screen blanked, then a media player window popped up and a video clip began to run.

Harry Gottlieb's face gazed out at them. He was seated at this very desk.

"Ah, there you are," he said. "Congratulations, both on plucking up the nerve to hit the key and on answering my password poser correctly. I imagine the one caused you no small consternation, whereas the other, I trust, presented no difficulty." His eyes sparkled with evident delight.

"Arrogant jerk," said Chase.

"You do realise he can't hear you?" said Theo.

As if to disprove that, Gottlieb then said, "Yes, Chase, I am whatever you just called me. I don't apologise for my character. I don't apologise for anything I do. Regret and self-recrimination are unproductive. They serve no purpose.

"You are watching this video," he went on, "because I have absented myself from my house. I am, in fact, absenting myself from Washington and from civilised society altogether, for the foreseeable future. I am going, as they say, 'off the grid'. Don't come looking for me. You will not find me."

He offered a smile that seemed equal parts smirk and sneer.

"'Why?' is the question that is plaguing your brains. Or perhaps not. Perhaps you've formed an opinion about me, and believe you already know my reasons for absconding. I'm talking to you, Theo, rather than your sidekick."

"Sidekick!" Chase exclaimed.

Theo shushed him.

"You are likely to have assumed," Gottlieb was saying, "that it is I who have been masterminding, even perpetrating, lethal attacks on our fellow demigods. This video message will do nothing to quash that suspicion. Quite the reverse; it must look as though I am running scared."

He paused, bending closer to the camera.

"Let me tell you that I am. I *am* running scared. But not from you and the Monster Hunter, Theo. From you two I have nothing to fear, so long as you understand that you have nothing to fear from me."

"I think I should be the judge of that," Theo muttered.

"You do realise he can't hear you?" said Chase.

Gottlieb said, "It so happens that some of the drone sorties I organised bore fruit sooner than anticipated. During the small hours of this morning, I was phoned by Langley. It was no imposition; I tend not to sleep much, or well. Brain too busy.

"At each of the three sites where CIA Unmanned Aerial Vehicles had so far carried out reconnaissance, I was told, there were clear indicators of recent human activity. To wit: tyre tracks, heaps of excavation spoil, and the detritus left behind by campsites.

"For the record, the sites in question are in the Taklamakan Desert; on Socotra Island; and amid the gorges of Motuo, a county in the Nyingtri Prefecture, which lies in that part of Tibet that China has claimed for its own and which I can assure you was fiendishly hard to get to when I made my way there the first time.

"Now, had it been just *one* of these locations that had been disturbed, I might not have worried too much. It could have been happenstance – archaeologists rooting around for relics, palaeontologists dredging up fossils. Even two of the sites might not have been cause for concern. Explorers are getting everywhere these days. But all three? And let's not forget these were just the first three sites surveilled by drone.

"Clearly all twelve hiding places had been visited. Meaning, of course, that the divine artefacts are now out in the world.

"Given the deaths you informed me about, I must conclude that we are under attack. We are the subjects of a concerted, systematic genocide."

"Shit," Chase breathed, while Theo only nodded. He felt chilled, but vindicated.

"And so I have taken what I consider to be the only sensible course of action," Gottlieb said. "Like the hunted fox, I am going to ground. It may not surprise you to learn that I had plans in place for just such an eventuality as this. It was always a possibility that the artefacts might come back into play. Long ago I prepared myself a refuge, in case of emergency – a safe place, well away from civilisation. I am departing in just a moment. My protection detail has been dismissed, as has my domestic staff. A town car is coming to spirit me to the heliport, and from there I head for parts unknown, at least as far as you're concerned.

"It's going to be hard to leave my Washington life behind. I've grown accustomed to it. I imagine that quitting my position as Presidential advisor so abruptly, without warning, will prevent me from resuming it once the danger is past. So be it. The balance of geopolitical power is shifting anyway. Perhaps it's time I looked east, or possibly south.

"You may, naturally, choose to disbelieve everything I have just said. I cannot have helped my case by being somewhat economical with the truth last night. I presume that you, Theo, have not forgotten about the copper cylinders and the instructions contained therein, although it's such a long time since we spoke about them. I would have made mention of them had it not been for Chase's presence. What passed between the two of us, that day at Piraeus, was meant to stay between the two of us, and I am very much in favour of keeping information compartmentalised. Still, I am aware that my caginess might be looked upon as deceit. Please believe me when I say it wasn't intentional.

"You'll recall that it was King Minos to whom I gave the cylinders for safekeeping at Knossos. Minos, or as he is nowadays known, Evander Arlington. A very rich man. I mean, we are all rich, aren't we? You can't have lived as long as we have and failed to accumulate a healthy balance of savings. Compound interest is an immortal's best friend. But Evander Arlington is in another league altogether. Possibly *the* richest person on the planet. Richer than even Croesus could have dreamed of being, and *he* was the greediest, most acquisitive bastard I've ever had to deal with.

"Does Arlington still have the cylinders in his possession? That I do not know. He and I have seldom communicated. He is even more of a recluse than I am.

"But if he still has them, and knows he has them, and has chosen to unstopper them...

"Well, Theo, Chase, I leave that with you.

"Perhaps we shall meet again. Perhaps not.

"In the meantime... Good luck."

The clip ended, freezing on Gottlieb's face and its look of what might even have been sincere concern.

Then the screen went blank again, and from the computer tower came a sudden frenzy of activity: a stuttering whir, a sudden blast from the cooling fan. *Now* the hard drive was erasing itself.

Outside the house, a police cruiser pulled up. Theo spotted it from the study window. The two officers inside looked at the partway-open gate, then one of them got on the radio. A minute later, both of them clambered out of the car, unclipping the poppers on their sidearm holsters.

By then, Theo and Chase were already skedaddling out of the house via the French windows in the lounge. They raced across the lawn, hurdled the back wall, and were soon lost from sight in the parkland beyond.

SIXTEEN

Xagar District, Somalia

"MAKE NO MISTAKE, this is going to be the hardest one yet," Badenhorst had warned. "The man is no pushover. Don't underestimate him. He will not go quietly. He will fight back. Don't fuck it up or he will fuck *you* up."

So far, however, Roy had seen neither hide nor hair of Daniel 'Iron Dan' Munro, the Myrmidons' next target. It was two days since the bus had dropped them off at the counterinsurgency-force training camp and Badenhorst had waved them goodbye, and in all that time the man in charge of things, Munro, had been notable by his absence. Roy expected at least to see him in the commissary tent, or else bump into him wandering through the compound. Munro was around; everyone said so. But he seemed never to leave the rickety trailer home which sat parked at the northern end of the camp. He hadn't come out to supervise the orientation of the new arrivals, or greeted them with a speech of welcome. He hadn't been there for the first day's backpack hike into the bush, or this morning's live-fire exercise. He appeared content to let his second-in-command, Lieutenant Alain Dupont, formerly of the French Foreign Legion, run the show. His presence seemed more rumour than fact.

The inhabitants of the camp, Myrmidons aside, were a mix of Somali soldiers and private security contractors – mercenaries – from a range of nations. The ratio of locals to foreigners was four to one, and altogether they totalled in the low hundreds, battalion size. Ostensibly the non-Somalis were there to mentor and tutor the indigenes, preparing them to combat the Islamist extremists who were taking over increasing swathes of the region. Funding for this operation came jointly from the government in Mogadishu and a consortium of businessman backers in the United Arab Emirates who rightly equated a rise in terrorism in Somalia with an increase in pirate attacks on cargo ships passing around the Horn of Africa.

In fact, of course, the non-Somalis were there to engage the enemy just as much as the Somalis and lend some developed-world heft. And the Myrmidons blended in easily among them. They all had military backgrounds. They all had service records that could be, and had been, checked out by the politicians and businesspeople sponsoring the camp. They all, in short, fit the profile of mercenaries, and no one they met had questioned their bona fides even once. They were treated as though they belonged. The more the merrier, seemed to be the philosophy. Come join the fun.

In the middle of the afternoon, when it was almost too hot to breathe and all formal activities were suspended until the sun began to go down, Roy went on a surreptitious recce. He ambled past Munro's trailer home a couple of times, noting the drawn blinds and the apparent lack of an air-conditioning unit. It must be like an oven in there, a sauna. How could Munro bear it?

He decided to make a third pass. Already he was formulating strategies for the mission. If Munro wouldn't show his face, then they would just have to compromise – and improvise. They would have to smoke him out of the trailer home somehow. When the bear was in his lair, you didn't go in to get him; you made him leave and face you in the open, on your turf rather than his.

As he approached the trailer for the third time, looking as though he was just sauntering by, he heard its suspension creak. Munro was moving around in there. Some heavy footfalls.

Then, all at once, the door was flung open.

"Who the fuck are you?"

Roy froze.

The man leaning out from the trailer home was huge and muscular, his bulk emphasised by the narrowness of the doorway. His combat fatigues strained around his upper arms and his thighs. He was unshaven, and appeared not to have showered for days. A beer bottle hung loosely from his fingers.

"I asked you a fucking question," said Daniel Munro. "I expect a fucking answer."

"Roy," said Roy. "Roy Young."

"Well, Roy, Roy Young, why the hell do you keep tramping to and fro outside? Like some motherfucking sentry?" Munro's accent was an odd mixture, mostly mid-Atlantic but with strong Scottish-brogue overtones and a hint of something more exotic underneath.

"Getting the lie of the land, that's all. I've only been here a couple of days. When I'm staying somewhere, I like to know the ins and outs of it. Especially the outs. Just in case, you know?"

Munro weighed up the explanation for plausibility. He took a swig of beer.

"Why aren't you sitting with your feet up somewhere in the shade?" he said. "Stupid time of day to be wandering about. Asking for heatstroke."

"Mad dogs and Englishmen," said Roy.

Munro thought about this remark and decided it was amusing. "Heh. Yes. I've met enough of your countrymen to know you're batshit, every last one of you. 'Barking', isn't that what you call it? Like mad dogs. You English run into firefights that any sane soldier would back away from. It's like you've all got a death wish."

"I guess when you live on a small island, you go a bit stir crazy."

"That'd explain it. Okay, Roy, Roy Young. You get a pass this time. But stop pissing about around my house." Munro thumped the trailer home's plywood side. "I don't like it. Makes me antsy. Got that?"

* * *

AT SUNDOWN, THE Myrmidons convened in a quiet corner of the camp, behind the corrugated-iron shed that housed the latrines. The smell there wasn't too bad, although it was hard to ignore, as were the swarms of flies it attracted.

"Tonight," said Roy. "We go for it tonight. Midnight."

"Doesn't give us much time to prepare," said Gunnvor Blomgren.

"It's not about preparation. It's about catching Munro with his guard down, when he's least expecting it. I've seen the bloke; I had a run-in with him this afternoon. Not only is he built like a brick shithouse, he's got sharp ears and a suspicious nature. We could leave it a day or so more, but my feeling is the longer we put it off, the more chance there is he might rumble us."

"How?" said Gavin. "If he never comes out of that crappy old caravan of his?"

"I don't know how. I just think he will. There's something about him. I've met a few mercs. Even the dumbest of them are savvy, and Munro seems far from dumb."

"He's kind of a legend to all the other mercenaries," said Jeanne. "You should hear them talking about him. He's got this rep like he's a goddamn superhero. The Australian guy I was chatting with yesterday…"

Roy felt an obscure pang of jealousy. He had seen Jeanne in conversation with that rugby-shouldered Aussie, who had the eyes and smile of a Hugh Jackman and a lot of the charm too, and who'd touched her on the arm more than once – just a friendly gesture, or so you might think, but such friendly gestures masked deeper intentions. There was nothing between Roy and Jeanne that gave him the right to be resentful if other men were interested in her. He hadn't even made a move on her yet. Still, he felt a certain possessiveness, and it had been tempting almost beyond endurance to go over and tell the Australian to back off, and force him to if he didn't of his own accord.

"He was saying how Munro's been in the security contractor game as long as anyone can remember," Jeanne continued. "And his thing is he's not scared of bullets. He never ducks down under fire, just stays standing and returns it. Duncan even said" – that was the Australian's name, Duncan – "that he once saw Munro take a round in the chest but wasn't fazed. Almost like he wasn't hit."

"Was he wearing a flak vest at the time?" said Sean Wilson.

"He was."

"There you go, then."

"But Duncan swears the round struck him here." Jeanne indicated her sternal notch. "Just above the collar of the vest. That's the extraordinary thing. It should have turned Munro's ribcage to oatmeal – should have killed him outright – but didn't."

"Ah, you can never tell. When the lead's flying, no one is paying close attention. It was a ricochet, maybe. Not a direct hit."

"All the same. Iron Dan. Sounds like he lives up to the nickname."

"These darn raghead troops are in awe of him," said Travis Laffoon, who came from Louisiana by way of the 82nd Airborne and a stint at a military correctional facility for insubordinate conduct and petty theft. He had a picture of Jesus tattooed on his right biceps and Satan on his left, and constantly chewed gum as though he was trying to gnaw it into submission. "Like, here's the Prophet Mohammed" – Laffoon held a hand level with his heart – "and here's Munro." He held his other hand level with his nose. "If he started a religion, you can bet they'd give up Muslimism and join his instead."

"Muslimism?" said Hans Schutkeker. "English is not my first language but I'm pretty sure that is not a word."

"If I use it, Shitkicker, then it is," said Laffoon. "You want to take it up with me, be my guest. I'm right here."

"Shitkicker. Ha, so funny. Because that is a bit like how my surname sounds."

"Yeah, it's funny. It's funny as goddamn hell."

Roy jumped in before the argument degenerated to blows. Schutkeker and Laffoon were destined not to get along. The snooty German and the rowdy Bible Belter were oil and water – or, indeed, petrol and fire.

"Munro," he said, "is the mercs' merc. Badenhorst told us as much during our briefing. If private security contractors had Oscars, Munro'd have a downstairs toilet full of them. He's awesome, and that's lovely for him. Hooray. But he's just a man, and we've got a bow and arrow with his name on it. Two sets of bows and arrows, actually. All we have to do is manoeuvre him into a position where our archers can get a clear shot. And here's how we're going to go about it…"

AND SO, AT midnight, they sneaked out of their dormitory huts. The sky was all stars, the moon a mere sliver of light balancing on one tip atop a dark far range of hills. The racket of a million cicadas and frogs made stealth almost irrelevant. The crunch of boot soles on gravelly soil and the soft clink of weapons belts paled into insignificance before the noise. You could scarcely hear yourself think.

Nonetheless Roy had advised the utmost caution. There was to be no comms. Hand signals only. Everyone had to stay within sight of at least two other Myrmidons at all times. Anyone who lost visual should retire to a safe point rather than blunder about trying to re-establish contact.

Take no chances was the motto of the night. If Munro was everything he was cracked up to be, they needed to nail him quickly and with minimum fuss, before he had an opportunity to retaliate.

Roy led a group of the Myrmidons to Munro's trailer home, fanning out as they approached. The archers took up positions to the right and left of the door, some ten metres away. They were Luis Rojas, from Andalusia, and Tzadok Friedman, an Israeli. Both had studied archery in their youth; Friedman had represented his country at an international level in the sport's Young Adult division. During their training as Myrmidons, they had practised long and hard with the antique bows provided by Badenhorst. These were things of crude beauty, a far cry from the modern compound bow with its carbon fibre limbs and cradle of cables and pulleys. They were recurved, fashioned from arcs of horn fastened together by bronze collars; their strings were leather thongs. Rojas and Friedman had complained bitterly about them at first, saying they were hard to draw and keep steady. After a week or so familiarising themselves with them, however, both men had to admit, if with some reluctance, that the bows were finely balanced, accurate and surprisingly powerful.

They each went down on one knee and nocked arrows, pulling the strings back to full draw. They aimed at the trailer home door, at right angles to each other, offering a perfect crossfire. The arrows were standard aluminium alloy shafts with 300-grain spines, 125-grain broadhead tips and helical plastic fletchings. Fired correctly, they were sturdy enough to bring down a bull moose.

The rest of the Myrmidons in the group arranged themselves in a rough semicircle around the trailer home, hunkering down in shadows.

Now it was time to wait.

Somewhere over at the southern perimeter of the compound, Gavin Martin was marshalling a second, smaller team of Myrmidons. They had helped themselves to some flashbangs and fragmentation grenades from the camp's armoury, which was not well-guarded, a prefab unit with windows that anyone with a combat knife and the inclination could jemmy open. Their goal was to make mischief. Specifically, to simulate a raid on the camp by hostile forces.

If Munro wasn't going to leave his trailer home voluntarily, Roy had thought, then they were going to have to give him no alternative. A veteran war dog like him couldn't – wouldn't – ignore an apparent enemy action.

At twenty past midnight the first explosions sounded. Balloons of light burst in the night sky, followed by drumroll detonations. These were chased up with staccato crackles of gunfire.

Within moments, people were stumbling out from the nearby dormitory huts. Voices were raised. There was confusion, commotion, shouts echoing across the camp. From a distance Roy heard Alain Dupont ordering troops to grab rifles, go and take a look.

The uproar grew. Mercenaries and Somali soldiers went sprinting past the Myrmidons' hiding places, not seeing them, too intent on responding to the attack.

From the trailer home, however, nothing. No light came on behind the blinds. The door remained shut.

Roy couldn't believe it. Surely Munro couldn't be sleeping through all this? He remembered the beer bottle in Munro's hand. Could he be *that* drunk?

He motioned to Almaz Beshimov, the youngest of all the Myrmidons, a one-time Kyrgyz army reservist who, although still in his mid-twenties, had seen action in Chechnya, South Ossetia and Ukraine as part of Russia's covert special forces. Roy forked fingers at his own eyes, then pointed to the trailer home door. Beshimov nodded assent and trotted forward, pistol at the ready. He sidled up to the door, reaching for the handle with his free hand.

A fist punched clean through the trailer home wall from within, emerging beside Beshimov's head. It grabbed the Kyrgyz by the neck and yanked hard, pulling him face first into the jagged opening it had created. Three times the young man's face was rammed against jutting spars of splintered plywood. Blood spurted from lacerated cheeks and nose. He shrieked as one of his eyeballs was gouged. A fourth and final yank, harder than all the rest, resulted in a brutal *snap* that silenced his cries of distress.

The fist let go and withdrew. Beshimov's lifeless body slumped to the ground.

Then the door flew out, kicked from its hinges, and Munro dived out after it, wearing nothing but a T-shirt and jockey shorts. He had a Glock 17 Gen4 in each hand and was firing even before he hit the ground. 9mm Parabellum rounds flew in all directions, with an accuracy Roy found uncanny and terrifying. It was as though Munro knew where the Myrmidons were situated; had known in advance, while still inside the trailer home. Now he was shooting at them, and although not every bullet found its mark, he still scored a fatality and two woundings with his initial salvo.

Roy loosed off with his Browning L9A1, emptying the entire clip in Munro's direction, but aiming high. Jeanne and Sean Wilson joined in.

"Suppressing fire!" Roy yelled. "Pin him down! Rojas, Friedman, what the hell are you waiting for?"

The archers, startled by the sudden ferocity of Munro's attack, tried to draw a bead on him.

Munro, meanwhile, scuttled away from the gunfire on all fours, not with the frantic urgency of a man fleeing for his life, more the air of someone avoiding an irritant.

A bowstring twanged. An arrow whizzed in his direction, released by Rojas.

And Munro did the frankly impossible.

He twisted round and caught it in mid-flight. Plucked the arrow from the air as though it had been hovering there, stationary.

Then he flung it back overhand at its sender.

The arrow transfixed Rojas through the neck, spearing his windpipe. The Spaniard dropped his bow and keeled over. As he lay on his side, gargling blood, his hands groped ineffectually, trying to tug the arrow out. Then they fell limp. He spasmed. His eyes rolled up. Dead.

Roy gaped helplessly.

What Munro had just done...

"Iron Dan" wasn't finished yet, however. He bounded over to Rojas's body, almost faster than the eye could follow, and snatched up the bow.

"This!" he bellowed, holding the weapon aloft and looking around him imperiously. "Whoever you are – where did you get this? Who gave it to you?"

Roy slapped a fresh clip into his Browning and stepped out in plain view of Munro. The mission had gone clusterfuck. Munro had completely wrongfooted them. The man was a beast. He could punch holes through wood. He had no fear under fire. He could catch arrows in mid-air and throw them like javelins. He was as agile as a puma. He was everything the other mercs had said about him and more.

All the same, there was a chance the Myrmidons could still pull this off. Out of the corner of his eye Roy could see Friedman. The Israeli still had an arrow nocked. He was taking careful aim, aware that he had one shot only and that a miss would be tantamount to signing his own death warrant.

Roy just needed to keep Munro distracted for a few more seconds.

"Answer me!" Munro demanded. "This is Orion's bow. I recognise it. You should not have it. You!" He jabbed the bow accusingly at

Roy. "Englishman. I knew there was something not right about you. Explain yourself."

Everything slowed to a standstill. Panic continued to reign in the camp, people hurrying to and fro, explosions and rifle reports from afar as Gavin and the other Myrmidons kept up their bogus assault and the Somalis and mercenaries rushed to mount a counteroffensive. But here, in these few square metres in front of the trailer home, as though in the eye of a hurricane, an eerie calm prevailed.

Roy levelled the gun at Munro. They were supposed to make the kill using the bows. Badenhorst had been quite insistent about that. Each and every one of their targets had to be eliminated with one of the ancient weapons.

An exception might have to be made here, however. Munro was too dangerous for the Myrmidons to rely on arrows alone. He had proved that beyond question. Roy needed to shift the paradigm somewhat.

"A gun," said Munro, staring at the Browning with contempt. "You're going to shoot me? Is that the plan?"

"It wasn't," said Roy, "but it is now."

"Go ahead then."

"As you wish," and Roy pulled the trigger.

Four rounds smacked into Munro at point blank range, all in the chest, centre of body mass.

The impacts staggered him, but he did not go down.

More astonishingly, he was intact.

He wasn't wearing *any* protection. No ballistic vest, nothing. Holes appeared in his T-shirt, but the bullets failed to perforate his flesh.

They literally bounced off him.

It was just...

Not...

Fucking...

Possible.

Next thing Roy knew, Munro had him by the throat. He hadn't even seen the man move. He was hoisted off the ground, Munro using lifting his entire bodyweight one-handed with next to no effort, as though he were a straw effigy. Roy heard the bow being chucked to the ground and felt the Browning being wrested from his grasp. He could do nothing to prevent it. He was choking. He clung to Munro's wrist, clutching and clawing, trying to unpick the fingers, prise the hand away. No use; the hand was locked solid, a steel pincer. Red bubbles began exploding in his vision. His ears were roaring. His chest heaved as he tried to suck in a breath that couldn't reach his lungs. So this was how he was going to die.

Then he felt the muzzle of the Browning being ground against his temple. At the same time Munro relaxed his grip on Roy's neck somewhat. His windpipe was still constricted, but he could just about breathe again.

"Here's the deal," Munro said. "You're going to tell me who sent you; who gave you that bow. Or else I will blow your brains out. And if you won't tell me, one of your pals will. Believe me, I will make it happen one way or another. How much do you want to live, Englishman?"

A lot. If Roy didn't live, there would be no payout. Josie wouldn't get to stay at the Gesundheitsklinik Rheintal. She would be jettisoned back out into the world, still fragile and now fatherless, powerless against her own dark impulses.

If he died, she died.

But then, were Roy to tell Munro what he knew, he would be sacked at the very least. Badenhorst wouldn't hesitate; assuming the Afrikaner remained alive long enough to do so. Given how angered Munro was, he didn't rate his employer's chances.

Whatever he did, he was screwed.

Fortunately, as Munro shook him, Tzadok Friedman had managed to edge round to a new firing position and now had a clear shot at the side of Munro's head. He resettled the arrow into position, balancing the shaft on his left thumb while he pulled the bowstring back with his right hand – slowly, ever so slowly, to prevent creaking. That, he thought, was what had given the game away when Rojas fired. Had to be that.

He drew a breath. Held it. Sighted along the arrow.

Exhaled.

Released.

Munro turned his head, dropped both Roy and the pistol. His hands came up.

He almost caught the arrow.

Almost.

The arrow embedded itself in his skull. It went into his cheek, its tip bursting out at the back through his parietal bone with a little spit of blood.

Munro teetered, incredulity in his eyes. He murmured words in a foreign language, the same language Anthony Peregrine had spoken when confronting the Myrmidons.

Then, like a felled sequoia, "Iron Dan" Munro toppled and went crashing to the ground.

THE MYRMIDONS WITHDREW, using the chaos in the camp for cover. Roy was dazed and bruised from his encounter with Munro; his head felt as though it was attached to the rest of him by a slender thread. Nevertheless he helped along one of the wounded, Mayson, whom Munro had shot in the arm, while Jeanne and Friedman supported the other, Corbett, who had taken a bullet to the thigh.

They were minus Beshimov, Rojas, and one other, a Peruvian called Gutiérrez. Despite the mission being a success, it was more a rout than an orderly retreat. They stumbled across the darkened savannah, putting distance between them and the compound. Gunfire rattled intermittently along the camp's southern edge, and parachute flares went up, shedding a wavery crimson glow over the landscape.

In time, the gunfire dwindled and died out. The camp was in ferment for the rest of the night, however. Its inhabitants scoured the scrubby desert, in jeeps and on foot with flashlights, looking for their attackers. At break of day they abandoned the search, giving it up as a lost cause. The raid had been short and sharp, and the perpetrators seemed to have vanished into the night as abruptly as they had appeared.

Gavin and his squad met up with Roy's while the sun was just breasting the horizon. The rendezvous point was a rock outcrop some two kilometres northwest of the camp, not far from the dirt track which was the only road access in and out.

Gavin was still buzzing from the adrenaline high of launching the fake raid. It had all gone to plan. Once soldiers started mustering at the camp perimeter, the Myrmidons had simply skirted round, slipped in alongside them and merged into their ranks. Soon they were all blasting away side by side at an enemy that wasn't there.

Sneaking out of the camp just before sun-up had, similarly, been child's play. The discovery of Munro's dead body had thrown everything further into disarray. Lieutenant Dupont had deduced, not entirely wrongly, that the attack from the south had been a diversion, enabling a second raiding party to infiltrate from the other direction and cut down the camp leader alongside three of the new intake. The radicals – the culprits could only be Islamist radicals – had shown an unprecedented level of nerve and ingenuity. Dupont was furious. But even with him now nominally senior officer, he couldn't fill the vacuum left by Munro, in whose absence the camp felt rudderless and incohesive. Gavin and the others had walked out without being stopped or questioned even once.

Gavin's exhilaration faded when he caught sight of Roy and what was left of the other group. Mayson's arm was in a makeshift sling; Corbett had a field-dressing bandage round his thigh. Roy himself sported dramatic purple contusions on his neck.

More than that, though, Roy was seething, and after he gave a hoarse-voiced account of the hit, Gavin understood why.

"That bloke Munro," Roy said. "He wasn't human. Seriously, Gavin, he was not a normal human being. Not by a long shot. He was like fucking Superman. I am not kidding. And Badenhorst expected us to go after someone like that with *those?*" He flapped a hand at the two bows. "With something out of the Dark Ages? That's taking the piss, that is. The piss is quite firmly being taken. There is stuff going on here that we're not being told about. We've been lied to. This is bigger and weirder than we've been led to believe."

"You're sure you saw what you're saying you saw?" said Gavin. "I mean, heat of battle, mate. You know it, I know it. Doesn't always seem real."

"It was real," Roy insisted hotly. "Ask Jeanne, ask Friedman, any of them. They saw it too. Munro was a Terminator. Beshimov, Rojas, Gutiérrez – they didn't stand a chance. Look at Mayson and Corbett. Look at the state of us. One man did this to us. *One man*. Badenhorst has got some explaining to do. When that bus comes..."

The bus did come, an hour later, in response to an encrypted text sent by Jeanne confirming that the mission objective had been achieved.

When the Myrmidons climbed aboard, however, Badenhorst was not there. Roy could only sit and fume as they drove back towards Kismayo. Every jolt of the bus sent a sharp pain daggering through his bruised neck muscles. Kindling for the blaze.

SEVENTEEN

Mexico City

As Theo ducked through the ropes into the wrestling ring, the thought uppermost in his mind was: *I have to lose this fight in order to win.*

In the opposite corner, his opponent was limbering up. The man wore a bright yellow leotard and matching boots, accented with gold trim here and there. The front of the leotard, stretched across large pectorals and the pronounced ridges of his abdominals, was embroidered with the image of a lion. His full-head PVC mask continued the motif, with tawny cat's eyes framing the eyeholes and carnivorous fangs snarling around the mouth hole.

This was the hulking, fearsome, much-loved *luchador* known as El León.

Better known, to Theo at least, as Heracles.

And he was not in a good mood.

It perhaps should not have come as a surprise to Theo that Heracles had found himself a niche in the world of Mexican wrestling. As

Chase put it, "Muscle men? The manly slap of male body against male body? A basic good-versus-evil drama played out before cheering crowds? *Lucha libre* might as well have been invented for Heracles, it's so him."

They were flying down from Washington to Mexico City aboard a privately chartered Cessna C750 Citation, and Chase showed Theo some YouTube clips of El León in action. Clad in his lion-themed costume, Heracles cavorted around the ring with gusto, executing drop kicks, bouncing off the ropes and grappling opponents into submission with complex, quasi-contortionist holds. Chase explained that in *luchador* terminology El León was a *técnico*, a good guy, who almost always won his bouts, but not before the bad guy facing him, the *rudo*, had come close to defeating him, often by playing dirty and sometimes blatantly cheating.

"He's really having to hold back," Theo observed. "You can see him trying to be as delicate as he can."

"No shit. Of course he is. If he used even a tenth of his full strength, he'd reduce the guy to mincemeat. Not that it matters. It's not an actual contest, you know, *lucha libre*. It's play acting."

"No shit. But there are elements of *palé* to it, still. Pins, hip throws. Three falls and you're out."

"Aw, are you getting all dewy-eyed about the good old days?" Chase adopted a crotchety old-timer voice. "'Bring back Milo of Croton and Leonskitos of Messene, that's what I say. Now *they* was wrestlers, them boys. Tough as all get-out, and they didn't mind a bit of bare-ass nudity. Referee didn't blow no whistle at 'em neither. They wouldn't behave, why, he'd just take a whip to their backs.'"

"*Palé* was at least exciting to watch. So was *pankration*. Genuine skill. Genuine pain. Genuinely high stakes. This…" Theo nodded at Chase's phone screen. "It's a cartoon. *Tom and Jerry* with actual people."

"It's loved by millions in Latin America," said Chase, "just like WWE is in the US. And the wrestlers are athletes, if nothing else."

Theo demurred. All he saw was theatre, a comic-book spectacle of heroes and villains. That said, there was an intriguing sociological subtext to *lucha libre*, in so far as the *rudos* tended to adopt identities that represented the forces of authority and oppression – politicians, police officers and mobsters – making the *técnico* a symbol of the common man as he stood up to the crooked and the corrupt and triumphed. Theo could, at this very simplistic level, find something laudable in that.

As the five-hour flight drew to an end and the jet began its descent towards Benito Juárez Airport, Chase once again aired his opinion that they were on their way to see the wrong demigod. "Don't want to harp on about it or anything, but isn't it Evander Arlington we should be trying to going after? Gottlieb pointed the finger straight at him. Said more or less that's where we ought to look. If Arlington has known all along where the weapons were stashed, stands to reason he's the one who's dug them up. Couldn't be anybody else."

"Couldn't it?" said Theo. "I explained this. We can't trust a damn thing Gottlieb says. Yes, he gave Arlington the cylinders, but even if Arlington still has them, it doesn't necessarily follow that he's opened them. That's only conjecture. And if he has retrieved the weapons, why? What does he stand to gain from deploying them against the rest of us? And why now, when he could have done it any time in the last couple of thousand years?"

"So we go see him and ask. Nicely at first, but if he doesn't co-operate…" Chase clenched a fist. "We get a little more convincing."

"He's not easy to get hold of, let alone meet face to face. According to you he has a dozen homes all over the world, apart from his Manhattan penthouse. He could be at any of them."

"Then we visit each and every one until we hit paydirt."

"That would take days – time we can ill afford, given the rate at which the deaths are coming. It would be pointless anyway; if Arlington is out there roaming the planet, bumping demigods off one by one, home is the last place we'll find him. Not that I think he's carrying out the killings personally."

"No, that isn't like him, is it? He'd have minions doing the dirty work for him."

"But maybe he's supervising the operation at first hand. He's got himself some paid assassins and he's leading them from victim to victim, siccing them like attack dogs when they're close enough."

"He'd need plenty of them, if you ask me. Neither Aeneas or Orion would have been a pushover, even if you caught them unawares."

"It still doesn't feel right, though," Theo said. "Doesn't feel like a Minos thing to do. I can't figure out what his motive might be. On top of which, Gottlieb could simply be using him as a smokescreen. Misdirection. We focus on Arlington and forget all about Gottlieb himself, leaving him free to continue orchestrating his big psychopathic masterplan."

"One or other of them, Arlington or Gottlieb, that's who we should be concentrating on," said Chase adamantly. "I can't see why you think Salvador Vega is more important than both."

"Salvador Vega is… was… has been my friend. He is, in old-fashioned parlance, a stand-up guy."

"He's also my step-grandson – and my half-brother, actually. I still don't think we should be bothering with him when there's an actual suspect we could be tracking down."

"Noted, but I want him with us anyway, because he'll provide some serious muscle. We may need it. More to the point, Salvador could well be in the firing line, and I could never forgive myself if I didn't at least warn him. Do you have a problem with that? I don't think you do, given how you agreed to come on this hideously expensive plane flight with me."

"What can I say? You fished out your black Amex and starting waving it around. I wasn't going to turn down the chance of a sweet ride like this, was I?"

As if to underscore his point, the Cessna hit a patch of low-altitude turbulence, but daintily, with none of the heavy, slithery bumping of a passenger airliner, as if there was nothing a sleek little jet like this couldn't take in its stride. Outside the cabin windows the most populous city on Earth sprawled in every direction, filling a plateau ringed by mountains and volcanoes. Irregular geometric blocks of buildings were divided by lushly tree-greened avenues and freeways, all overlaid with a thick brown pall of smog. It might not have been a very beautiful sight but, for scale alone, it was impressive.

"Anyway," Chase added, "I'm just the sidekick, like Gottlieb said. Robin to your Batman. You do the thinking, I tag along."

"You know that's bullshit. We're family. We're equals."

"I guess. And I do bring some much-needed flair and pizzazz to our partnership."

"And would a sidekick have a constellation named after him?"

"Nice of you to bring that up. A once-a-year meteor shower, too."

"Strictly speaking, the Perseids are named after your children."

"Wouldn't be any children if there wasn't a father."

"Can't argue with that," said Theo. "It's good to have you along, Chase. That's what it comes down to. I'd rather you were with me than do this alone."

"Coming from you, cuz, that's almost smushy. Are we having a bonding moment? Do... do we hug?"

"No. No, we do not."

"Thought not."

"I just like having someone around I know I can rely on – most of the time, when you're not being a jackass."

"And the moment is ruined."

"You have my back. I have yours. And if we can get Salvador on side, he'll have *both* our backs. Extra insurance."

"How easy do you think it's going to be, getting him on side?"

"Shouldn't be a problem," Theo said. "I hope."

FAMOUS LAST WORDS.

A television contact of Chase's who worked for the Azteca network had made some calls, done some digging around, and discovered where El León trained. It was a gym in the Tepito *barrio*, tucked up a side alley not far from the Tianguis street market. Chase's rusty Spanish and a fistful of pesos got them past the front door and into a large, yellowly-lit room with bare cinderblock walls and a strong reek of sweat and liniment. Here a dozen or so Mexicans with husky physiques were working out with weights, while in the ring that occupied much of the floorspace a pair of *luchadores* prowled, lunging at each other occasionally. The clanking of the weights was interspersed with grunts of exertion and the shuffle of boot soles on canvas.

The gym owner himself had given Theo and Chase permission to be on the premises. The bribe helped, but also he believed their claim that they were relatives of Salvador Vega. "There is a family resemblance, *cierto*," he said. "I can see it. Salvador will be here soon. Take a seat. Make yourselves at home."

The other Mexicans, however, were none too happy about the pair of *Americano* visitors. Theo and Chase weathered hostile stares and muttered comments about *gringos* as they waited.

Theo tuned it out, concentrating on the *luchadores* in the ring. It became apparent that they were choreographing an upcoming fight. They would plan a sequence of moves between them, which they would run through slowly at first, getting faster and faster with repetition until they had it down pat, at which point they would start putting together the next sequence. Neither was in costume, but distinguishing *técnico* from *rudo* wasn't difficult. The former had a clean, acrobatic style while the latter was more of a brawler and would resort to mouth hooking and crotch grabbing. Gradually, grudgingly, Theo was forced to concede that there was some artistry involved, and some physical courage. *Lucha libre* might not be a sport, but it was entertainment, and it was performed by people who were as dedicated to their craft as ballerinas, if not quite as graceful.

When Salvador Vega arrived, the mood in the gym changed in an instant. It had always been that way with Heracles. He never merely walked into a room. He boomed into it, pushing his presence before him like a ship's bow wave. He greeted his fellow wrestlers with handshakes and high fives, studiously ignoring Theo and Chase, even though Theo had seen the gym owner pointing them out to him. This, too, was typical Heracles. Knowing you had gone to some trouble to seek him out, he would give you the cold shoulder for a while before deigning to notice you. *Am I important to you? Well then, let's make you feel unimportant to me.* His ego was big, but it was also fragile.

Finally he strode over to them, and he was all grins and hearty back-slaps, as magnanimous as any monarch. He told them in Spanish how delighted he was to see them, what a surprise, it had been too long, how were they? As he said this he yoked an arm around each of their necks and steered them towards the locker room. To all appearances he had them in a friendly bear hug, but his grip was so powerful even Theo nor Chase couldn't have escaped.

The locker room was unoccupied, and as soon as the door swung shut behind them Salvador switched to English and lost the bonhomie.

"Who the hell do you think you are? Coming in here like that. This is where I work, you idiots; you can't just show up unannounced. Don't you know how that's going to look? A pair of well-heeled Westerners saying they're family. I have a reputation to uphold. I have to fit in. It's taken me years to establish myself here, to be accepted despite not being a native Mexican. Outsiders are not welcome in *lucha libre*. I had to work hard to prove I was worthy to belong and to earn my place. And now you've just gone and blown that in a minute."

"Whoa, whoa, whoa, big fella," said Chase. "First, get your arm off me or I'll break it."

"You?" Salvador laughed derisively. "Not a hope." But he let them both go.

"And second," Chase went on, "we didn't mean to damage your wrestler cred, if that's what we've done. We just needed to find you ASAP, and this was the only place we knew of where you'd be. So back the fuck off, you great hairy oaf."

"What Chase is trying to say," said Theo, "is that we're sorry to have blundered in the way we did, and we wouldn't have if it wasn't an emergency."

"Hmph." Salvador pretended to be unmoved by the apology, but he relented a little, dialling his anger down a notch. "You weren't to know, I suppose. An emergency? Really? What could that be?"

Theo explained as simply and succinctly as possible. Salvador listened, eyebrows knitting more tightly together the more he heard.

"If this were anyone else but you, Theo," he said at the end, "I would think it pure fantasy. But you always were a trustworthy companion. You sailed with me to Themiskyra. You were fearless and true even as a brat. I remember when I visited your school at Troezen: I took off my cloak and all of Pittheus's pupils fled in panic, thinking it was a real live lion – all except you, who attacked it with an axe."

Theo tried not to blush. "I did get a bit carried away, didn't I?"

"Carried away? You'd have chopped the damn thing to pieces, if it hadn't been indestructible. 'This youngster Theseus,' I said to myself, 'he'll go far.' And I was right. And now you reckon somebody has got it into their head to start slaying us demigods?"

"The evidence is stacking up."

"Then I can see why you'd need me. If it's reinforcements you're after, you can't do better than the greatest hero of all time."

Theo shot Chase a look, silencing the snarky riposte his cousin was poised to make.

"That still leaves us in a quandary, however," Salvador continued. "I can't let you get away with the harm you've done to my image. How can I show my face back out there, among the *luchadores* I train with on a daily basis, when they know I'm associated with *gringos* like you two?"

"You could have tried not being so polite to us in front of them," Theo said.

"I could not show a lack of *xenia*." Heracles, perhaps more than most, treasured the Hellenic principle of hospitality. "It would have been ungracious to spurn you, not least seeing as you are kin. All the same, I will never hear the end of this. Word will spread. There'll be whispers backstage at the Arena México. They'll be saying El León is a fraud. El León has connections north of the border. El León is as bad as any American."

"They will?"

"They will. It would be the next worst thing to having my mask removed in the ring, which is the ultimate insult in *lucha libre*."

"Then what do you suggest we do about it?"

"I have an idea."

IT WAS NOT a good one, but it was Salvador's, and he was disgruntled, and he needed to save face somehow, so Theo had no alternative but to go along with it.

Everyone in the gym gathered at the ringside to watch as El León and the gringo squared off. Theo was wearing borrowed boots, tights and leotard, none of which quite fitted, and he felt faintly silly in this get-up, but at least, small blessings, he hadn't had to put on one of those masks. In fact, it would have been an insult to *los enmascarados* everywhere if he had. A *luchador*'s mask was no gimmick; it was his alter ego, his emblem, his essence. Many wrestlers refused to be seen in public without theirs on, and amateurs certainly did not qualify for the honour of wearing one.

Salvador nodded to him from across the ring. He had warmed up. He was ready.

Theo nodded back. He wasn't ready. He wasn't looking forward to this at all.

But needs must. If a wrestling match with Heracles was what it took to keep the man amenable and cooperative, so be it.

All Theo knew was that he must not win. If he did, El León would lose even more face, and he would not take that kindly. He might never forgive it.

Theo wasn't even sure if he *could* win. He had some significant skill as a wrestler, but against Heracles he was seriously outclassed in terms of sheer strength.

He had to lose, but make it look good, so that El León looked good.

And whatever happened, however he did that, it was going to hurt.

EL LEÓN CAME at Theo like a freight train, piling into him at full tilt. He pounded him back against the corner-post padding and drove the air from his lungs.

The spectators cheered.

Theo retaliated almost without thinking. He planted a foot behind El León's ankle and tipped him over onto his back. The sound of 250 pounds of demigod slamming onto the canvas echoed to the ceiling joists.

The spectators jeered.

El León flipped up onto his feet.

The spectators cheered again. "El León!" they chanted. "El León! El León!"

Theo was left in no doubt who was the *técnico* in this particular fight and who was the *rudo*.

What followed was twenty minutes of tussling and pummelling, wrenching and squirming, crunching and crushing. Several times Theo found himself being pressed to the canvas, Salvador bearing down on him with his full weight. Always he managed to twist out of it, gaining just enough leverage to break the hold. Well, almost always. Once, Salvador managed to get him in a headlock he could not unpick. No matter how hard he pulled on the arms that were noosing his neck, Theo couldn't make him let go and was forced to tap out. Another time, Salvador lifted him bodily into the air and executed a grand amplitude throw, dumping him on his back with his legs in the air before securing him in place with a knee to the thorax. Theo could have interrupted the move with a reversal by scissoring his legs around Salvador's head, but he more or less gave Salvador the submission.

That was the line Theo was trying to tread, letting Salvador chalk up his three submissions but not making it obvious that he was letting him. And it wasn't easy. A part of him – a deep-seated part – rebelled at the idea of throwing the fight. He was Theseus, a champion. He did not like being the bad guy, even if it was just pretend. It offended his sense of himself.

As it dawned on Salvador that his opponent was not willing to be a complete pushover, he began to grin. He also began to use more and more of his immense strength. There was no tiptoeing around now, as there had to be during his matches with mere human wrestlers. No pulling punches, no need for the usual restraint. Delightedly he shoved Theo around the ring, flinging him to and fro, with as much concern for his wellbeing as if he was a crash test dummy.

Theo, in turn, became sneakier and craftier. He was considerably more nimble than Salvador and kept darting out of his clutches every time he tried to establish a solid hold. He would use Salvador's bulk against him, overbalancing and toppling him. He even tangled him up in the ropes at one point, though he stopped short of upending him and spilling him out of the ring. That would have been a severe humiliation for Salvador, and Theo didn't want to go the full *rudo*. He had standards.

Eventually Theo won two submissions of his own, leaving him and Salvador at level pegging. The next submission would be the decider.

All round the ring the spectators were going wild. They were aware that this was a proper fight, unrehearsed, nothing staged about it: a genuine grudge match. It thrilled them. They bellowed support for El León and insults at his gringo opponent. Chase joined in. Mostly he just swore – *¡pendejo! ¡cabrón! ¡hijo de puta!* – not aiming the expletives at either of the fighters in particular, but not wanting to be left out of the general hullabaloo.

As they circled each other in readiness for yet another clinch, Salvador murmured to Theo, "We should bring this to a close, my friend. You have done enough. Let's not drag this out any further than necessary."

"Easy for you to say," Theo replied, swiping sweat from his forehead. "You're not the one who's got to fold like a little bitch."

"Fold? I'm beating you fair and square. If you can't see that..."

"Funny. Kerkyon of Eleusis said much the same thing when I wrestled with him. That was shortly before I hoisted him up, smashed him head first onto the ground and broke his neck."

"Don't trumpet your Labours at me, sonny boy. Any of my Twelve beats all of your Six. Yours were just pleasant diversions. A man who wishboned people with pine trees? Try a swamp full of man-eating bronze-beaked birds. A host cutting up his guests to fit his bed? I have two words for you: Lernean Hydra."

"And I have two words for you," said Theo. "Shut. Up."

They crashed together, an impact of flesh on flesh so loud and hard that it startled the spectators briefly into silence.

Then it was the two of them locked in a stance, chest to chest, sinews taut, muscles cording, like something on a Greek vase or temple frieze, both of them straining, both of them resisting, the canvas vibrating beneath them, the entire ring shaking, the ropes quivering like plucked violin strings, and the noise from the spectators rose to a deafening tumult, and Salvador jockeyed for advantage and Theo jockeyed for advantage, and their teeth were bared and their eyes bulged and their knuckles cracked...

...AND SEVERAL HOURS later they were sitting together at a table in a cantina in the La Condesa district, along with the gym owner, the other *luchadores* and Chase. Salvador kept ordering fresh rounds of Tecate beer and ogling the waitress who brought them over, while everyone else joked and chattered and bantered. Music played on the sound system, a weird hybrid of mariachi and techno, and it was loud but their carousing was louder and their voices pealed out of the cantina's open windows into the sweltering night.

"Was that not an epic fight?" Salvador said to Theo repeatedly. "Was that not like something from the past? It should be noted. It should be celebrated! My victory, of course, was never in doubt, but you gave me a run for my money. Drink up. Drink up. You too, Chase. Drink!"

Chase didn't need much encouraging, but Theo was more hesitant. Under the present circumstances, he wasn't sure it would be prudent. What if the demigod killers were here in Mexico City? What if they were spying on the three of them right now? How much easier would their job be if their victims were pie-eyed and incapable.

But Salvador kept plying him with beer, and Salvador's joviality was infectious, and Theo gradually relaxed and got into the swing of things.

At one stage he and Salvador ended up pissing side by side in the cantina's gents washroom. In front of them, above the urinals, was a lavishly detailed mural. A large bejewelled skull gazed down on them with a broad grin, wreathed in flowers and surrounded by guitars, musical notes, beer bottles and human figures cavorting. A cigar was clenched between its tombstone teeth.

"Ah, Mexico," said Salvador, returning the skull's gaze. "Life and death intertwined. Celebrate the now because you don't know what tomorrow might bring. That's the Mexican philosophy. And that's how it should be for *us*, Theo. We're heroes. It should be all about fighting, feasting and fornicating. What is the point otherwise? There was a time, you know, when my one and only ambition was to earn a place in Olympus. That was all I wanted, to ascend to Olympus, to be welcomed into the bosom of my true family, to sit at my father's side, to be one with the gods. I thought that my heroic deeds would grant me that."

He zipped up and went to the washbasin.

"But it seems as though the gods had other ideas," he said, running the tap. "I was excluded; we all were. It was a cruel joke. There never was any intention among the Olympian order for us to join them. Somehow we got it into our heads that there was, but there wasn't. We were just their castoffs, their disinherited brats. Born on the wrong side of the blanket, and never destined to receive our due."

He moved to the paper-handtowel dispenser.

"But you know what? We are immortal. We *live*. Whereas the gods, they're gone. Nobody prays to them any more. Nobody offers them sacrifices or libations. Nobody *believes* in them. Other gods have taken their place. And without that human support, without belief, they have faded away, dwindled to nothing. I suspect that if you and I were to travel to Olympus right now – if that were possible – we would find nothing there. If we could fly on the back of Pegasus as Bellerophon did, through the clouds, above the bronze dome of the sky, what would be waiting for us? Nothing but ruins and skeletons. Celestial flesh turned to dust, blowing in the wind. Crumbling palaces littered with goblets of dried nectar and dishes of shrivelled ambrosia. An empty paradise."

"Bellerophon was punished for attempting to reach Olympus," Theo said. "He broke both legs and went blind, spent the rest of his days as a crippled hermit."

"A lesson to us all," Salvador said. "But it rather proves my point. It is far better to be us, I believe, Theo. To be a demigod rather than a god. We survive. We still have life. And fighting, feasting and fornicating – that's how to live it."

Hands dried, he left the room. Theo lingered, thinking.

Salvador, he decided, was right. After all, what was the harm in letting your hair down every once in a while? What good was immortality if you couldn't have a little fun? Theo seemed to have forgotten, in the million days he had seen go by, that those days were there to be enjoyed. The more so, given that he might die tomorrow. Might even die tonight. So drink the beer. Laugh. Revel in the company of others. Make the most of what the world had to offer. Live.

He returned to the bar and got the next round in.

HIS HANGOVER THE next morning, as he came to in one of the guest rooms at Salvador's apartment in the Polanco area, was so apocalyptically awful he wished he could die. He stumbled out onto the balcony to breathe some comparatively fresh air. The smart new high-rise block overlooked a leafy street and a park. The sun was sulphurous. The city droned.

He felt like shit.

Still, on balance, it was worth it.

EIGHTEEN

Gesundheitsklinik Rheintal, Switzerland

As SOON AS Josie had awoken in her room at the Gesundheitsklinik that morning, she had known it was going to be a Yellow Day.

Yellow Days were smooth and bright. They were for getting outdoors and taking in the scenery. They were days when it wasn't wrong to listen to some music on her headphones, maybe sing along to it if no one was within earshot, maybe even dance to it if no one was looking. They weren't as good as Green Days. Those were the best of the lot, plain sailing all the way, days of serenity and appetite. Nor were they as adventurous as Red Days, when Josie sincerely believed she could take on the world. But there were better than the Blue and Brown days, and infinitely preferable to the Black.

How she loathed the Black Days.

She was out roaming the grounds when Benedikt found her. The clinic sat in fifty acres of land, large enough that you felt you could get lost in it even though you never really could. Eventually, if you wandered far enough, you would come to the wall – the neat brick-topped fieldstone wall which bounded the property and was just tall enough that it could not be climbed – and you would be reminded that your freedom had limits. As long as you remained out of sight of the wall, however, the illusion held. The winding paths and neat flowerbeds, the benches and lakes, the trim lawns and evergreen glades, all seemed to exist just for your pleasure, and while occasionally you might come across a gardener or another patient, most of the time you had it all to yourself.

Josie liked Benedikt. Of all the orderlies he was by far the gentlest and the kindest. He had thick dark hair and enviably long, curly eyelashes. She had something of a crush on him, in fact, although relationships between orderlies and patients were strictly prohibited, and – more to the point – Benedikt was avowedly gay.

She beamed at him as he approached.

"Josie. There you are." A tone of mild reproof. "You didn't come to the dispensary for your medication."

"Oh, is it that time already? I'm sorry. I lost track."

"Never mind. Here, I have it."

"That's so nice of you. Thanks."

He gave her the pills. He'd had the foresight to bring a small bottle of mineral water with him too, so that she could wash them down.

They sat on the grass side by side. It was a quiet, sheltered spot where few of the other patients ventured. The Swiss summer air was crisp and smelled of meadows.

"And today is what colour?" Benedikt asked. His English was mannered and precise, and his *w*s had a slight *v* to them, which Josie found endearing. "No, don't say. Let me guess. Yellow?"

"Spot on."

He held up both hands in a double victory salute. "Yay me."

It was Dr Aeschbacher, Josie's primary therapist, who had suggested assigning colours to her moods. Josie never knew, until the day began, how she was going to feel, but once she realised what sort of frame of mind she was in, that was what she would be stuck with until bedtime. If she woke up and her head happened to be jammed full of dark thoughts, there was no shaking them. They crawled all over her like cockroaches, filling every crevice of her being with their prickly legs and insistent chittering. She feared they would suffocate her. The terror was almost beyond her capacity to bear.

Dr Aeschbacher was teaching her that her moods, even if they couldn't be changed, could be managed.

"Put a colour on them, Josie," she had said. "Then see only the colour. See that it is just a colour, nothing more. It is just red, or blue, or green, or whichever. Then the mood will not matter nearly as much. You understand?"

Josie was trying to follow the advice. Dr Aeschbacher was pretty and very wise, with thin rimless spectacles and an aura of calm that seemed to seep out of her and into Josie during their sessions together. Josie felt she could tell her anything and not be judged for it.

"As it is a Yellow Day," said Benedikt, "I feel it would do no harm to ask if you have heard from either of your parents recently. I know it is a sticky topic, but…"

"Mum Skyped last week. We spoke for an hour. She's doing okay. My dad…" Josie frowned. "He's not been in touch for a while. I think he's working. He works abroad a lot, off doing… stuff."

"I like him. He seems like a nice man, the times we've met."

"Yeah, well, he's not your dad, is he?"

"He is a computer consultant, yes?"

"Troubleshooter, he calls it. He's ex-service. After the Army he re-skilled, took some courses, and now does IT stuff for the rich and stupid. He has international clients. They pay him to sort out their systems, fix bugs, get everything running smoothly."

"So he is very busy."

"He is. I never saw much of him even when I was living at home. He kept getting posted to places. And him being away so much was why he and Mum split up. It wasn't the only reason, obviously. I'm…"

She faltered.

Benedikt did not touch her; physical contact was not permitted. But he gestured as though he would have patted her hand sympathetically if he could.

"I am glad it is a Yellow Day," he said. "You seem to be having more of them. And more Green and Red too; and Black, not so many. Have you noticed that?"

Josie had, sort of. She didn't keep track of the day colours. She didn't write them down in a journal or anything. Looking back, though, she could see that the Black Days, and the Blues and Browns as well, had been getting fewer and further between.

"Progress," said Benedikt.

"Progress," Josie agreed.

And then there was a tiny wet sound, like a fly splatting against a car windscreen, and Benedikt started staring at her in a curious way, as though he had something important he wished to share.

Whatever it was, he failed to say it. Instead, he slumped backwards onto the grass, and Josie wondered if he was being cute, if he was trying to be funny, and she laughed, but nervously, because she didn't quite get the joke, assuming it was a joke. Was he pretending to have fallen asleep? Was it some sort of comment about her boring him so much he had sunk into a coma? No, Benedikt hadn't a mean bone in his body. He wouldn't tease her like that.

Only when she saw the small fluff of cotton protruding from the front of his white tunic did Josie realise that Benedikt was not being witty or silly. He was... unconscious? Dead?

She looked up. Looked round. Panic stopped her throat. Her stomach lurched.

Men were coming.

Not orderlies. Not any kind of clinic employee. Nor her fellow patients.

Men in black jumpsuits and balaclavas. Crossing the lawn towards her. Running low and softly.

They had guns. Pistols with oddly long, thin barrels.

One of them pointed his gun at her and pulled the trigger.

There was a spike of pain in Josie's chest.

And her Yellow Day went completely dark.

NINETEEN

Benito Juárez Airport, Mexico City

WITH A COUPLE of hours to kill until their flight was scheduled to depart, the three demigods – Theo, Chase and Salvador – made their way to one of the premium lounges at Benito Juárez for an early lunch. Chase had been disappointed that Theo was not springing for another private jet. "Once you've travelled in that kind of luxury," he'd said, "it's hard to go back." But when Theo had suggested that Chase stump up the thirty grand charter fee this time, his cousin had been forced to admit that flying by mainstream air carrier wasn't so bad. They would still be turning left when they boarded the plane, after all. It could be worse.

Salvador helped himself to everything the lounge's lavish buffet bar had to offer. The attractive hostess staffing the counter made some remark about how she liked to see a man with a hearty appetite, and that was the cue for ten minutes of relentless and unsubtle flirting. Observing this, Chase said to Theo, "You've got to admire the guy. The way he goes on around women, you'd almost think he's straight."

"He is straight," Theo replied. "Basically. He just strays in the other direction from time to time."

"Um, Hylas? Philoctetes? Iolaus? And all the other, ahem, 'squires' he dragged around with him on his adventures? And the younger Argonauts he kept hounding after? That's a heck of a lot of straying."

"For every one of those boys there's been at least three women. He had forty-nine of King Thespius's fifty daughters, for heaven's sake, and would have made it a clean sweep if the fiftieth hadn't been so shy. That's in addition to his wives and his concubines, and more princesses and slave girls than you can count."

"He used to like fathering kids, that's for sure, but I never saw any woman who could make his face light up the way a pretty boy could."

"I guess in a place like Mexico, he's playing safe by staying vigorously hetero. Can't blame him for that."

"And the wrestling gets the other stuff out of his system," said Chase with a nod. "As long as he doesn't mistakenly pop a boner while he's –"

A ping from Theo's phone interrupted Chase, preventing him from taking this line of thought any further, perhaps mercifully.

"Email," said Theo. "Anonymous sender address. No subject heading."

"Spam. Delete it. Unless you want your user ID hacked."

"No, I don't, but..." On a hunch, Theo opened the email.

It read:

Not all twelve sites ransacked. One still intact: Novy Tolkatui.

HG

Beneath the text was a link which, when Theo tapped it, opened up a new tab showing a map location – a tiny village in the Krasnoyarsk region of Siberia.

"Gottlieb," said Chase. "Quick, hit reply. Ask for more details."

"No use. It's one of those one-shot disposable email service providers. The address expires the moment you use it."

"So what's he telling us?"

"What it says. Whoever has the artefacts missed one out."

"Probably because it's in Russia's answer to Buttfuck, Idaho, and whoever has the artefacts couldn't face going there and bailed. But what good is that info to us?"

"Depends." Theo delved in his pocket for the cocktail napkin from the Eighteenth Amendment. Novy Tolkatui was where Gottlieb had hidden Hades's Helm of Darkness.

"Hey, that was mine," said Chase. "My artefact. The invisibility helmet I wore when I went after Medusa. That's the only one of the twelve nobody wanted? I'm kind of insulted. I take that personally."

"Seems like Gottlieb wants us to have it," said Theo. "That's how I interpret this."

"Or he's setting us up. Laying a trap."

"A valid interpretation."

"I've a third. He's sending us on a wild goose chase, to keep us out of the way so he can carry on killing demigods without interference."

"Also valid."

"Maybe he and Evander Arlington are in cahoots. I love that word. Cahoots. It's always good to have a legitimate excuse to say it. They're in cahoots, scheming together against the rest of us."

"Unlikely, but not beyond the realms of possibility."

A thought occurred to Chase. "Hey, could this be a whole *Highlander* thing?"

"What?"

"*Highlander*. The movie. Think about it. Immortals killing other immortals. 'There can be only one.' Life imitating art – or rather life imitating 'eighties Hollywood sci-fi trash."

"As I recall, in *Highlander* the villain beheads the other immortals to harvest their power. I don't see how that could apply here. Our divinity isn't a transferrable resource."

"Transferrable resource?" said Salvador, re-joining them after his dalliance with the hostess, which had culminated in an exchange of phone numbers. "What are you talking about?"

Theo filled him in on the latest development.

"We must go," Salvador said simply.

"Huh?" said Chase. "Just like that? 'We must go'? Because Harry Gottlieb – who, let's not forget, may well be our Big Bad – says so?"

"If it's a trap, we spring it deliberately. Our enemy ambushes us, we get to see him face to face, we learn who he is, we have an opportunity to turn the tables and defeat him. Advantage us. If it isn't a trap, we gain the last remaining artefact. Advantage us again. A win-win."

"Yeah, unless our enemy kills us. Then it's more a die-die."

"Kills us? *Us?*" Salvador let out a roar of laughter, startling several of the other travellers in the lounge, most of whom were sedate executive types or brittle rich folk. "How can they kill three of the foremost champions of the Age of Heroes?" he continued at a more subdued volume. "We're more than a match for anyone, surely."

"Uh, divine weapons, remember?" said Chase.

"Pfah!"

"And so far they've managed to wipe out Aeneas and Orion, neither of whom was a slouch in the combat department. Orpheus, I grant you, easier meat – but Aeneas and Orion? That takes some doing."

"Even so, each died singly, alone. I defy any foe, however well armed, to overwhelm us three together. At worst, even if they prevailed, it would be greatly to their cost."

"He has a point," said Theo.

"He has?" said Chase.

"What else were we planning to do? We were going to go back to NYC and maybe start attempting to track down Evander Arlington. Gottlieb has landed something in our laps that we can use, something we can get proactive on, something tangible. I say we take the gamble and go for it."

"Well…" Chase deliberated. "All right. I'm going to bow to your judgement on this one, cuz. Being as it's my Helm of Darkness, that kind of influences my decision. One small hitch: travel visas to Russia are a bitch to get hold of. They take ages to come through. That said, I know someone at the Russian Consulate in San Francisco who might be able to speed things up for us."

"You are a mine of useful contacts, Chase," said Theo.

"This guy, Yakov, he helped when I wanted to make an episode about the Alkonost and the Sirin; they're these Russian monsters with the bodies of birds but the heads and chests of women."

"Or harpies, as they're better known," said Salvador.

"Similar, but with added Slavic bad temper. Yakov arranged permits and transportation for me and the crew to go all sorts of places, deep in the Russian interior. Can't say he came cheap, but if it's a quick turnaround you're after…"

"Call him," said Theo. "I'll start booking flights."

TWENTY

Kismayo, Somalia

BADENHORST HAD MADE himself scarce. It was almost as though he knew Roy was on the warpath and was avoiding him. When the Myrmidons got back to the hotel in Kismayo, Badenhorst wasn't there. He had left a message for them at the reception desk, telling them that he was off taking care of some business, they should stay put, he would be back soon.

So the Myrmidons had no choice but to hang around and wait. Mayson and Corbett were tended to by a local doctor who was willing to clean and sew up bullet wounds for cash, no questions asked. He gave them antibiotics and painkillers, strong enough to stun an elephant. They spent the time in their rooms, dazedly flicking through the blurry, badly-tuned TV channels, watching any British and American shows they could find even though the dialogue was invariably dubbed into Somali or Arabic.

The rest of the Myrmidons made the most of what the hotel had to offer, which wasn't much. The place, consisting of a set of two-storey concrete buildings arranged around a central courtyard, was reasonably clean and accommodating. Bright paintwork and some gaudy murals of animals lent it a certain amount of jollity but also couldn't quite disguise its fundamental resemblance to a prison camp. There was a swimming pool, half full of pale green, slightly stagnant water and home to frogs and lizards; the cabana bar served no alcoholic beverages whatsoever, only black tea and sodas.

After two days of tedium and stasis, Roy had built up a good pressure of steam. Who the hell did Badenhorst think he was, leaving them here to stew? How dare he just waltz off like that, not even staying to find out how the mission had gone? What kind of a boss was he? When he got back, there was going to be a reckoning. Oh, yes. Badenhorst had no idea of the shitstorm he would be facing when he returned. He would cough up some answers, or else.

Roy did try calling him a few times, but always it went to voicemail. He didn't leave a message. He didn't trust himself to stay coherent; and besides, what he wanted to say to Badenhorst needed to be said in person.

He also tried calling Josie, but met with a similar lack of success. With her, he did at least leave messages, saying to ring him back when she had a moment, but she didn't respond. He wanted to talk to her, to prepare her for the possibility that she might have to leave the Gesundheitsklinik. He had enough money saved up to keep her at the clinic for another couple of months, but if he lost this job – which was not inconceivable if things did not go well with Badenhorst – he wouldn't have a penny to show for it. Worse, he'd be blacklisted, unemployable.

When Josie was having one of her bad spells, she tended to shut down, refusing to speak, neglecting her phone and falling off social media. Roy checked her Facebook: she had last posted on it over a week ago, some innocuous status update about a Pixar movie she had just watched. Her Twitter and Instagram accounts had lain fallow for nearer a month. With any ordinary teenage girl this would have been a cause for concern; in Josie's case it wasn't unusual. Even if she was doing well with her treatment, the Gesundheitsklinik's administration frowned on patients being too active in cyberspace or interacting too freely with people beyond its walls. In order to heal soonest, they needed to think less about the outside world and more about themselves. Some of the clinic's clientele were high-profile CEOs and celebrities who needed to remain contactable, so phones, laptops and tablets weren't banned outright, but their use was discouraged. Exposure to external influences could be a distraction, placing speed bumps on the road to recovery.

On the second evening, Roy ended up having a late-night drinking session with Gavin, Jeanne, Sean Wilson and Travis Laffoon. The sale of alcohol was banned in Somalia, and unlike in some other Muslim countries there were no exceptions to this rule, not even in hotels and restaurants frequented by Westerners. Black market booze could still be bought, however, and Wilson and Laffoon had enterprisingly gone out and sourced some generic-brand rum and vodka, which they mixed with coconut milk and pineapple juice to create an approximation of a piña colada. The concoction was both sickly sweet and frighteningly potent. By the third glass Roy was hammered, and by the fifth he was having something like an out-of-body experience. For a time his anger at Badenhorst seemed far removed and ill advised. Shouldn't he drop it? Shut up and just do the job? Weren't there more important things to care about?

He barely remembered getting to his room. Jeanne helped him, though. He was sure of that. He had a clear recollection of finding the stairs very difficult to climb and Jeanne holding his arm and instructing him to keep putting one foot in front of the other. He recalled, too, her steering him to his bed and forcing him to drink water even though he was not at all thirsty. He then made a pass at her, telling her she was amazing and he was lonely. She turned him down flat, but in a way that implied that another time, perhaps when he was a tad soberer, she might consider it.

His dreams were feverish, hellish. A parade of paid murders; his greatest hits. Bullets smacking into heads from afar, splitting them open like watermelons, as seen through the reticle of a sniper scope. Knives sneaking across throats or slipping through intercostal muscles, a hand over a mouth. The snicker of a suppressor in an elevator. A hanging, once, dangling an obese tinpot dictator from a rafter by a rope, then watching as the man's neck began to elongate, the sheer weight of his body stretching it and stretching it until, with a sound like tearing canvas, the neck snapped in two and the body collapsed to the floor, leaving the head wrapped snugly in the noose, penduluming to and fro, dripping gore in a monochrome Jackson Pollock on the terracotta floor tiles. A couple of drownings: elbow-deep in bathwater, holding the person down, waiting for the thrash and gargle to subside, the last few air bubbles to leak from the mouth, the stillness to settle in.

How could he do this, year in, year out, and still stand before a mirror and look himself in the eye?

Why was he not screaming all the time?

BADENHORST APPEARED SHORTLY after breakfast the next morning, sauntering into the hotel insouciantly, as if to say, *So what if I've been away? Fuck you.*

Roy, in the grip of a wretched hangover, happened to be looking out of the window of his room when a taxi pulled in below and the Afrikaner stepped out. Badenhorst under-tipped the driver and swaggered through the lobby entrance, and Roy stumbled downstairs to intercept him.

He was coming nicely to the boil by the time he reached the lobby. Badenhorst had no idea what he was in for. Badenhorst had some questions to answer. Badenhorst was going to come clean, whatever it took.

"Ah, Roy. Just the man I wanted to see. Come to my room."

Roy was brought up short. This wasn't how he had foreseen the confrontation playing out.

But Badenhorst's room? Why not? His grievances were better aired in private than in public anyway.

"You're looking rough, may I say." Badenhorst shut the room door behind them. "Slept well?"

"Listen, Badenhorst…"

"I'm going to stop you there. You seem like you have something to get off your chest. We'll come to that. First, there's this."

He held up a phone.

"A little clip I want to show you. Our last little chat – well, it didn't end altogether satisfactorily from my point of view. I got the feeling you were being insubordinate, and we all know where insubordination leads to, if it isn't taken care of. So watch the clip, then decide where you want to take things from here."

He tapped the *Play* symbol.

On the phone, Josie's face appeared in tight close-up.

Roy's breath caught in his throat.

Josie had been crying. Eyes puffy and wet.

She looked pale and terrified.

"Dad?" she said. "Dad. These people… I don't know who they are. I don't know where I am. They're recording this. They want me to give you a message. They've told me to tell you I'm fine. I'm being looked after. I'm not a prisoner, but they're not going to let me go. Not yet."

She sniffed hard, damply, tremblingly.

"I'm scared, Dad. Really scared. What's happening? What *is* this? They – they took me. From the clinic. Knocked me out with a tranquilliser dart or something, and… And Benedikt. They got Benedikt too. Dad, please do whatever they ask. Please, Dad. I really think –"

The clip ended abruptly, cutting her off mid-sentence.

Ray made a grab for the phone.

Badenhorst snatched it out of his reach.

"Uh-uh, Roy. I'm allowing you one look at it, and one look only. That's your daughter, *nè*? Your Josie. We're not disputing that, right?"

Numbly Roy shook his head.

"Good. Okay. So you know we have her and she's well – as well as can be expected – and we're not mistreating her. *Ja*? I was there when we snatched her. It was quick and clean and no one got hurt. Do you believe me?"

Numbly Roy nodded.

"So here's the reasoning behind this," said Badenhorst. "You're a valuable asset, Roy. You're a natural leader, and the other Myrmidons respond well to you. They're happy to have you telling them what to do."

Roy said nothing.

"What it boils down to is: I can't afford to lose you. The team can't. You've made yourself indispensable. So in order to guarantee you stay on board and don't rock the boat, I've had to take out a little insurance policy. I've got hold of the one thing in your life you can't do without, the one thing you cannot afford to lose. Lovely young *choty goty* Josie. And I'm going to keep her until the project is done. I promise you – cross my heart, swear to God – no harm will come to her. She is completely safe. Look into my eyes and know that that is true. I will make sure she continues to get her pills and is looked after properly. I have seen to that. But know this too."

Badenhorst's face hardened.

"If you do not play ball, if you misbehave in any way from now on, you will never see her again. I can't put it any more plainly than that. There are places where pretty teenage girls can disappear to. Places they can be sent where they'll never be found. People who will pay good money for them."

A cracking, grinding sound. Roy clenching his teeth.

"In a way, my friend, this is your own fault. If you weren't so damn good at what you do, it wouldn't matter to me if you stay or you go. Any of the others, they spoke to me the way you did back in England, I'd've cut them loose, no problem. So long, *totsiens*. But you – you're the alpha dog in the pack, and if I have to give the leash a good hard yank to keep you in line, I don't mind. That's just how it has to be, hey?"

Badenhorst shrugged.

"You could say this is kind of an extreme step to be taking, and I agree. But there's a proverb in Afrikaans: *Wie nie waag nie wen nie.* 'He who doesn't take risks doesn't win.' And that's me. A winner."

Now Badenhorst smiled.

"You've been quiet for so long, I'm starting to get uncomfortable, Roy. What do you have to say to all this? Any thoughts?"

"I suppose," Roy said eventually, "that if I kill you now, Josie will die too."

"I think that's taken as read. If I fail to check in with the men looking after her at a set time every day, a command will be executed, blah-blah-blah, you know the drill."

"Then rest assured, when all this is over, *then* I will kill you. With my bare hands. I will beat the life out of you, slowly, bit by bit, and I will relish every fucking second of it."

"Roy." Badenhorst was imperturbable. "When all this is over, you will be a very rich man and you will never have to worry about your daughter's future again, and you and I will be living somewhere far, far away from each other and we won't have to see each other or even think about each other ever again, and we will both be happy, and that is that."

"Want to bet?"

"Not a gambling man, Roy. My father was; wager on anything, my *ouballie* would. Who could drink the most, who could piss against a wall the longest. He even once bet a friend which of us, me or one of my brothers, would start crying soonest when he leathered us. Anything. Kind of put me off the whole notion. So no, I don't want to bet. Because also I know. I know that we are going to part as friends after we're done with this business. Smile and shake hands and off we go our separate ways. Anything else would be an unwise move on your part."

Badenhorst let the sentence hang in the air for a moment. Then he said, brightly, "But enough of that. What is it you wanted to talk to me about? You're the one who came to find me. Something to report? I'm all ears."

Roy was utterly defeated. Badenhorst had him firmly by the balls. Josie... The bastard had kidnapped her. Flown to Switzerland and abducted her from the Gesundheitsklinik and spirited her off to God-knows-where. From the sound of it he had also kidnapped the orderly, Benedikt Frankel, the one Josie liked best. That was something, at least. Someone to be with her, who was trained in psychiatric care and could oversee her wellbeing and medication.

Clinging to this tiny piece of good news like a shipwrecked sailor clinging to a scrap of flotsam, Roy said, "Our targets."

"What about them?"

"You haven't told us everything you can. If I'm to continue to lead the Myrmidons, as I seem to be doing, and do it to the best of my ability, I need full operational intel." Every word he spoke was sticking in his craw. It was difficult not to howl at the top of his voice, to resist the urge to bury his thumbs in Badenhorst's eye sockets and gouge his eyeballs out. "They're not normal, are they? There's something unusual about them, *exceptional*. I need – *we* need – to know what it is."

Badenhorst cocked his head. "Hmm. *Ja*, this was bound to happen, wasn't it? You were bound to notice sooner or later. I have two options here. Either I can explain in full, and you'll have trouble believing me and you might even think I've gone off my rocker, or I can just say 'Get on with the *blerrie* job, man' and leave it at that. On balance, I'm going to go with number two. Do you really have to know everything? I think not. It's far simpler if you just accept that these people are not your everyday hits. They are in a class of their own."

"But you know who – what – they actually are?"

"I do, and let me tell you, it took a while getting used to the idea. It's the sort of thing that entirely rewires your understanding of the world, and while I imagine you're the kind of guy who could eventually get his head around it, I'm not sure I can say the same for some of the others. It might be too much for them, especially limited folks like Travis and Hans, you know what I'm saying?"

"Then fill me in. Just me. I won't share. I'll simply factor it into the planning on future missions. We got our arses handed to us back there, courtesy of Daniel Munro. I don't know if you're aware of that."

"I had a feeling you might. I did warn you."

"We were lucky to get away with as few casualties as we did."

"Lucky? Luck had nothing to do with it. It was skill, Roy. *Your* skill. Besides, you made the hit. You pulled it off. All's well that ends well, eh? Everything's hundreds."

"Still, wouldn't it make sense to give me everything I need to prevent the same thing happening again? Or are we that expendable?"

Badenhorst shook his head, none too convincingly.

"That figures," said Roy. "I know what a Myrmidon is, after all. I looked it up the day you first mentioned the name, while we were in training. A Myrmidon isn't just the term for a kind of Ancient Greek infantryman. It's based on the Greek word for ant. Ant person. Which is how much you value us. We're insects."

"It was my employer's choice. It seemed to tickle their fancy. Whatever the word means, though, don't take that as a benchmark of my esteem for you. Quite the opposite. All of you Myrmidons, but you especially, Roy, have my full respect. Despite all this antagonism between us."

"If you respected me at all, you'd let my daughter go free."

"Let's not go there. I thought we'd settled that. No, my decision stands: you will have to make do with such intel as I give you each time. Like using ear plugs on the Del Karno mission. Any more than that is irrelevant. If you don't like it… Well, I would say you can take a hike, but you can't. Not you. So you're just going to have to suck it up instead. Too bad for you."

If Roy had not turned around and left the room at that moment, he might not have been responsible for his actions. He would have vented every last bit of the white-hot fury he was feeling, and Badenhorst would have been lucky to survive the onslaught.

OUTSIDE ON THE landing there was an elderly fridge-sized ice dispenser which served the entire floor. It buzzed and churned constantly but never seemed able to fulfil the purpose for which it had been built. Roy took out his frustration on it, pummelling the front of the machine with his fists until it was deeply dented and his knuckles were bleeding.

Then he phoned the Gesundheitsklinik and asked to be put through to Dr Aeschbacher. She hesitantly confirmed that Josie had been absent from the clinic since yesterday morning.

"Do you have some idea of her whereabouts then, Mr Young? Is that why you called?"

"No."

"Then who told you she was gone?"

"I… learned about it from a third party."

"Who?"

"None of your business. I also know that a member of your staff, Benedikt Frankel, is absent too. What I'd like to know is why I wasn't notified about any of this immediately."

"The management did not wish to alarm you unduly and, as the case may be, unnecessarily," said Dr Aeschbacher. "Often in these instances, when patients abscond, they come back within twenty-four hours, forty-eight at most. The standard procedure is not to classify them as 'missing'" – Roy could almost see her doing air quotes – "until at least three days have elapsed."

"That's crazy."

"Mr Young, patients at the Gesundheitsklinik are not inmates at a sanatorium, they are voluntary participants in a programme of wraparound, holistic therapy, and if one of them wishes to take a break from that at any time, unannounced or otherwise, we have no legal right to stop him or her."

"Legal right? What about moral duty?"

"They are not prisoners. We are not their jailers."

"But Josie's a fifteen-year-old girl, for fuck's sake."

"There is no call for bad language. And Josie turned sixteen last month, actually. That seems to have escaped your notice."

It had. Roy cursed himself. He had been preoccupied. Idiot!

"In some Swiss cantons," Dr Aeschbacher said, "that makes her of age to vote in elections."

"All the same, she's only a kid."

"And we are only a private mental health institution. We are not a school. We are not, as I have said, a prison. We provide a paid-for service which clients are free to opt out of whenever they wish."

"I've heard some mealy-mouthed bollocks in my time…"

"We are concerned about Josie's welfare, Mr Young," Dr Aeschbacher said, silkily, professionally. "But since Mr Frankel disappeared at the same time as she did, our concern is mitigated."

"It should be heightened, surely."

"You think he and she have… eloped, is that the word? Unlikely, given Mr Frankel's sexual orientation. I believe this is, if it is anything, a kind of Platonic *folie à deux* that they have concocted between them. In which case, if that is so, then rest assured we will be implementing the appropriate disciplinary sanctions against Mr Frankel when he and Josie return. We will –"

Roy cut the connection. He couldn't listen to Dr Aeschbacher trowel on this crap a moment longer. Fuck her, the smooth-talking corporate drone. Doling out bullshit on a spoon like it was honey, covering the clinic's arse.

The ice dispenser came in for further punishment. This time, to spare his hands, Roy gave it a thorough kicking.

TWENTY-ONE

Novy Tolkatui, Russia

"WELL, HERE WE all are, freezing our asses off in Siberia," said Chase as he removed yet another layer of clothing. He was now down to his undershirt, the armpits of which bore glassy blooms of sweat. He stuffed the baseball shirt into his backpack, where it joined a lightweight cotton tracksuit top.

"Did you honestly think it snows here the whole year round?" said Theo. "Even in midsummer?"

"No, but I didn't think it'd be so damn hot either. I mean, Jesus, this is like California."

"Only with more flies," said Salvador, swatting at the cloud of pests which had descended on them within twenty paces of leaving the Mil Mi-8 civilian transport helicopter and had accompanied them ever since.

"And worse humidity," Chase added.

Salvador turned to Theo. "He complains all the time, doesn't he? I forgot that about him."

"Not all the time," Theo said. "Sometimes he gripes. Every so often he bitches."

"I do not," said Chase. "I just point out when things aren't going the way everyone would like. That's performing a useful public service."

"Is it," said Salvador, blandly.

They had landed at the edge of a dense, sprawling forest, having flown across a vast expanse of scrubby barren steppe dotted with the occasional smallholding and flyspeck hamlet. This spot was the closest the pilot could get them to Novy Tolkatui. From there it was a five-mile trek through the forest to the village along a rutted, overgrown dirt track. Pines towered on either side of the route, and now and then the three demigods would see a small lake glimmering through the trees. Krasnoyarsk, the nearest true civilisation, lay 150 miles to the south. They had arrived at the city's Yemelyanovo Airport the previous evening and spent the night at a hotel where every single member of staff, right down to the bellboy, had offered to fix them up with hookers and drugs.

They walked on, still attended by the black flies that seemed to regard them as a mobile smorgasbord. After a while even Chase stopped talking. The silence of the forest was as oppressive as the heat and flies. No wind stirred the tree branches. A yawning primordial stillness held sway.

During the helicopter flight, both the pilot and the co-pilot had been inquisitive, wanting to know why three Westerners were interested in Novy Tolkatui, of all places. The Krasnoyarsk region had so much to offer tourists: the granite rock formations of the Stolby Nature Reserve, the Paraskeva Pyatnitsa Chapel with its panoramic hilltop views, the hydroelectric dam on the Yenisei river at Divnogorsk. What was it about a tiny, incredibly remote, no-account village that attracted them? It wasn't as if anybody even lived there any more, at least not to the pilot's and co-pilot's knowledge. Like many old settlements in the area, it was reputed to be deserted, its inhabitants abandoning their homes to find a livelihood and, indeed, a life. There might still be one or two families lingering on, but if so, they'd be hunters or subsistence farmers, grubby, inarticulate, inbred – not the sort of people who welcomed outsiders.

Chase had spun them some yarn about scouting for a TV documentary on the subject of isolated, semi-abandoned communities, relics of a bygone age, untouched by the modern world, etc. This seemed to satisfy their curiosity. The word 'television,' properly wielded, had magical power. It could open doors, quell dissent, and make even the awkwardest customers pliable.

The first sign that Theo, Chase and Salvador were nearing Novy Tolkatui was the rusted husk of a Soviet-era tractor sitting by the side of the track. Weeds had grown up through its engine block. Its tyres had perished away to nothing.

Further on they came to a small shrine, a lopsided wooden thing that would have once housed an ikon for peasants to kneel before and venerate. A Russian Orthodox cross perched on its roof, and an orange-breasted barn swallow perched on one arm of the cross, flicking its tail as the three demigods went by.

A minute or so after that, Chase addressed his two companions softly.

"Don't look round. Be cool. Just keep walking."

"What is it?" said Theo, equally softly.

"We're being followed."

Salvador turned his head.

"I *said* don't look round," Chase hissed. "What part of that did you not understand, you big ape?"

"But I can see no one."

"Doesn't mean they're not there. They've been behind us ever since the tractor. I wasn't sure at first, so I didn't say anything. I am now."

"How many?" said Theo.

"Two, I think. They're in the woods and they're being very sneaky, and at the same time very careless."

"Both at once?"

"I can't quite make it out myself," said Chase. "It's like they can't agree on how they're supposed to be stalking us. I've only got the sound of their footsteps to go on, but one of them's super stealthy, the other's trampling like an elephant. I've been trying to catch a glimpse of them out of the corner of my eye, get a fix on where they are, but they're not obliging."

"I vote we attack," said Salvador. "Rush at them. Flush them out of hiding."

"For once Mr Musclebound talks sense," said Chase. "But I'm going to hazard a guess that Captain Cautious here will say we should just keep on walking."

"You know me so well," said Theo.

"Unfortunately."

"Why startle them? They're not being actively hostile."

"Not yet," said Salvador. "But I for one do not like being stalked like game."

"Not bothered about that so much," said Chase. "Me, I'm more worried that these are local yokels. What if this is some sort of Russian *Deliverance* scenario? Or maybe *The Texas Chainsaw Massacre*? They're hillbillies out to rape us or eat us, or maybe both, and not necessarily in that order."

"They can try," Salvador growled, "and they will fail."

"What's the Russian equivalent of banjo music? Balalaika music? There's going to be a lot of that in our future if we're not careful."

"Will you two just calm down?" said Theo.

But he couldn't deny that he was more than a little creeped out. Once, in a forest not dissimilar to this one, he had faced Sinis, a bandit who liked to strap hapless travellers by the wrists and ankles to a pair of bent pine trees and then released the trees so that his victims were ripped in half. Theo had been young then, still on his way to becoming a fully-fledged thief beater and crook killer. He remembered vividly the unnerving experience of coming upon the remains of Sinis's handiwork littering the forest floor: decaying corpses, skeletons picked clean by scavenging animals, each two distinct parts separated by some distance. It had simultaneously sickened and enraged him, and after overpowering Sinis and bringing him to his knees, he had had no compunction about executing him in the exact same manner. There was no justice like poetic justice.

"If they're locals," he added, "then they have much more to fear from us than we do from them."

"And if they're not locals?" said Chase. "What are you thinking, Theo? That it might be the demigod slayers?"

"It might be. We might be straying into Gottlieb's trap, just as he hoped."

"All the more reason to take them out now," said Salvador. "Make our move before they make theirs. Element of surprise."

"Or," said Theo, pointing ahead, "we draw them in to a place where we can find a defensible position and hole up."

They were rounding a corner and Novy Tolkatui was coming into view, a pitiful cluster of wooden shacks and huts in various states of dereliction. Few windowpanes were not cracked, and some windows had fallen out altogether and been replaced by sheets of cardboard or fibreboard. Moss and ivy vied to see which could cover more surfaces.

"Then let's make a run for it," said Chase. "All together. On my mark. Three, two, one, go!"

They were in the heart of the village within seconds, and even more quickly inside one of the sturdier-looking structures, Chase kicking the door down and raising a great cloud of dust by doing so. The three demigods scattered to different corners of the single room that occupied the entire interior of the hut. They stationed themselves beside different windows and peeked out through the grime-caked glass.

"Hear anything?" whispered Theo. "See anything?"

"Not a thing," said Salvador.

"Me either," said Chase.

"Okay." Theo returned to the entrance, righted the door, and reinstalled it in its jamb, securing it in place by leaning a crude table of warped, splintery planks lengthwise against it. The light in the hut became dimmer and hazier, and the smells of damp and rotting wood seemed to strengthen.

"What now?" said Salvador. "Haven't we just made ourselves sitting ducks?"

"Think about it," said Theo. "If it's the demigod slayers out there, what weapons do they have? Bow and arrows, axe, sword, spear, scythe, trident. They can't hit what they can't see, so arrows are out. That leaves only one option: they're going to have to charge. Which means they're going to have to show themselves, and when they do, it lets us see them, gauge their numbers, and counterattack – meet them head-on."

"I like the sound of that, Theo," said Salvador. "What appears to have been rank cowardice, the act of mice scurrying away from the cat to their hole, is in fact shrewd cunning."

"I'll take that as a compliment. I'm sure it was meant as one."

Long minutes passed.

"Come on, you bastards," Chase muttered. "Come and get it. We're waiting."

Another minute.

Then...

"I see movement," said Chase. "Over there. In that barn. Someone's –"

Theo looked in time to catch a glimpse of a body in motion. Fast. A whirlwind.

Then the door and the table supporting it flew inward, and there was suddenly a fourth person in the hut, and before any of the three demigods could react the person alighted on the nearest of them to hand, Chase, and spun him around, sending him reeling headlong against a rickety shelf where sat a tarnished copper samovar and some enamel crockery, all of which crashed to the floor, as did Chase.

Salvador lunged across the room at the interloper and was flattened by an artfully placed blow, an elbow jab to the back of the neck that seemed to steal all the rigidity from his body. He flopped onto his belly like a wet fish, with a cry that was half grunt, half yelp.

The intruder placed a foot on Salvador's back, pinning him prone, and turned to Theo.

"You're next, Theseus. Or do you surrender?"

Theo gaped.

"Queen Hippolyta?"

"JUST HIPPOLYTA, IF you please," said the one-time ruler of the Amazons. "The race I reigned over are gone. Or you can call me Sasha Grace, as the mortals do now. And again, your surrender. Shall I have it, or must I incapacitate you as I did these two lummoxes?"

Salvador groaned on the floor beneath her foot. Chase, meanwhile, was picking himself up, but Sasha Grace snapped a telescopic baton out from her hand and tapped the back of his head with its tip.

"I'd stay put if I were you, Perseus," she warned. "Unless you want me to crack your skull open."

Chase stiffened. Theo could see him weighing up his options. Could he disarm her before she struck? Was he quick enough? Whose reflexes were swifter, his or hers?

From personal experience, Theo knew the answer to that, and it wasn't Chase.

"Do as she says," he told him. "This woman does not mess around."

"Listen to your cousin," said Sasha Grace. "He speaks wisely for someone with a cock and balls."

Theo studied her. Lithe, slender, with steely eyes and a haughty beauty. Still every inch a queen, even in jeans, biker boots, a leather jacket and a white halterneck T-shirt, with her hair tied back in a ponytail.

"You're trying to remember when we last met," Sasha said. "London. 1888. You were going by the name of Templeton Stevens, consulting detective. I had adopted the alias Meg Adams."

"No need to remind me. I was hunting the Ripper. You were fishing for him. We pooled our resources and caught him together."

"Caught him and punished him for his crimes against females. I cherish the memory of how he pleaded for his life in that deserted wharf we took him to. How he howled and sobbed as I carved off parts of him and lobbed them into the Thames. How long did he last? It was fairly impressive. Nearly an hour before the life left him."

Her eyes flashed in the gloom of the hut, and Theo felt a small chill. Not much scared him quite like this bloodthirsty warrior woman did.

"And he was such a nobody, too," she went on. "All those grand theories that have sprung up since, about royal doctors and prominent lawyers and heirs to the throne, and he was just a common-or-garden dockworker who, as he told us himself, couldn't get it up and thought a knife an adequate substitute for a limp dick."

"We parted as friends, though, didn't we, you and I?" said Theo.

"Allies, perhaps."

"But on good terms."

"Yes. I believe I told you that you could consider yourself forgiven for your role in the theft of my girdle. Him, though..." She ground her foot harder into the small of Salvador's back. "Him I find it harder to forgive."

"I can rise from this position at any time," said Salvador. "You know that, don't you? You do not have the better of me."

"Keep telling yourself that, Heracles, if it salves your wounded pride."

"But why are you here?" Theo asked her. "What brings you to Novy Tolkatui?"

"Duh!" said Chase. "Can't you see, cuz? It's her. She's the one. She's the demigod slayer. It all makes perfect sense. Every victim so far has been male. Madame Ballbreaker here hates males, but especially the ones who wrong women. Aeneas – skipped out on Dido. Orion – king of the rapists. Orpheus – got those Maenads mad at him, and as Del Karno he wasn't exactly the poster boy for feminist sensitivity awareness training. Sasha Grace has embarked on a one-woman vendetta, getting payback for the abuse her gender has suffered at the hands of –"

"I'm going to stop you there," Sasha said, "before you make an even bigger asshole of yourself than you're already doing. One-woman vendetta? I've never heard such a load of horsecrap. What do you take me for?"

"Uh, a crazy broad who starts wars over stolen underwear?"

"For your information, I launched the Amazonomachy because I was trying to get my sister back. I was under the impression – mistaken, as it turned out – that Melanippe had left Themiscyra with Theseus against her will. She had not. She had *actually* taken a liking to him."

"Thanks for the note of surprise," said Theo. "I'm not without my charms."

"The matter was settled amicably, once the first skirmishes between Amazons and Athenians were over and Theseus and I were able to parley. As for my girdle, it was not 'underwear', it was a ceremonial belt symbolising my regal authority. If you don't know that…"

"He does," said Theo. "Chase just enjoys pushing people's buttons. It's his thing. But if you're not here to kill us, Sasha, what are you here for?"

"The same reason as you."

"And that would be…?"

"So sly. Wanting me to be the one to tip their hand first. Very well. Odysseus sent me. I'm here to collect the Helm of Darkness. And unlike you three clowns, I actually have it."

AN UNEASY TRUCE was reached. Sasha let Salvador up off the floor and put away the baton. Chase and Salvador retreated to a corner of the hut and tried not to look as though they had just been humiliated, while Sasha explained to Theo how she had come to Novy Tolkatui. Long story short, she had received an email from Harry Gottlieb sketching out the situation with regard to the divine artefacts and the demigod killings. He had recommended that she join the expedition to recover the twelfth artefact, giving Theo and Chase the benefit of her assistance.

"Good old Gottlieb," said Chase. "Didn't think we could manage on our own so he drafted in backup."

"That or he wished to ensnare yet another of us in his trap," said Salvador. "Four birds with one stone."

"If this is a trap," said Sasha, "where is it? Where are our enemies? I did wonder whether Gottlieb's email was a ruse of some sort; never trust the man of stratagems. For that reason I took a circuitous path through the forest to get here. There's nobody in the vicinity. Nobody for miles around."

"Doesn't mean the killers couldn't still spring an ambush," said Chase. "Maybe parachute in or something."

"All the more reason to grab the Helm and go," said Theo. "Where is it, Sasha?"

"Hiding in plain sight. Come with me."

The Amazon strode outside and crossed to the barn where she had been lurking prior to storming the hut. The doors stood wide open, but within there was nothing except a few scraps of straw, some antique farm implements, and roughly a million cobwebs.

"There," she said.

"Where?" said Chase.

Sasha rolled her eyes. "The very man who used the Helm, and he still doesn't get it."

"I do," said Theo. "As we walked to the village, there were two people following us. Remember? One of them was stealthy, making an effort not to be noticed. The other was being less subtle about it. 'Trampling like an elephant' you said, Chase. It seems that the two of them weren't together. I'd go so far as to say that at least one of them had no idea of the other's presence."

"It's so delightful watching a man puzzle something out," said Sasha. "It's like an infant learning how to eat its food, slow and sloppy."

"The stealthy one was you, Sasha."

"Bravo. I heard your helicopter coming in and latched onto your whereabouts more or less as soon as you landed."

"And the other one, the 'elephant,' was an ordinary man who didn't feel the need to move quietly because he knew he couldn't be seen. Because —"

Before Theo could finish, Sasha stepped smartly towards the centre of the barn and reached out in front of her. Her groping hand found what it was looking for. She grabbed at thin air at waist height and swept her hand up, and all at once a man appeared. He was sitting slumped and cross-legged on the packed-dirt floor, his arms and legs bound with a length of mouldy old rope. He was shaggy-haired and emaciated, with a long tangled beard and clothes held together by patches and twine. He looked up and blinked blearily around, as though surfacing from a deep sleep.

Above his head Sasha was holding a bronze helmet with a nose protector, tapered cheek guards and a pointed crown. It seemed like something any Hellenic soldier might have worn in battle, an unremarkable piece of armour made of humble beaten alloy — and yet it exuded a strange dark radiance, a feeling of oppression and claustrophobia, like a sky heavy with thunderclouds.

Sasha dropped it neatly back onto the man's head. Tendrils of blackness shot down from the helmet, enveloping him, and he vanished. There was just an empty space where he had been.

She lifted the helmet off, and both it and the man popped back into visibility.

He was wide awake now, and anxious. His eyes focused on the four demigods and he began to babble in Russian. Theo knew some of the language, but the man was speaking too rapidly for him to understand everything he was saying, and anyway he kept stumbling over his words and stuttering. The gist seemed to be that he was ashamed. He was begging for forgiveness. He had done something wrong. Please don't hurt him.

Sasha, in fluent Russian, told him to take a deep breath, calm down, put his thoughts in order, then start talking again.

The man did his best. He said he was sorry; he should not have used the helmet. It was forbidden. For generation after generation in his family, there had been one key rule: you never put the helmet on. You kept it safe, you told no one about it, but above all you never ever put it on.

But now look at him. He was the last of his line. Gennady Ulyanov, the last of the Ulyanovs of Novy Tolkatui. The last man still living in Novy Tolkatui, period. All alone. No wife, no children, no family, nothing. Stuck here while everyone else had left. Stuck because of his duty to look after the helmet. This had been the Ulyanovs' solemn, sacred responsibility since as far back as anyone could remember. Since Novy Tolkatui was just plain Tolkatui. Since before that, when it was a clearing in the forest inhabited by a tribe of elk herders. Since the day, way back at the dawn of time, when a traveller had come from far, far away and left the helmet with the tribe's chieftain, with strict instructions that it be kept hidden for all time.

From father to first-born son, the secret of the helmet had been passed down along the family line. Through wars and empires and conquests and pogroms. Then came *glasnost* and *perestroika*. The villagers, liberated from the yoke of Communism, feeling freer than at any time they could remember, began to migrate to the towns, the cities. One by one they went until in the end only Gennady – stalwart, unswerving Gennady – remained.

That was eleven years ago, and not long afterward Gennady had broken with tradition and started using the helmet when he went hunting for food. How much easier it was to sneak up on a deer or a rabbit when his prey could not see him. And there was no one around to tell him not to do it. No one to know what the helmet could do, how it miraculously masked the wearer from sight. Just him. The only living soul in this great wilderness. Until now.

Theo wondered why Odysseus had chosen to use human beings, this once, to protect an artefact. Did he run out of inspiration? More likely he just didn't consider the Helm of Darkness to be as dangerous as the rest. It wasn't bladed or pointed. It wasn't something for bashing or smashing. It was a passive weapon, and of the twelve, least consequential to him; and so he had expended the least effort on securing it.

"So you were out hunting," he said to Gennady, "and you spotted us and decided to follow us, using the helmet's power?"

"That's right. That's right. I was curious. Your helicopter made such a din. 'Gennady,' I said to myself, 'who has come to Novy Tolkatui? Who has come to your village, where no one but you has set foot for many a year?' I had to see for myself. And then, as I was tracking you through the trees..." He tipped his head in Sasha's direction. He was so tightly bound, it was the only part of his body he could move. "This woman came. Out of nowhere. Somehow she found me even though she could not see me."

"Wasn't hard," Sasha said with a shrug. "No disrespect, Gennady, but your personal hygiene leaves something to be desired. I just followed my nose."

"An arm around my neck. I remember nothing after that. I blacked out. And now you, all of you," said Gennady, "you want the helmet. You were not surprised by it. By what it is capable of. You knew already its power. You have come for it."

"We have," said Theo. "I know you've been entrusted with its care, but..."

"No. No. Please. I insist you take it. Do. Then I can at last be rid of it."

"You don't mind?"

"Mind?" Gennady's gaunt face brightened with joy. "Don't you realise what this means? I am... free! I can leave this goddamned shithole village. I can go somewhere – anywhere. I can have fun. Meet people. Get a girl. My life can start! At forty-one years of age, Gennady Ulyanov finally can *live*."

"So you're saying we'd be doing you a favour?"

"How can I stop you making off with the helmet? Even if I wasn't tied up like this, there are four of you, one of me. There is only so much I can do to prevent it being stolen. Only so much I am capable of. I am supposed to be willing to sacrifice my life to keep it safe, but fuck that. Take the damn thing. Take it with my blessing. It has only ever been a burden. I have just one small request."

"What's that?"

"May I have a lift? If you can find room for me in your helicopter, take me with you. Drop me off wherever you like. Anywhere is better than here. Please?"

OUT OF GENNADY'S earshot and eyeline, they discussed his fate.

Sasha was all for killing him. He knew too much. She would make it quick: grab his head, twist it around on his neck. He wouldn't feel a thing.

Theo strongly objected. The man deserved a break. All those years on his own. The last in a long line of protectors for the Helm of Darkness. It was only fair that Gennady got some sort of reward for that. Besides, who would believe him if he told them about the Helm? He would come across as half-crazed.

Sasha relented, reluctantly. As a compromise, she said that Gennady would not travel with them, but he could have the rented trail bike she had used to get to Novy Tolkatui. It was parked a couple of miles away. She went to fetch it while the villager, now released from the rope tying him, gathered up his few meagre belongings. She showed him how to ride it, and told him the name of the street where he could find the rental agency in Krasnoyarsk, instructing him to deposit the bike back there.

Gennady was thrilled. Grinning toothlessly, he set off along the track on the bike. He crashed almost immediately, but he was back in the saddle in a trice and speeding off once more, full throttle.

"If he gets to Krasnoyarsk without killing himself," said Chase, "it'll be a fucking miracle."

"That might be my plan," said Sasha.

THEY WALKED TO the helicopter, four of them now, Chase with the Helm of Darkness tucked into his backpack. He treated it with a proprietorial air. It was his; he should carry it.

The pilot and co-pilot were startled to learn that they were now expected to take an extra passenger. First, a man had emerged from the forest on a trail bike. Then this. Where had the Westerners found the woman, out here where nobody in their right mind went? What was going on?

Chase expanded on his television-documentary story. By coincidence, they had run into a fellow location scout. What were the chances? And her motorbike had been stolen by that man, so she needed a lift home.

The pilot and co-pilot were unconvinced, but a stunning-looking woman was a stunning-looking woman, however dubious her provenance. There was, anyway, plenty of room for her in the cabin. An Mi-8 could seat twelve; she would add a little weight, but not enough to throw out their fuel calculations. Welcome aboard!

As the helicopter took off, Theo cast a sidelong look at Sasha. He was a little less enthusiastic. He couldn't tell if she had joined them for the duration, as a fourth member of the team, or was merely hitching a ride and would desert them once they got to Krasnoyarsk. She herself hadn't made it clear and, being long accustomed to doing exactly as she pleased and answering to nobody but herself, felt no compunction to. A queen never explained – or excused – her actions.

And for all her claims to the contrary, Sasha Grace was still a queen. The way she sat in her seat, she made it look like a throne, lap-belt and plastic upholstery notwithstanding. The way she held her head erect, you could imagine a crown perched on it rather than a set of ear defenders. There was regality in her posture, her every gesture.

Danger, too. Theo didn't trust this woman any further than he could throw her. For as long as Sasha Grace stayed with them, he would be keeping a very close eye on her.

TWENTY-TWO

Krasnoyarsk

AFTER THE MI-8 landed at the heliport on the outskirts of Krasnoyarsk, Sasha gave no indication that she had anywhere else to go. She accompanied Theo, Chase and Salvador in a taxi to their hotel, which stood among the concrete high-rises in the city centre. Only when she checked herself into a vacant room did it become apparent that, for better or worse, she was remaining with them. The one-time ruler of the Amazons did not deign to divulge why or for how long; she told them she was going upstairs to take a shower and have a rest, and they would meet up for dinner later to discuss things.

"What's her angle?" Chase asked as Sasha disappeared into the elevator. "What does she want?"

"To help?" Theo ventured.

"Then why the damn hell doesn't she say so?"

"Because she has dignity. Or arrogance, which she thinks is dignity."

"I dislike her," Salvador said. "And that has nothing to do with the fact that she and I have history."

"It's got everything to do with the fact that she and you have history," said Chase. "There's no other reason. You nearly killed her for that girdle."

"She nearly killed me too," Salvador retorted. "It was a close-run thing."

"Still, history. She's not the bygones type and neither are you."

"She's seriously upped her game since," said Theo. "She was always badass, but today she barely broke a sweat subduing you two. It was almost indecent, how easy she made it look."

"It wasn't fair." Salvador rubbed the back of his neck, where a large bruise had formed. "She played dirty."

Chase nodded in sympathy. "I could have taken her. I only didn't because you told me not to, Theo."

"Sure, sure."

"It's true. So you reckon it's okay that she continues to tag along with us?"

"I think she could be an asset," Theo said. "I think there are worse people I could have by my side. But," he added, "I think there are better people I could have at my back, if you get my drift."

THEY WENT OUT for dinner as a foursome that night, just as Sasha decreed. Theo saw it as an opportunity to probe her gently and gauge her motives and intentions. The concierge at the hotel recommended a restaurant on the Yenisei embankment with a terrace overlooking the river. "Best Siberian cuisine you will ever eat," he told them, and the food *was* good, especially the beef dumplings and the sturgeon broth, although the aspic-covered meat jelly was more of an acquired taste.

Sasha remained aloof and tight-lipped for much of the evening, but Theo nonetheless managed to prise a few nuggets of information out of her. Currently she ran a personal security service for high net-worth women – business executives, movie stars, supermodels, trophy wives. Based in London, with branches in Los Angeles, Moscow and Dubai, it was called Wonder Women and it supplied close protection details for clients who preferred not to have a hulking male goon hanging around them the whole time. Sasha's employees were skilled in combat and the use of small arms, and were attractive and well groomed and could therefore blend in better with the client's lifestyle. They were inconspicuous, and that made them more effective. Quite often, Sasha said, client and bodyguard formed a personal bond, the latter becoming as much sister as protector, which she found heartening and gratifying.

"So once again you're head of a band of warrior women," Theo said, "only now the title's CEO rather than 'your majesty'."

Sasha was obscurely, royally amused. "Not badly put."

"Don't these Wonder Women of yours need you right now?"

"The company can manage without me for the time being. I have efficient subordinates who know the workings of the business as well as I do. I keep in constant touch. I don't have to be in the office to supervise."

Theo decided to go for broke. "I suppose what I want to know is how long you're –"

At that moment a gaggle of other diners in the restaurant, local young professionals, came up to the demigods' table brandishing phones. Once of them, elected spokesman by the rest, tapped Chase on the shoulder.

"You are Mr Chase Chance? Of the TV show? The man who is doing the monster hunting?"

"Guilty as charged."

"Hey! It is you! I knew it!"

The group begged for selfies, and Chase was only too happy to oblige. He had downed a few vodkas during the course of the meal, so his grin was wide and goofy as he posed with an arm around the youngsters' shoulders, the twilight sky and the broad, burbling river forming a scenic backdrop to the shots. He even put on a good show of cowering in terror as one of the group loomed over him with fingers clawed and a snarling expression like a movie werewolf or vampire. It was all very good-natured and rowdy, and Chase was charged up when it was over.

"See?" he said to Theo. "Happens in Russia too. Anywhere in the world I go. That's properly famous, that is."

"It's the same for me in Mexico," Salvador said, "when I am out with my mask on. They queue up to shake my hand and take a picture. The women – sometimes they can't restrain themselves. The places they grope me!"

Chase wagged his eyebrows at Theo. Theo just rolled his eyes.

"Hey, cuz, I've got an idea." Chase patted his backpack. Inside was the Helm of Darkness. He couldn't bear to be parted from the artefact, now that he had it back. "I'll go the restroom and put the helmet on. Then I'll come back, you wave your hands about above the table, and I'll lift up cutlery and plates and stuff in the air to match your movements, and it'll look like you're a Jedi using the Force."

"No."

"Come on! It'll be hilarious. Can you imagine their faces? They'll freak."

"Still no."

"You can say things like 'I find your lack of faith disturbing' and 'If you strike me down, I shall become more powerful than you can possibly imagine.'"

"Or no."

Chase pouted. "Seems such a wasted opportunity."

"It would draw attention to us that we don't want. Your adoring fans are bad enough. If we start doing parlour tricks…"

"You can always pretend afterwards that you're a stage conjuror."

"Really, it's not going to happen."

"Spoilsport."

"If I have to be."

Chase moped, but not for long. A couple more rounds of vodka saw to that.

Sasha said to Theo, "I presume you have a theory who is carrying out the attacks on us."

"I do."

"You would not be Theseus if you didn't. Care to tell me?"

"Two likely suspects. Harry Gottlieb is one."

"It's always sensible to assume Odysseus has a hidden agenda."

"If it is him, he's playing us even now by sending you to join us. But I don't see what that gets him, other than the pleasure of pushing people around like chess pieces. What is the bigger picture? What's his endgame?"

"Simply messing with us and having us try to second-guess his motives might be enough for him, for now."

"I'd be more certain that Gottlieb was our man if Novy Tolkatui had turned out to be a trap after all. Since it didn't and we got the Helm, it could mean I've misjudged him."

"Or he was using you – us – to obtain the twelfth and final artefact, saving him the effort."

"And then, at his leisure, he can inveigle us into handing it over to him. It's plausible."

"Who's the other suspect?" Sasha asked.

"Evander Arlington. You might know him better as –"

"Oh, I know exactly who Evander Arlington is. I work for him."

Theo was startled and not a little alarmed. "Run that by me again?"

"Not for Arlington himself. I should be more specific. For his wife. She is a Wonder Women client. Has been for several years. Arlington, of course, foots the bill. Keeps us on a handsome retainer. At twelve hours' notice I can have a bodyguard at his wife's side anywhere in the world, wherever and whenever she needs one. He is insanely protective of her, but then that's hardly surprising."

"Why?"

"You don't know who Mrs Evander Arlington is?" Sasha said archly. "And you call yourself a detective!"

"Crimefighter, actually."

"Well, you used to call yourself a detective."

"In another age. Technically I'm not even a crimefighter any more. Just a writer."

"Yes, I've seen your books on sale, chiefly at airport terminal bookshops. Can't say I've been tempted to pick one up."

"So who is Mrs Arlington? Probably some glamorous actress I've never heard of."

"Glamorous yes. Actress? Debatable. In the broadest definition of the word, perhaps. Still not a clue?" Sasha was enjoying his ignorance.

"Chase is the one who seems to know what everyone's up to. He's our resident Demigod Wiki. Chase?"

"Yeah?"

"Who is Evander Arlington married to?"

"No idea. Someone beautiful and high-maintenance, would be my guess. I didn't even know he was married. I thought, like the rest of us, he'd given up on getting too close to mortals. We've all seen so many loved ones grow old and die; who wants to have long-term relationships with them anymore?"

"Amen to that," said Salvador, and he and Chase clinked glasses together, spilling quite a bit of vodka in the process.

"Arlington has got around that issue," said Sasha.

"His wife a sex doll then?" said Chase. "I can see how it might work. Non-perishable rubber. Never wears out. Lifetime guarantee."

He and Salvador roared with laughter.

"No," said Sasha, lip curling in distaste. "He married one of us."

Theo thought fast. Based on Sasha's hints and insinuations, one candidate came to the fore. "Helen."

Sasha rewarded him with a nod that could scarcely have been more patronising. "Helen of Sparta, daughter of Zeus and Leda, sister of Castor, Pollux and Clytemnestra, and wife of Menelaus until her abduction by Paris, which gave her the name she's better known by."

"Helen of Troy," said Salvador.

"And also," Chase said to Theo, "your one-time girlfriend."

Theo shook his head ruefully. "Don't remind me. I've made some mistakes in my time, but..."

"Making off with a girl who'd barely started her monthlies," said Sasha, "while you were in your sixth decade of life?" She sneered. "No, I can't imagine *that* going wrong at all."

THESEUS HAD FALLEN for Helen the very first time he saw her, which was at the temple of Artemis in Laconia, just outside the city of Sparta. In a fit of high spirits, he and his friend Pirithous, King of the Lapiths, had drawn lots to decide which of two divinely sired beauties they would attempt to sleep with. Pirithous had got the short straw: Persephone, wife of Hades. Persephone was loveliness incarnate, with cherubic cheeks and fecund hips, but being married to the god of the Underworld made her by far the greater challenge of the two, and ultimately Pirithous failed dismally. Helen, famous throughout Greece for her astonishing good looks but also young, free and single, had seemed the safer bet, so Theseus was happy to travel to the land of the Spartans and court her.

He had not been prepared for just how remarkable her beauty was. A lightning bolt from Zeus himself could not have left him as staggered and dumbfounded. At the sight of her he felt utterly unmanned, and at the same time aroused to a degree he had never known before. The way her peplos clung to her figure, its folds caressing her curves, its open sides revealing glimpses of her perfect breasts ... The inviting shape her mouth seemed to fall into naturally when at rest ... The strong planes of her cheekbones and coquettish tilt of her chin... Unlike most women of noble birth, Helen eschewed cosmetics. She did not need them. Her lips were red enough on their own, her eyelids naturally smoky, her skin pale and soft.

She moved among the temple's columns, bearing a votive offering of cheese, which she placed beside similar offerings at the feet of the *xoanon*, the wooden effigy of Artemis. Then she took her place among the priestesses and joined them in the *diamastigosis*, in which adolescent males tried to get at the offerings and were driven back by women armed with ceremonial whips. Even the glee and narrow-eyed ferocity with which Helen lashed at the youngsters did not dampen Theseus's ardour; quite the opposite, in fact.

The young men seemed to feel the same. Helen's whipping drove them into a frenzy. They competed with one another to receive blows from her rather than from any of the priestesses. They hurled rivals out of the way for the honour of feeling the bite of her whip, and showed off the bloody weals afterward as badges of pride.

Theseus was soon to discover that Helen's tongue was a vicious as any scourge. Her behaviour at the temple ought to have given him a clue, but he was too smitten with her. He *had* to have her, and so he pursued her relentlessly, in secret, without the knowledge of her adoptive father King Tyndareus. He lavished gifts on her, boasted to her of the life of luxury she would lead at his palace back in Athens, danced to her whims, prostrated himself before her, and promised her anything and everything it was in his power to grant. In hindsight he made a complete fool of himself, but at the time, with lust and adoration raging through him like a lava flow, it all seemed sensible and appropriate and right, the only way to be.

She succumbed in the end, and agreed to go with him to Athens. They stole off from Laconia one night and he installed her in his palace as though she were the greatest prize a man could ever win.

What a bitch she turned out to be.

For perhaps three weeks their life together was bliss. They made love at least three times a day, sometimes twice as often as that, and Theseus had never known such ecstasy. The feel of her was like silk. The scent of her was like perfume. The taste of her was like ambrosia.

Then she became demanding. The sex tailed off; she shrank from his touch. She wanted more slaves, more jewellery, more clothing. Better food. Better wine.

Theseus complied, of course. Anything to keep his Helen happy. The bliss lingered, still just tangible, within sight, recapturable. There were moments when he could kid himself that nothing was wrong and that she was as passionate about him as he was about her. He believed that the squalls she brought to the household would pass, and balmy sunshine would return.

But then she started casually beating servants. She had a slave flogged within an inch of his life for the crime of dropping a dish of olives. A cook was branded with his own iron tongs for making her a cup of goat's milk too hot to sip. A gardener was dismissed for pruning a shrub back too far for her liking.

Theseus could not let her get away with this. He prided himself on the unusual decency with which he treated his domestic staff, and Helen had offended his sense of fair play.

He was unable to bring himself to hit her. Most other men in his position, in that day and age, would have, but he did not even scold her. Instead he tried to reason with her. He implored her to stop abusing and upsetting the servants.

The result? A blistering hour-long diatribe from Helen, full of insults and swearing, followed by a sulk of epic proportions that lasted well over a week. No amount of blandishment could jolly her out of it; all the begging in the world could not pry her from her bedchamber.

The affair – because Theseus now saw that that was all this was, an affair, not the glorious eternal union he had thought it would be – limped on for another couple of months. There were brief reconciliations between longer and longer bouts of bitter, stony estrangement. He became increasingly disenchanted with Helen and resigned to the idea that she would have to go. Seldom did she have a kind word to say to him. Mostly she called his masculinity into question and complained that he was not the person he had made himself out to be back in Laconia.

Then her brothers Castor and Pollux came from Sparta to retrieve her, and they did not arrive a moment too soon. They thundered into Athens with a retinue of hoplites and cavalry, threatening war and retribution. It was widely believed in Laconia that Helen had been taken by Theseus against her will, much as had been the case with Melanippe and the Amazons. Theseus, however, was able to convince the twins otherwise, and that he was only too willing for them to take Helen back home. To sweeten the deal, he gave them fifty head of cattle, a hundred amphorae of wine, and sackloads of gold and ivory. He did not consider this too high a price to pay for getting rid of her.

"Look at that damn face," said Salvador, breaking in on Theo's reverie of reminiscence. "So sour. There's a man who knows how it feels to be screwed over by a woman."

"It was not," Theo admitted, "my finest hour. In my defence I will say that at least I didn't start a ten-year war over her that cost thousands of lives. The only one who really suffered on my account was yours truly. And now Evander Arlington has her in his life?" He gave a hollow laugh. "I almost feel sorry for the old bastard."

"She is difficult still," said Sasha. "I can't say Hélène Arlington – she pronounces her name the French way nowadays – is my favourite client. Some of my Wonder Women work for her once and refuse to do so ever again. The more robust ones can handle her, though, and are compensated accordingly. No one could accuse her husband of being ungenerous. But it all begs the question, why would Evander Arlington be killing other demigods? What leads you to that conclusion, Theo?"

Theo explained about the record of artefact locations Odysseus had left with King Minos. "That's all I've got to go on so far. If I could just find Arlington to speak to him, then I might be able to eliminate him as a suspect, or otherwise. That's generally what we've been hoping to do. This trip to Russia has just been a detour. And…" He looked at Sasha levelly. "Now that we've met you, it looks like we have an 'in' with him. Which is fortunate." He almost said *fortuitous*.

"You'd like me to set up a meeting with Arlington, via his wife?"

"You're in contact with her, aren't you?"

"I have ways to get in touch with her."

"Bingo. Then you're the man for the job."

"Woman for the job."

"That's what I said. Would you? Pretty please?"

TWENTY-THREE

Airspace above the eastern Mediterranean

THE EMBRAER LEGACY 650 tipped its wings and banked to starboard, veering away from the setting sun in a smooth arc. Holger Badenhorst, closing the cockpit door behind him, turned to face the cabin. With three of them dead and Corbett and Mayson invalided out, eleven Myrmidons remained. He cleared his throat and waited until he had their attention. The last of them to look his way was Roy Young, and there was death in the Englishman's stare. If looks could kill…

Well, tough shit, my friend. Feel about me how you like, I have you by the balls and you know it.

"Ladies and gentlemen," he said. "You'll have noticed we have just made a significant course correction. We aren't heading for the States any more. I've received new instructions from our employer. The American mission has been postponed. We're going for someone different."

"Where?" said Gunnvor Blomgren.

"Russia."

"Shee-it," said Travis Laffoon. "Russia?"

"You sound aggrieved, Laffoon," said Hans Schutkeker, from three rows behind. "Have you ever been to Russia?"

"No, but I ain't heard one damn good thing about the place. I was looking forward to stepping foot on US soil again, getting some decent down-home grub inside me. Russia? They got nothing there. No food, no money, no cars."

"I think you will find it's not as bad as that," said Schutkeker.

"I think you'll find I don't give a rat's ass about your opinion, Shitkicker."

The German sprang from his. "All right, that's it. I have had all I can stomach from you, you mouth-breathing moron."

"Mouth-breathing moron? Oh, snap! I need some lotion for this *burn*."

Schutkeker lumbered down the aisle, hands outstretched, and the Louisianan reared up to meet him.

Roy rose between them.

"Sit down," he said, his voice soft. "Both of you. Sit back down right now."

Both Laffoon and Schutkeker tried to shove past him to get at each other.

All at once Roy had both of them by the throat, his fingertips digging hard into their windpipes.

"Do as I say, or so help me I will throttle the life out of you."

He looked left and right, holding each man's gaze for several seconds.

He was not kidding. There was a dark and hideous glint in his eyes. The Myrmidons were all killers, but Roy Young, at that moment, was a stone-cold murderer.

"Hey, hey, we're all tired," Badenhorst said, moving down the aisle. "Crossing all these time zones. Don't know whether it's *blerrie* night or day." He laid a hand on Laffoon's shoulder, but his focus was on Roy. He had to keep the tone light; the standoff had the potential to go very wrong. "Tempers start to fray. There's friction, especially with all the forceful personalities we have here. Only to be expected. Let's just back down, *nè*? All of us. Got a long flight ahead, seven hours plus. Probably this is the time to get some shuteye so we're nice and rested for work tomorrow. How about it?"

"Yes, how about it?" said Roy to Laffoon and Schutkeker. "I'm going to let you both go, on the understanding that if there is any more of this bollocks between you, I will take it personally, and you will not like that."

Laffoon and Schutkeker nodded.

Roy released them.

They retired to their seats, sullen as scolded schoolchildren.

Badenhorst leaned in and said in Roy's ear, "Good job. Asserting your authority. I told you you're the leader."

"Glad to be of service," Roy replied coolly.

Badenhorst mentally translated that as *fuck you*, and fixed the Englishman with a huge smile.

As he strode back to his seat, the Afrikaner felt pleased. If Roy could channel into the Myrmidons' remaining missions the same deadly energy he had just brought to defusing the row between Laffoon and Schutkeker, then success was assured. Badenhorst had had his qualms about kidnapping Josie Young, but now he was certain it had been the right move. His employer had taken some persuading; but Roy was becoming a loose cannon, and Badenhorst had managed to re-secure him, and all was cool. All was hundreds.

The jet hurtled eastward, into the gathering dusk.

TWENTY-FOUR

Krasnoyarsk

ONCE AGAIN, CHASE wanted to go on a monster hunt.

"It's like an addiction with you," Theo said, after his cousin announced at breakfast that he fancied another expedition into the wild to track down a local semi-mythical beast. "You can't leave it alone."

"What can I say? I'm a creature of habit, and my habit is creatures."

Salvador chuckled, sipping ferociously strong black tea. "See what he did there? Wordplay. Clever."

"Maybe," said Theo, "but wandering the countryside is less clever."

"Why not?" said Chase. "We've got time to kill, and let's face it, Krasnoyarsk isn't exactly party city. Half an hour by hire car and we can be out in the back of beyond. You know the Stolby Nature Reserve? The place the helicopter pilots mentioned, with the rock formations? It's got several rivers running through it, including the Bazhaika. Up there last year there was a sighting of a vodyanoy."

"A what?" said Salvador.

"Water elemental. Looks like an old man but with webbed fingers, long green hair and a frog's face. You don't want to piss one off.

They've been known to sink dinghies and rowing boats and drag people into the water to drown. This guy claims he encountered one while fishing on the banks of the Bazhaika. It grabbed his line and tried to reel him in, and he let go of the rod and ran like a son of a bitch to his pickup. Only just got away, he said, and he was so terrified that he drove the truck into a tree on the way home."

"What's the betting he'd been drinking?" said Theo.

"That's what the cops who arrested him thought. And I'll be honest, he did fail the breathalyser."

"Of course he did."

"But the police report said he seemed genuinely shit-scared. He stuck to his story and wouldn't be shaken from it. He'd had a run-in with an amphibious monster."

"Okay," said Theo. "Maybe there is a vodyanoy out there. But there's *also* someone out there who appears determined to wipe us out. We're being hunted too."

"Weren't they supposed to have got us yesterday, these demigod slayers, in Novy Tolkatui? Wasn't that their golden opportunity?"

"I just feel we shouldn't push our luck."

"Oh, come on. What harm can it do? It'll only be a few hours. I'm bored, and I could do with letting off some steam. Plus, I've got the you-know-what." He pointed to his backpack, by his side as ever, with the Helm snug within. "How can they find me if they can't see me?"

"I want to go too," said Salvador. "Sounds like fun. I haven't confronted a monster in I can't remember how long. It's as much in my nature as it is in Chase's. Defeating chthonic creatures, that's my specialty, and this one sounds like one."

Sasha had arrived in the hotel dining room in time to catch the tail end of the conversation. "Why not let them, Theo?" she said, helping herself to scrambled eggs, kolbasa sausage and blinis from the buffet. "If they're so keen."

"Because I don't think it's a good idea, that's why. We shouldn't make life easy for our enemies."

"Can you be sure our enemies are even here in Russia?"

"I can't. But if Gottlieb knows where we are, it's a possibility we shouldn't discount. Did you get hold of Evander Arlington, by the way?"

"Not yet. I've left a message on Hélène Arlington's voicemail, and emailed her for good measure. She isn't always terribly quick responding, if it doesn't suit her. Conversely, she hates it if you don't answer a request from her immediately. She is imperious in her ways."

Takes one to know one, Theo thought.

"I'll try a follow-up call if I don't hear back from her by lunchtime," Sasha added. "Best I can do."

"Appreciated."

"So?" said Chase. "Not that I have to have your permission, cuz, but can me and Salvador go on a vodyanoy hunt? Is it okay with you, 'Dad'?"

"Why not accompany them, Theo?" Sasha suggested. "If you're worried they might run into trouble, wouldn't it be better if you're there too? Safety in numbers, and so on."

"Yeah, awesome idea," said Chase. He clasped his hands together like a child begging for a treat. "C'mon, Theo. Please? *Pleeease?* I'll do my chores and make my bed and, and..."

Theo had misgivings.

But then, he always did. These days, it seemed he couldn't be certain about anything.

Sasha's argument had merit, at least. The three of them together were a formidable proposition. Theseus, Perseus and Heracles. You'd have to be crazy to tackle that trio all at once. Even an Olympian god, were any still active, might think twice about taking them on.

"In no way enthusiastically," Theo said, "all right."

TWENTY-FIVE

Stolby Nature Reserve, Krai region, near Krasnoyarsk

THE ROCK PILLARS – *stolby*, in Russian – which gave the national park its name were soaring projections of mottled-grey volcanic syenite. They thrust up above the treetops, some stepped and pyramidal like ziggurats, others sheer and columnar and arranged in ranks like skyscrapers. They were stone islands amid a sea of dark green taiga.

The great majority of the nature reserve's 47,000 hectares was closed to the public, restricted to park rangers only. That did not deter Chase. For a time he led Theo and Salvador along the marked paths, like good little tourists. Once they were well away from the car park and the crowds, however, he struck off into the forest, setting up a jogging pace which his two companions dutifully matched.

They covered several miles at speed, forging across undulating terrain. They skirted areas of swamp, leapt streams and waded through shallow rivulets. The dense fir canopy provided shade from the broiling sun. Startled ground squirrels fled from their approach. Musk deer bucked into the undergrowth. A saker falcon shadowed them from above for a while, before losing interest and wheeling away.

As they paused to rehydrate, Chase consulted his phone's GPS map. "Bazhaika river's about three more miles thataway," he said. "We walk from here on. I'm the pro, so pay attention to me. If I say stop, stop. If I say shut up, shut up. Tread softly at all times. I don't know how skittish vodyanoys are, but I'm not taking any chances. If ours hears us come crashing through the woods, it might just scare him off before we can get within range."

Drenched in sweat from running, they resumed their journey, ambling now but alert.

Soon the noise of a great smooth river was audible and there was the smell of fresh water in the air. Chase slowed further, his head swivelling left and right. Theo noted how serious his cousin had become. Gone was the habitual facetiousness, the perennial easygoing smile. Chase was listening intently, watching like a hawk, his nose raised to catch the breeze. His movements were fluid and economical, his footsteps light and graceful. This was him in his element. This was Perseus in pursuit of quarry. It was riveting to behold.

All at once Chase's hand shot up. Theo and Salvador went stock still. Chase prowled forward a few paces in a half crouch. They were very near the river now; Theo could see its tawny glint ahead through the trees, like a road paved with topaz.

Chase motioned for Theo and Salvador to stay put. Then, slowly, painstakingly, he unshouldered his backpack and extracted a combat knife, which he snugged into his belt. Delving into the backpack again, he brought out the Helm of Darkness.

The moment the helmet appeared, Theo became conscious of the vibration it gave off, a sombre thrum that you felt rather than heard, like a subsonic note.

The three Uranian Cyclopes – Brontes, Steropes and Arges – had forged the Helm for Hades as a thank-you gift for his part in freeing them from captivity during the Titanomachy, the war between the gods and the rebel Titans. Hades had then infused it with his own dark numen, to create the invisibility-bestowing item of apparel it was now. He had lent it to Perseus to aid him on his quest to kill the Gorgon Medusa and thus fulfil a somewhat rash promise to the brother of his adoptive father, King Polydectes, who had believed it would be a suicide mission and would leave the way clear for him to seduce Perseus's mother Danaë. In addition Perseus had been bequeathed various other handy items: a polished shield from Athena, which he used as a mirror to guide him to Medusa and avoid direct line of sight with her literally petrifying gaze; a *kibisis*, a magic carrying-bag, from some nymphs, in which he stowed the Gorgon's decapitated head; and a sickle and a pair of winged sandals from Hermes. Shield, *kibisis* and sandals had all been handed back after the quest was completed, but the Helm and the sickle Perseus had retained, until the day Odysseus had proposed his divine weapons amnesty.

Chase lodged the helmet on his head and almost instantly shimmered out of sight. He padded off. Theo was able to track his progress only by the slight disturbances in the layer of pine needles on the forest floor, and soon he could no longer even see them. Chase was gone.

Theo and Salvador stood like statues for several minutes.

"This is ridiculous," Salvador said eventually. "Does he expect us to stay put and not move a muscle the whole time 'til he comes back?"

"Shh," said Theo. "Dial it down."

"But are we here to help him or not?" Salvador said, marginally more quietly. "Is he going to catch this vodyanoy thing all by himself? Won't we be allowed to share in the glory?"

"He's probably not thinking of anything right now except bagging his beast."

"He's forgotten about us?"

"You saw him – how laser-focused he got. We're nothing more than a distraction to him now. Not even that."

"Well, this has been a waste of our time, then, hasn't it? I was hoping at the very least that I'd be grappling the vodyanoy to the ground, perhaps pinning it in place so that Chase could finish it off. And what happens? I'm left standing around like a lemon while he goes off and has all the fun. This..." He groped for the word. "This *sucks*."

Theo suppressed a smile. The look of petulant disappointment on Salvador's face was almost laughable.

Something shifted.

It was barely perceptible. A zephyr-like waft in the air, a whisper of movement.

Theo's hackles rose.

"Move!" he yelled at Salvador.

The muscled giant was slightly slow off the mark, but he moved nonetheless, breaking out of his static pose, lunging forward.

An arrow thunked into the tree trunk right next to him and quivered there, sticking out like a new-grown branch.

Theo and Salvador scrambled downslope towards the river.

Another arrow whizzed between them, past them, arcing down to land with a *plop* in the Bazhaika's shallows.

The two demigods reached the river's edge a moment later. Theo Chanced a look behind him.

People were coming through the trees.

Paramilitaries.

Padded body armour. Crested battle helmets. Their bodies garlanded with guns and grenades.

Some of them carried older, more basic weapons. An axe. A trident. A sword. A spear.

Theo glimpsed a patch on their upper sleeves. An insignia. The letter M.

He had no idea what the M actually represented, but right then and there, as far as he was concerned, it stood for Murder.

GUNFIRE.

Bullets whined and buzzed all around them.

Theo and Salvador were sprinting along the river's muddy shore.

Salvador had wanted to go on the offensive. At first sight of the paramilitaries he had puffed up his chest, stuck out his arms and bellowed defiance.

But then the paramilitaries had pulled and cocked pistols, and Theo had seized Salvador's wrist and yanked him away. He had sized up the opposition and known immediately what their tactic was going to be: cripple him and Salvador with bullets first, then deploy the ancient handweapons to finish the job.

Those weapons were divine artefacts, there was no question about it. They radiated numen. The paramilitaries were the killers, and they were out in force.

Inwardly Theo cursed Chase. Foolhardy idea, going monster hunting somewhere so isolated and remote. Asking for trouble. His cousin should have known better, and he, Theo, should have put his foot down.

He and Salvador soon put a safe distance between them and their attackers. They arrived at a bend in the river and abandoned the shore for the sanctuary of the forest. They ran on for a few hundred metres more until Theo became aware that Salvador was flagging.

"Can't slow down now," he said. "Dig deep. Keep going."

"I would," came the reply, "but my leg and back say otherwise."

"What do you – ?"

Blood was leaking down Salvador's jeans. More blood spilled from his midriff, soaking his shirt.

"I've been shot," Salvador said. "Didn't realise until a moment ago, when the adrenaline wore off and the pain finally kicked in. Didn't even feel the impacts. They got me. One's in the damn butt cheek, what's more. The ignominy."

"Okay. Okay. But you can still run. Grit your teeth and work through it. You're a demigod. We're built to take punishment."

Salvador attempted a few steps, but stumbled to his knees.

"Fuck! Fucking fuck!"

"Arm around my shoulder," Theo said, proffering himself. "I can take your weight."

"Have you seen how big I am?"

"No arguing. I'm strong."

They forged on together through the trees, side by side, Theo supporting, Salvador limping. Behind them Theo could hear footfalls, low voices exchanging observations, the clank of gunmetal. The paramilitaries were in pursuit, and from the snippets of conversation he could make out, they knew they had winged one of their targets. He even overheard a comment from one of them about picking up a trail of fresh blood. "Piece of cake, following them now," the person said.

Under normal circumstances he and Salvador could have outrun the paramilitaries without any difficulty. No human could match a demigod's speed, or a demigod's stamina. Going full tilt, they could have left their attackers far behind in their wake and kept up the pace for a full hour before needing to slacken off.

As it was, they were moving at not much above a brisk stroll. The paramilitaries were gaining on them.

A granite boulder loomed ahead, the size of a large car. Theo steered himself and Salvador into its lee. He lowered Salvador to a sitting position. Salvador, wincing, perched at an awkward angle with one buttock slightly off the ground.

"Let me take a gander at those wounds."

The damage to Salvador's backside looked painful. A sizeable chunk of flesh had been torn away. As for the bullet hole in his back, Theo reckoned the round had nicked his ribs and perforated his colon. It was the less immediately debilitating of the two injuries, but the one he would take longer to recover from.

"We can't stay here," Salvador said. "They're coming."

"We can't go on either, not with you hobbling like that. They're going to catch up with us either way. Our best bet is to hole up here, let them pass, and then head back the way we came."

"That won't work. They'll spot us. We're hardly hidden from view, are we?"

"If we're lucky…"

Salvador shook his head. "In another age, I might have prayed to the gods to preserve us. And they would have answered, no doubt, unless my father's wife was in one of her moods."

"We can't call on them now. We have to rely on ourselves. I just hope Chase is okay, wherever he's got to."

"I'm sure my grandfather is fine. With his Helm of Darkness, he'll have been able to elude them. As for us, there's only one sensible option." Salvador hauled himself to his feet, using the boulder for leverage. "No point in us both dying when one of us can help the other live."

"Salvador, no."

The sturdy giant stooped to pick up a fallen fir branch, as long as a baseball bat and twice as thick.

"Not quite my warclub of old," he said, hefting it, "but it'll do in a pinch."

"Don't do this. Really. We can still –"

"Theseus. You don't mind if I call you that? For old times' sake? Theseus, you must run now. Run like you've never run before. Get out of here and survive. I'm asking this of you because you're the one who can prevent them killing any more of us. You can get to the bottom of this affair and end it."

"No. I mean yes, I can. I think I can. But it'll be easier with you backing me up, Heracles."

"Not going to happen. Listen. They're very near now."

They were. The paramilitaries were, by Theo's estimation, no more than a couple of hundred metres away, and closing in rapidly. They were moving in a line, stretched out through the forest like a net.

"I can provide a distraction," Salvador said. "Buy you time. You have to get away, rendezvous with Chase, regroup, retrench, and then destroy these fuckers. Kill every last one of them. For me. I will count it a personal favour. Promise?"

Theo's mouth had gone dry. His eyes stung. "Promise."

"We had some times, didn't we?" Salvador said with a smile that did not seem forced. "Our exploits will live on, even if we don't. Fighting, feasting and fornicating. I always thought, if I went out, I'd go out doing one of those things. Now it looks like I am. I'd have preferred feasting or fornicating, perhaps, but if this is the way it has to be…"

He stepped out from behind the boulder, brandishing his makeshift club.

"Come on, you bastards," he called out. "Here I am. Come and get me."

There was a rush, a hiss.

Now an arrow was protruding from Salvador's meaty pectoral muscle.

"Is that all you've got?"

A second arrow whizzed into him, piercing his thigh clean through.

He staggered but regained his poise, and strode on towards the paramilitaries.

Theo turned and began loping off in the opposite direction, pausing after a few steps to look back.

Gun reports rippled. A hail of bullets came Salvador's way. He was hit two, three, four times. He tottered on, remorseless.

One of the paramilitaries hurtled into the open, swinging a sword.

Salvador swept the man aside with a bludgeoning blow from his fir-branch club. The paramilitary flew through the air like a toy. He hit a tree trunk head first, with neck-snapping force, but was probably dead already, chest stove in and heart crushed as soon as Salvador struck him.

"Who's next?" Salvador shouted, coughing blood. "Who wants some?"

He trudged onward, but then all at once crumpled, as though his legs had been cut from under him. He sprawled prone on the forest floor, the arrows snapping beneath his weight. The club rolled from his grasp.

He forced himself to his hands and knees but couldn't get any further. He was crimson all over with blood.

"This is not fair," he murmured. "This is not how it should be at all. You –"

More bullets thudded into him.

Theo was sickened. It wasn't even murder any more. It was slaughter.

He felt an almost overwhelming impulse to go to Salvador's side. He couldn't simply let his friend – his kin, his companion in adventure – be hacked to pieces by these animals. Every cell in his body cried out at him to defend Salvador, help him, save him.

But he knew, if he did, he would most likely wind up dead too. His overriding imperative was to make sure Salvador wasn't sacrificing *his* life in vain. That meant leaving him to his grisly fate.

It was the hardest thing Theo had ever had to do, turning away. His final glimpse of Salvador – Heracles – etched itself into his memory. He resolved, on the spot, never to forget it. He wanted it crystal clear in his mind, so that next time he faced these paramilitaries – and there would *be* a next time, and it would be at his initiative, not theirs – he would have fuel to keep the fires of retribution well-stoked.

The paramilitaries had Salvador surrounded. There were a half-dozen of them. The one carrying a trident hoisted it above his head, prongs downward.

It was a trident very much like Poseidon's own, that symbol of authority with which the sea god could trigger earthquakes and shatter rocks to make springs of water flow forth. This one, smaller but otherwise identical, had been gifted to one of Poseidon's many half-human sons; Theo could not remember which one. At this moment, it hardly mattered. What mattered was that the trident was lethal. To anyone, but above all to a demigod.

Theo didn't stay to watch the trident descend, but he heard it. The wet *thunk* of the prongs piercing flesh, a scream which trailed off into a gurgling choke. Silence.

The forest became a blur around him. He was aware he was running, but just that. The rest was a welter of grief and rage.

IT WAS PERHAPS a minute later that he found himself once more at the river's edge and stopped to take his bearings. When he and Salvador had made their bid to escape from the paramilitaries, they had headed downstream, with the water's flow. It made sense for him to continue in that direction, so that he would be moving away from the enemy, not towards – although he was sorely tempted to go straight back and just lay into the paramilitaries, punching them, strangling them, breaking their limbs, taking as many of them as he could with him before they inevitably finished him off.

On his own, it would have been a suicide run. Had Chase been with him, he might have given it serious consideration. They would, at worst, give the the killers something to think about. At best, they'd wipe the floor with the lot of them.

Damn his cousin, wandering off like that when he did. Talk about irresponsible.

As he prepared to set off again alongside the river, Theo spied movement at the periphery of his vision.

He wheeled round.

There was someone lurking amid the trees, in a patch of shadow.

"Chase?"

The dim, silhouetted figure moved out into the light: one of the paramilitaries.

Without hesitating, without even thinking, Theo charged at him. The man raised both hands above his head.

"Stop," he said.

Theo skidded to a halt, inches from the man. He could, if he wanted to, smash his fist into his face, shatter his skull like an eggshell. He wouldn't even see the blow coming.

"You're Theo Stannard," the paramilitary said. He had an English accent. Not a Londoner's, but close to it. Estuary English, was it called?

"So what if I am?"

"You're the author."

"And you, pal, are a dead man. You and your cronies just killed one of my oldest friends back there, so you'd better give me a damn good reason why I shouldn't rip your head off and —"

"I surrender."

Theo frowned. "Say again?"

"I surrender. Take me prisoner. But do it quick. The others know I'm on your tail, but I'm maintaining radio silence. They don't know I've caught up with you and they're not worried about me yet. Not if their comms chatter's anything to go by. They're busy setting up a perimeter around your friend's body. As far as they're concerned, I've gone ahead solo to scout for you, see if I can't flush you back towards them. You're a loose end. If they don't hear from me in five minutes or thereabouts, they're going to start wondering whether I'm okay. At least two of them will come looking for me. I am no threat to you. I just want to talk. I want some answers."

Theo studied the Englishman's face. The guy was sincere; every instinct he had was telling him that. It wasn't a trick. The Englishman really was surrendering. He really did want to talk.

Still, Theo's desire to kill him was almost unendurable, a primal urge. Blood called for blood. It had been that way back in the Age of Heroes. You killed those who killed your kin, to restore the balance, to right the injustice. Theo could snuff out the Englishman's life and feel not so much as a twinge of conscience. The cold-blooded murder of Heracles demanded nothing less.

On the other hand…

Theo wanted some answers too.

Tamping down the white-hot loathing that seethed inside him, he said, "Okay. You've got five minutes. Talk."

TWENTY-SIX

Banks of the Bazhaika River

"OKAY. YOU'VE GOT five minutes. Talk."

Roy lowered his hands a fraction.

"No," said Theo Stannard. "Keep those up high. The further they are from your sidearm, the better – for you."

Solemnly, obediently, Roy lifted his hands back where they had been.

He still could not quite believe what he was doing, the risk he was taking. Had the man before him been anyone but Theo Stannard, he wouldn't even have contemplated approaching him. When he'd caught sight of Stannard's face as the Myrmidons were homing in on their target, he had been stunned. He had recognised him from the publicity headshot on his Amazon author page. Why was Stannard, of all people, accompanying the target, Salvador Vega? What connection did he have to the big bearded *luchador*? Roy had to find out. There was, he felt, something about this situation that he might be able to use to his advantage.

"I've read one of your Jake Killian books," Roy said.

"So? You a fan?"

"That's irrelevant."

"Not a fan, then."

"My point being, I reckon you're someone I can reach out to, maybe even trust. You're also someone who may well be able to explain what's going on here."

"You got that from reading my novel?"

"Writers reveal a lot about themselves in their writing, without always meaning to. The author of the Jake Killian series strikes me as a moral person."

Stannard looked at him askance. "Which one?"

"Huh?"

"Which Jake Killian?"

"*Killian's Rage*. Third in the series, I think. Does it matter?"

"Just curious. Asking myself if there's anything special about that one, anything that particularly screams 'trustworthy'. Can't think of anything."

"It's the main character. The protagonist. A bad man trying to do good. A black knight turned white. I suppose, in a way, I identify with that."

"You're part of a paramilitary unit that's going around killing people."

"It's complicated," said Roy.

"I'll bet it is. So is this a book club? Are we spending this truce discussing my fiction, or are we using it to get some shit sorted out? Who are you, anyway? Give me a name."

"Roy Young."

"From the UK?"

"Yes. And who are you?"

"You know that."

"No." Roy put some force into his voice, as much as he dared. "Who are you really? Who is the Theo Stannard who I've just watched run three times faster than an Olympic sprinter? Who *are* these people, who have such speed and strength and endurance? In fact, the question I should be asking is *what* are you?"

"And maybe the question *I* should be asking," Stannard retorted, "is who's sent you after us? And where did you get those weapons you're using? Not the guns, the other ones. The old-fashioned ones."

"Who's sent us? I can honestly say I don't know."

"That's convenient."

"I mean it. I know who I answer to, but he's just a middle man. He answers to someone else, and who *that* is I have no clue. As for the weapons" – Roy shrugged – "we've been given them, instructed to kill our targets with them. Don't know why; no one's told us. Above my pay grade, as they say. I have some theories, but they're vague."

"Go on."

"At first I thought the weapons were symbolic," said Roy, "although I couldn't figure out what of. Now I reckon they have some direct relevance to you and your kind. They're the only things that can really hurt you. They're your – at the risk of sounding daft – kryptonite. Like stakes and crucifixes to vampires. Which leads me to wonder…"

Roy was almost embarrassed to carry on. If he hadn't seen the things he'd seen, the things that Daniel Munro had been capable of, the things Vega and Stannard had shown they could do …

"*Are* you vampires?"

Stannard snorted a laugh. "Yeah, no."

"Standing out in broad daylight like this," Roy said. "Obviously you're not. I just thought maybe the legends didn't tell the whole story, or else you're a new breed of vampire, resistant to the sun, or…"

Stannard stared at him.

"Forget it. Forget I said anything at all. But you definitely have this whole superhuman aspect to you. I'm not wrong about that, am I?"

"We're… different," said Stannard. "It's complicated."

"Government experiment? Advanced black-budget military programme? Genetically enhanced super-soldiers? Am I even in the right ballpark?"

"Why does it matter to you?"

"Normally it wouldn't. Normally this would just be a job to me and I couldn't give two shits who my targets were or what sort of people, or why I'm being paid to kill them. Now, though, I'm feeling used and manipulated. The contract doesn't sit right with me at all. It's not my habit to worry about this sort of thing: don't judge, don't question, just do. But I can't help thinking I'm somehow on the wrong side of this fight. For the first time in my career I have the impression that whoever I'm working for is someone I really shouldn't be. As if to prove it, they've started blackmailing me in order to keep me under their thumb."

"My heart bleeds."

"I'm not asking for sympathy. In my line of work you do deals with wankers all the time. Goes with the territory. You should expect the occasional back-stab. But there's more. I've never before been made to feel that I'm a henchman. That grates. Like I'm one of those disposable goons in a James Bond movie whose sole purpose is to throw themselves at the hero and get mown down."

"Still not exactly tugging at my heartstrings, Mr Young. Mowing you down is something I would deeply love to do right this minute."

"Hear me out, Stannard," Roy said. "What I'm trying to say is that I'm not innocent, God knows, but nor am I the villain of the piece. My boss's boss is. He or she is sending us Myrmidons against a group of people whose have exceptional abilities or powers or I don't know what, and it strikes me that we're going after an endangered species. White tigers, snow leopards, mountain gorillas, that sort of thing. Rare creatures on the brink of extinction."

"No one's ever described me as rare before," said Stannard. "Or endangered."

"Far as I'm concerned, you're both. Someone really seems to have it in for you and your kind. They're throwing a ton of money at eradicating you."

"To the extent of having bespoke Hellenic-style helmets made for their private army of assassins. And is that what the 'M' on the arm is for – Myrmidons?"

"Yes. Ant soldiers. So's we know just where we sit on the scale of importance."

"Myrmidons were well-respected, back in ancient times. Brave, feared in battle. I'm not saying that to boost your ego, just stating a fact."

"Do you have any idea who you might have pissed off so badly that they want you dead?"

"Me personally? I could name a couple of people, perhaps. But us as a group? My 'kind,' as you put it? Who would want us *all* dead?" Stannard rubbed the back of his neck. "Again, I could name a couple of people, but it's still a puzzler. I just can't see what the benefit is. *Cui bono*, as the lawyers say. It means –"

"I know what it means. 'Who benefits?'"

Stannard eyed him with surprise and a glimmer of curiosity.

"I may be a henchman," said Roy, "but I'm not brainless."

"So I see. Are you the only one among you Myrmidons who's uneasy like this? Are you the sole bearer of a conscience?"

"So far, none of the others seems bothered. If they've realised we're up against superhumans, they don't care. I haven't canvassed opinions, but the general mood is that as long as we're getting paid in the end, you lot could be green tentacled Martians and it wouldn't matter."

"Your colleagues aren't as smart as you."

"Oh, they're all pretty smart." Roy thought of Travis Laffoon. "Almost all."

"Then they're less observant."

"Or can compartmentalise better. But I think it's beginning to dawn on them, even so, that there's something unusual going on."

"Do you think you can use that to your advantage?"

"In what way?"

"Well…" Stannard took a step back, so that he was no longer in Roy's face. "Let's say you and I may be able to find some sort of common interest."

"You mean apart from me having read one of your novels?"

"Was that a joke?"

"It was trying to be."

"Then don't do it again. I am still only an inch away from ending you. But if we can both agree that we aren't actually enemies, then perhaps we can be useful to each other."

"I like the sound of this," Roy said. He was thinking of Josie. Since her kidnapping, he had been preoccupied with his daughter. Barely anything else mattered. Theo Stannard might prove a valuable ally; certainly a powerful one. With his help, his knowledge, there might be a way for Roy to apply leverage on Badenhorst and get the Afrikaner to reveal where Josie was. That or he could enlist Stannard himself to look for and rescue her. This – something like this – was why Roy had thrown himself on Stannard's mercy in the first place. It had been a desperate measure, but these were desperate times. "Go on."

"What if," Stannard said, "you could turn the other Myrmidons? Bring them round to your way of thinking?"

"Tall order."

"But...?"

"Doable. I can think of at least two of them I could make headway with. Get them on side, and the rest might fall in line. You want me to start a revolution within the team?"

"It would degrade the Myrmidons' effectiveness and give us an edge."

"If I were to do that..." Roy began.

"You'd expect something in return. Of course. Such as?"

Roy was about to answer when he felt something snaking around his neck: an arm, heavily muscled. But the crazy thing was he could see nothing there. There was fabric pressing against his skin, warmth from another's flesh, and his clawing hands found solid flesh to grab onto – but whoever had seized hold of him from behind was invisible. Was *not there*.

Even as his mind attempted to fathom the anomaly, the arm applied pressure. Intolerable, choking pressure. Roy had already had Daniel Munro try to strangle him once recently. Now someone was doing it again.

Stannard's expression showed confusion, which rapidly became alarm. Roy heard him shout, "Chase, no! Don't!" But it sounded as though his voice was coming from deep within a hurricane. Everything for Roy was a churn and a roar and a thunder.

And an abrupt, engulfing blackness.

TWENTY-SEVEN

Location Unkown

IT OUGHT TO have been a Black Day. The days preceding it had been Black Days, very Black, but today it seemed as though something had given way inside Josie, like a plank breaking under too much weight, and she was just empty.

Give it a name, she heard Dr Aeschbacher say inside her head. *Give it a colour*.

But it had no colour, this nothingness, this lack of caring.

So it was White.

A new kind of day.

A White Day.

The room where she was being held prisoner was beautiful. The ceiling had leaf patterns moulded into its plasterwork. The walls had marble panels. The floor was laid with carpet so thick it was like a mattress. The upholstery on the furniture was silk brocade, the wooden parts painted gold. The bed was a handsome oak four-poster. There was a vast mirror above the fireplace and a glistening glass chandelier overhead. Josie had never stayed anywhere so ostentatiously, opulently rich. If only she were here of her own free will. If only she was not a prisoner in this gilded cage.

The room was part of a large suite; that much she had been able to work out. It was either an apartment or belonged to a swish, exclusive hotel. Double doors led to a living area, where her jailers resided. They were on guard duty in there, and seemed to spend most of their time watching football. All day long the TV blared the cheers and boos of stadium crowds, a sound that rose and fell like waves crashing on a beach. Every so often they would switch to a music-video channel for a change, or else porn, but generally it was football. From the way they yelled at the screen, the games seemed to exasperate them more than bring them enjoyment. The players on the pitch were, to a man, cripples and incompetents, except when one of them scored a goal, which elevated him to godlike status.

Josie caught only glimpses of the jailers, who all communicated in English with a variety of accents, most of them Baltic-sounding. Now and then, when the doors were opened, she would see them sprawled on the sofas – big men, blockily built, with rugged faces and meaty complexions, stubbly scalps and a variety of beards and moustaches. There were always three present, and the roster changed constantly. She guessed there were ten of them in total. Ten men, just to keep little her under lock and key.

Why did she need that many jailers? Why did she merit such a lavishly grand prison? What was this all about? Why on earth would anyone hold Josie Young captive? What had her father done?

Since waking up in the suite three days ago, these questions had raged around her head. It was agonising. She had spent most of the time in bed, curled up, her stomach in knots, a hand over her mouth to stop herself from screaming. Meals came, meals went; sometimes she ate, sometimes not.

After three days, however, resignation set in. She didn't have the energy to stress over the situation any more. She just had to accept it. This was where she was, and this was how things were. She couldn't alter it. She could only live with it.

Thank God for Benedikt. On several occasions Josie had looked at that splendid gilt-framed mirror and thought how she could smash the glass and use a shard to open up a vein. Without Benedikt, she would have done it.

Benedikt had been provided with a camp bed in a corner of the room. He had been asked for a list of the medications she needed, and doled out the pills as and when required. He never left her except to fetch a meal tray from the other room or go to the bathroom. He was a constant, levelling presence.

He was scared. He admitted that to her on the very first evening, shortly after she was forced to record the video message for her father. He had no more idea than she did what was happening and he hated being trapped here. But, he told her, his primary goal was to look after her. That consideration overrode all others.

Still, she had noticed his hands trembling as he uncapped a bottle of her lithium tablets, and seen how his shoulders hunched whenever he went into the other room and spoke to the men. Bravery had its limits. Benedikt was saying all the right things, but inside he was as close to snapping as she was.

ON THIS WHITE Day, when Josie realised she no longer felt anything, not even afraid, she began to think hard about where she was.

What the purpose was for her being here.

Her mind was working with uncanny clarity. It was as though the Whiteness of the day had somehow freed up a mental logjam. Instead of returning again and again to her obsessions – herself, her inadequacies, her mistakes, her shortcomings, the general pointlessness of her existence – she found she was paying attention to things outside her. She was making connections, letting logic drive her.

It was midmorning. Bright sunlight filtered in around the edges of the curtains, which were kept shut by order of the jailers. Josie and Benedikt were forbidden from opening them and looking out, and so far they had both obeyed the edict.

Now Josie padded across the spongy-carpeted floor to the windows. Benedikt was dozing on the camp bed, his breathing heavy and slow. Josie cast a glance at his sleeping form, then at the double doors. It was football in the other room, of course; the fans were roaring their tribal chants.

She knew already that she was in a city. She had heard traffic grumbling outside and church bells chiming the hours. She knew it was a city in mainland Europe, because the sirens of the emergency vehicles gave a tinny two-tone toot you didn't get anywhere else. But which city?

She raised the curtain edge ever so slightly and put an eye to the chink. The suite was high up, on perhaps the seventh or eighth storey. It had a commanding view of a broad avenue, some monumental-looking buildings, tram tracks, a slow parade of smart, clean cars. There was a palatial office block across the way. Down at street-level Josie saw shops – branches of chains that sold high-end goods – and a couple of coffeehouses. The people passing along the pavements were well dressed and almost exclusively white. A crocodile of schoolchildren threaded along behind a teacher. A walking-tour group followed their guide in a gaggle, taking photos.

"What are you doing, Josie?"

She dropped the curtain shut. Benedikt was awake and frowning.

"They said do not touch the curtains," he said. "Do not even go near the windows."

"I had to have a look."

"What do you think they would do if they caught you? It would not be good."

"Well, they haven't caught me." She walked back to the four-poster. "And even if they had, they wouldn't hurt me."

"What makes you so sure?"

"Because I'm a hostage, aren't I? They need me alive and well."

"But not so much me, eh? You they might leave alone, but me, I am not so important. Poor old Benedikt Frankel might suffer while Josie Young does not." He laughed hollowly, uncertainly.

"I wouldn't let that happen."

"How would you prevent it?"

"I would threaten to kill myself if they even raised a finger against you."

"You mean it."

"I do."

Benedikt pushed himself up to a sitting position. "Are you all right, Josie?"

"Fine."

"You just seem… It is not like you to be so bold. So assertive. Not like the Josie I have known. Not that this is bad, far from it."

"Listen, Benedikt. I've been thinking. About this whole fucked-up situation we're in. I don't know what these men want with me. They haven't said, and won't say. But I have my suspicions."

"We should not even be talking about this. What if one of them walks in?"

"Football's on. They're busy. But if you're worried, come and sit next to me over here. We'll keep our voices low."

Benedikt, with a furtive glance over his shoulder towards the next-door room, joined her on the bed.

"Why me?" Josie said. "Why, out of everyone at the Gesundheitsklinik Rheintal, all those celebs and execs, did they go for the least valuable patient? Doesn't that strike you as odd?"

"Your father. You told me he's an IT specialist. A troubleshooter, yes? He has wealthy clients. He must also be quite wealthy himself if he can afford to meet the clinic's fees. So they are ransoming you to him."

"But it still doesn't make sense. By Gesundheitsklinik standards Dad and I are small fish. There are people there from families worth billions."

"Perhaps one of his clients is displeased with his work. They have gone to these extreme measures to get him to finish a piece of coding that didn't meet with their standards."

"Bit far-fetched."

"Or perhaps somebody wishes to learn the secrets of somebody else, a rival. What is it called? Industrial espionage. Your father might know how to access the computer system of some corporation, and another corporation would like to him to reveal that knowledge. You are the method for persuading him. They are using you to twist his arm."

"I'd buy that, only…"

"Only…?"

Josie took a deep breath. "I'm not sure my dad actually is in computers."

Benedikt's eyes narrowed. "It is a lie? A cover story?"

"Maybe. I think so."

"So his real work is perhaps not so legitimate? At the clinic we hear rumours about this sort of thing. Clients whose money is not honestly earned. Their bills are paid by transfer from bank accounts in unusual places, like the Cayman Islands. They're businesspeople, but it is not clear what business they do. The rule for us staff is not to worry about it, definitely not ask questions about it. So possibly you should not tell me anything more."

"But if I'm right about him, you ought to know. Because it's relevant."

"Okay," said Benedikt warily.

IT HAD NEVER been much more than a hunch, but over the years Josie had become increasingly less convinced that her father did what he said he did for a living. The older she got, the better idea she had of how an IT specialist looked and behaved. Whatever the image of a computer expert might be – bespectacled, nerdy, somewhere on the autistic spectrum – Roy Young was not it. He did not fit the stereotype.

When she was younger, just a kid, and her parents were still together, she had watched her father leave on his business trips. Every couple of months he would disappear for a week or so, and each time there was something about the grimness of his expression that made her feel he wasn't simply going off to fix some company's software bugs or set up an intranet, whatever he claimed. He looked like a soldier going into battle. Her mother, too, became tense whenever he was away. She tended to drink more wine than usual, and every now and then Josie would hear her crying in the night.

Then there were the arguments. Her parents would start rowing over stupid things, inconsequential things, and sometimes it would escalate and Josie would overhear comments she was not supposed to. Once, her mother said, "If you just had a bloody normal job, Roy, I could be a normal wife to you, the wife you want. But you don't. You go abroad and you, you... do what you do... and how am I meant to deal with that? How am I meant to look you in the eye when you get back, knowing where you've been and why?" To which her father replied, "I was straight with you from the start, Alison, when I got into this. Maybe I should have just kept schtum. I thought you deserved to know everything. You didn't seem to mind back then. But now it bothers you? How I keep a roof over our heads and food on the table? How I pay for a big house in Highgate and the lifestyle you enjoy so much? My mistake. What a fool I was. I apologise." It didn't sound like an apology to Josie, lying in bed upstairs; it sounded pained and angry.

The first time Josie attempted suicide, her mother managed to pin the blame for it on her father. As Josie lay in a cubicle in A&E, sedated, wrist bandaged, she was dimly aware of her parents holding a whispered conversation at her bedside. The specifics were unclear, but at one point her mother, between muffled sobs, said to her father that it was hardly surprising the daughter of a man like him would try to kill herself. "It's in the blood," she said. "Death is in the blood." Josie realised later that, woozy and groggy as she had been, she might have imagined this. Why would death be in her blood? What could that possibly mean? There was every chance she had misheard, or misunderstood. But the phrase stayed with her nonetheless. *In the blood*.

When her parents finally divorced and her father moved out, her mother went into a spiral of depression, becoming a borderline alcoholic. One evening, well into a second bottle of prosecco, she wandered into Josie's room and ranted about her ex-husband, calling him destructive and false. "Everything about him is tainted, Josie," she said. "I can't stand to be in this house, knowing how the mortgage is paid for. Our home is huge and beautiful and horrible. I'm surprised the taps don't drip blood. These clothes I'm wearing, the car I drive, my own body... Everything he touches is polluted by him. Polluted. Except you, my sweet," she added, enfolding Josie in a wine-pungent hug. "You're perfect. You're holy. Never forget that. You mustn't let his stain infect you. You must stay pure. It's too late for me, but not for you."

The truth was, no parent could ever wholly keep secrets from their child. Everything came out in the end. Father Christmas, the Tooth Fairy, where babies came from, the cracks in a marriage, problems with domestic finances – parents could lie about these to their kids, but the kids would figure it out for themselves sooner or later. They picked up the clues, put them together, made sense of them, drew conclusions. It was inevitable.

Josie knew there was more to her dad than met the eye. She knew there was something dark and dangerous about him, a side to him that he did his best to disguise. She colluded in the deception. She didn't want him to know that she knew. He pretended he was an IT specialist, and she pretended to believe him.

"HE WAS IN the Army," she said to Benedikt. "He served overseas. Afghanistan. I guess he must have killed people there. But that was when I was tiny, a baby. After he re-trained, he became a civilian. No more killing. Or so I thought."

"But these arguments you have just told me about," said Benedikt, "they took place after he was not in the Army any more."

"Exactly. Mum was talking about his work in the present, not the past. When she was referring to how the mortgage was paid for, she meant right then. Besides, she's never described Dad's military life in negative terms. She was always proud of him being a soldier, serving Queen and country. What she hated – still hates – is whatever he's been doing since. That's where all the 'tainted,' 'polluted' stuff comes in."

"Unless she has a real loathing of computers."

Josie laughed, perhaps louder than the quip deserved. Benedikt ought to be rewarded for trying to joke, under the circumstances.

"It's obvious my dad is no saint," she said. "I can only assume that that's what's got me into this mess and, I'm sorry to say, you too."

Benedikt gave a little bow, both acknowledgement and absolution.

"But," she went on, "you can bet your arse that if he knew where I am, he'd come and get me. He's not one of those dads who stop caring about their kids. He'd do anything for me. Hence him paying an arm and a leg to keep me at the clinic. I'm still his princess. And if he's even half what I think he is, he'll stop at nothing until I'm safe. Whoever's behind this knows that too. Why else are those men out there, those brick-shithouse doormen types? Why else are there so many of them on call?"

"They have guns, too. I've seen them. In holsters under their armpits."

"Tranquilliser-dart guns? Like the ones they knocked us out with?"

"The other kind."

Josie suppressed a shiver of dread, although she was not wholly surprised. "There you go," she said. "They don't need those for you and me. I'm just a girl and you, no offence, aren't Arnold Schwarzenegger. You're lovely but I don't see you kicking their butts all over the place."

"You are harsh but unfortunately accurate." Benedikt held up a slender hand. "I once punched a boy at school. He was a bully and he called me *Schwuler*. It means 'faggot'. I broke my finger on his jaw. See?" The top joint of his index finger was slightly crooked. "It did not set straight. Also, he then beat the hell out of me. That was the first and the last time I ever hit anyone. I learned my lesson."

She took the finger and kissed it, as though a kiss might retroactively heal the injury.

He smiled. "I suppose we are past the clinic's rules about no physical contact between patients and staff."

"We are. And if the guys out there have no reason to feel threatened by you and me, which they don't, then what are the guns for? More to the point, who?"

"You think your father."

"I think it's the only explanation."

"Josie, do you have a plan?" He sounded heartbreakingly hopeful. "Do you believe you can get us out of this?"

"I believe my dad can. We just have to get a message out to him somehow. Give him our location. He'll do the rest."

"But how to do that? They have confiscated my phone."

"Mine too."

"And we don't know where this place is, this building."

"It's in a major European city."

"That does not narrow it down."

"One where German's the main language, judging by the shop signs out there."

"Still not much help. It could be Germany, the German-speaking parts of Switzerland, Austria…"

"Trams."

"I am no expert on European cities, but many of them have tram systems."

"Do you think you'd recognise it if you saw it?"

"You are asking me to look out of the window."

"Quick peek."

"But they have told us never to open the curtains."

"Technically it's not opening them."

"All the same…"

"There are offices opposite. They don't want us standing at the windows trying to signal someone over there for help. That's all. They can't really expect us not to at least get a little curious about where we are."

"Did I not mention the guns?"

"If we're not meant to look out, they'd have stuck newspaper over the panes or something."

"They have not done that because it might alert people that something strange was going on in here."

"I still reckon the curtain thing is more a guideline than a rule."

Benedikt sighed. "Josie, I don't know that I would be able to tell what city it is, just by looking."

"You stand a better chance than me. You're from round these parts."

"Even if I *can* tell, how does it make any difference?"

"Just trust me," she said. "I'll be standing guard by the doors, listening. If I hear anyone coming, I'll warn you. Five seconds. That's all I'm asking. Please, Benedikt?"

She wore him down, stubborner than he was circumspect. He gave in eventually. He snatched a look outside, and they reconvened on the four-poster.

"Well?"

"Let me catch my breath. My heart is beating so fast."

"Mine too."

"I do not like fear."

"I'm so used to it, I'm beginning to get sick and tired of it. All my life I've been scared of something. My parents splitting up, not meeting up to people's expectations, my reflection in the mirror. Now, when I've got a genuine reason to be frightened, all I am is pissed off. I want to do something about it."

"Being kidnapped is a form of therapy?" Benedikt said. "Is that what you're saying?"

"I wouldn't recommend it as a treatment," she said, "but it does sort of put things into perspective."

"Well, for what it is worth, I believe we are in Vienna."

"Vienna?"

"Capital of Austria."

"I know what Vienna is. How can you tell?"

"Not far from here I saw a… *Kirchturm*, in German. What is the English word for the tower on top of a church?"

"Steeple?"

"Yes. Steeple. I also saw some of the roof of this church. It has very colourful tiles which form a pattern – diamond shapes and zigzags, green, gold and purple. I may be mistaken, but there is only one church with a roof like that. St Stephen's Cathedral in Vienna. And did you not see the flag flying on a building not far from there?"

"A red and white one with an eagle in the middle?"

"That is the Austrian flag. Ninety-nine per cent, I am sure this is Vienna."

"Vienna," Josie said. "Is Vienna a big city?"

"Not so big, I think. Not on the scale of London or Paris. Why?"

"There can't be many smart districts in it like this one."

"Probably not. Maybe no others apart from this."

"Good. That narrows it down."

"You hope that your father will be able to find this place somehow? This building we're in? This room?"

"If we give him all the clues we can."

"And then he will come for us, and fight his way through those men next door, and rescue us?"

"He'll do something, that's for sure."

"Josie, believe me, I want to be out of here as much as you do. I want your father to be some one-man army who can save the day, like Bruce Willis or Liam Neeson. But we must be practical. We must not dream. We must face facts. This is real life. We should just leave our captors to go through the process of ransoming you, if that is the point of all this. We should sit tight and behave and wait for money to change hands or your father to do whatever these people demand. Let it play out. That, for sure, is better."

Josie gnawed her lip. "I'm not prepared to do nothing. For so long I've done nothing, except feel sorry for myself. Enough's enough."

"Fine," said Benedikt. "But we still have the same problem. No phones. Even if your father can do all you think he can, it's no good when we have no way of contacting him."

"There is a way."

"How?"

"You've been in that other room."

"I have. So?"

"Am I right in thinking there's a phone in there?"

"I don't know."

"I'm sure I saw one, through the doorway. Over in the corner on a sideboard."

"A sideboard is…?"

"A table against the wall. You know the one I'm talking about. It's wooden, varnished. Has curved legs and clawed feet."

"Okay, I know the table. A phone?"

"A landline. Handset, base unit, maybe with an answering machine. Old-fashioned setup."

"We call your father with it?"

"One of us does."

"And the men stand aside and permit this?"

"Of course not," said Josie. "The other of us gives them something else to think about. A distraction."

"What do you have in mind?"

"You're not going to like it. Professionally, personally, on every level."

"This does not surprise me," said Benedikt, resigned. "The new Josie Young I am seeing appears to be a crazy woman."

"Wasn't I always crazy? Isn't that why I was at the Gesundheitsklinik?"

"I apologise." He shot her a look of contrition. "It was a wrong thing to say."

"I'm only teasing," Josie said. "There's bad crazy and there's good crazy. I've done the first. Been there, got the T-shirt. It's about time I tried the second."

TWENTY-EIGHT

Central Krasnoyarsk

"HE SHOULD BE dead. Why isn't he dead?"

These were the first words Roy heard as he came to. The voice was a woman's, unfamiliar, dripping with disgust.

"Good question," said a man's voice, also unfamiliar. "If I'd had my way, he would be. But old Peter Purepants here stopped me before I could finish him off."

"With justification," said a third voice: Theo Stannard. "He's not our enemy."

"Could have fooled me," said the woman. "There were a dozen of them, you said. All dressed like him, all armed like him. They murdered Heracles. How is he *not* our enemy?"

Heracles?

"Because," said Stannard, "before Chase so rudely interrupted, Mr Young and I were establishing a rapprochement."

"Big word," said the other man, presumably Chase. "Is that a fancy way of saying you were going to let the bastard go?"

"It's a fancy way of saying he could be useful to us. Isn't that right, Mr Young? I know you're conscious. Your breathing has changed."

Slowly Roy raised his head. His thoughts were sluggish.

He was in what appeared to be a hotel room – functionally furnished, décor making a stab at tasteful. He was tied with strips of torn-up towel to a tubular-steel chair. Stannard was perched opposite him on the end of the bed, elbows on knees, chin on fists. The woman, austerely beautiful, leaned against the windowsill, arms folded below her breasts. The third – Chase – was pacing agitatedly to and fro. Roy had the nagging feeling he knew his face from somewhere.

Heracles, though. Unless he had misheard, the woman had said, *They murdered Heracles.*

The big man with the beard; the target. Salvador Vega, also known as the *luchador* El León.

Heracles?

"Shit," said Roy thickly, croakily. "Is that who you people are? It can't be. You can't be. That's just not…"

"Not what?" said Stannard. "Who are we, Young?"

"It's insane. It's impossible."

"What's he yammering on about?" said Chase.

"I believe he overheard Sasha referring to Salvador by his original name just now. I believe the penny is dropping."

"He knows? About us?"

"Sure. Why not?" said the woman called Sasha. "He must do, or why would they have the artefacts?"

"No," said Stannard. "Remember what I told you? Young and his fellow Myrmidons are pawns. They've been kept in the dark about the true nature of their victims. Only now, right now, is he putting it all together."

"And you're cool with this?" said Chase. "That he's rumbled us?"

"I would be concerned had he not shown himself to be an intelligent, reasonable man, someone who's willing to listen and compromise."

"I still say we should kill him." Chase took a step towards Roy, and Stannard restrained him with a hand.

"I say we should interrogate him first," Sasha chimed in. "Pump him for information – don't have to be nice about it. *Then* kill him. There was little love lost between Heracles and me, but still he was one of us. This man should be held to account for his death. An example should be set."

"Heracles was closer to me than he ever was to you," said Stannard, "and *I* say Roy Young should not be harmed."

"Demigods," Roy said. "Greek demigods." His head was gradually clearing, like a fog lifting. "Or else you're pretending to be Greek demigods."

"I suspect you know we're not doing that," Stannard said.

"No. As explanations go, it's nuts, but it's still an explanation, as good as any. And the four before Vega – Peregrine, Merrison, Karno, Munro…"

"Munro?" said Chase. "*Daniel* Munro? You got him too?"

Stannard raised an eyebrow.

"Achilles," Chase said, shaking his head. "Fuck me. Fucking *Achilles*."

"Right," said Roy. "They're all demigods too."

"*Were* all," Stannard corrected.

"Until you people decided to start bumping them off," said Chase.

"What, for kicks? I don't think so," said Roy.

"What, then? Just a job?"

Roy held Chase's angry glare calmly. "Of course it's just a job. I'm a soldier. A pawn, like Stannard said."

"Henchman, to use your own word," said Stannard.

"Henchman," Chase spat. "Sure. Means you aren't to blame. Well, hench *this*, motherfucker!"

Roy's head snapped sideways and his cheek erupted in an explosion of pain. He hadn't seen Chase move. One second Chase had been standing beside the bed, a couple of metres away. The next – *wham!*

He craned his head back up. The whole of the left side of his face throbbed. He wondered if Chase had fractured a cheekbone. Certainly felt that way. Cracked a molar, too, he thought.

"Stand down," Stannard said to Chase, glowering at him. "We aren't hitting Young. We aren't torturing him. We're trying to work things out. Get some trust going."

"That'll be why I'm tied to his chair," said Roy. "Trust."

"Chase's idea."

"Damn right," said Chase.

"I agreed to it because I felt it would be to your benefit," said Stannard. "If you weren't under restraint, you might do something foolish like attack us, try to fight your way out of here. That, I can assure you, would not end well for you."

Roy looked at the strips of towel binding him. "For my own protection."

"Very much so. Now, you've figured out who we are, and I've confirmed it. The next step is you telling us a bit more about yourself and the people you work for. Quid pro quo."

"I already said, back there in the forest, I don't *know* who I'm working for. I don't know who's handing down the orders and footing the bill."

"You really have no idea?"

"There are layers of deniability in the kind of work I do, firewalls between the people pulling the trigger and the people wanting the trigger pulled. You have intermediaries who set everything up; sometimes even *they* don't know who's ultimately running the show. That way, if anyone gets hauled in by the authorities, there'll be gaps in the paper trail."

"Backsides covered."

"Yeah. And can I just say that talking is hurting like a son of a bitch? Your friend Chase has a hell of a right hook."

"Plenty more where that came from," Chase said, flexing his fingers and balling them into a fist.

"Which one are you, by the way?" Roy said to him. "If Vega was Heracles, you are...?"

"I'm Mister Fuck-You-Up. That's all you need to know about me."

"Can't say I remember *that* myth."

"Seriously, guy, you want me to punch you again?"

"Young," said Stannard, "you'd best not get Chase riled. He's got a mean streak."

"We all do," said Sasha.

"Okay, okay," said Roy. "But if you're demigods, that means you've got to be ridiculously old."

"Three and a half thousand years," said Stannard, "give or take a century."

"Looking well on it."

"Good genes."

"But I thought you lot died. That's what the stories say. Heracles – it's been a while since I read a book about him, but wasn't there some business with poisoned clothes? He put something on and it killed him?"

"A tunic stained with the blood of the centaur Nessus," said Stannard, "and also with the venom of the Hydra, from the arrow Heracles shot Nessus with. While Nessus lay dying, he convinced Heracles's then-wife Deianeira his blood was an aphrodisiac. She persuaded Heracles to wear it, thinking it would make him fall back in love with her and stop him chasing after Iole. The envenomed blood burned him, ate his flesh – but didn't kill him."

"He limped off to Mount Oita in Trachinia," said Sasha. "Built himself a funeral pyre, set it alight, but didn't actually climb onto it. He hid out for weeks while he recovered from the poisoning. By then the word had gone round – he was dead. He used that. A chance to make a new start. Untangle himself from the mess his philandering had got him into."

"That was a test, wasn't it, Young?" said Stannard. "Checking to see if we are who we say we are."

"Kind of," Roy admitted. "You're either well-rehearsed in your character stories or you're the real deal. But I honestly did think you grew old and died, like everyone else. The myths got it wrong?"

"Myths are malleable. Truth can be manipulated, rumours started. That's what Heracles showed us. He was the first to fake his death, but the rest of us quickly realised we could do the same. Living forever has its plusses, that's for sure, but it has it drawbacks too, and one of them is mortals noticing that you don't age, you don't change, you don't get infirm as the years go by. Another minus is outliving the mortals you love."

"So you keep slipping out of one life and into another," said Roy. "Like a snake shedding its skin."

"In a nutshell."

Roy started to shake his head disbelievingly, then stopped with a wince. Chase's punch had wrenched muscles in his neck.

"Part of me's going, 'This is insane, Roy,'" he said. "'You're still unconscious. You're dreaming all this bollocks.' But I'm not; you exist. I'm looking right at you. You, Stannard, you're Theo Stannard the author, but you're also... Let me guess. Theseus?"

Stannard sat back. "Not bad."

"I heard you say you were close to Heracles. Theseus and Heracles went on adventures together, didn't they? They were pals. And the name was a clue. Now, Sasha over there, she's a trickier proposition. She mentioned there was no love lost between her and Heracles. That might make her one of his female conquests, one of the many exes he left in his wake, but I'm going to go out on a limb and say she's Queen Hippolyta of the Amazons."

Sasha's face remained impassive, but her eyebrows arched ever so slightly, which Roy took to mean he had scored a hit.

"As for you..." He looked at Chase. "You I haven't the foggiest about. I do know that you're someone reasonably famous today. I've seen your face on the telly. I think it was on a trailer for a show. You present a programme on one of the satellite channels somewhere high up the listings, the ones that most people don't watch. But I'm still drawing a blank."

"You don't need to know who I am," said Chase. "You only need to know that I'm this close" – he held up thumb and forefinger, their tips a centimetre apart – "to ripping your head clean off."

"We killed your friend," said Roy. "I get it. For what it's worth, I'm sorry."

"Not just Salvador," said Stannard. "You so-called Myrmidons have killed four others. Four that we know about. Could be more."

"Just four."

"So your 'sorry' doesn't make a damn bit of difference," said Chase. "You wouldn't even be saying it if you weren't stuck in that chair pleading for your life."

"I'm not pleading for my life," said Roy. "Have you heard me do that? Even once?"

"Well, you should be."

"I'm with Stannard. Theo. Can I call you Theo?"

"Maybe."

"Like Theo, I want this to be over. Not this nice chitchat; the whole thing. The Myrmidons, the killings. I've taken on a job that I've realised is a shitty one. And I speak as someone who's done his fair share of shitty jobs. Even by my standards, this one sucks. Massacring immortals – it's immoral."

"A conscience," said Stannard. "Rare in someone in the wetwork business."

"We don't call it that. Not these days."

"Wetwork's what you do, though. Your trade."

"I'm an outcomes facilitator."

"Dress it up in a fancy name," said Chase, "it's still killing people."

"Euphemisms serve a purpose."

"Sure they do. In your case they make you feel better about murdering for money."

Roy nodded, acknowledging the point. "But now have a chance of ending this before it goes any further. I'm willing to co-operate with you, Theo. The other two as well, if they'll let me. We put our heads together, and maybe we can figure out who's pulling the strings, and what we can do to stop them."

"Theo," said Chase, "you're not actually considering this, are you, cuz? Tell me you're not."

"I'm keeping an open mind."

"How can we trust this man?" said Sasha. "He's in fear of his life. He'd say anything right now."

"We can trust him," Stannard said, "because he surrendered to me."

"But what if that was just a ruse?"

"We can also trust him," Stannard continued, "because his employers have a hold over him. They're blackmailing him."

"So he said."

"I don't think he's making it up. What is it, Roy, that they're blackmailing you with? You never got round to telling me."

Roy swallowed hard. "My daughter. They have my daughter."

Stannard looked at him evenly. "They've kidnapped her? They're threatening her?"

"Exactly that." Roy's voice had gone husky. "If I don't play ball, she's... Well, you can guess what happens."

"You can't bring yourself to say it."

"Could you?"

Chase grunted and flapped his hands in exasperation. "Really? That's it? He says someone's got his daughter, and we're expected to roll over and give him our bellies to rub?"

"Look at him," Stannard said. "No one can fake the way he looks right now. That anger, that depth of hatred. He's not lying."

Sasha unfolded her arms and pushed herself away from the windowsill, moving to Stannard's side so that she had a clearer view of Roy. "Daughter, you say?"

"Josie," said Roy. "Fifteen. No, just turned sixteen. My only child."

"They would use a sixteen-year-old girl as leverage? They would be that callous? That cruel?"

"Apparently they would."

"Then they have made an enemy of you."

"Something of an understatement."

"And my enemy's enemy..."

"I'm not your friend," said Roy. "Don't want to be. But if I agree to help you stop the killing, and you agree to help me get Josie back before they can harm her, that's a kind of contract, at least. Quid pro quo. Eh, Theo? What do you say?"

Stannard deliberated a while.

A long while.

Roy knew his life hung in the balance. Chase was itching to kill him. Sasha had been inclined that way too, but Josie's plight seemed to have swayed her. Stannard had the casting vote. The group clearly had no leader *per se*, but Stannard was the canniest of the three and the other two seemed to defer to him when it came to strategy. And judgement calls.

Roy's fate – perhaps Josie's too – rested in his hands.

TWENTY-NINE

Central Krasnoyarsk

THEO MADE HIS decision. He hoped he wouldn't regret it, but he didn't think he would.

He undid the knots on the strips of towel. Young rubbed his wrists and articulated his fingers to restore circulation.

"Thanks," the Englishman said.

"You're welcome."

"So, what now?"

"Now, you tell us everything. Everything we need to know. How many there are of you, what weapons you've got, how you're getting about. Anything else that might be helpful."

"Okay."

Young began reeling off facts. The Myrmidons were down to eleven now, Vega having reduced their complement by one shortly before he died. They were all ex-military, a range of nationalities, high-end paid assassins. They had been recruited by a South African, Holger Badenhorst, who'd offered them more money than anyone could rightly refuse. Badenhorst was the linchpin of the operation, receiving commands from above. He seemed aware that the Myrmidons' targets were demigods, but how much more he knew, Young wasn't sure. Best guess, the Afrikaner had no idea whom they were working for. Someone with cash to burn, no doubt about it, and a serious grudge against demigods. Aside from that, who could say?

"Badenhorst's also the man behind Josie's kidnapping," Young said. "That's on his initiative. For which reason, I get to kill him once I have her back safe and sound. I'm going to make the cunt suffer."

Sasha shot him a look. "You should know that I don't care to hear that word used in that way."

"Make the *prick* suffer. How's that?"

"Better."

"Do you know who the next target is?" Theo asked.

"No," said Young. "We work on a case-by-case basis. We don't find out who's next on the list until after we're done with the previous mission. Sometimes it seems like the choices are made on the fly."

"How so?"

"Well, for instance, coming here to Russia, that was a last-minute thing. We'd been heading in the opposite direction 'til Badenhorst got a call and we changed course."

"Short notice?"

"Very. Only last night, in fact."

Theo pondered this. "And it was Salvador Vega you were after? Just him?"

"Just him," said Young. "No one told us there'd be any more of you than that."

"Odd, because Russia wasn't Salvador's stamping ground. He'd been in Mexico for the past – how long, Chase?"

"Couple of decades," Chase said. He looked more than a little disgruntled that Young had been freed. Theo would have some ego-massaging to do once he was finished with Young.

"Yet you came to find him here."

Young shrugged. "Our employer evidently has up-to-date intelligence. He's tracking you somehow."

Theo thought of Harry Gottlieb. A man who could commandeer the resources of the CIA would have had no trouble pinpointing Salvador's whereabouts, or the whereabouts of any of the other demigods. There were few places they could go that he could not find them.

But it might be more straightforward than that. Gottlieb had, after all, sent Sasha to join Theo's group. Was she reporting back to him? Spying for him, right under their noses? It made a horrible kind of sense. The Myrmidons had gone looking for Salvador in the Stolby Nature Reserve. They had known his exact location. How? Because Sasha Grace had told Gottlieb that was where he would be.

She caught Theo looking at her, and he flicked his gaze back to Young. He had begun to believe that Gottlieb was on their side. All at once he was revising that opinion and dusting off his theory that Gottlieb was behind the killings. The former Odysseus had the contacts and the resources to wage a campaign like this. The question was, why? What did he get out of it? Perhaps it was the sheer sadistic pleasure of snuffing out demigods' lives. He didn't count himself as one of their kind, after all. *I am not, by the strictest definition, a demigod*, he had said to Theo and Chase. Was this his way of proving himself? Showing them that, while he didn't have the same physical capabilities as the rest of them, he could still beat them? That his labyrinthine intellect gave him the edge?

"Well," Theo said to Young, "if your employer is determined to wipe demigods out, including the three of us, then our best tactic is to make it easy for him. We present him with an irresistible target, and get him to commit everything he's got. Then turn that to our advantage and mount a last stand."

"Sounds risky," said Chase. "As in suicide risky."

"Not if we have an ally in the enemy camp," Theo said with a nod at Young. "Someone in a position to blunt the Myrmidons' attack."

"I'd have to tread carefully," Young said. "If Badenhorst got wind that I was working for the other side, one call is all it'd take. One call to whoever he's got holding Josie."

"I realise what's at stake for you. I've no wish to jeopardise your daughter's life. But if you can aid us surreptitiously, without it looking like that's what you're doing…"

"I can damn well try."

"Then all we have to do is figure out how to set the agenda – how to make it seem as though we're still prey when we're actually predator. I have some ideas in that direction, but I'm open to suggestions. Chase? You're a hunter. I'd welcome your input here if you have any."

Before Chase could answer, a phone double-beeped: Sasha's. She took it out and squinted at the screen.

"Text," she said. "From Hélène Arlington. Finally she's got back to me."

"What does it say?" Theo asked.

"She's okay with setting up a meeting for us with her husband. They're in Greece at the moment and expect to be there for the next few days. She wants to know what our business with him is."

Theo thought fast. Even if he was inclining back towards Gottlieb as the culprit, that didn't mean Evander Arlington was off the hook. It would still be worthwhile confronting him in person.

"Tell her it's important."

"That's all?"

"Why else would I be bothering? It's not as if I'm Arlington's favourite person in the world. Or he mine, for that matter."

"You want me to put that?"

"No. Say this. If he doesn't know what it's about, then he should be told, and if he does know, then we're presenting him with an opportunity he'd be foolish to turn down."

Sasha's thumbs tapped away.

"That should pique his interest," Theo said. "The acid test will be how he responds. If he refuses to see us, odds are it's because he knows we're on to him and he's scared to face us."

"Or he's just being his usual snotty self," said Chase.

"There is that, but I figure, if he's innocent, his arrogance won't let him give us the brush-off. He'll want to know why we – me in particular – are importuning him like this. High-and-mighty Evander Arlington couldn't pass up the chance to have Theseus, Perseus and Hippolyta come before him like petitioners at court."

"Perseus," Young muttered, looking at Chase.

"And if he's guilty," Theo continued, "if he's our guy and he does consent to a meeting, he'll be expecting us to beg for mercy. Which he can choose to grant, or not. Either way, he gets to feel all smug and lordly."

"Or alternatively he can set a nice little trap for us," said Chase. "We can waltz in, and the Myrmidons will be waiting."

"But we'll be ready for them, and Roy will be our ace in the hole. This, potentially, is the endgame."

Sasha's phone emitted a swooshing sound. "Sent," she said.

"Who's Evander Arlington?" Young asked.

"Possibly your boss," said Theo.

"I gathered that. I assume he's one of you."

"Minos."

"King Minos? Of Minotaur fame?"

"None other."

"And Hélène, his wife. Is she just any old Hélène, or is she one of you lot?"

"One of us."

"I'm going to guess Helen? As in *the* Helen, as in 'of Troy'. The Face that Launched a Thousand Ships."

"And launched a thousand doomed love affairs as well," said Sasha. "The kind of woman who toys with men's affections and leaves chaos in her wake."

"You disapprove, Sasha?" said Chase. "I thought a bunny boiler like Helen would be right up your street."

"Using your looks to take advantage of men is hardly difficult. There's no skill in it. It's a mark of the feeblest kind of female. I favour a woman who can snare her own bunny rather than boil someone else's."

"That's that metaphor stretched."

"I thought I was being quite witty."

"For you, yes. But I'm the gold standard for wisecracking around these parts."

"So you believe."

"It's all part of the Chase Chance charm."

"Charm?"

Young cleared his throat. "Excuse me. Hate to butt in when you're having so much fun, but I should be getting back." He consulted his watch. "I've been gone nearly four hours. Best-case scenario, the Myrmidons reckon I'm dead. Worst-case, Badenhorst assumes I'm AWOL and looking for Josie."

"All right," said Theo. "Let's you and me swap phone numbers. Then we can keep each other abreast of what we're up to."

"Agreed."

"One question. What are you going to tell your colleagues?"

"You mean what's happened? I suppose I can say I got lost in the woods. Had a comms malfunction, couldn't radio for help."

"Think they'll buy it?"

"Hope so. Might be pushing it with the comms part, though. Speaking of which, where is my helmet? And my weaponry?"

"I had to strip it off you," Theo said. "Couldn't very well carry you to the Stolby car park like that."

"Okay. I'm sure I can get replacements. But it's going to make my cunning cover story somewhat harder to swallow. 'Oh, and by the way, I dropped all my gear too!' You have a better suggestion?"

"Well, it might be more plausible if you claim you ran into me and came off worse."

"That's have the ring of truth, if nothing else," said Young. "It'd also account for the ruddy great bruise I can feel forming on the side of my face."

"This South African, Badenhorst, he sounds like a shrewd customer."

"Doesn't look like one, but yes, he is."

"I don't think a single bruise is going to sell the story."

Young's face fell. Then, with grim resignation, he nodded. "I take your point."

"In a stand-up fight you'd be lucky to have got away from me alive. You'd never have managed it without it costing you."

The Englishman positioned himself directly in front of Theo, arms hanging by his sides. "Get it over with, then."

"Nothing personal," Theo said. "This is for the sake of authenticity only."

"Of course. And just so's you know, I didn't much like your book."

"You've picked a fine time to tell me."

"I didn't hate it. Just didn't love it. If this was Goodreads I'd probably give it three stars."

"Could be worse. I'll take that."

He punched. Young staggered.

"I felt," Young gasped, "that you... you have a strong grasp on plotting... but your characters are... formulaic. Ciphers."

Theo punched again. Young reeled, but recovered.

"Apart... from Jake Killian, that is," he said. "He... he's fairly believable. The rest... seem just kind of there to... to service the storyline."

Theo landed a couple of sharp blows in quick succession.

Young collapsed to his knees. Somehow he was able to keep talking.

"As for your prose... Not as elegant... as it could be."

Thump. Thump. Thump.

Young was on all fours, heaving for breath.

"Meat-and-potatoes stuff. Could do... Could do with a little... garnish."

A toe-kick to the ribs.

"But still... I'm tempted... to read... one of the others... in the series."

Another kick.

THIRTY

Prospekt Mira, Krasnoyarsk

ROY HOBBLED ALONG the street until he found a pharmacy. He spoke almost no Russian, but was able to communicate to the woman behind the counter that he needed some sort of strong painkiller. Not that she couldn't have guessed from the way he held his ribs and winced at even the smallest movement.

He dry-swallowed four of the tablets there in the shop, before limping back outside. He slumped onto a pavement bench and waited for the chemicals to work their magic. After what seemed like far too long, the throbbing of his injuries began to subside.

Theo Stannard had worked him over pretty thoroughly. Roy felt like he had been rolled around in the back of a cement truck then dropped off a building. It hurt simply breathing. Stannard had been careful, however; solicitous, even. No bones broken. No inner organs damaged. As beatings went, it had been a judicious, forgiving one. Roy was still mobile, and as long as he kept himself topped up with analgesics, he should be able to function more or less as normal. The bruises, however, were already impressive and were on their way to becoming spectacular.

He fumbled out his phone. He was on a busy shopping street at mid-afternoon and expected that he might draw some stares. It seemed, however, that a man in black paramilitary fatigues sitting on a bench looking the worse for wear was not a noteworthy sight in Krasnoyarsk. Well-dressed passers-by spared him the occasional glance, but no more than that.

Badenhorst picked up after the second ring. "Roy! Man, I didn't think I'd be hearing from you again. What in hell's name happened to you? You disappeared on us. We assumed the worst."

"Kind of a long story. Look, I'm not in great shape. Where are you?"

"We're getting set to leave for the airport. Where are you?"

"One of the old districts of Krasnoyarsk. Lots of trees. Nice buildings. Hang on."

Roy caught the attention of a blonde woman in high heels, laden with carrier bags. She spoke enough English to be able to answer his query.

"I'm on Prospekt Mira," he said to Badenhorst. "Can you come and collect me? I'll explain everything when you get here."

"No problem. Stay put. I'll be there as soon as I can."

"Don't worry, I'm not going anywhere."

"Glad to hear it, Roy. Glad to hear it."

A QUARTER OF an hour later, a taxi pulled up; the rear door opened and Badenhorst beckoned from within. Roy clambered stiffly in, joining the Afrikaner on the back seat. The car's interior reeked of pine air freshener, which was fighting a losing battle with the pungent odour of the driver's cigarettes.

As the taxi moved off, Roy noticed that Badenhorst had one hand inside his jacket, holding something pointed at him. It was small, but not so small that it couldn't have been a gun – a Beretta Px4 subcompact, for instance, or a Kahr P380. The kind of backup automatic that could fit comfortably in a pocket or an ankle holster.

"Jeez, the state of you," Badenhorst said. "You look like *kak*. And where are your weapons? Your helmet?"

"Somewhere in the forest," Roy replied. "Left them there along with my dignity, it feels like." Every word counted. Every word had to be right, and convincing. "There was a second man, Badenhorst. Salvador Vega had a friend."

"I know. The others said."

"The second bloke – I went after him. Tried to head him off. He got the drop on me."

"Yes?"

"And he was... Well, whatever the other targets are, he was one too. You know, strong, fast, all that. He disarmed me. Just tore off my belts, helmet, everything, then started to give me the kicking of my life. I got in a few licks myself, but really, it was like Mike Tyson versus, I don't know, Bambi."

"But he let you live."

"I wouldn't say that exactly. When I realised how deeply I was in the shit, how badly it was going for me, I broke free and ran. Ran and hid. No helmet, no comms, so I'd no way of contacting the rest of the team. It's taken me all this time to find my way out of the nature reserve and hitch a ride back to town."

"And you couldn't have rung earlier to let us know you were okay?"

"No signal out there in the forest. Here is the first place I've been able to get any bars."

Badenhorst weighed this up and nodded.

"You might not think it," he said, "but you should count your blessings, Roy. You could have come off a lot worse from that encounter. A *lot* worse."

"Don't I know it. I hate to run away from a fight, but frankly it was that or get beaten to a pulp."

"I have to say, though, it was rash of you to go after him alone."

"Seemed like a good idea at the time."

"And without one of the artefacts, either, which would at least have given you a sporting chance. I've never pegged you as rash before, my friend."

"Maybe I'm not thinking straight," said Roy, inserting a slight edge into his voice. "Maybe when someone is dangling my daughter's life over my head, the old rationality isn't what it ought to be."

"The ever unflappable Roy Young, feeling the pressure?" Badenhorst's upper lip curled sceptically.

"You should be proud. There aren't many people who've managed to get under my skin. Just you and my ex."

"I can't have you anywhere except at the top of your game, Roy. If this business with your daughter is becoming a distraction…"

"Maybe you should have thought of that before you snatched her."

"Don't get snitty with me, my friend." The object hidden under Badenhorst's jacket twitched; the Afrikaner wanted Roy to see that he had it and was ready to use it if need be. "Don't forget who's in charge."

"I'm committed," Roy insisted. "I'm here to see this thing through to the end. You know that. For the money, of course, but more than that, for Josie. You've got me exactly where you want me. I've accepted that."

Badenhorst fixed him with an appraising look. Roy returned it with a stare that contained both compliance and defiance, a mixture gauged to show the Afrikaner that he was acquiescent but no pushover. If he gave in too easily, the other man might suspect something; but if he was too insubordinate, Badenhorst might elect to terminate his contract – and perhaps him as well.

The taxi wormed through Krasnoyarsk's outskirts – crumbling concrete low-rises, patches of tangled waste ground, dense webs of overhead cable.

Badenhorst broke into a sudden grin.

"Very well, then. You're still on the team. Just don't let anything like this happen again, *nè*? I need my Roy Young. I need him clear-headed and in full working order."

"You've got him."

"Good."

Badenhorst withdrew his hand from inside his jacket. He was clutching, not a snub-nose automatic, but a phone. There was a brief text message on the screen and his thumb was crooked over the Send icon.

"If our conversation had gone in a direction I didn't like," he said, "or you'd tried something foolhardy, all I would have had to do was press. The tiniest motion, but it would have had huge consequences. Instead…"

With a couple of keystrokes, he erased the message.

"As if it never was," he said.

"A kill order," said Roy.

"Correct."

"To the people who've got Josie."

"You thought maybe I had a gun aimed at you? No. Just my phone – a far more effective deterrent, I'd say, in the circumstances."

Roy bit his tongue. Fought down the urge to turn the heel of his hand into a battering ram and drive Badenhorst's nasal bone up into his brain.

He forced himself to think of Theo Stannard. Theseus, and his allies Perseus and Hippolyta. Greek demigods. If he helped them, they would help him. That was the deal.

Just a little longer. He could stick this out. He could hold on.

Just a little longer, and then…

Then there would be a reckoning.

When Josie was no longer in danger, Holger Badenhorst would get what was coming to him. Everything he deserved, and more.

THIRTY-ONE

The Aegean Sea, southeast of Athens

THE BOAT POUNDED across an Aegean as blue as a kingfisher's wing: a 25-foot Sea Fox Walkaround, propelled by a pair of 150-horsepower Yamaha outboards. At the helm was Rosalind, one of Sasha Grace's Wonder Women. Another, Melina, was below decks in the compact forward cabin.

Theo sat at the stern, feeling the drumming of the engines through his buttocks and thighs. Sasha occupied the passenger seat next to Rosalind, beneath the boat's sunshade. Chase perched at the bow, legs dangling overboard, like a living figurehead. He was wearing a pair of Aviators and had both hands braced on the guardrail to steady him against the leap of the waves.

The wind that tore at Theo's hair was humid and salty, and carried scents that were achingly familiar. The vista, likewise, was achingly familiar: azure water, horizon speckled with islands, sky a cloudless blue firmament, sun flaring magnesium-white. He had not visited Greece – mainland or islands – for many years. Greece was home, and there were memories associated with the place, and the majority of them were good, but were outweighed by the minority that were painful.

Hippolytus, for one. His first, last and only child, taken from him while still in the bloom of youth.

His wives, dead too.

And then there was the general deep-seated pang which most people felt for their distant past, for an era that was innocent and irrecoverable, a simpler time.

The Age of Heroes was gone. Theo was feeling it more acutely than ever now that Heracles was dead. That great, garrulous man, a slave to his appetites, voracious in every respect, had been the holdout, the one who had kept the spirit of their generation alive, the one who had modernised least. Theo was close to Chase, but in many ways he had felt closer to Heracles, for all that the two of them had had little contact over the centuries. The great warrior had steadfastly continued to embody the image of who he was, while other demigods shifted with the flow of history, matching their colours to the times, like chameleons. Theo had done his best to emulate Heracles's example, staying true to himself, and had succeeded, so he thought, right up until the late 1970s. Only then – after what Chase liked to refer to as his "midlife crisis" – had he at last admitted defeat and become something other than a crime solver and justice upholder. Only then had he remoulded himself to fit the world, rather than try to force the world to suit him.

Now he was feeling something of the old fire in his belly. A glowing ember rather than a full blaze, but it was good to have it there again. Not since his "retirement" forty-odd years ago had a sense of righteousness sung quite so loudly in his ears. There were deaths to be avenged, punishments to mete out. Villains to vanquish.

Life was beginning to make sense once more.

IT WAS FORTY-EIGHT hours since he had given Roy Young a beating and turned him loose.

The first twenty-four of those were spent in a kind of limbo. There was no reply from Hélène Arlington. Nor was there any word from Young. Theo, Chase and Sasha passed the time in Krasnoyarsk with nothing better to do than drink, eat, sleep, and wait. Theo juggled with ideas for the next Jake Killian, made some notes, but couldn't really concentrate. An email from Cynthia – "*Just your agent checking in, wanting to know why her favourite author hasn't been in touch lately*" – went unanswered. He had nothing to tell her that wouldn't sound vainglorious or dismissive. The whole notion of writing a novel seemed cheap and trivial just then, like taking a photo of life and pretending it was the real thing.

Then wheels began turning.

Hélène Arlington texted. Her husband would see them. He and she were staying at their island home in the northern Cyclades. How soon could they get there?

Theo checked airline schedules. Aeroflot could fly them overnight to Athens via Moscow, a thirteen-hour trip including the stopover, arriving midday the next day.

That was acceptable to Evander, Hélène replied. Did they require picking up from Athens? She could send the helicopter.

Theo told Sasha to say thanks, but no. They would make their way to the island under their own steam.

"We climb aboard the Arlingtons' helicopter," he said to her and Chase, "and from that moment on we'd be effectively prisoners. We'll hire our own helicopter instead. No, better yet, a boat. That way we've always got an easy escape route off the island."

"I can help there," said Sasha. "Two of my Wonder Women call Athens home. I'll get them to make the arrangements."

"Can you also ask them to source some weapons for us?"

Chase cocked his head. "Guns?"

"What else? I'm not going to go into this half-assed. In the event that the Myrmidons are there waiting for us at *Casa* Arlington, I'm sure as hell not taking them on unarmed. I want the odds to be as even as possible."

"I believe I can do guns," Sasha said with a tiny, feral smile. "Any particular preference? Make, model, calibre?"

"I'm no expert. Whatever's easy to use. If there's such a thing as an idiot-proof gun, that."

"Semiauto pistols, then. Glock or Ruger. Virtually point-and-shoot. Nine millimetre for stopping power, so even if you miss central body mass or the head you're likely to incapacitate your target. I'm fairly certain my ladies could get their hands on some Uzis, if a rapid-fire alternative is what you're after."

"Let's have those too. The more the merrier."

"Theo, this isn't like you," said Chase. "Getting all NRA all of a sudden."

"This isn't like any situation I've had to deal with before," Theo said. "Up until now, being a demigod has always been enough. I haven't had an adversary I wasn't the better of. This time is different. You didn't see the Myrmidons taking down Salvador."

"No," said Chase. "No, I did not."

"I did. Heracles, the strongest of us. The one who most loved a good scrap. And they mopped the floor with him. They got Achilles, too. The greatest warrior who ever lived. Next to either of them, I'm small potatoes. At least with a gun in my hand I stand a chance."

"You won't be alone either," said Sasha. "I'm coming with you."

"I see."

"You don't sound enthusiastic."

"Just surprised. Didn't think you cared enough."

"About Heracles or any of the others, not so much. But as a point of principle, this matters to me. And really, you need me. It isn't open for negotiation."

"Okay," Theo said, thinking that at least he could keep an eye on Sasha if she was close by. "I didn't want to presume, but if you're in, you're in. Great."

"I'm in also," said Chase. "I've had your back this far. It'd be rude not to see it all the way through."

"Thanks. I hoped you'd say that."

"Besides," Chase added, "you know you can't do shit without me. I'm the wind beneath your wings, cuz."

"And now I'm feeling just a little bit nauseous."

Chase grinned. "Mic drop. Chance out."

TWO FLIGHTS AND a taxi ride later, they were boarding the rented Sea Fox at Piraeus. Athens simmered in the noonday heat, loud and crowded and a far cry from the city Theo once knew. The symphony of temples and palaces he had presided over had become a cacophony of apartment blocks and traffic-clogged streets, gross and clanking. He was repelled by it, yet couldn't help feeling a perverse pride too. A sapling he had nurtured and cultivated had grown into *this*. Sprawling, unruly, smog-shrouded, but still alive, still vibrant, still important. Athens remained a player on the world stage even after three millennia. How many other ancient cities could you say that about?

Melina, the shorter and darker of the two Wonder Women, was a native Athenian. Rosalind, her taller, paler-skinned girlfriend, was Scottish by birth but lived here now. Both were accomplished martial artists, specialising in krav maga and jeet kune do respectively, and proficient in the use of firearms.

After they had hugged Sasha warmly, Rosalind apologised that they'd been able to gather together "only a few wee weapons" in the time available.

This proved to be British understatement. Down in the cabin there were two large canvas duffel bags crammed with ordnance and ammunition. Theo estimated there to be thirty guns all told; pistols mainly, but a half-dozen stubby submachine-guns as well, the Uzis that Sasha had mentioned. He noted, too, the presence of black military-grade ballistic vests.

"That should do it," he said.

Melina gave him and Chase a crash course in firearms handling. The two demigods knew a little about the subject already. Theo had toted a revolver during both his London consulting detective period and his Los Angeles gumshoe phase, and had done homework on guns while researching for the Jake Killian novels. Chase, for his part, had a rifle permit for hunting. They quickly got the hang of the basics of semiautos – how to load a clip, rack a slide and clear a breech jam.

When they emerged above decks, the Sea Fox was nosing its way out of the harbour, threading a course between tankers, cruise liners and container vessels, a salmon among whales.

* * *

NOW, AS THEY homed in on the island owned by Evander Arlington, Theo recalled how he had journeyed to Crete to meet the man for the first time.

Athens was being forced to pay tribute to King Minos after he conquered it in revenge for the murder of his son Androgeus at the Panathenaic Games. The tribute, a kind of war reparation, consisted of seven young men and seven young women to be sent to Crete every nine years as fodder for the Minotaur. Theseus volunteered to be one of the next consignment, after arriving at Knossos, killed the Minotaur in its labyrinth lair, with more than a little help from Minos's daughter Ariadne. He returned to Athens in triumph and assumed the throne recently vacated by the late King Aegeus.

Having met Minos and seen first-hand how a monarch ought not to behave, Theseus made it his mission to be the opposite. Where Minos was petty and temperamental, Theseus was wise and patient. Where Minos ruled through fear and intimidation, Theseus ruled with fairness and justice. He copied him in only one respect. The Cretan navy was then the largest in the Mediterranean, and cemented Minos's power in the region. Theseus commissioned the building of an Athenian navy that would not be just the equal of Crete's but its superior – the mightiest single fleet, in fact, that the world had yet known. Never again would Athens be held to ransom by its enemies.

The ocean became Athens's empire, its unchallenged domain, and by securing peace and prosperity for his subjects through naval strength, Theseus laid the foundation for the thriving cultural hub the city soon evolved into.

It was, and perhaps would always be, his supreme achievement. And in a roundabout way he had Minos to thank for it.

THEIR DESTINATION LAY midway between the islands of Kea and Gyaros: a flat-topped rocky outcrop, two kilometres across at its widest point. Seen from above, is resembled a heart, hence its name: Kardionisi.

The inlet between the lobes of the heart formed a natural deepwater harbour, and Rosalind guided the Sea Fox into this and towards a concrete jetty where a sleek 150-foot superyacht was moored. Crisply-dressed domestic servants appeared and caught the ropes she and Sasha tossed to them. Within seconds the boat was tethered, and Rosalind killed the engines

Theo, Chase and Sasha disembarked, each with a handgun secreted somewhere under their clothing. Chase was also toting his backpack, with the Helm of Darkness inside. Rosalind and Melina stayed aboard to guard the Sea Fox and its cargo of armaments. Should Sasha summon them, they were to come running with as much of the arsenal as they could carry. By the same token, they should have the boat ready to depart at a moment's notice. The Sea Fox was the demigods' lifeline, in case the worst should happen. The Wonder Women knew enough about the situation to understand that their boss and her friends were relying on them. Theo had the feeling they could be trusted to do their part; their loyalty to Sasha was a fierce mixture of admiration and love. They would not let her down.

"I am Ioannis," said one of the servants, grey-haired, the most senior of them. He spoke Oxford English, with barely a trace of a Greek accent. "The Arlingtons' major domo. I'm here to show you to the house. Would you like me to carry your pack, sir?"

He held out a hand to Chase.

Chase shook his head. "It's not heavy. I'm good."

"As you wish. Kindly follow me."

Ioannis led the three demigods to a funicular elevator whose track climbed the gradient from the jetty to the island's brow. The ascent was slow and smooth and took them through a field of photovoltaic panels, their faces tilted to the sun.

"Kardionisi is powered by solar energy," he said. "It also has a desalination plant for water. We are almost entirely self-sufficient, except for food. That arrives every week from the mainland by boat."

"Nice set-up," said Chase. "This were my pad, I'd be tempted never to leave. Mind you, if this were my pad, I'd be a James Bond villain."

Ioannis blithely ignored the remark. "Mr and Mrs Arlington spend at least part of every summer here. They have houses in the

Hamptons, on Mustique and in Cannes, so you could say they are spoiled for choice, but I like to think that Kardionisi is their favourite, the place where they feel the most relaxed and carefree."

The elevator halted and Ioannis slid the door open. Ahead, a broad, crushed-seashell footpath wound through a grove of oleanders. At the end sat a rangy, multi-level house built of whitewashed stone. The architecture was modern with Hellenic flourishes: fluted Doric columns, porticoed doorways, temple roofs. Overall, though, the lines were clean and unfussy. Plate-glass picture windows gazed out over the sea in every direction.

Ornamental gardens surrounded the house – clipped hedges, hibiscus bushes, urns, cornucopias, and various items of statuary, a mixture of the figurative and the abstract. An infinity pool nestled beside a clay tennis court. Just visible was a helicopter pad, where a silver Westland passenger chopper was parked. There was even a maze, formed of trained cypresses.

Chase nudged Theo. "Couldn't help himself, could he? Had to have a labyrinth somewhere."

"It's kind of his signature, I guess," Theo said.

Yet he couldn't suppress a small shiver as he thought of the actual labyrinth on Crete, the Minotaur's lair. All that cold damp subterranean stone, the tunnels hollowing into darkness, the countless sharp turns and dead ends, the floors littered with cracked bones, and at the centre something that stamped and snorted thunderously and every now and then bellowed a terrible, near-human cry. Daedalus himself had designed it, and Theo recalled thinking that he was not simply up against the brute strength and savagery of the Minotaur but also the mind of the greatest inventor of the era. The labyrinth was tricksy and deceptive, full of repeating patterns that confounded you, staircases that doubled back on themselves or headed nowhere, and inclines that went up when you were expected them to go down and vice versa. Everything about it was intended to make you feel lost and hopeless, constantly retracing your steps, until despair and claustrophobia robbed you of your wits, leaving you easy pickings for its half-man, half-animal inhabitant. If Ariadne hadn't given him a thread to unspool as he entered the labyrinth, to mark his path back to the exit, he might well have ended his days in there, gibbering, starving.

As they neared the house, Theo sneaked a look at his phone. Still nothing from Roy Young, not a peep. He chose to take this as a good omen. If the Myrmidons were on Kardionisi, or at least making their way here, Young would surely have warned him by now.

Unless Young had run into difficulties. What if Holger Badenhorst hadn't been fooled by his story, and had rewarded his disloyalty with a bullet in the head?

Young was too wily for that to happen, Theo thought. But then again, how well did he know the Englishman? Perhaps he had placed too much faith in him.

Regardless, he was at Evander Arlington's home now, about to meet the man face to face. If this was the lions' den, he was firmly in it. There was no backing out. As with the labyrinth on Crete, the only option was to forge on, head for the middle, and be prepared for whatever might come.

Ioannis ushered the three demigods through the main entrance into a cool, airy atrium. From there a short flight of steps led up to a spacious reception room furnished with low leather sofas, marble tables and a tasteful smattering of *objets d'art*. The broad windows showed other Cycladean islands near and far, each apparently suspended on a cushion of heat haze, hovering like a ghost.

"May I fetch some sort of refreshment?"

"What have you got?" Chase asked.

"What haven't we?"

"Whisky, maybe?"

"Macallan Lalique single malt scotch. Will that do?"

"Sounds expensive."

"Could not be more so."

"Then I'll have a shot of that," Chase said, adding, "On the rocks."

Ioannis's expression soured just briefly before reverting to its previous imperturbable state. "On the rocks. Of course. Any other requests? Madam? Sir?"

Sasha and Theo declined. Ioannis glided out of the room.

"I know, I'm a monster," Chase said. "But it's worth ruining good liquor just to see the way that snooty asshole's face fell."

"He's not snooty," Theo said. "He's professional."

"Same difference." Chase ambled over to the nearest window and pressed his nose against it. "Seriously, this is how to live. Look at the place. It's like Elysium on Earth. It's as close as you can get to being a god without, you know, actually being one. You have to hand it to Arlington. He's got it made. If I was a one-per-center like him..."

"A one-percenter?" said a woman's voice, with a disdainful chuckle. "Evander? Hardly!"

Theo turned to see Hélène Arlington standing in the doorway.

SHE WAS STUNNING. As stunning as she had always been. Flawless skin, lustrous eyes, gleaming hair. A swanlike neck; an imperious nose.

She occupied the doorway as though she was a portrait and it was the frame. One leg was poised slightly ahead of the other, so that her hip was cocked and her torso in three-quarter profile, showing off the curves of her figure to their best advantage. Her dress was square-cut and sheer, the neckline revealing a discreet measure of cleavage. There was jewellery – a lot – but all of it chic, unflashy, expensive without proclaiming itself to be.

If there was one significant difference between the Helen enshrined in Theo's memory and the woman in front of him, it was the changes in her skin tone and hair colour, the one darkened, the other lighter. In Ancient Greece a pale complexion was prized in females. It betokened wealth and leisure, the mark of someone who did not have to toil in a field for a living, someone who spent only as much time outdoors as she wished. Hélène, by contrast, sported a perfect all-over tan, golden bordering on bronze. Her hair, meanwhile, was no longer a tumble of black curls, but arranged in two straightened swoops and burnished with coppery highlights. She was glossily metallic, almost literally a trophy.

"He's the one-percenter's one-percenter," she said. "Everyone envies and despises the mega-rich, but Evander's one of the people the mega-rich envy and despise."

She broke her pose and strode into the room.

"Theseus," she said. "Long time no see."

She extended a hand to him, fingers downturned. He shook it.

"What, you're not going to kiss it?"

"Times have changed. People don't do that anymore."

"Well, they should."

"And it's Theo. Not Theseus."

"Of course. And Chase. Dear Chase."

Chase, somewhat to Theo's surprise, did kiss the proffered hand, although not without an impish glint in his eye.

"And last but not least, Sasha Grace. How are you, my love?"

The two women air-kissed, cheeks touching lightly, briefly.

"I must say, I rarely have cause to complain about the bodyguards you send," Hélène said. "They are interesting and accomplished girls. One or two might be somewhat less than polished, but for the most part you choose well."

"All part of the service."

"Such a clever idea. Male protection details can be so dreary. It's like dragging a refrigerator around with you all day, only with worse conversational skills. A Wonder Woman, on the other hand, isn't just a bodyguard but a companion. You can ask her opinion on wardrobe, makeup, hairstyle, anything, and at the same time you know she'll see off pests and keep you safe from harm. I recommend your agency to all my friends, you know."

"Grateful for the business."

"Did you happen to bring any of your girls with you today?"

"Rosalind and Melina. They're down with our boat."

"How delightful. Melina's one of my favourites. She has the rough beauty of the Greek peasant stock. Reminds me of one of my handmaidens back in Laconia. I'll see to it that they get something to eat. I'm sure they'll appreciate it."

"Thank you."

Sasha was not enjoying the chitchat, or the near-toxic levels of condescension. Her smile remained amicable but her eyes were saying *bitch*. Hélène knew it, too, and didn't care.

"Your husband...?" Theo said.

"Theseus. Theo. You're so hasty. So impatient. Always in a rush. That was your great failing when we were together, as I recall. Couldn't wait to get to the climax."

Chase suppressed a snigger – or at least tried to.

"Evander won't be a moment," Hélène continued. "He's on his way. He just has some business to attend to. Am I not enough in the meantime?"

The look she fixed Theo with was radiant, dazzling, devastating. All at once it was as if he was back at the temple of Artemis, seeing her for the first time. He forgot about how everything had gone wrong between them, how their love had shrivelled and curdled after just a few short weeks. He could think only of prostrating himself before her and begging her to be his again.

He wanted to reply, *More than enough*. What he managed to say, with effort, was, "It's him we've come to talk to."

"Of course. I'm just the wife; the old ball and chain. Nobody's interested in me."

"I wouldn't say that. I only –"

"I'm used to it. Evander's the multibillionaire. All I do is hang off his arm at parties looking ravishing. It's all I'm good for. That and putting up with his male friends pawing at me when their wives' backs are turned."

"I didn't think Evander Arlington was the partying kind. He seems somewhat reclusive."

"Oh, we socialise. Just not with anyone you'd know, and far from the public gaze. Our circle of acquaintance is very rarefied, a club open only to the apallingly wealthy. I don't think you can belong if you don't own at least a private island."

"Obviously I need to up my earning potential."

"With those silly little potboilers you turn out? I doubt it. Authors, however well they sell, aren't in our league. Even the British wizard woman is a pauper by our standards. Evander has had *centuries* to amass his fortune. If you started now, you might just catch up sometime around the year 4000 – but by then he'd have increased his worth further, so you'll never actually be his equal. Chase wasn't wrong to say it's like being a god. When you can command any luxury, any possession, any object, any*one*, without even having to think about it. Throw in immortality as well, and... If the gods on Olympus were watching us now, they'd be spitting with envy."

"But they aren't watching, are they?" said Chase. "They're dead. Dead and gone. We know that because if they weren't they'd still be meddling in our affairs."

"Quite," said Hélène. "If they were around nowadays, they surely wouldn't allow someone like Evander to prosper to the extent that he has. Jealousy alone would spur them into action. There's always a punishment for those would rival them."

"Aren't you doing that right now?" said Theo. "By saying what you're saying, you're all but daring the gods to smite you."

"And where's my bolt of lightning?" Hélène looked around her theatrically. "Where's my just desserts, my ironic doom? Let's see if I'm turned into a stag and ripped apart by my own hunting hounds, like Actaeon. Or maybe into a cow and have a gadfly sting my backside forever, like poor Io. Or blinded like Tiresias, or have my liver pecked out daily like Prometheus. Hmmm. No? Nothing? Guess nobody up there is paying attention."

A tiny part of Theo was appalled. As a youth he had been taught to respect and dread the gods. You didn't provoke them, not if you knew what was good for you. Stories of their almost whimsical cruelty abounded, and had left their mark on him. No matter how old and jaded he became, he couldn't entirely shake off the notion that it was a mistake to flout their will.

Not that he believed the gods were still alive. Far from it. Hercules' description of a desolate, skeleton-strewn Olympus was, though speculation, all too plausible.

At the same time, Hélène's open defiance touched a nerve. It was weirdly thrilling. Here she was, inviting her own downfall. Clearly it would never come, but still, it felt bold, transgressive. Three thousand years ago Theo would have run for cover if anyone had spoken like this in his earshot, for fear of being caught in the fallout of the inevitable divine retribution. For all that the times had changed, the instinct remained ingrained.

There were footfalls on the stairs from the atrium, and in came Evander Arlington.

His first words were, "Now, now, Hélène my love. Such hubris in front of our guests? You must stop showing off."

His tone was gently chiding. Hélène preened in pleasure and sidled up to him, nuzzling her head against his. Arlington snaked an arm around her waist. Stocky, besuited, hair tidily trimmed, he looked every inch the plutocrat, right down to the manicured tips of his stubby fingers. There was the froglike jawline Theo remembered, and the pouchy-lipped mouth and the surprisingly small teeth, and the grin that appeared welcoming but also seemed hungry, as though the world was a feast and he was ready to eat his fill.

He was hardly handsome, the man who had been King Minos, and a couple of dozen extra pounds around the midriff didn't help. But like many a tycoon, Evander Arlington knew that homeliness didn't matter if you had a fantastically glamorous woman by your side. Her beauty reflected on you. Hélène, more than anything else in Arlington's life, was a symbol of his status. Perhaps that was why he gripped her waist so hard; it was a display of ownership, a man staking his claim.

He acknowledged each of the three visitors with a nod, saving the last and least courteous for Theo.

"How good of you all to journey here," he said. "I trust it wasn't an inconvenience, the Mohammeds coming to the mountain, as it were. I can only say that if you're intending to stay, you'll be well looked after. Enough to recompense you for the trouble you've gone to. We have several guest cottages on the island, all quite superb. It's not quite the old palace at Knossos, but you'll want for nothing."

"No plans to stay," Theo said. "A few moments of your time, that's all we're after."

"Yes. And I wonder what that would be about, eh? What is it that has brought Theseus, Perseus and Queen Hippolyta to my door? What has prompted this unexpected reunion of the Class of 1500 BCE?"

"You sound like you already know."

"I do. I do. But not for the reason you might assume."

"Oh?" said Theo. "And what reason would that be?"

"The wrong one," Arlington said adamantly. "I know why you're here simply because I have been told about it. The artefacts, the killings, everything."

"By?"

"Me," said a cultured, urbane voice. A very familiar voice.

And in walked Harry Gottlieb.

THIRTY-TWO

Vienna

"YOU DO NOT have to do this," Benedikt said. "In fact, I insist you do not. I say that both as your medical caregiver and your friend. It is craziness. What you are risking…"

"I know what I'm risking," said Josie. "You've only told me a hundred times. Permanent kidney dysfunction, seizures that could leave me with tissue and nerve damage. What's the other one? Cognitive impairment, that's it. Brain fucked. But it's got to be done. There's no other way."

"There is. There must be. Why not let me be the one? Why don't I do it?"

"Sweet of you, but no. It's me those bozos out there have to look after. You said it yourself: you're not nearly so valuable to them. If something serious happened to me, I don't think their lives would be worth living. And that's what we're counting on. We need them to start freaking out, headless-chicken style. Now come on, hand 'em over."

Reluctantly Benedikt passed her four tablets. Josie cupped them in the palm of her hand, one eye on the door connecting the bedroom to the suite's main room. As ever, a football match was blaring on the TV. It was late afternoon and her daytime jailers were coming to the end of their shift. They would be replaced in an hour or so. At this point, after twelve hours on duty, they would be bored and inattentive, thinking about getting outside, fresh air, how to spend their evening. The last thing they would be expecting, or prepared for, was an emergency. They would not handle it as well as they would if they were at the beginning of their shift.

It was now or never.

Josie tossed the tablets into her mouth and washed them down with a swig of water.

"Okay," she said. "Okay. No going back. You've got this, haven't you, Benedikt? Tell me you have."

"I have."

"You can cope?"

"I can."

"What's my dad's number?"

Benedikt reeled off the digits from memory.

"No. You've got the five and the seven the wrong way round."

"Sorry. I am so nervous."

"Try again."

He recited the number, this time correctly.

"You've only got one shot," Josie said. "You can't blow it."

"I shan't. But... What if it goes bad?"

"You mean what if I've just taken too much lithium? But you said you've gauged it. A non-fatal overdose."

"Yes. I am sure it will not kill you. Pretty sure."

"*Pretty* sure?"

"No. Sure."

"You better be."

"The worst thing that can happen, I think, is you will fall into a coma."

"Oh, is that all? Well, as long as that's the *worst* thing that can happen."

"Josie, *du gehst mir voll auf den Sack*."

"What?"

"I said you're really busting my balls here."

"Too right I am," she said. "Because we're committed now, and I was fine until a moment ago, but now I'm worried. This is the plan we agreed on."

"And it is a poor plan."

"Maybe, but it's also our only plan, and it's too late for you to go all wobbly on me. Promise me you won't. Swear to me you'll keep your shit together."

Benedikt took a deep breath. "I swear I will keep my shit together."

"Good, because it's all on you from this point forward, Benedikt. I've done my bit. You have to – Ow."

"What is the matter?"

Josie clutched her stomach. "Cramp."

"It is starting already."

"All right. Action stations."

Benedikt moved off towards the other side of the room.

Josie caught his wrist.

"If this doesn't work…"

"Don't."

"But if it doesn't, I just want to say thanks. For being with me."

He glanced around the room. "As if I had a choice."

"Not just here. At the clinic too. You're a nice man, Benedikt. You have such a good heart. You've helped me as much as Dr Aeschbacher and the medication. I'm glad to have known you."

"Josie…"

She let go of him. "That's all. Now please…" Her stomach cramped again, painful enough to make her hiss and double over. "Let's do this fucking thing."

TWENTY MINUTES LATER, Josie began convulsing. She heard Benedikt let out a cry of alarm. After that, she blacked out.

The next thing she was aware of was someone patting her cheek.

She prised her eyes open to see Benedikt leaning over her.

"Benedikt. Did…?"

"Be calm. Do not try to speak. You are okay. You are going to be fine."

He flicked his eyes sideways. Josie understood this to mean they weren't alone in the room. She turned her head to see one of the day-shift jailers loitering by the doorway. He had red hair and a huge droopy moustache like a walrus.

All at once she felt an overpowering urge to vomit. She ran to the bathroom.

When she was finished, she flushed the toilet, rinsed her mouth out and staggered back to the bed. She felt wretched. Her ears were ringing, her head ached, her throat was sore and her insides roiled.

"That's a good sign, yeah?" said Ginger Walrus. "The puking?"

"It means she is getting the last of the salt water out of her, that is all," Benedikt replied. "I cannot yet tell how badly she has been affected. I will have to keep monitoring her."

"Stupid girl," Ginger Walrus muttered. "Taking an overdose. Silly little bitch. What was she thinking?"

"Salt water?" Josie said. Benedikt had told her he would have to bring her round somehow. He hadn't mentioned anything about salt water.

"I had to get the lithium out of you," said Benedikt. "This man and his friends would not let me call for an ambulance. They refused. They told me I must fix you. They said if you died, I would too. So I – what is the word? Improvised. I got them to fetch some rubber tubing, a bucket and some table salt, and I performed a gastric lavage."

"A what?"

"A stomach pump. I passed warm salty water down your oesophagus into your stomach and siphoned it out again."

"That'll be why my throat hurts."

"I think it did the trick." Benedikt took her pulse. "Your heartrate is steady. Strong. It was touch-and-go, but I think the danger has passed."

"Thank you," Josie said thickly. She wanted to ask about the landline phone next door. Had he managed to get to it? Had he contacted her father? The purpose of her apparent suicide attempt was to cause panic and confusion. While the guards were preoccupied with her, Benedikt could sneak into the other room and quickly make the call. She was desperate to know if he'd succeeded.

As long as Ginger Walrus was present, however, Benedikt could not tell her. She searched his face for clues, but he was keeping his expression impassive, giving nothing away.

Drowsiness closed in on her. She felt wrung-out, exhausted. Sleep offered a refuge from pain. Unwilling, but grateful all the same, Josie sank into it.

THIRTY-THREE

Kardionisi

THEY DINED ON a terrace jutting out a hundred metres above the sea. A warm breeze stirred the damask napery and the leaves and flowers of the jasmine trellis that lined the parapet. A crescent moon rose into the dusky sky, seeming to ignite the stars as it passed.

The wine was a pale Boeotian retsina, nicely chilled, not too coarse or sharp. The food was meze. The conversation was stilted. Hélène did most of the talking, keeping to generic, inoffensive topics: celebrity scandals, property prices, political elections. She played the perfect hostess, making sure her guests were well looked after and wanted for nothing.

Theo wasn't even sure why he, Chase and Sasha were still there. By now, they could have got what they'd come for and be sailing back to the mainland. An hour ago he had had not one but both of his main suspects – Evander Arlington and Harry Gottlieb – standing right in front of him, ripe for interrogation. Before he had been able to open his mouth to begin, however, Hélène had butted in. It was getting late. Nearly time to eat. Why didn't they do this like civilised people? All sit down together and have a meal? There were important matters to discuss, no question, but wouldn't it go better around a table, with bellies full?

"An excellent suggestion, my dear," Arlington had said, stroking his rounded gut like a favoured pet.

"Hear, hear," Chase had said. "Don't know about anyone else, but I could eat a horse. Actually, we were just in Russia, so I probably have."

Theo had protested, knowing it was futile. Hélène's mind was made up, and Helen of Troy always got her way.

As servants gathered up the dessert course dishes, he laid a hand on the table, firmly enough to make a small thud.

"Time we addressed the elephant in the room."

"Not that we're in a room," Chase chipped in.

Hélène dismissed the servants.

"So, we're alone," she said. "Theo has been itching to get to this point all evening. It's quite rude of him, how unappreciative he's been of Evander's and my *xenia*. Sitting there all sulky and surly through dinner. But I'm prepared to forgive. Theo, the stage is yours. Speak. These so-called Myrmidons; tell us about them."

"I won't beat around the bush," Theo said. "Evander, Harry. I'm quite convinced one of you is responsible for the deaths of Aeneas, Orion, Orpheus, Achilles and Heracles."

Arlington spluttered. Gottlieb merely pursed his lips.

"Really!" Arlington said. "That's why you're here? You come all this way, you take advantage of my hospitality, just to bandy about wild accusations? How insulting. I knew this was going to be about the killings, but I had no idea you'd be implicating *me* in them. I'd like to know what you base this – this *preposterous* allegation on."

"Simple. It requires a great deal of money and influence to mount the kind of paramilitary operation we've been seeing, to send a top-notch hit squad jetting all over the world. Money and influence are something you both have in abundance. Then there's the twelve artefacts. Only two people have ever had access to the details of where they were buried: Harry, who did the actual hiding, and you, Evander, the guy he gave a list of the locations to as a failsafe." Theo shrugged. "Honestly, it's no more complicated than that. It's got to be one or other of you. Unless..."

"Unless what?"

"The fact that Harry is here, when he told us he had gone to ground, opens up a new possibility. The pair of you have been conspiring together."

Gottlieb's expression remained smugly, aggravatingly enigmatic, while Arlington grew redder in the face. He seemed to swell up in his indignation.

"You can't even decide which of us to pin the blame on, so you're hedging your bets and going for *both?*" he said. "Why not bring Hélène in on it while you're about it? Chase too? And Sasha? Why not embroil all of us in this little paranoid fantasy of yours? I'm absolutely flabbergasted that you have the temerity to speak to me like this, in my house. I should have you thrown out, at the very least, although I can think of far worse fates I'd like to visit on you."

"The more you bluster and threaten, the more I think I'm right."

Arlington stood, shoving back his chair, bumping the table with his thighs, making the cutlery and glassware jump. "All you have done is insinuate," he said, jabbing a forefinger at Theo. "Where is the proof? Bring it to me now. Show me, beyond any doubt, why you believe I have organised a campaign of murder against the demigods – against my own brethren."

"Other than the logical reasons I've just set out, I don't have anything concrete linking you to the Myrmidons, Evander."

"Precisely. It's all just circumstantial. Conjecture."

"But," Theo continued, "what I would like you to tell me is where you keep the copper cylinders Harry gave you, the ones containing directions for finding the artefacts."

Arlington, still standing, narrowed his eyes. He was thinking.

"Now that you ask, I'm not sure. It's been ages since I last saw them."

"You're kidding me. Perhaps the most important items you've ever had in your possession, and you don't know where they are?"

"Do you have any inkling how much stuff I own? How many works of art, pieces of memorabilia, treasures, trinkets?"

"But the cylinders are none of those things. They're *life or death* for us. They're not something you just leave carelessly lying around. If you really have forgotten where they are, you're either breathtakingly irresponsible or the biggest fool that ever lived."

"And you, sir, are as impertinent as they come!" Arlington thundered.

"Oh, sit down, Evander," said Hélène. "Stop beating your chest. Theo isn't the slightest bit intimidated. We can work this out without slapping our dicks on the table, can't we?"

Sasha chuckled, as did Chase.

Arlington hesitated, then took his seat again. His wife had defused much of the tension, though far from all.

"Not that you wouldn't win that particular competition," she added with a decorous leer.

Her husband, in spite of everything, was unable to quench a smile.

Finally, Gottlieb spoke. "I hate to say it, Evander, but Theo has a point. You ought to know where the cylinders are. Is it conceivable that you've lost them?"

"No. I don't think so. I'm fairly certain they're at my place in New York. Stored in the safe there."

"Only *fairly* certain?"

"If not, then at the castle in the Cairngorms, in the cellar. One or the other. Hélène, I don't suppose you have more of an idea?"

"How long have we been married, darling?"

"Forty years."

"Closer on fifty, but who's counting? I've been by your side all that time. I've shared three different surnames with you. But I've never heard about any copper cylinders before today."

"Have I never mentioned them?"

"Not once. Must have slipped your mind."

"Well, there you go, Theo. That exonerates me. I'm not even sure where the damned cylinders are, and my wife says they've never once come up in conversation. I can't say I've even thought about them in recent times. I remember, when Harry gave them to me, telling myself that I should be careful with them, make sure they never fell into the wrong hands. But time passed, I had other things to focus on, and the cylinders became just part of the baggage I carried around with me."

"Anybody else thinking of the ending of *Raiders of the Lost Ark*?" said Chase. "No? Just me, then."

"Assuming you're telling the truth, Evander," Theo said, "that doesn't mean you never looked at what's inside the cylinders."

"But I never did."

"So you say."

"Won't take me at my word, eh?"

"I'm not in the mood to trust *anyone* at present, you least of all."

"Less than Harry? I'm genuinely hurt."

Theo turned to Gottlieb. "That's a point: why *are* you here, Harry? I thought you had some bolthole you'd run to."

"See that yacht down there?" Gottlieb gestured in the direction of the jetty, just visible from the terrace. The superyacht bobbed on the evening tide. A crewman was out on the foredeck, polishing chrome trim. "That's it. That's my bolthole."

"I assumed the boat was Evander's."

"Mine?" Arlington snorted. "Even the smallest of the three I own is twice the size. *That's* a dinghy."

"It's a hiding place that allows me to go where I like," said Gottlieb. "Rather than being confined in one spot, I can be anywhere – and nowhere. Fully crewed, all mod cons, a floating home from home. I have to dock at port every couple of weeks to refuel and resupply, but otherwise I can just keep cruising indefinitely, unfindable. It's the perfect refuge for weathering a storm. A figurative storm, that is. An actual storm, too, come to think of it."

"I should have guessed," said Theo. "Odysseus roaming the Mediterranean again. Why not?"

"There is a certain symmetry to it, yes. A certain irony as well."

"Just be careful which islands you put in at."

"There are far fewer hazards for the traveller in the Med these days. No Sirens, no Scylla and Charybdis, no Circe. All those have gone. The most I have to worry about is colliding with a boatload of refugees in the dark. But to go back to your question: I decided to pay Evander a call for the simple reason that I felt he should be given a heads up. I knew that you, Theo, would be gunning for him. I thought the least he deserved was some forewarning."

"You couldn't have Skyped him? Sent a text?"

"Some things are better done in person. I was in the area anyway, and Evander and Hélène are such excellent hosts. You can't fault me for wishing to partake of their generosity." As if to illustrate the point, Gottlieb plucked the retsina bottle from the ice bucket and refilled his glass.

"You have to admit," Theo said, "it doesn't make you look innocent, you being here. Doesn't make Evander look innocent, either."

"You seem convinced that we're in cahoots."

"There's that word again," said Chase. "Cahoots. Love it."

"What you've yet to explain," Gottlieb continued, "is why. Why would we collude in the killing of demigods? What do we get out of it? I personally had nothing against Aeneas, or Orpheus, or any of them."

"Neither did I," said Arlington.

"My interactions with each of them have been sporadic at best. There was never any longstanding animosity."

"I guess not," Theo said.

"Put it another way. Of the five demigods who've been killed, I harboured a grudge against none. And the same is true of Evander. The only demigod I can think of whom *he* might have cause to resent, Theo, is you."

Arlington bowed his head briefly in acknowledgement.

"And you," Gottlieb said, "are most assuredly alive."

"So where does that leave us?" Chase said to Theo and Sasha.

The three of them were making their way to the guest cottages at the southern end of the island, the pointed of the heart. Ioannis was escorting them. The paths were lit by parades of knee-high lights.

"Back at square one," said Sasha.

Theo shrugged. He didn't want to talk about it any further until they were alone again, unaccompanied.

Ioannis showed them to a row of blocky, self-contained apartments, like huge sugar cubes set in a straggling line. Each had a king-size bed draped in Egyptian cotton bedlinen, a balcony and a spacious bathroom.

"Have a look round," he said. "They're all made up. You may choose whichever you like."

"Except Harry Gottlieb's, presumably," said Chase.

"Mr Gottlieb isn't staying here."

"He has his yacht," said Sasha.

"As a matter of fact, Mr Gottlieb is staying up at the house," said Ioannis. "There is a bedroom there reserved for – ahem – special guests."

"That'd be about right," said Chase sardonically. "Harry Gottlieb wouldn't slum it with *hoi polloi* like us."

"You'll find a selection of nightwear in the closets which you're welcome to borrow. Fresh towels too. If there's anything else you need, whatever the hour – food, drink, anything – simply press the intercom button. Someone will respond. If that will be all? *Efcharisto. Kalinichta.*"

After the major domo had departed, the three demigods reconvened outside.

"We should just go," Theo said.

"Are you shitting me?" said Chase. "I don't know what your cottage is like, cuz, but there's a whirlpool bath and a multi-jet shower in mine. The drinks cabinet's stocked like you wouldn't believe; so's the fridge. There's about a billion channels on the TV. The last thing I want to do is get on that goddamn boat and spend six hours schlepping back to the mainland. Screw that. I was on a long-haul plane last night. Tonight I want a decent sleep in a comfortable bed."

Theo couldn't argue with his logic or the force with which he expressed it.

"Sasha?"

"We can head back to Piraeus in the morning. I'll instruct Rosalind and Melina to stand down until daybreak. One thing, though, Theo."

"Yeah?"

"How long have you suspected that Harry Gottlieb might be behind the killings? It wasn't something that occurred to you just this evening. You weren't grilling only Arlington. It was both of them."

Theo could see no point in lying or prevaricating. "Gottlieb's been on my radar since Chase and I met up with him in Washington. The way he bailed on us was kind of a red flag."

"So you would have considered me tainted by association, since it was Gottlieb who sent me to join you in Russia."

"Can't deny it."

"Yet you never said anything."

"I might have been wrong. I was playing the odds. And trying to avoid pissing you off."

"Do you still have misgivings about me?"

"Want me to be honest?"

"If you wouldn't mind."

"You weren't with us in Stolby, and you were the only one who wasn't. You stayed behind."

"The whole exercise seemed futile to me."

"But you encouraged us to go anyway."

"Chase needed to let off steam."

"I did," Chase said.

"You all did," said Sasha. "Men are not the masters of their feelings. They need an outlet for all those emotions they cannot express. I judged that the three of you would benefit from getting out in the open air and hunting for a while. Whether you caught Chase's beast or not, it would be cathartic. Of course I regret my decision now. With hindsight, I wish I'd been with you. It might have made a difference."

"It might," said Theo, "but probably not."

"But you believe – what? I sent you with him and set the Myrmidons on your trail?"

"I'd be an idiot if it didn't occur to me. They came right to where we were."

"It could have been coincidence that I chose not to go."

"Maybe, but I don't like coincidences. I don't believe in them."

"*Was* it you, Sasha?" said Chase. "I mean, let's be direct about this. Look us in the eye and tell us you weren't involved?"

"I had nothing to do with it," Sasha said. "Believe that or not, I don't care. I know I am telling the truth. If I'm not on your side, how come I'm still with you? How come I have got you transportation and guns? Answer me that, either of you."

Chase was silent. Theo deliberated. He wanted to think Sasha was being up-front with them, but her personality made it difficult. Someone as prickly and aloof as her always seemed to have a hidden agenda, even if they didn't.

"You can't," she said. "Thought as much." And she spun on her heel and disappeared into her cottage.

Chase looked at Theo. "Get some sleep, cuz. That's the best remedy. You're tired; so am I. We'll start again in the morning, all bright-eyed and bushy-tailed."

He clapped him on the shoulder and, somewhat drunkenly, ambled off.

THEO TRIED TO sleep, but couldn't. Frustration knotted his stomach. Thoughts whirled round in his head.

If it wasn't Arlington or Gottlieb, then who? Who was sponsoring and masterminding the killings? How had they got hold of the artefacts' locations? Why were they going to all this expense and trouble to exterminate demigods? What was the point?

He had been so close to a resolution, or so it had seemed. Kardionisi was where everything would be tied up, he'd been sure. But now, as Sasha had said, they were back to square one.

Eventually he did doze off.

Only to be woken sometime around 3AM by a beep from his phone.

A text message, from Roy Young.

Four short words.

Be ready. We're coming.

THIRTY-FOUR

The Aegean, south of Kardionisi

A TRIO OF black Zodiacs scudded across the nighttime waves in triangle formation.

Roy was in the leading boat. With him were Gavin and Jeanne, the latter driving. The remaining eight Myrmidons were divided equally between the other two boats.

The Zodiacs – fast, low-profile inflatables – were a mile from their destination, a small island now rising on the horizon. Distant lights twinkled on its summit, outnumbered and outshone by the myriad of stars scintillating above.

Just as Roy downed the last two of his Russian painkillers, his phone vibrated. Theo Stannard had answered his text.

I'm the next target?

Quickly Roy tapped out a reply, gloved thumbs clumsy:

You and anyone who gets in our way.

Stannard came back with:

> How many of you?

Roy:

> The lot.

Stannard:

> I should be flattered. How long do I have?

Roy:

> Not long. We're nearly there. I'll do my best at this end. Haven't been given much time to prepare. Just stay alive so you can keep your side of our bargain.

Stannard closed the exchange with:

> You help keep me alive and I will.

Roy tucked his phone away and turned to Gavin and Jeanne.

"Stannard's been alerted," he said above the outboard's rumble. "You two sure about this? You're still with me?"

Gavin said, "I'm not happy about the money. In my head, all I can see is a bloody great big wedge of cash flapping away from me on wings. I had plans. That villa in Malaga…"

"It's just money," said Jeanne. "We can earn more another time, another way. Badenhorst is a son of a bitch. He crossed a line when he kidnapped Roy's daughter. What kind of shitstain does that?"

"The kind we shouldn't be working for. The same kind who'd bullshit us, holding back the full intel we needed. That's just plain rude; the worst kind of unprofessional. I know people in our line of work are not always what you'd call honourable, but still, there's a code of ethics. A rule book."

"The whole project has been a fog of secrets and misinformation," Roy said. "Kind of goes with the turf, I know, but this is on an altogether different scale."

"The pay was too good," Jeanne said. "Too good to be true."

"Yeah, we were blinded by it. I know *I* was."

"What I still can't get my head around is that our targets have been actual Greek demigods," Gavin said. "I used to love those creaky old movies as a kid, the ones with Ray Harryhausen animation, *Jason and the Argonauts*, *Clash of the Titans*, all that. And they were about actual living people? The same people we've been going after? It's just plain bonkers."

"It's just a shame you've only got the two of us to back you up, Roy," said Jeanne.

"You're the only two I know I can trust," said Roy. "Schutkeker, Laffoon, Blomgren – I just don't think I can rely on them. Sean Wilson, maybe; I thought about it. But when it came down to it, you two were the only ones who seemed like you'd do the decent thing, once you knew about Josie. You'd put your consciences ahead of lining your wallets."

"Too right," said Gavin. "I've got kids. My boys. I like it that I can afford to give them a good life. My wife, too. Makes the job doable. But if I thought for one moment that there was going to be blowback, that I was going to put them in danger... Well, I don't know what I'd do. Go ballistic, most like. I'm amazed you're managing to hold it together, mate. Iron will."

"Not so much that as the idea of nailing Badenhorst's bollocks to a wall after this is over."

"While they're still attached to him or not?"

"No particular preference. Either'll do." Roy tapped the pressure button on the side of his helmet to activate the Myrmidons' universal comms link. "Everyone, we're half a klick out. Decelerate to dead slow. There's enough chop in the water to mask the sound of our engines at low rev."

Minutes later Jeanne was nosing the Zodiac into the island's natural harbour. She cut the motor and the inflatable coasted up silently alongside the two boats moored at the jetty – a midsized launch and one of those floating gin palaces beloved of the global elite. Both were unlit and quiet. Anyone aboard was most likely asleep.

During the mission briefing Badenhorst had advised the Myrmidons that there were civilians on the island. Travis Laffoon had asked the inevitable question: "What do we do about them?" Badenhorst had said leave them alone unless they showed themselves to be hostile.

Roy felt the point was worth reiterating. "Target Alpha is Theo Stannard," he said over the comms as the other two Zodiacs sidled up to the jetty. "We do not shoot at anybody who isn't a direct threat. No collaterals on this one if we can avoid it."

He leapt onto the jetty. Strapped to his back was the ancient double-bladed battle-axe he had used to slash open Isaac Merrison at Chapel Reef. As then, he seemed to feel the weapon vibrating where it touched him, trembling like a greyhound in the slips, eager for action. It was almost as though the axe was alive and thrilled at the prospect of bloodshed. Last time, he had dismissed it as nonsense, a figment of his imagination. Now, he was not so sure. In a world where demigods were real, all bets were off. Did the special weapons the Myrmidons were using have magical powers? It made a crazy kind of sense. Supernaturally boosted implements for killing immortals. Why the hell not?

The island's sides were sheer. The only practical way to get to its summit was the funicular elevator, which currently stood at the top of its track. There was a button for summoning it, but the noise was liable to cause a disturbance and wake people. Fortunately, a set of concrete service steps ran parallel with the track.

"Gavin, Jeanne, with me," he said. "The rest of you, stay put."

"Uh, actually that's a no-can-do, Roy boy," said Laffoon, clambering onto the jetty.

"I'm sorry, what?"

"I said that's a no-can-do. We're all of us going with you."

"You are not. I'm team leader. I give the orders. And I'm telling you, this is just me, Gavin and Jeanne. The three of us will be enough. Everyone else, remain here on the jetty. Hunker down and wait 'til we return."

"No, that ain't how it's gonna happen."

"Yes, Roy," said Hans Schutkeker. "You give us orders, but someone higher than you has also given us orders."

"Badenhorst?"

"Yes."

"We're in the field," Roy said. "In the field, I'm in charge, not him."

"That is true in every respect but this one."

"Shitkicker and I don't see eye to eye on much," said Laffoon, "but on this we're simpatico. It's not that we don't respect you as a commander, Roy..."

"We just do not like you," said Schutkeker. "Badenhorst thought you might try to go it alone. He has overruled you, and he has asked Laffoon and me to enforce his decision on behalf of the rest of us. It is something we are happy to do. Also he has told the two of us, Laffoon and me, to accompany you at all times on the island. 'Do not let him out of your sight. Watch him like a hawk.' His exact words."

"So everybody's coming," said Laffoon. "All for one and one for all."

Shit.

Bloody Badenhorst. The Afrikaner had gone behind his back. It was something he should have foreseen. Their relationship had been rocky since Josie's kidnapping, and events in Russia had done nothing to stabilise it. Roy had practically had to beg to be allowed on this new mission, and Badenhorst had agreed to let him lead it only after persistent lobbying.

"Maybe you're not match fit, Roy," Badenhorst had said. "All beaten-up like that. A spell on the benches might do you good."

"Or maybe," Roy had said, "I've got something to prove. The person who did this to me, kicked the shit out of me, he was one of these superhumans, right? And now it turns out that Theo Stannard is as well. But I think maybe you knew that about him all along. That's why you gave me a funny look that time you caught me reading one of his books."

"Very perceptive."

"A mediocre thriller writer who happens also to be physically advanced, improved, whatever it is these people are. I owe him and his kind a bit of payback, and now I have a chance to take it. That makes me the ideal candidate to spearhead the mission. This is personal for me."

"Too personal, perhaps."

"Look, Badenhorst, you're not going to find anyone here more dedicated, more focused. I'll get Stannard for you. I want one of those fuckers' heads on a platter. Might as well be his."

The Afrikaner eyed him speculatively. "Well, I suppose I can understand that. Vindictiveness is a powerful motivator."

"Vengeance, more like."

"Tomayto, tomahto. Okay then. You're still boss-man. Just don't disappoint me, Roy. That's all I ask. That's all Josie would ask, too, don't you think, if she were here?"

The words "thank you" had never been harder to say. Forcing them out of his mouth had felt like coughing up a lung.

But Badenhorst, it turned out, didn't trust Roy at all, not any more. Laffoon and Schutkeker resented him; Badenhorst could not have chosen better.

Roy thought of the Afrikaner back there in Korissia, the small fishing port on Kea which the Myrmidons had set out from an hour ago in the Zodiacs. He imagined him right now, some ten kilometres across the water, sitting pretty in his hotel room, laughing smugly.

He managed to keep his face placid, his breathing steady.

Just.

"Come on," said Laffoon. "We ain't got all night. Let's do this. Lead the way, limey."

Roy turned and set off up the steps.

The other ten Myrmidons followed in a column, single file.

How was he going to help Stannard now? If it had been just him, Gavin and Jeanne, then no problem. Now, though, he had eight other people to factor into his calculations, and two of them were going to stick to him like glue throughout the mission.

How the hell was he going to salvage anything useful from this mess?

THIRTY-FIVE

Kardionisi

THEO SWAPPED SILK pyjamas for his daywear and raced next door to Chase's guest cottage, tucking the Glock 9mm into his waistband as he went.

Chase didn't answer his knock, so he let himself in.

His cousin was nowhere to be seen. A bottle of Jack Daniel's and a tumbler rested on the marble coffee table in the middle of the room; Chase had sat up to drink a nightcap and watch some TV. The bed, however, looked as though it had not been slept in. Chase was a slob. Every time he stayed at Theo's, Theo had to go round picking up after him, putting damp towels back on the drying rail, wringing out washcloths he'd used, hanging up the clothes he left strewn on the floor. It drove him nuts. Chase would not have left the bed as tightly immaculate as this one was. Never in a million years.

Theo felt a pinch of disquiet in his stomach. Where had he got to?

He headed round to Sasha's guest cottage. It was, he felt, just conceivable that his cousin had gone to visit her. There was friction between the two of them, and Sasha did not hold Chase in the highest esteem. Yet Chase had his ways. He could switch on that boyish, winning smile of his and swerve past almost anyone's defences with it. Drunk, horny and ambitious, he might well have tried to put the moves on Sasha, and there was the possibility – the very remote possibility – that he might have succeeded.

Sasha came to the door in a dressing-gown, sleepy-eyed, wary.

"Theo? What – ?"

"Are you alone?"

"Why shouldn't I be?" The penny dropped. "No. Seriously? You think Chase and I…? You honestly think I would even…?"

"Sorry. It's just, he's not in his cottage, and they're coming."

"Who are coming? The Myrmidons?"

"The Myrmidons. Roy Young texted me a few moments ago. They're heading here. They may even be on the island already."

"To kill who?"

"Me."

"How do they know where you are?"

"Isn't it obvious? Arlington; Gottlieb. I was right all along. One or other of those two has called them in. Whichever it is, he must think I'm trapped, vulnerable."

"Then we'll have to disabuse him of that notion," Sasha said. "Give me a minute."

She returned shortly, dressed. Her phone was in her hand and she was scowling.

"What's up?"

"It's strange. I can't raise Rosalind and Melina. I've called them both, but neither's replying."

"Asleep?"

"They'd have their phones with them even so, right beside them."

"On silent?"

"I should damn well hope not. They know I might need them at any hour. They should have picked up."

The pinch in Theo's stomach was becoming an ominous pang. "I hate to say it, but maybe the Myrmidons have got to them."

"That's what I'm thinking, or trying not to think. My Wonder Women are good, though. I train them myself. They're not the sort you catch unawares easily."

"The Myrmidons are no slouches either."

"Damn it!" Sasha's eyes flashed angrily in the dark. "I have to get down to the boat. I have to know what's happened to them."

"I agree. Also, that's where the majority of our guns are stashed. There's eleven Myrmidons and only two of us, and with just a single pistol each we're outmatched. That's not even taking into account the artefacts."

"Eleven hitmen, just for you?"

"I know. I'm trying to look on it as a compliment. Mostly, though, it's scaring the crap out of me. And I don't know where Chase is, and that's scaring the crap out of me too. He could be anywhere on the island and he has no idea that a massive shitstorm is on its way."

"Theo. Calm down. Chase may be an idiot but he's a dangerous idiot, especially in a tight spot. He can look after himself. You, meanwhile, have the Queen of the Amazons on your side. We've got this covered."

For the first time since Sasha had swanned back into his life at Novy Tolkatui, Theo felt unconditionally grateful for her presence. He hoped it wasn't just because Chase was missing and he was desperate to have someone – anyone – in his corner.

"Far as I'm aware, there's only one way up onto the island," he said. "The elevator. That's how the Myrmidons will be getting up here. It's also our only way down to the boat."

"In other words, we're bound to run into them somewhere between here and there."

"Unless we're sneaky. One advantage we have is that we know the lie of the land better than they do. If we're careful we can avoid them."

THEY FOLLOWED THE island's eastern perimeter from north to south, hugging close to its precipitous edge. The sea clashed and thrashed below, creamy white breakers throwing themselves against Kardionisi's rocky flanks as they had done for eons, long before the place ever had a name. It was an hour or so after moonset, but the starlight was plentiful, more than enough to see by.

Suddenly Theo froze and went into a crouch, signalling Sasha to do the same. He had glimpsed figures silhouetted against the sky, threading through the gardens toward the main house. They were a couple of hundred metres away, but he was able to make out the distinctive profiles of their crested helmets. They walked stealthily, steadily, with purpose. He counted half a dozen of them before they were screened from view by some shrubbery.

As he and Sasha moved off again, he drew the Glock. It was cold and solid in his hand. He flicked off the safety catch. He would shoot if he had to, but only as a last resort. Gunfire would attract attention.

They arrived at the elevator some ten minutes later. Theo scanned the scene and straight away spied two Myrmidons, standing not far from the head of the funicular track. Sentries. There to prevent anyone getting off the island.

He reapplied the safety and slipped the gun – which he was coming to think of as *his* gun – back into his waistband. Then, turning to Sasha, he nodded at the two Myrmidons and put a finger to his lips. He made a fist. Sasha gave an 'okay' sign.

They crawled on all fours, side by side, using a ridge of rocks for cover. Soon they were within five metres of the sentries. A normal human could not leap that span of distance in a single bound from a standing start.

A demigod could.

Theo counted down on his fingers. Three. Two. One.

Simultaneously he and Sasha sprang.

They crashed down onto the Myrmidons from behind, flattening them. Theo yanked back the head of the one he was straddling, then slammed it face first into the ground. Neither of the Myrmidons was Roy Young. Theo knew that much. Not tall or lean enough to be Young. He and Sasha didn't have to hold back.

It took a couple more impacts to render the Myrmidon insensible. Sasha dealt with her Myrmidon somewhat more brutally. A twist of the head, a crackle of snapping vertebrae – the assassin shuddered and lay still.

"Two down," Theo whispered.

"Why didn't you kill yours?" Sasha said. "He would never have shown you the same courtesy. Can we afford to be merciful to these people?"

"The guy's out of commission. Won't come round for a good long while. If I need to kill, I will, don't worry."

Sasha rummaged through the corpse's weaponry and equipment. "What have we got here?" She tugged a short-handled hammer from a loop in the Myrmidon's belt. "Hephaestus's. Must be. You can feel the pounding when you hold it – metal being forged on an anvil. It reeks of furnaces and sweat."

Theo held up a stubby wooden club which his Myrmidon had been carrying. "Dionysus's. Feels like… stale wine and indolence. I doubt the god of revelry ever wielded it in anger. It was more a phallic symbol than anything."

"You'd have thought he'd have made his phallic symbol a little more impressive."

"It's large enough to cosh someone with. There aren't many men who can say that."

Sasha grinned, looking genuinely amused, for once. In general she found something funny almost in spite of herself, as though it were an effort. But not this time.

"They gave these two the least effective of the artefacts," Theo said. "Either nobody was expecting them to run into trouble…"

"Or they're the two most expendable Myrmidons."

They dragged the bodies – dead and unconscious – behind the rock ridge, out of sight. Then, artefacts in hand, they set off down to the jetty. Theo had spotted the service stairs earlier, during the daytime, and Sasha agreed that this was the quieter and more sensible way to descend.

At the bottom, they crossed over to the Sea Fox and stepped aboard. Sasha softly called out Rosalind's and Melina's names; there was no response. She bent down and grasped the handle of the door to the cabin.

The door opened only part-way inward before budging up against something. Sasha had to put her shoulder to it to shove it all the way open.

The obstacle was a body. Rosalind's.

The Scottish Wonder Woman was lying diagonally across the cabin floor, face down. The coppery tang of spilled blood wafted out through the doorway, accompanied by a faint, dull whiff of decay.

Rosalind's head had been caved in, the back of her skull sporting a tennis-ball-sized depression.

The other Wonder Woman, Melina, sat at the small fold-down table which nestled within the boat's prow. Her head was canted back at an ugly angle, resting against the inside of the hull. A jagged crimson halo surrounded it. Her eyes were empty.

On the table there was a tray. Two plates of food sat untouched. Dolmades, spanakopita, stuffed tomatoes, feta salad, olives in garlic oil. A selection of the same meze the demigods had had for dinner.

"No…" Sasha breathed.

The Wonder Women had been dead for several hours, to judge by their pallor and rigidity.

And the duffel bags holding the guns?

Gone.

THIRTY-SIX

Kardionisi

A FIGURE LOOMED in the darkness.

At first Roy mistook it for one of the many statues dotting the grounds of the house, until he noticed its clothing was rippling in the night breeze.

He whipped out his handgun and took aim.

"Halt right there."

The figure raised its hands. It was a woman. A woman in a chiffon-and-lace nightgown that clung to her body sinuously and suggestively.

"P-Please," she stammered. "Please. Don't hurt me."

"Who are you?"

"Hélène. Hélène Arlington. I – I live here. This is my house."

Hélène. Formerly Helen of Troy. And she was every bit as beautiful as the legends said.

But she was also one of *them* – a demigod.

Roy lowered the gun, but only a fraction. "Your husband owns this place, yeah?"

"Yes. Evander. Have… Have you come for him?"

"No."

"Oh, thank heaven. He's a very rich man. I always feared someone might try to kidnap him. I thought you –"

Laffoon stepped forward, brushing past Roy. He too had a gun out. "Lady, we're looking for a guy name of Theo Stannard. You got five seconds to tell us where he is or I plant a bullet in you."

"Theo? You want Theo?"

"Clock's ticking."

"He's… I can show you where he is. I can take you right to him. Just please don't kill me."

"Cool." Laffoon looked at Roy. "See? That's how it's done. None of this tea-and-scones chitchat. Cut the shit. Get to the point."

"The guest cottages," Hélène said. "They're just along here."

"Wait," said Roy.

"Jee-zus!" Laffoon hissed.

"Just a second. Mrs Arlington, it's four in the morning. Why are you outside?"

"I'm not a good sleeper," she replied. Her smile, though forced and tentative, was still entrancing. "I wake up at odd hours. Sometimes a quick turn round the garden helps. Fresh air, peace and quiet. It's a beautiful night for a stroll, isn't it?"

"We ain't here to admire the weather," Laffoon said. "Get your ass moving."

"All right. All right." She turned. On slippered feet she led the Myrmidons along a path. Laffoon followed her so closely, the two of them could almost have been dancing.

Rounding a corner, they came within sight of a row of small cubic buildings. Hélène Arlington halted and pointed.

"He's in one of those, I don't know which. I didn't bring him down here. That was Ioannis's job. Ioannis is our major domo."

"Okay," said Roy. "Everyone, two groups of four. Take it door by door. One group start at that end, the other the other. I'm staying with Mrs Arlington. Someone needs to look out for her in case all hell breaks loose."

"Make that two groups of *three*," said Laffoon. "Shitkicker and I are staying with Mrs Arlington too."

Outwardly Roy shrugged; inwardly, he groaned. Whatever he said, however he organised things, it was clear Badenhorst's pair of obedient little lapdogs weren't going to leave him alone. He only hoped Stannard was elsewhere by now. If the man had any sense, he'd have hightailed it out of his guest cottage and holed up someplace with sightlines and more than one exit, someplace defensible.

"We have two other guests as well," said Hélène.

"We're not interested in anybody but Stannard," said Roy.

"You won't hurt them? Promise?"

"Not unless they give us any bother."

"Roy, is this a good plan?" said Jeanne.

"Splitting up to search for Stannard? I think so."

"Maybe you should come with us." Jeanne flicked a glance at Laffoon and Schutkeker. "Help us."

"I'll be fine." To all of the Myrmidons he said, "Whoever finds Stannard – if he's here – withdraw, give a yell over the comms and wait for the rest of us to converge. Do not engage him until we're all there."

As three of the assassins went one way and three another, Roy turned back to Hélène. Only he, out of all of the Myrmidons, knew who she really was. Even Gavin and Jeanne had no idea. He hadn't mentioned her to them when telling them about his encounter with Stannard and the bargain he had struck with the former Theseus.

He wondered if Hélène Arlington was as dangerous as the other demigods. She didn't look it. Unless sheer beauty was a weapon, of course; then she was one of the deadliest creatures he had ever laid eyes on.

"Why?" she said. "Why does Theo Stannard have to die?"

"It is not for us to ask," said Schutkeker. "We are people paid to do a job, that is all."

"Has he done something bad? Is he being punished?"

"You talk too much," Laffoon spat. "You need to shut up, or I'll shut you up myself."

He pressed his gun to her head.

Hélène cringed.

"Back off," Roy told Laffoon. "Remember what I said? No collaterals."

"Yeah, not really seeing the dedication from you these days, limey," the Louisianan said. "It's like your heart's not in it any more. Maybe you're the one I should be shutting up."

He swung the gun from Hélène to Roy.

"Put that bloody thing down, you moron."

"How's about I put *you* down instead? Do us all a favour. Then we can have someone in charge who isn't compromised. Someone who has more of a handle on the situation."

"Someone like you, you mean? Don't make me laugh."

"I'm not the one who ran off in that forest and got his ass handed to him. Tell me, what exactly went on there? Been meaning to ask. 'Cause there's a lot about your story that don't add up."

So that was it, Roy thought. Badenhorst hadn't tasked Laffoon and Schutkeker simply with keeping tabs on him. He'd told them to stage a mutiny.

And idiot that he was, Roy had presented them with the perfect opportunity. It was just him, them and Hélène Arlington, all alone. Everyone else was busy, six Myrmidons here at the guest cottages, the other two back at the head of the elevator where he'd stationed them on guard duty. Laffoon and Schutkeker could execute him on the spot and there would be nobody to prevent them.

Out of the corner of his eye he saw Hélène looking avidly at Laffoon, at the gun he was directing at Roy.

He could have sworn that she ever so briefly licked her lips. But perhaps it was just a nervous tic.

"It's funny," Laffoon said. "Shitkicker and I both got a gander at that fella in Russia, the one you skedaddled off after on your own. We both reckon he looked like Theo Stannard. When we saw a pic of Stannard at the briefing earlier tonight, we both made the connection. Didn't say anything then, but we went and spoke with Badenhorst after. Told him what we thought. Guess what he said? He said you never ID'ed the guy, even though he left you as battered as a used piñata."

"But you would have known," said Schutkeker. "You would have known it was the same person as soon as you saw the picture. And you said nothing."

"So were you just not paying attention? Or is there something else going on?"

"What really happened after you caught up with him in the forest? Did you recognise him? Is that why you went after him? If so, why did you not say anything at the time, or straight after when you got picked up in Krasnoyarsk?"

"These are the big-bucks questions, you see, buddy. They speak to a certain... unreliability, if you know what I mean."

"I'm hardly likely to sell out to someone who left me in that state, now am I?" Roy said.

"'Sell out'. Your words, not mine."

"It's what you're implying."

"Could be you got yourself all beaten up to cover your ass. So's it wouldn't look like you and Stannard made a deal."

"That's crazy. Do you know how crazy that sounds?"

"I've heard crazier."

"Why would I make a deal with him?"

"Because you want out of this," Schutkeker said. "You were reaching out to someone you hoped would be an ally."

"And that's why Stannard's now on the hit list," said Laffoon. "This has become a test. For you. A test of loyalty."

The Louisianan's finger tightened on the trigger.

Roy had perhaps a second remaining.

Keep bluffing? Stall for more time? Or go for the gun? Try to disarm Laffoon, then take out him and Schutkeker?

He tensed.

"Clear," came Jeanne's voice over the comms. "We've checked all of our buildings. They're all clear."

"Clear this end, too," said Sean Wilson. "Nobody in."

"Everyone regroup," said Jeanne.

The Myrmidons jogged back towards Roy and the others.

Laffoon slowly, disappointedly lowered the gun.

"Seems like you caught a break, 'old chum,'" he said. "But don't get too excited. It's only a reprieve."

"When we do find Stannard," said Schutkeker, "then we will see."

THIRTY-SEVEN

Kardionisi

"WHO... DID... THIS?"

Sasha's face was as hard as granite. Each word was a compressed nugget of rage.

"One of us," Theo said. "A demigod. Has to be."

"How can you be so sure?"

"Look at Rosalind's head. That's a single blow to the occipital. The indentation is more or less the size of a fist. And Melina. Someone grabbed her and slammed her against the wall hard enough to flatten the entire back of her head. Nobody human can do that. Nobody human could have pulled this off, especially against two skilled martial artists. The attack was sudden, unexpected, and carried out by someone with exceptional strength and speed."

"Gottlieb?"

"No. Harry Gottlieb is human-nominal in almost every sense, apart from his immortality. He doesn't have our capabilities."

"Then Arlington."

"More likely. Think how it must have gone down. The tray of food. Somebody brought that to the boat from the house. They knocked on the cabin door. Rosalind and Melina let them in. The person placed the tray on the table, then attacked. The women's guard was down. They never saw it coming. It was someone they knew, and trusted."

"That would be Arlington. He fits the bill. They've both met him before, a number of times."

"Or else Ioannis."

"The butler man? Is he a demigod?"

"Not so far as I'm aware, but that isn't to say he couldn't be. There are dozens of random demigods out there whose faces I've never seen and whose names I've forgotten, if I ever knew them in the first place. Somehow I can't imagine Evander Arlington delivering meals in person. It's beneath him. Ioannis, on the other hand..."

"Hélène did say she would send food down to the boat. But if Ioannis did this, why?"

"Boss's orders," said Theo. "Arlington must have guessed we'd brought weapons. Couldn't bear to see the playing field levelled even slightly. That or he thought he'd whittle our numbers down by two and then Ioannis removed the guns on the spur of the moment, showing initiative."

"Arlington would never get his own hands dirty, would he?" said Sasha.

"Not if he could help it."

"We go back to the house, then. Find Arlington and Ioannis and tear them into more pieces than can ever be put back together."

"Aren't you forgetting something?"

"The Myrmidons?" Sasha sniffed dismissively. "Let them get in the way. See how well that works out for them."

THEY JOGGED BACK up the steps, Sasha in front.

At the top, she almost collided with someone. She raised Hephaestus's hammer and would have brought it down with lethal force if Theo hadn't grabbed her wrist and stopped her.

"No. Don't."

It was Gottlieb. He stood stock still with his hands raised defensively, mouth fish-gaping in alarm.

"Why the hell are you creeping around like that?" Sasha challenged.

"I might ask the same of you," said Gottlieb.

"You could have got yourself killed."

"I'm all too aware of that, Ms Grace, but thanks to Theo's swift reflexes I live to draw another breath. There are intruders on the island. Clearly you know that already. I was fortunate enough to be alerted to the fact by one of the crew on my yacht. He was disturbed in his sleep by the sound of people on the jetty, looked out of a porthole and saw figures in battle fatigues with guns. He went and woke the captain, who called me. I advised him to stay below decks, prepare the boat for departure and wait for me to come."

"You're getting off the island?" said Theo. "Just sneaking away?"

"Damn right I am. Unlike you, I don't thrive in situations where my personal safety is endangered. I've no desire to be killed. I've enjoyed a long and prosperous life and I'd very much like for it to continue."

"And you've no problem with abandoning the rest of us? Leaving us to fend for ourselves?"

"You have your own boat. I'm surprised you haven't used it. Where is Chase, by the way? Is he not with you?"

"We don't know where he's got to. That's one reason we're not fleeing. We have to find him before the Myrmidons do."

"Another reason," said Sasha, "is that Evander Arlington is an evil prick and must die."

Gottlieb nodded sagely. "Evander's finally tipped his hand, has he? I had a feeling he might. As soon as he mentioned yesterday that you three were en route to Kardionisi, I sensed he might make a play."

"You mean you knew he's behind the killings?" said Theo.

"Why else do you think I'm here? I came to sound him out."

"I thought you wanted nothing to do with any of this. That's why you ran and hid. Your priority is and always has been saving your own skin."

"Quite so, dear boy. But I could never resist the lure of intrigue. I wanted to know for myself whether it was Evander pulling the strings. Call it intellectual satisfaction, if you like. Now, had I just invited myself to the island out of the blue, he might have smelled a rat. If, however, he was under the impression that I was a refugee, frightened, desperate, he could welcome me in and be none the wiser, safe in the assumption that I was no danger to him."

"So the cowardice thing was only a ploy."

"A good one, if it convinced the wily Theseus. But isn't it obvious that I've been trying to help? Who was it who brought in Sasha to assist you? You needed an extra pair of hands."

"You can understand, surely, why I might have had misgivings about that," Theo said. "Coming from a guy who'd just crapped out on us..."

"Never trust Greeks bearing gifts, eh?"

"I'm no 'gift'," Sasha said.

"Figure of speech, my dear. Calm yourself." Gottlieb cast an anxious glance over his shoulder. "Well, much though I'd love to stand here all night talking, there is the small matter of a bunch of demigod-slayers on the loose. It's time for me to pursue the better part of valour. I wish you both luck in your endeavours."

He paused on his way to the steps.

"Oh, and I stumbled across a couple of Myrmidons lying on the ground just over there. Your handiwork, I presume. Small suggestion, offered in a spirit of cooperation and supportiveness. They're roughly the same size as you."

As GOTTLIEB DISAPPEARED down the steps, Sasha looked at Theo.

"That's..."

"Really not a bad idea," Theo said. "Wish I'd thought of it."

"I was going to say 'grim'. The one who's my size is dead."

"Well, you shouldn't have killed him."

"Hindsight is a beautiful thing."

"I never had you pegged as the squeamish type, Sasha."

"I'm not. I'm not. And if you don't wipe that stupid smug look of your face right this instant, Theo Stannard, I'm going to show you just how un-squeamish I am."

THIRTY-EIGHT

Kardionisi

"THEO STANNARD MUST still be on the island," Jeanne said. "He can't have gone far."

"Yes, but where is he?" Roy said.

"More to the point," said Schutkeker, "why is he not where he was supposed to be?"

"Maybe she lied," Roy said, eyeing Hélène Arlington.

"At gunpoint?" said Laffoon. "This woman? Nah."

"Or maybe," said Schutkeker, "Stannard knew we were coming. Maybe someone warned him."

"I recommend you don't take that thought any further, Schutkeker."

"Ha! Have I touched a nerve? Hit the hammer on the head maybe?"

"Nail," said Laffoon. "It's nail on the head, not hammer, you dumb Kraut. But I have to admit it looks kinda iffy, Roy. Say you and him *are* friends now. You'd drop him a line beforehand, wouldn't you? Tell him the shit is about to hit the fan."

"Theo came by boat," Hélène offered. "It could be he's trying to get to the jetty, to escape."

Laffoon wagged a finger at her approvingly. "Now, her ladyship here has got her head screwed on. A smoking hot babe, and smart with it." The Louisianan appeared utterly smitten with Hélène, like a schoolboy mooning over the class beauty. She could do no wrong in his eyes.

"If he's gone that way," Roy said, "he'll run into Serge and Dragomir. We'd have heard from them, if they'd seen him."

"Sure, 'less Stannard saw them first. How about we call in and find out how they're doing?" Laffoon tapped the side of his helmet. "Hey, Serge, Dragomir. Travis. How's things with you? ...Serge? Dragomir? Guys, do you copy? Are you reading me?"

He looked at Schutkeker, then at Roy.

"There's your answer. Serge and Dragomir are no longer with us. Meaning Roy's new BFF Stannard is making for his boat. We'd better hustle. Everyone! Haul ass back the way we came."

It seemed that Travis Laffoon has usurped command of the team right from under Roy's nose. The other Myrmidons barely even questioned the fact that he was giving the orders now. They understood that Roy had fallen from grace, and responded to Laffoon's decisiveness.

The exceptions were Gavin and Jeanne. As everyone else broke into a run, the two of them looked to Roy for a prompt. He mimed resignation.

"What are you waiting for?" Laffoon snapped at them. "Move! You too, Roy."

Schutkeker seized Hélène by the arm, and Roy, Gavin and Jeanne fell in step behind him.

Events were spiralling out of control. Roy wasn't sure how he was going to bring them back on track, or even if he could.

AS THE MYRMIDONS trekked back across the island at a fast lick, Roy considered his options.

He could break away, make a bid for freedom. But then the others would hunt for him, egged on by Laffoon and Schutkeker. He was on a tiny island. There weren't that many places to hide. He doubted he could reach the jetty and take one of the Zodiacs without getting caught.

Alternatively he could try to take down Laffoon and Schutkeker, reassert his authority that way. With Gavin and Jeanne backing him up, he might just manage it.

But hovering over all of his decision-making was the thought of Josie. Roy remembered Badenhorst in the taxi, thumb just millimetres away from pressing Send. A single text message from the Afrikaner could shatter his life forever. If Josie died, Roy would be destroyed. In return, he would annihilate Badenhorst and everything he ever cared about, assuming there *was* anything he cared about. But after that orgy of retaliation, what then? There would be no future worth speaking of. How could you go on if your only child was dead? Roy had asked himself this question several times when Josie was self-harming and making suicide attempts, and the only answer he could come up with was: you couldn't.

He was stymied. Nothing he could do now would not have dire repercussions for her. Badenhorst could crush him like a bug.

Halfway to the elevator, something odd happened.

Roy, Gavin and Jeanne had been straggling along at the tail end of the column of Myrmidons.

Then, all at once, two more Myrmidons appeared behind them.

One moment they weren't there. Next, they were. They had just kind of slipped into place.

He wondered if Laffoon had sent back a couple of people from the front to keep an eye on him. He might have missed the order. The pair could have taken a roundabout route, stepping into shadow, then out again to fall in line at the rear.

He saw that one was carrying a hammer, the other a club.

The two artefacts that Serge and Dragomir had been carrying.

Then he caught sight of their faces in the glow of a pathside lamp.

He turned his head to look forward once more.

He said nothing, but there had been a nod of acknowledgement from Theo Stannard and a steely, determined look from Sasha Grace.

Roy jogged on, braced for action.

*   *   *

A BEND IN the path. They were now perhaps half a minute away from the elevator. Roy had no idea when Stannard and Sasha were going to make their move or what form it would take. He knew, however, that they had to hurry. It was only a matter of time before someone else noticed that the Myrmidons were somehow magically back to a complement of eleven.

He grasped the haft of the battle-axe behind his back. He did it in an obvious way, so that the two demigods would see.

Then, surreptitiously, he pointed a finger at Gavin, and at Jeanne. He smoothed the air horizontally.

He hoped the message was obvious: *these two are okay, don't hurt them.*

It was all he could do.

At that moment, Hélène Arlington happened to glance round. Her gaze rested briefly on Roy before straying past him to the two Myrmidons beyond. She said to Schutkeker, "It seems we've picked up some hangers-on. You might want to watch out."

Schutkeker wheeled, saw Stannard and Sasha.

Letting go of Hélène, he went for his gun.

The night erupted into conflict.

THIRTY-NINE

Kardionisi

As soon as Theo and Sasha heard the Myrmidons approaching, they sought cover. The cypress maze was near to hand, and they dashed to its entrance and took refuge just inside.

Peering out, they saw the Myrmidons quick-marching past, with Hélène Arlington in their midst, being dragged along by one of them.

"Shit," Theo said. "They've taken her hostage."

"What for?"

"Leverage, I guess. They think they can use her to smoke us out."

"'Show yourselves or the simpering bimbo gets it.' Maybe we should call their bluff. See how that pans out."

"You really don't like her, do you?"

"Men are fools, but the woman who encourages them in their foolishness is worse. Why pander to male fantasies in order to control them? It may seem like domination, but it's just another form of subservience."

"Okay, but we've still got to rescue her," Theo said. "That's a given, right?"

"If you insist."

"Are you ready to take on nine Myrmidons?"

"As a warm-up before we deal with Evander Arlington and Ioannis? Yes."

Theo felt the Myrmidons were more of a threat than she gave them credit for. Each was a professional killer, bearing an artefact that could kill them...

"Then let's do this before common sense kicks in."

He padded out from the maze, Sasha beside him. They merged with the column behind the rearmost Myrmidon. Roy Young.

A few paces further on, Young looked over his shoulder.

Their eyes met.

Young turned back round. Theo saw his spine stiffen, his shoulders straighten.

When Young grasped the haft of Ares's battle-axe, that clinched it. He was ready. Theo read the hand signals he made. If he interpreted right, the two Myrmidons immediately ahead of Young were friendly. Young had said at Stolby that there were a couple of members of the team who he felt could be persuaded to turn against their paymaster; must be these two.

Theo established that Sasha had got Young's message too. When he looked back round, his gaze locked with Hélène's.

He was about to offer her some covert sign of reassurance, but too late. She addressed the Myrmidon gripping her arm. She told him that she thought Theo and Sasha were impostors.

Theo was dumbfounded. Hélène had looked straight at him. The Myrmidon helmet did not hide his face. She had recognised him. He had seen it in her expression.

And then she had warned her captor about him and Sasha.

And now the man – big, slab-faced, pug-nosed – was drawing his sidearm.

Theo overcame his shock. Fear kicked in, a jolt of adrenaline banishing everything except the need to fight, to win, to survive.

He accelerated to a full sprint. Past Young, past the other two Myrmidons, full tilt at the man with the gun. Dionysius's club aloft and humming in his fist, singing a song of wild abandonment, of high revels and low morals, of boundaries exceeded.

He struck before the man could loose off a shot, bringing the club down on the wrist holding the gun. He smashed every bone in the wrist. The Myrmidon shrieked in sudden agony, and the gun fell with a clatter. His hand hung limp from his forearm like a bird's broken wing.

The club swung again, a blow to the shoulder. More bones shattering, the sound of flattened meat. Another shriek.

A third blow cracked the man's helmet. His head snapped sideways and he crumpled to the path. Blood gushed from his nostrils, giving him a dark crimson moustache.

Affixed to his back by Velcro ties was a bident. It gave off a sombre gleam redolent of caverns and misery.

Hades's.

A superior weapon to the club. Theo wrested it off the Myrmidon's body – unconscious? dead? He didn't care which. He hefted the bident in one hand, stowing the club in his belt with the other.

Sasha was running past him, her sights set on the next Myrmidon along.

Theo whirled round to Hélène.

"What the hell is with you?" he snapped. "You saw my face, you saw Sasha's. And you *outed* us?"

"A new Trojan War, Theo," she replied.

"A new – ?"

"Stannard!"

Roy Young lurched past Theo to intercept a Myrmidon running at him, trident levelled at Theo's midsection. Young diverted the trident with a swipe of his battle-axe. The weapons clanged against each other.

The trident holder rounded on Young. "Showing your true colours at last, huh, Roy?" he said in an accent from somewhere south of the Mason-Dixon. "I knew all along you were a slippery son of a bitch. Guess Stannard musta turned you, back there in Russia. Offered you even more money not to kill him."

"You have no fucking idea, Travis," said Young. "Money is the last thing this is about."

"Could be I don't give a flying fart what this is about. Could be I see myself getting a nice fat bonus if I run you through with this here pig-sticker."

The Myrmidon called Travis rammed the trident – seething with Poseidon's numen – at Young. Young deflected with the battle-axe. The two of them swung, thrust and parried.

Sasha was engaged with another of the Myrmidons, this one wielding a scythe. He was deft with it; the long, curved blade flashed in criss-cross patterns, keeping Sasha at bay, giving her no opportunity to land a blow with Hephaestus's hammer.

Theo spotted yet another Myrmidon drawing a bead on Sasha with a bow and arrow. He yelled out a warning, and Sasha ducked. The arrow zinged past her head with centimetres to spare.

The two Myrmidons who were Young's allies started shooting at their own team. The gun reports were as loud as thunder. The other Myrmidons scattered. Some returned fire.

"You?" said Theo to Hélène. *A new Trojan War.* It could mean only one thing. "*You* instigated all this?"

"Theseus, my love, my *first* love," she replied, tenderly. "Aren't you thrilled? Isn't it exciting? Doesn't it get your blood pumping? It does mine."

Theo tightened his grip on Hades's bident. Its twin points shone darkly.

"You wouldn't," Hélène said.

"You have no idea what I would do."

"Your sense of fair play is too strong."

"After seeing Heracles die – cut down like a dog – my sense of fair play isn't what it was."

"Would you really destroy this?" Hélène indicated herself with a sweep of her hand: her face, her figure, her exquisiteness. "The body you once worshipped and adored? Desecrate it with that thing? I think not."

There was an abrupt scream close by, to Theo's left.

He saw one of Young's two allies – the man, not the woman – hurtling through the air as though thrown. He could not make out who or what had struck him.

The man landed with a *crunch* against an abstract bronze statue. He rose awkwardly, crookedly to his feet.

The woman cried out, "Gavin!"

Gavin had lost his gun but he was armed with a sickle, which he drew from his belt. Theo could feel Hermes's numen emanating from the weapon, an aura of swiftness and sharpness.

Gavin waved it in the air. From the way he was standing, favouring his left flank, he appeared to have several broken ribs on that side.

Suddenly he was flat on his back, as if an unseen cable had pulled him over.

The sickle flew from his grasp...

...and disappeared into thin air.

It was then that Theo finally realised what was going on. A broad grin on Hélène's face told him that she knew too.

He leapt forward, shouting, "Chase! No!"

At the same moment, Gavin's belly seemed to unzip itself. A scarlet gash opened at his crotch and travelled up to his sternum. Innards spilled out over its jagged lips. Gavin screamed in helpless, wretched agony.

Theo, with his free hand, made a grab for where he knew an arm to be. His fingers closed around the limb and he hoisted it upwards.

"Chase, didn't you hear me? I told you not to. That man isn't –"

"I know what he is," said Chase's voice from somewhere about half a metre in front of Theo's face. "Or rather, *was*. He was the bastard who had my sickle. And now I've got it back."

Gavin, neatly eviscerated, shook and shuddered on the ground. His eyes were fading. He was passing beyond help, beyond everything. Blood dripped from a point in midair, where the tip of Chase's sickle must be.

"I mean he was on our side," Theo said.

"Oh, I know that as well," said Chase, yanking his arm out of Theo's grasp. "It's what *you* don't know, cuz, that really matters. That's the big deal here."

Chase sounded unlike Theo had ever heard him before.

He sounded *serious*.

"Take the Helm off," Theo demanded. "Let me see you."

"I'd prefer to stay invisible, if you don't mind. It's working for me."

There were grunts and cries behind Theo, gunshots, the uproar of battle.

But all he paid attention to was Chase.

Chase and the terrible understanding he could feel dawning inside.

"Tell me I'm wrong," he said. "Tell me you aren't in league with her." He jerked a thumb in Hélène's direction.

"Cahoots," came the reply. "Can't you use 'cahoots' instead? It's so much funkier."

"How…?"

"How could I? How did I? How *dare* I? Which is it?"

"All of them."

"Come on, Theo. You're the smart one. Famous for it. You're the Holmes, I'm the Watson. You figure it out. Meantime, while you're doing that, I'll be… over here…"

Chase's voice was suddenly fainter, further away.

"Me and my sickle and my helmet, together again… just like old times."

Theo lunged after him.

"And keeping me out of your reach… so you can't grab me and beat the crap out of me… like you're itching to."

Theo ran on, following the dwindling sound of his cousin's voice.

"Chase! Chase, get back here!"

No reply.

"Chase!"

The fighting was now a good distance behind him. Theo halted, listening intently.

There. The merest whisper of a footfall, dead ahead.

He set off again at a sprint.

"Chase, I don't want to hurt you. I just want to – to understand. I just want you to explain."

"And *then* you'll hurt me," Chase said. "I know you, cuz."

The words were coming from beside the entrance to the cypress maze. Theo made a beeline for it.

A corner of square-trimmed cypress shivered, rustling.

Chase was gone into the maze.

Theo, barely pausing, hurried in after him.

FORTY

Kardionisi

ROY WAS HOLDING his own against Travis Laffoon, but only just.

The Louisianan was fighting like a man possessed. Like he had everything to lose and everything to prove.

Back and forth they went, jabbing, feinting, clashing. The battle-axe and trident were a match for each other, and so were the men wielding them.

Except – the painkillers were wearing off. Roy's limbs were getting clumsy and tired. He was stiffening up.

Laffoon, on the other hand, was in fine fettle.

And he could tell that Roy was weakening. He redoubled his efforts. The prongs of the trident came ever nearer, ever closer to spearing Roy, while the battle-axe grew ever heavier in Roy's hands.

Finally Laffoon got past his defences. One tip of the trident cleaved through the flesh of Roy's upper arm. Roy recoiled, panting, gasping. The battle-axe sagged, blade meeting the ground.

"Got a boo-boo, huh?" Laffoon jeered. "Well, it ain't nothing compared to the boo-boo you're about to have."

He pulled the trident back for a finishing thrust.

Well, Roy thought, *if I die, at least they'll have to let Josie go. No point in hanging on to her if I'm not around anymore.*

It was some consolation.

It was also an unrealistic hope. The simpler course of action for Badenhorst would be to kill Josie and dump the body far from where anyone might find it. That way she would tell no tales.

Roy *had* to live. For her sake.

He hoisted up the battle-axe. Somehow he got the haft of it in between two of the trident's prongs, halting the thrust. Laffoon drove harder. Roy resisted with everything he had.

"Can't you just goddamn *die?*" Laffoon snarled.

"Not while arseholes like you still get to suck air. Wouldn't be right."

Roy shoved, and Laffoon staggered backwards, tripping over one of the pathside lights and crashing back onto his behind. Roy twisted the battle-axe to tear the trident out of his clutches, then lofted the axe and brought it down on Laffoon's head.

A hand darted out and caught the haft before the blade hit home.

The hand was slender, delicate-looking, with flawlessly manicured fingernails.

But phenomenally strong, too. It pushed the battle-axe back up at Roy, and all he could do was twist out of the way of the oncoming blade, which sheared past his head so close it almost lopped off an ear. Next thing he knew, he was no longer holding the weapon.

Hélène Arlington was.

"You'll be my third tonight," she said. "I'd rather watch killing than do it myself, but needs must. Sometimes a girl can't just sit on the sidelines and spectate. Sometimes she's got to muck in with the boys."

The axe blade shimmered through the air, destined for Roy's neck.

Then a Myrmidon rammed into Hélène from the side, shoulder-barging her. Caught by surprise, she stumbled, and the blow from the battle-axe flew wide.

She recovered to find herself face to face with Jeanne Chevrier.

A grim-faced, very pissed-off Jeanne Chevrier.

Who plucked a combat knife from her belt and raised it in an icepick grip, thumb on pommel, tip down.

"No gun, my dear?" said Hélène.

"Out. No time to reload. This will do."

"Careful, Jeanne," said Roy. "She's one of them."

"I figured."

"And you don't have an artefact," Hélène sneered. "Just a bog-standard army knife. Might as well come at me with a potato peeler."

"It'll be enough."

"In your dreams. I have an axe with the essence of a war god in it. I can see this fight going only one way."

"Bitch, please. Just shut up and give me your best shot."

The battle-axe whirred, lightning-swift.

Jeanne reared back out of its path.

Hélène swung again. The axe seemed bamboo-light in her hands. Her speed was breathtaking.

But she wielded the weapon with a kind of disdain, as though loath to touch it. She had every intention of killing Jeanne with it, but at the same time appeared uncomfortable with the whole messy business of murder. She was Jeanne's physical superior, but lacked her skill and experience.

Jeanne ducked under the axe swing and slashed with her knife. Hélène was too quick for her and avoided the attack, but the evasion threw her off-balance, giving Jeanne another opportunity. Jeanne pivoted and delivered a backhand strike, opening up a slit in Hélène's nightgown at waist level and drawing blood from the flesh beneath.

Hélène hissed, more in outrage than pain. "Oh, you unmitigated *cunt*. I can't believe you did that."

"Cut you?"

"Ruined my Oscar de la Renta. Evander loves me in this. A chunky great oaf like you wouldn't understand the importance of designer sleepwear. I bet you go to bed in boxer shorts and a tanktop. You look the type."

With a grunt Hélène launched herself at Jeanne again, the axe above her head.

Roy would have waded into the fray, but Laffoon was back on his feet and had picked the trident back up. All at once Roy was grappling with him, the two of them fighting for possession of the weapon.

Roy couldn't carry on much longer; there wasn't a part of him that wasn't taut and aching and begging for rest.

Only the thought of Josie kept him going.

And in the end, even that wasn't enough.

Laffoon prevailed. He wrenched the trident free from Roy's hands, simultaneously booting Roy in the chest so that he collapsed in a heap.

"'Bout time this was done and dusted," he said.

Roy fumbled for his handgun even as the trident descended.

Then there was a deep wet crunching sound.

The trident halted in midair, quivering.

Lafeyette stood rigid with a look of incomprehension on his face that deepened into incredulity.

He had been impaled on a scythe, entering him through the spine and emerging from his solar plexus like an upturned talon, glistening with his blood.

As he sagged, Roy saw Sasha Grace standing behind Laffoon. She lowered his body to the ground with the scythe, then slid the blade free with a single deft tug.

Roy offered her a look of profound gratitude.

She barely registered it, instead turning towards Hélène and Jeanne.

Roy turned too and saw to his dismay that Hélène had gained the upper hand in the fight. Jeanne had somehow lost her knife. Hélène was propelling her backwards with rapid to-and-fro swipes of the battle-axe. It was all Jeanne could do to stay clear of the axe's double-bladed head as it whipped left to right, right to left, in front of her.

"Hélène!" Sasha bellowed.

"What?" Hélène replied.

"I have a bone to pick with you."

"Can it wait? Little busy right now."

"It was you, wasn't it? Rosalind and Melina. I heard you: 'my third tonight'. You killed them, you cow. *You.*"

"And if I did? What are you going to do about it?"

"What do you think?"

Sasha charged at Hélène with the scythe.

Hélène spun to meet her.

Helen of Troy, a princess of Sparta, and Hippolyta, queen of the Amazons, both brandishing god-powered weapons, clashed together.

FORTY-ONE

Kardionisi

A MAZE. A monster. Again.

Only this time Theo was outdoors, not hemmed in all around by stone. And the monster was not a Minotaur but a man.

His cousin.

His friend.

His best and perhaps only friend in the world.

The cypress maze was not a patch on Daedalus's labyrinth, but its pathways were still convoluted and confusing. It the size of a sports field, and its walls of neat, dense evergreen foliage rose four metres from the ground.

Somewhere in its depths Chase lurked. He was invisible, thanks to the Helm of Darkness, and armed with the sickle Hermes had once given him, a weapon he was more than adept at using. He was a proficient hunter, too, his expertise honed over centuries.

Theo, for his part, still had Hades's bident and Dionysius's club, plus the Glock in his waistband. He knew a thing or two himself about killing. Nevertheless he felt he was outclassed, in all respects except one: he was smarter than Chase.

He hoped that would be enough.

At every junction and corner he tensed in anticipation. An attack could come at any moment, almost literally out of nowhere. He trod stealthily, senses hyper-alert. He was sure Chase had a fix on where he was. Chase might even be right behind him, stalking him, close as a shadow, silent as a ghost.

Pink streaks had begun appearing in the sky. Dawn was stealing across the Aegean, borne on the breath of a new day. Theo heard shouts and screams echoing across the island, the sounds of continuing combat.

Hélène's "new Trojan War".

This time not a decade-long siege conducted by great armies, but a petty little tussle between small groups. A conflict devised and orchestrated by Hélène for what reason?

Theo resolved to find out, once he had dealt with –

He moved almost without thinking about it.

Something smacked through the cypress wall to his left and he recoiled, shrinking to the right.

He couldn't see what had punched a hole in the foliage, but he was certain it had been Chase's sickle.

"Chase, stop this, I beg you."

Silence, but Theo knew his cousin was just the other side of the leafy green barrier. He could hear his breathing.

"I don't want to fight you."

"And I don't want to kill you," Chase said.

"A sickle nearly landing in my head says otherwise."

"I knew you'd get out of the way."

"No, you didn't."

"Well, I hoped you would. I can't expect you to forgive me, cuz. I'd like you to, but I know it's going to be a stretch."

"Forgive you for stringing me along? For lying to me from the start? Duping me and misdirecting me?"

"Yeah, that."

"I'm only just putting the pieces together, but I'm beginning to realise I've been a great blind idiot. You were never my ally. You were there to make sure I never got too close to the truth."

"But to keep you involved, too. Getting you involved in the first place. Helping you out when you needed it, like flying down to Argentina to fetch the pathologist's report on Aeneas. Being a sounding board for all your theories and suppositions."

"But why?" said Theo. "Why go to all that trouble?"

"For you, mostly."

"Me? How do you figure that?"

"The aim was to bring you back to who you were," Chase said. "To remind you that you used to be Theseus – motherfucking *Theseus* – and could be again."

"That's it? You dragged me into this whole mess because – because you felt I wasn't living up to my full potential?"

"You write *books*. What a waste of your talents. You were a crimefighter, a hell of a good one. You used to save lives. You used to make a difference. You used to be a hero."

"Maybe I'm happy not to have that burden of responsibility anymore."

"You trying to convince me or you?"

"But this hasn't only been about saving me, has it? It's been about what's in it for you too. I know you, Chase. You never fail to put your own interests first."

"I... I just want things to be more like the way they were." Chase had started to move, pacing steadily along on his side of the wall, and Theo kept in step with him. There was an intersection ahead, a break in the cypress hedgerow linking the parallel paths they were on. "That's what she was offering. Hélène. She approached me with her plan – a way of making people like us matter again, she said."

"Why you? You in particular? Out of all the demigods she could have chosen?"

"I don't know. Didn't ask. Guess she felt I was the right man for the job."

"And you were flattered as well, to be singled out."

"Kind of hard to say no to someone like that. Anyway, I liked her idea. I saw what I could do with it. Work it to my advantage, and yours."

The intersection was just a couple of metres away. In a moment,

Theo would have direct unimpeded access to Chase and vice versa. The bident seemed to sense this and was quietly eager.

"But I guess you wouldn't understand," Chase added sullenly.

"Then make me understand," said Theo. "Talk to me."

"That's the trouble with you nowadays, cuz. It's all words with you, not deeds. I'm sick of words."

Theo dived through the gap in the cypress wall, bident to the fore. He hoped not to have to stab Chase with it. He was brandishing the weapon chiefly in self-defence.

"Chase? Chase?"

He listened. Faint footfalls, fading.

His cousin had scurried off back the way he had come.

"Chase!"

Theo had no alternative. He set off in pursuit. He had to make his cousin see reason, to bring him to his senses. Chase had become dangerously unpredictable. Someone needed to rein him in – and that someone could only be Theo.

HE PLUNGED DEEPER into the maze. The day was brightening fast, the sky baby-blue, innocent.

All at once he emerged into a kind of clearing, an open space of lawn the size of a university quadrangle. This was the centre of the maze – the solution to the puzzle, as it were. There were two ways in: the one Theo had used and another directly opposite.

In the middle of the lawn stood yet another of Kardionisi's many statues. This one was a larger-than-lifesize representation of the Minotaur, no less. Cast in bronze, it perched on a squat stone plinth and rose perhaps three metres from base to apex. It must have weighed the best part of a metric tonne.

The man-bull was depicted hunched over, horns lowered, shoulders bunching, thigh muscles knotted, as though preparing to charge.

Minos's hybrid stepson, conceived on his wife Pasiphaë by a white bull given to him by Poseidon. A hideous, unnatural beast whose savagery and bloodthirstiness meant it had to be confined to the labyrinth for the safety of everyone on Crete.

The sculptor had done a good job capturing its ugliness and ferocity. Theo was brought up short when he first laid eyes on it. His breath caught in his throat and he reflexively thrust the bident out in front of him, ready to meet the Minotaur's attack.

"Yeah, handsome brute, ain't he?"

Chase's voice came from beside the statue.

"Took me a second or two, like you, to realise he's not real," he added. "Evander must've secretly been quite proud of the actual Minotaur, despite the fact it showed the world his missus fucked a bull behind his back. Had this statue made to remind him of the glory days, when kings could demand human sacrifices and no one objected."

"*I* objected," said Theo.

"You would."

"Hélène wanted to recapture *her* glory days too. That's the impression I'm getting. But she needed an accomplice, someone to help set up the murders."

"No, the murders were nothing to do with me. That was all on her."

"All? What about Heracles?"

"She found where he was the way she found where the others were: by looking them up online. Remember the restaurant in Krasnoyarsk? The selfies those locals took with us? They posted them online almost straight away. Hélène's been running searches using facial-recognition software. It's not rocket science. The internet makes keeping a low profile difficult for anyone these days. Aeneas, Orion, Orpheus, Achilles – that's how she tracked them all down. Then it was just a case of lining up the troops and sending them in. Same with Heracles."

"But still... In Stolby. When he was making his stand against the Myrmidons. He just fell over, for no apparent cause, and I heard him say, 'This is not fair. This is not how it should be at all.'"

"So?"

"Was that you?"

With a touch of remorse, Chase said, "Might have been."

"You had your Helm on, tripped him up at the crucial moment. That's what he was saying: it wasn't fair because *you* interfered."

"Heracles could have done a lot of damage. The Myrmidons can handle most demigod situations, but not him. Someone had to lend a hand. I was there, I was invisible. Seemed appropriate."

"But Heracles?"

"Never liked the guy much."

"*I* liked him. A lot. Does that not count for anything? I guess not, seeing how you were playing me all along."

"I was never playing you, Theo. I was just... encouraging you. Nudging you in the right direction."

"For my own good."

"Yeah. And don't you feel better? More yourself? Hasn't all of this given you back some sense of purpose?"

"Who are you to decide whether I need purpose or not, and what it should be?"

"Someone who cares about you. Someone who hates to see you being less than you can be."

"Take off the Helm," Theo said firmly. "It's just us, Chase. You and me. You don't have to hide. Let's look each other in the eye."

There was a long pause. Then Chase, sliding the Helm of Darkness off his head, shimmered into sight.

They faced each other across the open space, with the Minotaur statue glowering down at them.

"What now?" said Chase. "You try to kill me?"

"I'm tempted."

"You'll see that I did this for you, cuz. In the long run, you'll be grateful."

"You keep trying to justify it to yourself. Maybe one day it'll work."

"Is it so bad, wishing the world hadn't changed so much, wishing things were more like they used to be?"

"It is, if people get hurt and killed because of it."

Chase looked stricken. "I really hoped you'd see the situation from my point of view."

"Then you really hoped wrong."

"You're not going to let me off the hook, are you?"

"Chase." Theo's stomach was churning; his heart was breaking.

"If I thought for one moment that you felt regret – sincere regret – over what's happened…"

"I don't."

"Then there's nothing more to be said. No more words. You want deeds? Here's deeds."

Theo broke into a run.

So did Chase.

They hurtled towards each other, cousin versus cousin, demigod versus demigod: Theseus and Perseus.

FORTY-TWO

Kardionisi

SASHA GRACE DID not find Hélène Arlington the pushover she had thought she would be.

Roy could tell that within a few seconds.

Sasha had anticipated an easy victory. Hélène was one of the idle rich, right? Refined, sophisticated. Unaccustomed to violence. Whereas she, Queen Hippolyta, was a born warrior. No contest, surely.

Not so.

Overconfidence cost Sasha the use of one arm and nearly her life. Hélène leapt over a low sweep of the scythe that would have lopped off her feet if it had connected. The battle-axe slammed down on Sasha's shoulder, blade embedding several centimetres into the trapezius muscle. Sasha howled as blood gushed over her chest and back. Hélène cackled with delight and worked the axe free. Sasha staggered away, left arm dangling.

Hélène pressed home her advantage. The scythe was a two-handed weapon, but Sasha did her best using her remaining arm, slashing it to and fro, fending off her opponent. Shock and pain were taking their toll, however: Hélène's axe was coming nearer and nearer to finding its mark, and bringing Sasha's immortality to an end.

Even as the duel unfolded, Roy was conscious of the other Myrmidons closing in. Only three remained, aside from him and Jeanne: Gunnvor Blomgren, Sean Wilson and an Italian, Marco Valente. Wilson and Valente had the bows, Blomgren the spear, but they had stowed them in favour of pistols, which they now levelled at Roy and Jeanne.

Roy and Jeanne stood shoulder to shoulder, pistols levelled also. Jeanne had had time now to slap a fresh magazine into hers.

The other three halted a few metres short of them.

Impasse.

"Okay," said Roy. "You have a choice. You can kill us, or we can call a truce and attempt to sort this shit out. Because, however it may look, Jeanne and I are not your enemy."

"Who is, then?" said Wilson. "Them?" He indicated Sasha and Hélène with the barrel of his Beretta M9. His focus, like Blomgren's and Valente's, was as much on the fight between the two demigoddesses as it was on Roy and Jeanne. "What are we supposed to do here?"

"I'm still in charge of this mission. Laffoon – that was a blip. He and I have... something personal going on. But the fact is, there is no enemy. There isn't even a job any more, as I see it. We've all been played for fools, and it ends here, today."

"And how do you reckon that?"

"That woman..."

Hélène, teeth bared, hair flying wildly, spattered with blood, her own and Sasha's.

"...I think she's at the centre of all this. I think she's our employer."

"Her?" said Blomgren.

"Hard to believe, but I don't think I'm wrong. We're just tools she's been using in some sort of elaborate scheme of revenge, or hate, or I don't know what."

"So shouldn't we be trying to kill the woman who's trying to kill her?" said Wilson. "If she's the one signing our payslips..."

"No, because that other woman is on our side."

"But she killed Laffoon," said Blomgren. "I saw her. To save you."

"I am so feckin' confused right now," said Wilson.

Roy said, "All I'm asking is for you to lower your guns and we'll lower ours. Let things play out between those two. This isn't about us. It's something old and deep-rooted and... above us."

"That makes no sense," said Blomgren. "But then, things stopped making much sense when we set foot on this island. So for now..." She holstered her pistol. "Truce."

Wilson and Valente followed suit, as did Roy and Jeanne.

A scream from Hélène brought the attention of all five Myrmidons back to the fight.

Sasha had managed, in spite of her useless arm, to turn the tables. Hélène was on the ground. The point of the scythe had pierced her hand. The battle-axe lay beside her, just out of her reach.

Hélène writhed, hissing in agony, struggling to free her impaled hand.

Sasha simply leaned on the scythe handle with her good arm, increasing the pressure, driving the blade further through Hélène's hand and into the soil beneath.

Hélène lashed out with her feet, but Sasha seemed impervious to the kicks.

"How do you like that, you pampered whore?" Sasha jeered. "Rosalind and Melina were each worth a dozen of you. You preyed on their trust. You betrayed them."

"And I'd do it again, in a heartbeat," Hélène gasped. "Know why? Because they don't matter. *We're* the ones who matter. We're the ones *they* should be fighting over, dying for. It's what they're there for."

"They? Mortals?"

"Of course, mortals! There was a time when they'd go to war because of us."

"Because of you, you mean."

"Thousands and thousands of men, slaughtering and suffering, all in my name. All for *me*."

Sasha's lip curled. "You can't be serious. Is that it? You miss the Trojan War? After all this time, you haven't moved on? This whole little stunt of yours was what – nostalgia? To bring back that feeling again?"

Hélène gave up struggling. A weird serenity settled over her.

"Why not? I could, so I did. I was bored. Life is boring. Sometimes you crave a bit of excitement. Something to liven up the endless days. When I came across those cylinders in the cellar at Evander's Scottish castle…"

"The list," said a man, emerging onto the path from the direction of the main house. He was rotund and double-chinned, and even though he seemed to have got dressed in a hurry – shirt misbuttoned, a pair of wrinkled, baggy slacks that were probably the first thing that came to hand – there was an air of authority about him.

Roy would have bet good money this was yet another demigod. He was beginning to recognise them; they had a certain look in common, an agelessness they exuded from every part of them – except the eyes.

"Help me, Evander," said Hélène. "Look what they've done to me."

Evander. Her husband. Who, if Roy remembered rightly, had once been King Minos.

"From what I've been hearing, my dear," Evander Arlington said, "you've brought it on yourself."

"But don't you see how I've been injured? Damaged? You can't let them get away with it."

"Stop wheedling for a moment, Hélène, and give me an honest answer. You found the list by accident and you used it. Is that right?"

"I'm not ashamed."

"No, you don't know the meaning of the word, do you?"

"Evander…"

"You hired people – these people in uniforms – and sent them to murder our own kind. All for your entertainment."

"Evander, don't speak to me like that. You're my husband. Haven't I been good to you all these years? Haven't I been the perfect wife? Given you everything that you could ever want from a woman?"

Arlington squatted beside her on his haunches. "You have, and more. But this?"

"It was something for myself. Something to prove I was more than just Mrs Evander Arlington. I didn't think you'd mind. You were once a great king! Your word was law, men bowed before you. Don't you hanker for those times again?"

"I am still great," Arlington said. "But the world has changed. Kings take different guises now."

"You can't begrudge me my fun, though."

"My darling Hélène, you know I could never refuse you anything."

"And to cap it all, I brought Theo Stannard here. Your oldest enemy, the thorn in your side. The man who humiliated you."

Arlington shook his head sadly. "I'm over it."

"You still talk about him with anger in your voice. I've heard you."

"Hardly. I think you're confusing your contempt for him with mine. In a way, Theo did me a favour. The Minotaur was an embarrassment, a stain on my reputation."

"You have a statue of it on the island. I assumed..."

"To remind me of my fallibility. Mine and Pasiphaë's. I was supposed to sacrifice that bull, the one she slept with, but in my greed I kept it. The Minotaur was punishment for my hubris. So, in his way, was Theseus, but he taught me a lesson also. Thanks to him I ceased to take my kingship for granted. I learned to value the approval of my subjects. I owe him for that, although I've never told him so."

"You... don't hate him?" Hélène's brow furrowed in perplexity.

"He may not be my favourite person," said Arlington, "but no, I don't hate him."

"You don't want him dead?"

"Not him, nor any of the others you ordered killed. Hélène, Hélène, Hélène... It's like you don't know me at all. Forty years together..."

"Fifty."

"Fifty, and am I still such a mystery to you? Or have you seen in me only what you wanted to see? The complacent, compliant husband with the ever-open chequebook, the bottomless credit card?"

"I hate to interrupt this touching marital moment," said Sasha, "but I *am* about to kill your wife, Evander. Just thought you should know."

"No, you're not."

"She deserves to die, and I very much doubt you're man enough to prevent me."

"You are quite correct on that front," said Arlington. "I am nowhere near swift enough, nor strong enough, to stand in your way. It would be unwise of me even to try."

He reached for the battle-axe.

"I ask instead," he said, "to be permitted to do the job myself."

Hélène gaped. "Evander?"

"Kindly hold her still, Sasha."

After a moment's hesitation, Sasha planted a foot on Hélène's chest, pinning her down.

"Evander, please…"

"Hélène, I love you dearly, but I cannot ignore the trouble you've caused, the deaths you are responsible for. I cannot turn a blind eye. The account must be balanced; debts must be settled."

He straightened up, axe in hand.

"You have brought disgrace on my household and on my name," he said. "You have shamed me as much as Pasiphaë did, if not more. I cannot condone or forgive your actions."

The axe rose, bloodstained twin blades glinting in the brightening daylight.

Hélène's expression switched from disbelief to defiance.

"Go on, then, you bastard," she said. "If you've got the balls."

Up until the very last instant, she never thought Arlington would go through with it.

Neither did Roy.

And then the axe came down, severing Hélène's head from her neck in a single clean chop.

FORTY-THREE

Kardionisi

THEO AND CHASE drew apart, both bloodied, wounded, breathing hard.

"One final time," Theo said. "Let's stop this."

"We both know it's gone too far for that," said Chase. "You won't let me live, and I don't want to die."

"Maybe there's a compromise. A middle way."

"Don't kid yourself, cuz. I knew all along there was a good chance we'd wind up exactly this way. You were going to figure out sooner or later that I was dicking you around, and you wouldn't take it well."

"What I still don't get is what was in it for you. You must have had a motive of your own for siding with Hélène. I don't believe you went along with her scheme just because of a bad case of nostalgia. There has to be more to it."

"Okay. Yeah. You've got me. It's... complicated."

"Try me."

Chase let out a heavy sigh. "The gods."

"The gods?"

"They don't notice us. They don't care."

"That's because they aren't there," Theo said impatiently. "The gods are gone. Dead or – or dispersed, or I don't know what. But they aren't up in Olympus, keeping an eye on us. Not anymore. They've moved on. To Elysium, perhaps."

"And left us all alone." There was a plaintive note in Chase's voice, something like the despair of a lost child. A touch of petulance. "They're our parents. They should be looking out for us. Every time I kill a monster, I pray. Did you know that?"

"You never said."

"It's an offering. I call on Hermes and Athena, but mostly I call on my father. I let Zeus know that I've hunted and killed this beast on his behalf. For *him*. And what do I get back?"

"Nothing."

"Zilch. Nada."

"Why would you expect anything else?"

"Why wouldn't I?"

"The gods are our parents, sure," Theo said. "But parents aren't expected to raise their kids forever. Comes a point when the next generation have grown into adults and are supposed to be making their own way in the world."

"Zeus *never* gave a shit about me. He knocked up my mom – as a shower of golden rain, for fuck's sake – then disappeared."

"You're upset because you have a deadbeat dad? Join the club. Most demigods are semi-orphans from the get-go. It's par for the course. But you didn't have to rope the rest of us into your misery. You didn't have to get people killed, just because you're acting out your resentment."

"Acting out my – ? Screw you, you sanctimonious asshole! Just because *you've* let the world neuter you, doesn't mean it has to happen to all of us. Some of us can still be heroes."

"That's how you see yourself? Funny. From where I'm standing, you look like a villain."

Face contorting with rage, Chase flung himself at Theo. A flurry of sickle blows rained down. Theo parried with the bident, bracing it in front of him double-handed like a quarterstaff, until all at once he was holding two pieces of it. Chase had cut through the haft with a particularly powerful strike.

Theo retreated, dropping the bisected bident and drawing Dionysus's club from his belt.

Chase pressed forward, hacking relentlessly with the sickle, his eyes clouded with bloodlust. Theo wondered if his cousin was seeing him or some sort of beast he felt it was his sacred duty to eradicate.

He realised he was being backed into a corner. He couldn't afford to be pinned down; club or no club, it would be the end of him.

He barged past Chase, side-swiping him with the club as he went and narrowly missing. He darted across the lawn, aiming for the exit, the route he had entered by. There was greater safety in the maze, surely.

Chase caught up with him halfway there. Theo jinked to the left and a moment later the sickle cleaved through the air where his spine had been. Chase was between him and the nearer exit; Theo diverted towards the other, his cousin hot on his heels.

In the shadow of the Minotaur statue, Chase at last made contact. Theo felt an abrupt spike of agony in his flank. The sickle had dug between two of his ribs, deep into the intercostal muscle, snagging him, pulling him up short.

He twisted like a fish on the hook, feeling flesh rip as he tore himself free. He stumbled woozily for a few steps before his legs caved under him and he fell prone.

Chase strode over and straddled him, a foot either side. Theo began crawling, trying to stand upright. Every time he made it to his hands and knees, however, the pain in his side overwhelmed him and he sagged. He could hear himself making urgent grunting noises in the back of his throat. He clawed his way across the dewy grass. Chase stayed with him. At any moment, the coup de grâce would come. The sickle would slice through his neck or sink into his heart and that would be that.

Finally he could go no further. With the last of his ebbing strength he rolled over onto his back.

His gaze met Chase's.

"You don't have to," he croaked. "This isn't you. You're better than this."

"I wish I was, cuz," Chase said with a rueful grimace. "Truly I do."

He readied the sickle for the killing blow with an almost solemn air – dutifully, like finishing off a badly wounded beast.

He glanced up at the pristine dawn sky, as though looking for a sign.

Then, steeling himself, he tensed his arm.

Blinding whiteness. A deafening *bang*.

Is this is? Theo thought. *Is this what death feels like?*

His vision cleared, his ears still ringing.

Chase was frozen in position, just as startled as Theo was.

Behind him, the Minotaur statue seemed to have come alive. It was trembling, teetering. Tiny crackles of electricity coruscated over its bronze surface. Its lower legs were charred, blackened. Its feet, on the plinth, were more or less destroyed.

The statue creaked resoundingly.

"Chase! Move!"

Even as Theo spluttered out the warning, he himself was moving. Somehow he found the energy to rise to a crouch, to scramble away on all fours.

The statue bowed forward, tumbling towards where Chase stood. Chase either hadn't heard what Theo said or was too startled to do anything about it. He only turned round.

The bronze Minotaur seemed almost to pounce on him. The tortured groan of twisting, rending metal reminded Theo, for a moment, of the beast himself.

The impact was earth-shaking.

THEO ROSE TO his feet, unsteady, groggy. His ears were whining as though there were cicadas trapped inside them, and it was hard to catch his breath. One side of his ribcage felt on fire.

The Minotaur statue lay flat on the lawn, prone. He tottered towards it. He didn't want to look. He had to look.

The sickle lay on the grass, inches from Chase's outstretched hand. Of Chase himself there wasn't much visible, but what there was told Theo all he needed to know.

Crushed, pulverised.

Such thorough destruction that even a demigod couldn't survive it.

Theo raised his head.

The sky was empty. Not a cloud in sight. Just the endless unsullied blue of the firmament.

But something had hit the statue from above and toppled it.

Something that had blazed, something powerful from the heavens.

Something like...

A thunderbolt?

FORTY-FOUR

Kardionisi

EVANDER ARLINGTON SPOKE to Roy, Jeanne and the other three Myrmidons. For a man who had just ceremonially beheaded his wife, he seemed remarkably calm. A cold fish.

But then, King Minos, to the best of Roy's knowledge, had been a despot. Obviously the lives of others, even the life of someone he professed to love, meant little to him. He could snuff them out and square it easily with his conscience.

"Ladies, gentlemen," he said. "You have seen things today that perhaps you ought not to have. You have been party to events beyond your accustomed sphere of experience."

"Does that mean you're going to kill us, too?" said Gunnvor Blomgren. "To silence us?" She drew her pistol, chambered a round and aimed at Arlington.

Roy waved at her to back off. "I don't think that's where he's going with this. Let's hear him out."

"I'm merely saying that you have been victims of my late wife's machinations," said Arlington. "As her husband, I bear the responsibility for that. It is…"

He took a deep breath, and Roy noticed his hands were trembling ever so slightly. There was turmoil beneath the sanguine façade. Arlington was not as emotionless as he wished to appear.

"It is only right that I make reparation," he continued.

"Oh, so you're *buying* our silence," said Blomgren.

"Gunnvor," Roy said, "for Christ's sake, will you just shut up and let Minos speak?"

Arlington raised an eyebrow. "You know who I am."

The name had just slipped out. "Who you *were*," Roy amended.

"Of course. Quite right. Who I was. What the legends don't tell you is that I am very much a man of honour. Perhaps not back then, but now. My wife was paying you handsomely, I'm sure. I will see to it that you each receive every cent you are owed, plus extra."

"Can't say fairer than that," said Sean Wilson with a shrug.

"In return, you will surrender those weapons to me, the antiques. They are worthless in every respect except the one that, as far as I and my kind are concerned, counts. I cannot leave them in your hands. I must round them up and make absolutely sure that they –"

He was interrupted by a sudden flicker of fiercely bright light, followed an instant later by a *crack* so loud it made everyone jump.

For a moment nobody spoke.

Then Jeanne said, "What the hell was that? Was that... lightning?"

In the corner of Roy's eye there was an afterimage – a zigzagging vertical yellow line.

The bolt of lightning, if that was what it had been, had struck somewhere over in the hedgerow maze.

Out of a clear blue sky.

"Where's Stannard?" said Roy, looking around. It was the first time he'd noticed that Stannard wasn't anywhere to be seen. "I thought he was still here, but... in all the confusion..."

Sasha Grace, without a word, broke into a run, heading for the maze.

FORTY-FIVE

Kardionisi

THEO WAS TIRED, bone-deep. So tired he couldn't face the thought of navigating back through the maze to the exit.

Instead he employed the sickle, putting it more or less to the use a sickle was intended for. He hacked a path straight through the hedgerows. In one cypress wall after another he carved out a doorway for himself, until at last he staggered clear of the maze's perimeter.

Sasha was waiting, scythe in hand.

She lowered it when she saw him.

"Theo."

"Don't sound so surprised."

"You're alive."

"Just about. You look as bad as I feel. That's a nasty cut."

She glanced at the gash in her shoulder as though it was of no consequence. "What about Chase? I saw you run off after something – something I couldn't see. I assumed…"

"You assumed correctly. And Chase is… He met his nemesis."

"Oh," Sasha said. "I'm sorry. I know how close you two were."

"Apparently not as close as I thought. Same ideals, different wavelengths. What about Hélène?"

Sasha shook her head. "She met *her* nemesis."

"Crazy woman. Thinking she was triggering a second Trojan War. You know the saying about history repeating itself first as tragedy, then as farce? It's…"

Everything greyed. All at once the world seemed distant, as though behind gauze.

Sasha snaked an arm around him, catching him as he sagged, taking his weight.

"Thanks," Theo said. "Bit dazed. I guess, from the sound of it, the fighting's over."

"It is. I think we're done. Listen, Theo, there's something I have to say."

"Can it wait?"

"No. It's just – I may have judged you too harshly. A long, long time ago, when you eloped with my sister, I couldn't for the life of me understand what she saw in you. I thought you were a prig and a deceiver, too crafty for your own or anyone's good. I… I was wrong. All the bad blood it caused, the rift between Melanippe and me, not to mention the Amazonomachy. I've always regretted it, but I've never apologised for it. I'm doing that now."

"Better late than never, I suppose. For what it's worth, Melanippe always loved you, in spite of everything. Why else did we name our son after you? It was her idea. A token of respect."

Sasha nodded sombrely. "You're a far better man than I have given you credit for. It's a shame it's taken something like this for me to realise that."

"I grow on people," Theo said. "Like fungus. Shall we re-join the others?"

"Sure."

They began walking, Sasha supporting Theo despite the additional pain it caused her.

"What happened back there?" she asked. "We saw what looked like lightning."

Theo grimaced. "There's a name for it, and it's something I never expected to hear myself say in this day and age."

"Which is…?"

"Divine intervention."

FORTY-SIX

Kardionisi

ROY COLLECTED THE antique weapons off the other Myrmidons.

"I'm sure there is a reasonable explanation for all of this," Gunnvor Blomgren said as she handed him the spear. "I'm sure it all makes sense somehow."

"It does," said Roy. "I'll fill you in when I can. You might have trouble believing it at first, but..."

"Oh, I don't think we'll have trouble at all," said Sean Wilson. "The strange shit we've seen and heard tonight, and before tonight, for that matter."

Roy presented the weapons to Evander Arlington. "That's the lot."

"No, it isn't. There should be twelve."

"Stannard and Sasha Grace have some of the others, maybe the rest, I don't know. Do you have a checklist or something?"

"Not on me right this moment, but I have a friend – a guest on the island, in fact – who might be able to help." Arlington frowned. "To be honest, I'm surprised he isn't up and about. All the commotion – I doubt he could have slept through it. I wonder where he's got to."

"Might I ask a question?"

"Hmmm? What's that? A question?"

"I realise this isn't the best time, you have other things to think about, but... I have a daughter, and she's in grave danger."

"That concerns me how?" said Arlington sniffily.

"It concerns you," said Roy, "because your wife was responsible for her being in danger, sort of."

"Ah. How so?"

"Does the name Holger Badenhorst mean anything to you?"

"Not a thing. Who is he?"

"Your wife never mentioned him?"

"It would seem that Hélène" – Arlington flicked his gaze to the decapitated corpse – "was keeping more than a few secrets from me. I assure you, upon my word, I do not know any Badenhorst."

"Shit. I suppose it was a long shot. He's her fixer, you see. The man she got to recruit us Myrmidons and make arrangements. And he's – he's..."

"He has placed your daughter in jeopardy somehow. Would that have been with or without my Hélène's connivance?"

"I don't know. Maybe."

"If it was without, then I doubt I can help you in any way. If not even Hélène knew about it, then..."

Arlington's brow creased.

"Wait a moment," he said. "These past few weeks my wife has behaved absolutely normally. Nothing she did struck me as curious. But just the other day Hélène enquired about one of the properties I own, an apartment. Over breakfast, as I recall. It was out of the blue, à propos of nothing. 'Are you intending to use the place in the near future?' she asked. I wanted to know why, and she said, 'No reason.' She said she was considering a trip, to do some shopping I think, and was wondering if the apartment would be available. Nothing odd about that. Hélène likes – *liked* her shopping trips. I told her I had no plans to go there. The apartment was free for her to use if she wished. And that was that."

"Did she go?"

"Not to my knowledge, but it was only a few days ago. The trip may have been scheduled for next month, or may have been cancelled and she didn't tell me. It could have no relevance whatsoever to the situation with your daughter."

"Or it could be exactly what I'm looking for," said Roy.

At that moment Theo Stannard and Sasha Grace limped into view. Stannard looked battered, shellshocked, dead on his feet.

"Please," Roy said to Arlington, "if you could tell me where the apartment is…"

He was clutching at straws, he knew it. There was every chance the information would be useless. Wherever this apartment was, there was no guarantee Josie was there.

"You truly think there is some link between it and your daughter?" Arlington said.

"Your daughter, Roy?" said Stannard. "You know where she is?"

"I hope so," Roy said.

"I'm not convinced myself," said Arlington.

"Listen, Evander," Theo said to him. "If you know something – anything – that gives Roy a chance of rescuing his kid, you damn well tell him right now."

"All right. All right." Arlington raised his hand. "I never said I wouldn't tell him. The apartment is in Vienna. I can give you the address."

"Please do," said Roy, politeness only just containing a screaming sense of urgency.

"I can also lend you my helicopter to get you to the mainland," Arlington said. "This is clearly a matter of some emergency. I can have my private jet waiting for you at Athens International, fuelled and ready to fly."

"You'll do that for me?"

The multibillionaire shrugged expansively. "I have moral obligations. There is a need to compensate."

"How soon can I leave?" said Roy.

"How soon can *we* leave?" said Stannard.

Roy looked at him.

"We had a deal," Stannard said.

"But you can barely walk."

"You don't look any better yourself."

"I'll manage."

"So will I."

"I'm coming too," said Jeanne.

"How many can your helicopter take?" said Sasha.

"It seats six," Arlington replied.

"Then count me in."

"This could just be a wasted journey…" Roy began, but he knew, seeing their faces, that they didn't care. They were accompanying him to Vienna regardless.

"I'll make the necessary calls and rouse the pilot," Arlington said, turning towards the house. "Wheels up in under an hour."

FORTY-SEVEN

Vienna

Josie had recovered, both from the lithium overdose and the failure of her plan. Her resilience surprised her. She hadn't lapsed back into despair after learning that Benedikt had not managed to make the phone call after all. A Black Day had beckoned, but she had refused to let it consume her. She had shaken off its tentacles, forced herself to let go of her disappointment and look ahead. Try again. Come up with another plan.

Benedikt, however, was despondent. He was ashamed that he hadn't been able to reach the landline. After Josie had passed out, the guards hadn't left him alone for a moment. They'd insisted he stay by her side and keep a close eye on her, even while one of them was off fetching the materials for the makeshift stomach pump, which took well over an hour. A couple of times Benedikt had begged for a reprieve, a minute alone to collect his thoughts and compose himself. No dice. The guards were terrified of Josie dying on their watch.

"It wasn't your fault," Josie told him again and again, afterwards. "It was a shitty, half-arsed plan anyway. We both knew there was only a slim chance it was going to work."

In the event, it did bring captors and captives together. The realisation that Josie posed a threat to herself made the guards, especially Ginger Walrus, much more attentive: they had come painfully close to losing her, and it was a calamity they had no desire to see repeated. The doors between the bedroom and the main room were now never shut. Josie was under constant surveillance, the guards monitoring everything she did. She and Benedikt were able to snatch the occasional whispered conversation in private, but for the most part they behaved formally towards each other, as though they were nothing more than what they were meant to be, carer and patient.

And the day-shift guards held Benedikt in higher esteem than previously. He had saved Josie, and in doing so saved their skins. They had begun to treat him with a certain respect, allowing him to come and go between the two rooms as he pleased, even inviting him to sit and watch football with them. He was a fan and fairly knowledgeable; a fragile bond developed. Josie often heard him participating in their arguments over team managers and star signings. He had gained their trust.

So when, this morning, he offered to make coffee for them, the guards happily let him. They asked for it strong. Benedikt was keen to oblige and heaped spoonfuls of coffee grounds into the cafetière.

Josie watched through the doorway as he added something else to the cafetière before pouring the boiling water in. None of the day-shift guards noticed.

It had been her idea. A far better idea than the last one, although it wouldn't have been possible but for the last one, either. Her overdose had paved the way for this: giving the guards themselves an overdose.

Benedikt had palmed at least fifteen lithium tablets into the cafetière. The water would dissolve them in no time. The taste of the coffee would disguise what little flavour they had. The guards were about to get a dose of Josie's own medicine.

* * *

THEY DRANK THE coffee. Benedikt sat beside them, staring intently at the TV, not looking at them at all; he feared his face might give the game away. He focused on the football.

Josie waited. Benedikt waited.

How soon before the tablets started to take effect? Had Benedikt introduced enough of them into the coffee? Would being dissolved lessen their potency? Would the guards realise something was amiss when they all started feeling unwell at once?

So much could go wrong, but Josie and Benedikt were both agreed that it was worth the gamble.

Minutes ticked by, achingly long minutes, and then one of the guards put a hand to his belly. He said he felt odd, gassy. He had eaten Chinese last night, maybe that was it. He went to the cloakroom beside the main entrance, where there was an additional toilet.

When he didn't return after five minutes, another of the guards went to check on him, collapsing after he had taken five steps.

The last remaining guard, Ginger Walrus, rose immediately to his feet, groping for his gun.

"What is...?" he began, then doubled over with an agonising stomach cramp.

Josie's and Benedikt's gazes met through the doorway.

This was their one – their only – chance.

Josie sprang from the bed and hurtled into the main room. Benedikt leapt from the chair. Ginger Walrus straightened, making a grab for Josie, but she shoved him hard and he stumbled over a low marble table and crashed to the floor.

Benedikt was already halfway to the exit. Josie was right behind him.

They had done it! They were going to escape!

The door lay ahead. Just as they reached it, it opened.

In came a man neither of them had seen before. He wasn't one of the guards. He was large, ruddy-complexioned, bull-necked, and clad in casualwear, shirt and jeans, but with an unusual accessory: a kind of furry tunic, like an animal pelt, draped around his torso.

He stared at Josie and Benedikt, blocking their route with his bulk. He sized them up, and a sudden huge grin split his face. He seemed friendly. Like someone who might help.

"Please," Josie said to him. "These men have been keeping us prisoner. We have to get out of here."

She wondered if he was Austrian and didn't speak English.

"Benedikt, tell him what I said in German. Maybe he didn't understand."

"Oh, I understand just fine, *choty goty*," the man said in a South African accent. "And I'm sorry to say you've made a bit of a mistake. I know these men have been keeping you prisoner. I'm the one who's been paying them to."

JOSIE COULD HAVE screamed. So near and yet so far.

Instead, a wild animal instinct overcame her. She hurled herself at the man, fists flying. Benedikt joined in.

The man just laughed as the blows rained down on him. He appeared not to feel a thing.

Then he grabbed Benedikt by the neck and slammed him face first into the nearest wall. The nurse slumped to the floor with a groan.

The man clamped one meaty hand around both of Josie's wrists. She kicked him in the shins, but as before he seemed immune to pain. He thrust her roughly back into the room, at the same time pulling a pistol from a holster beneath his armpit.

"You, missy," he said, "you're a resourceful little minx. I don't know how you disabled these men, but I'm impressed. I'd never have thought you had it in you. You're supposed to be a basket case, *nè*?"

"I'll basket case *you*," Josie snarled. The line made no sense but sounded good to her. "Let me go, you fucker."

"Ah-ah. No call for bad language. Pretty young thing like you should watch her mouth. Men don't like women who swear."

Josie rammed a knee into his crotch.

The man only laughed. What was up with this guy? Was he made of titanium or something?

"Now, then," he said. "It seems your papa Roy has been a naughty fellow. I haven't heard from him and the people with him since last night – radio silence, no calls returned – and my gut feeling is he's betrayed me, even though he knew what the consequences would be if he did. It's that or everything has gone tits up with the job he's doing for me. Either way, I'm not taking any chances. I need you, Josie. You're my insurance policy and you're coming with me."

"Am not."

"I don't recall offering you a choice. This is a Vektor SP1 nine-millimetre, and it says you're doing as I tell you and you're not going to kick up a fuss. I have a car waiting downstairs. We're going to get lost in Europe, you and me. Your dad can come looking and he'll never find us. We'll have a lovely long vacation together, you and me. Maybe in that time we'll get friendly. You'll grow to like me. I already like you; I like girls with the dew still on them. You'll come to appreciate the touch of an older man."

"I will never let you touch me. I'd rather die."

"You say that now, but in a week or two –"

A gunshot.

The sound spiked into Josie's ears. For a moment she could hear nothing else a high-pitched ringing.

The man with the South African accent wheeled round, taking her with him.

At the entrance – Josie almost couldn't believe her eyes – was her father. He stood in a half crouch, arms extended, a pistol in his hands.

With him was a second man, dark-haired, dark-eyed, lithe.

Taking careful aim at the Afrikaner, her father fired the gun again.

Something shattered – a vase on a side-table.

The man next to Roy Young said, "Save your bullets. That thing he's wearing? The Aegis of Zeus."

"*Ja*, the Aegis of Zeus," the Afrikaner said. "Handy little trinket, don't you think, Roy? Makes you invulnerable, and once you put it on, it can't be unfastened except by the person who fastened it in the first place. So our employer told me. I suppose I could have let you Myrmidons use it on your missions, but it seemed unfair, one of you being immune to harm and the others not. So I kept it for myself, in case of need. And here's need. Carry on shooting, by all means. The bullets will just bounce off. One of them might even hit your pretty daughter. Wouldn't that be a pity?"

"Badenhorst..." said Josie's father.

"Now listen up." The Afrikaner – Badenhorst – pressed the tip of the gun against Josie's temple, holding her neck with his free hand, fingers digging in paralysingly hard. "This is what's going to happen. You and Mr Stannard there are going to move aside and let me and Josie leave. Otherwise... Well, I don't have to spell out the 'otherwise', do I?"

"Don't you dare hurt her."

"Or what, Roy? You'll kill me? Not as long as I've got this on."

Two women now arrived in the room behind Josie's father and the man called Stannard.

"He isn't dead?" said one of them. She had the same colouring as Stannard and looked pure badass, an impression that her heavily bandaged shoulder did nothing to dispel. "We heard shots. How could you have missed?"

"The Aegis, Sasha," said Stannard.

"Oh, shit. Of course. You thought he might have it."

"Jeanne," Badenhorst said to the other woman. "So you're in on this too. *Ach*, I should have known you'd side with Roy. I could see the two of you developing a soft spot for each other. Anyway, it makes no difference. You all can just get the fuck out of my way. I'm coming through with Josie here, and any of you tries to stop me..." He ground the gun into Josie's head. "Bang."

"Go on, then," Josie said. "Shoot. Pull the trigger."

"That's not the attitude, girl," said Badenhorst.

"I don't care. I want to die."

"No, you don't."

"I fucking do. Of course I do. If you know anything about me you'll know that I've tried to kill myself like half a dozen times. I keep screwing it up. You can do me a favour right now and put a bullet in my brain. End it all for me. Put me out of my misery."

"Josie," said her father, appalled. "Don't. Don't do this."

"Dad, you know I don't want to live. The treatment hasn't

worked. I hate myself. I hate everything about myself. The world's better off without me."

"She's just talking," said Badenhorst. "She's as keen to live as anyone."

"How do you know, you fucking wanker?" Josie yelled. Tears streamed from her eyes. "Don't you tell me what I want. You don't know how I feel. Go ahead, just do it. Just fucking shoot me."

She grabbed the gun and pressed it to the centre of her forehead.

"I don't care!" she said. "Finish it. I don't want to live any more. Pull the fucking trigger."

Badenhorst's face registered confusion and alarm. A hostage who wanted to be sacrificed? It didn't compute.

He pulled the gun away from her face. He seemed scared in case it went off by accident and he was left without his bargaining chip. His grip on her relaxed involuntarily.

In that tiny lull, that brief instant of indecision, Stannard leapt.

He threw himself at Badenhorst with such force that both of them flew across the room, straight into the still blaring television. The screen shattered, silencing the football at long last. Both men tumbled to the floor. Josie was left standing where she was, astonished at how fast Stannard had moved.

Stannard began beleaguering Badenhorst with punches. His arms were a blur, like the blades of an electric fan. They did no damage to the Afrikaner, but the sheer repetitive impacts pinned him in place, helpless.

The woman known as Sasha darted over to join him, holding Badenhorst down with her good arm while Stannard kept up the onslaught.

It seemed as though the beating might go on forever, with the man on the receiving end unharmed but unable to retaliate.

Then something changed hands between Sasha and Stannard. It was a short pole, perhaps half a metre long. One end seemed to have been sheared off, while at the other there were a pair of slender blades, like two knives in parallel.

"The aegis can't be unfastened," Sasha said to Badenhorst, "but it can be removed, if you have the right equipment."

Badenhorst's eyes widened, becoming panicky.

Stannard sliced through the Aegis, cutting it free from Badenhorst's body. He threw the fragments of furry material aside.

Badenhorst tried raising his gun, but Sasha disarmed him with a simple twist of the wrist.

Now the Afrikaner was very frightened. Stannard and Sasha hauled him to his feet. He no longer had the aegis to protect him. He was as vulnerable as any person.

"Roy?" said Stannard. "He's all yours. You have the right. You have the responsibility."

"Jeanne," Josie's father said, "would you take Josie outside?"

Jeanne grasped Josie gently by the shoulders and steered her towards the exit. As they passed Josie's father, he reached out and brushed a hand across her cheek.

"I don't want you to see this, honey."

"I know. I kind of don't want to see it either – although I also do."

"You were bluffing, weren't you? With the gun. I could tell. You – you're different. You look different. You look…" He searched for the right words. For an articulate man, he often had trouble saying what he really meant. "Healthy. Better than in a long time. You look like my Josie again."

"And you look like my dad. Same as always. Apart from the bruises."

"I'll see you in a little while. We'll catch up."

"It's okay, Dad." Josie threw a glance at Badenhorst, who was whimpering now, pleading with Stannard and Sasha to let him go. "I can wait. Take as long as you need."

Her father gave her a smile, wan but paternal. Loving.

Jeanne escorted Josie into the corridor outside, down in the elevator, out onto the street. Vienna simmered in summer heat. Josie breathed in city smells: traffic fumes, stonework, garbage rotting in a bin, a passer-by's cigarette smoke, the aroma of cooking from a nearby bakery.

Freedom.

The world was good.

Life was good.

THREE MONTHS LATER

EPILOGUE

Paris, France

FORGET SPRING, AUTUMN was the best time of year in Paris. The oppressive heat of summer, gone. The city filling up again after the annual August exodus, Parisians returning from their country homes and seaside resorts to reclaim the boulevards from the tourists. Slow, radiantly golden sunsets over the Seine.

Thomas Sinclair locked the door of his walk-up apartment in Montmartre and headed downstairs. He picked up a coffee and croissant to go at a café, then took the Métro Line 12 from Abbesses station to Saint-Lazare.

Today was a big day. A fresh start. The beginning of something. A new venture.

Thomas's office was in the 8th Arrondissement, just off the rue La Fayette. It sat on the third floor of a large, venerable Haussmann-era building with a central courtyard where, once upon a time, horses would have been stabled. An archway gave access from the street, large enough for coaches to have passed through.

He arrived there just past nine. Already his co-director was at his desk.

"First day of business and you're at work before I am," Thomas said. "Hope you're not trying to make me look bad."

"I'm not trying to," said the other. "I'm succeeding."

Thomas took his seat at a desk on the opposite side of the spacious, airy room. The two men faced each other.

"Do you think we're going to get any clients, Theo?"

"Thomas. Remember? It's Thomas now."

"Sorry. I'll get the hang of it, I swear."

"At least you're still Roy. Makes my life easier."

"Mine too," said Roy Young.

"And as for clients... Have faith. Wait and see. It'll be one or two at first, dribs and drabs, but once words get around, the floodgates will open."

With that, Thomas sat back, thinking.

It had taken far less time than he'd predicted, relocating to France, setting up the business. There was plenty of red tape to cut through, but he had access to a fairly hefty pair of scissors in the shape of his company's financial backer, Evander Arlington. French bureaucracy worked with remarkable efficiency if the right people were paid off in the right way. Arlington's bountiful wallet was more than up to the task.

The hardest part of the whole process had been turning down the Simon & Schuster two-book deal and walking away from the life and career of Theo Stannard. Thomas had quite enjoyed that incarnation, and he had disliked upsetting Cynthia, whose main source of income his novels were. She had alternately pleaded with and cajoled him to write the next Jake Killian, plus *The Golden Thread*, and *then* call it a day, but he had stood firm. He'd told her, regretfully, that publishing was no longer for him; he felt the need to retire from the industry and pursue other interests. He'd bought her a five-star Caribbean cruise as a parting gift, a thank-you-and-farewell, which she accepted with graceful reluctance.

Now, in Paris, Theo Stannard was Thomas Sinclair, and he and Roy had a company to run and a remit to fulfil.

All morning, the telephone did not ring and no emails arrived in their inboxes except for spam. The post brought nothing but a couple of circulars, some fast-food menus and a Good Luck card from Harry Gottlieb: *Thinking of you as you embark on this brand new ODYSSEY.*

"Early days," was all Thomas said.

They chatted about this and that to while away the time. Thomas enquired about Josie. She was doing well, Roy said. He might almost describe it as "thriving". She had just started her first term at a boarding school in Kent and said she was enjoying it. He had worried that she would find the adjustment hard, but it seemed that there was nothing she couldn't take in her stride these days. He visited her most weekends. The journey was only a couple of hours on the Eurostar. Every time, he saw a changed girl. Josie's future seemed bright.

"Shame it took getting kidnapped and almost shot to do for her what the most expensive mental health clinic in Switzerland couldn't," Roy said with an ironic shrug. "But there you go. She stays in touch with that orderly, Benedikt Frankel. He was the one who really made a difference to her. I owe him more than I do Dr Aeschbacher or any of those fucking overpriced shrinks, that's for sure."

"Badenhorst broke his nose, didn't he?"

"Yeah, badly, and it's set wonky, so Benedikt isn't as pretty-boy handsome as he used to be, but he says it adds character."

"All scars add character."

"And you don't have any."

"My scars are inner and they are many. I have huge amounts of character."

They chuckled, and Thomas marvelled at the thought that, not so long ago, one of them had been paid good money to kill the other. But then, it had never been personal for Roy, so how, really, could Thomas hold a grudge?

The phone rang. Each man had an extension on his desk. They grabbed for the handsets simultaneously.

Thomas's faster reflexes meant he got there first.

"Hello. Herculean Feats International. How may I be of assistance?"

The caller was a woman. She said she was in deep trouble and had been given this number by Sasha Grace. She was being threatened by a man – a wealthy man, a dangerous man. Her husband. He had contacts, connections to some shady and unscrupulous individuals. He was also an abuser, free with his fists, and she had finally had enough of being knocked about by him, so she had left and taken their kids with her and gone into hiding. She knew he would be looking for her, and with the people he was in league with aiding him, the resources they had, it was only a matter of time before he found her.

She was scared and she needed help, and Sasha Grace, from whom she had hired Wonder Women a few times, had told her Herculean Feats International was the place to go. She just wanted herself and her children to be safe, she said. She didn't want to spent the rest of her life on the run, constantly looking over her shoulder.

Thomas jotted down all the relevant details: names, addresses, locations. Roy was listening in on the other line. When the woman asked about their fee, Thomas said there was none. The company was privately funded, a kind of charity.

Evander Arlington, setting up a vast trust in their name.

"We can sort this all out for you," he told the woman. "I promise you, within a week you'll have nothing to worry about."

He put down the phone.

"Ready, Roy?"

"Sounds like someone has to be killed who deserves to be killed. I'm ready."

Thomas stood up.

The Age of Heroes was far in the past. The world had moved on. But that didn't mean the world didn't still need heroes.

ACKNOWLEDGEMENTS

I OWE A huge debt of thanks to Jonathan Oliver and David Moore for doing yet another bang-up editorial job. Unless you're a writer you may not realise what a difference good editing makes. Even seasoned old scribblers like me need a firm guiding hand to shape and hone our prose, and I'm lucky to have it.

I'm grateful, too, to Martin Wagner for a bit of help with my German, and to Patrick Mahon who's been a staunch supporter and pal for a while now.

Above all else, I'm grateful to my readers, not least the ones who've taken my Pantheon series to their hearts and made it such a success. These books are a hell of a lot of fun to write, and part of that fun is knowing they're going to be read and appreciated by such a wide range of people. To everyone who's sent me positive feedback over the years, suggested ideas for new Pantheon novels, chipped in with helpful comments, played the game of "casting the movie" with me, or just simply bought and enjoyed the books – a massive, heartfelt, semi-divine THANK YOU.